A Hate Crime in Brooklyn

David G. Secular

Disclaimer

A Hate Crime in Brooklyn is a work of fiction. All the names, characters, businesses, places, events, and incidents in this book are the product of the author's imagination or used in a fictitious manner. Any resemblance to actual persons, living or dead, or actual events is purely coincidental.

Published by Central Park South Publishing 2024

www.centralparksouthpublishing.com

Typesetting and e-book formatting services by Victor Marcos

ISBN:
978-1-956452-64-8 (pbk)
978-1-956452-65-5 (hbk)
978-1-956452-66-2 (ebk)

This novel is dedicated to my mom and dad.

My mom read every version of my story and even turning 100 until her passing continued to support me and our family more than we ever took care of her.

My dad enabled me, was the kindest soul and was loved by all. I only wish they could have been here to rejoice in their lawyer turned author's first published novel.

"Life is not like water. Things in life don't necessarily flow over the shortest possible route."

—Haruki Murakami ,1Q84#1-3

A Hate Crime in Brooklyn

The bullet, made entirely of silver, is precious. The laws of the Kanun command that every woman present a silver bullet to her husband on their wedding day as part of her dowry. It is to be used to take her life if she's ever unfaithful.

The bullet must not be found. So, she hides it inside her vagina wrapped in a tampon.

She has just arrived in America. The airport building is eerily white with sheer glass walls and ceilings stretching as far as the eye can see. There are a multitude of travelers, yet not a sound can be heard. Trapped in a speeding current of nameless faces, she yells for her mother and father before being stopped, pulled aside, and ordered by a homeland security officer to walk through an enormous metal detector.

The silver bullet sets it off.

"Më fai! it's not my fault," she desperately tries to explain.

She is 15 years old. She is speaking Albanian. They don't understand.

She is 35 years old. She has lived in Brooklyn for twenty years. She speaks perfect English. Why don't they understand?

She looks into the different colored eyes of the officer and freezes.

"Victor!"

Her blood curdling screams bounce off the walls of her bedroom. Sofia awakens.

Prologue

April 14, 2018
Brooklyn

"Shavua tov, my good friend. Best wishes for a great week."

The first call David Sherman received every Saturday night, the moment his Sabbath ended, was from a Special Agent of the Federal Bureau of Investigation. The Jewish greeting from Agent Ford, an African American, always brought a smile to Sherman's face.

David Aaron Sherman, maintained a small law office in downtown Brooklyn for close to forty years, specialized in criminal defense, and often represented indigent clients. Yet, despite being on opposing sides of federal prosecutions, Sherman and Ford had a special friendship. Sherman never forgot the trial where he uncovered a crucial flaw in the government's proof, which Dan Ford as the lead agent did not attempt to whitewash even though it assured an acquittal. Whenever they ran into each other in the hallways of the federal courthouse, they found time to chat and occasionally even grab lunch. Ford unhesitatingly agreed to serve as a reference for Sherman's niece Sharron when, as a young attorney, she applied for a position as a federal prosecutor.

Following the call, sitting in his favorite red leather armchair, watching his family gather around the living room after devouring his wife Elaine's legendary brisket and potato pancakes, Sherman felt blessed. His spacious home in Crown Heights, Brooklyn easily accommodated dinners for his entire extended family: his wife of almost 50 years, his daughter a teacher, son a doctor, each with two middle school children, an older sister and two younger brothers, their wives and children, all of whom were deeply bonded.

Sherman's cell unexpectantly rang again – this time with the chime reserved for Victor Hushemi's number. The fire in the pit of his belly, the one that was always lit by his number one client, ignited. In 1987, Sherman successfully defended Victor in a high-profile racketeering case. Years later, after Victor had established several successful, and seemingly legal businesses, he offered Sherman an annual retainer so lucrative, he couldn't refuse. Through the years, far too often he wished he had.

"Sherman, this can't wait. My driver's on his way to pick you up. I'm at my brother Edward's apartment."

"Victor, I apologize. But the Sabbath just ended. My family is here, and we just finished *Melaveh Malkah*, our Saturday night dinner. It must wait."

"I waited until after sunset. They and God will forgive you. My driver will be there any minute. Be ready."

Sherman's apologies for having to rush away were met with warm embraces of understanding by his family. Bending over the crib and planting a goodbye kiss on the forehead of his adorable grandniece Samantha, the only baby in the family, Elaine summoned her husband to the kitchen.

The first and sole love of David's life, Elaine was steadfastly supportive in all matters other than Victor. "My God, won't you ever stand up to him," she pleaded. While she scrubbed pots, pans and dishes in the kitchen sink, and opened and slammed shut the refrigerator, Sherman apologized, pecked Elaine on the forehead, and reluctantly trudged up the stairs to his bedroom. After putting on a white shirt, suit jacket and pants, he was in the middle of knotting his tie when he looked in the mirror. Staring at his white beard, the unrelenting wrinkles on his face, the rings under his eyes and his thinning face, he could not help but think, "I'm. way too old for this." Just then, the horn from Victor's Lincoln Navigator clamored.

Sherman quickly went downstairs and reached into the hallway closet for his tan spring trench coat. Sighing, David made his way down the front steps of his house to Victor's driver, Adem Hajdari, who jumped out of the vehicle to help Sherman step up into the passenger seat of the steep SUV.

"Sorry, Mr. Sherman," Adem apologized, "I know it's your people's holiday, but you know the boss."

"Sure do, no apologies necessary," Sherman said with a kind smile as he leaned back and buckled his seat belt.

As they neared Flatbush Avenue, the street was clogged with demonstrators. Thousands upon thousands held signs, marching and chanting, "Say his name! Say his name! Sylvester Stanley!"

"These *zezaks* are coming out the woodwork aren't they Mr. Sherman, Like rats," Hajdari said, laughing at his comparison.

"Adem, take a look," Sherman, his mood abruptly taking a U-turn, replied. "There's just as many whites as Blacks out there. The shooting was senseless and sick. White or Black, I'm sure Victor would agree."

Holding up his right hand while his left remained on the steering wheel, Adem caught himself, recalling that Sherman frowned on his feelings about people of color.

"Didn't mean to offend, Mr. Sherman. And I get it too. If a white guy was shot in the park, no way this case wouldn't be solved. They say the shooters had an accent... maybe even one of us. If it was some white guy shot, every Albanian in New York would be locked up until they had 'em. I hear they're not even sure he'll survive. Heard any updates Mr. Sherman?"

"Last news report has him still unconscious at New York Presbyterian, chances of survival touch and go. Police are supposedly tearing up the city looking for the shooters and to identify the woman in the costume. Unless the feds get involved, I'm almost willing to bet they'll come up empty."

Sherman kept quiet for the remainder of the ride. There was no point in telling Hajdari that he knew Sylvester. He had represented him in the past and, in fact, admired him. If he were ten years younger, and his knees not riddled with arthritis, Sherman thought, he wouldn't have just joined the march, he would have led it.

When Adem finally made his way through the crowded streets and dropped Sherman off, Victor was fuming in the hallway. Almost six feet, with a thin athletic body the envy of men half his sixty-seven years of age, Victor wore a light blue shirt, tan dress pants and a matching leather jacket. His sharp angular face commanded attention while his eyes made it impossible to turn away. Victor was heterochromatic. His right eye was blue and his left dark brown. Unheard of for an Albanian.

"Where the fuck have you been counselor? Your place is just a few miles from here. There better be a reason."

"I was in Adem's car the second he arrived. The streets are blocked everywhere by demonstrators."

"Fucking idiots," Victor sneered.

Without paying any attention to Victor's words, Sherman silently followed him into his brother Edward's apartment and was startled to find Victor's sister-in-law, Sofia, curled up on the living room couch with tears streaming down her cheeks. Her dark brown eyes were bloodshot and recessed far back into her normally fine-featured face. Her strong, solid frame looked frighteningly frail. Whatever trouble was brewing, Sherman couldn't imagine the devoted wife of Victor's disabled brother having a role in it.

Victor bent over Sofia and gently but firmly placed his hand on her shoulder, "Tell him. Tell him everything Sofia."

Victor threw Sherman a fierce look.

"Calm her down counsel. She's talking nonsense. Talking about speaking to the police. Reason with her Sherman, earn your damn retainer."

Knowing that being a witness to a conversation between Sherman and a client, even Sofia, could come back to haunt him, Victor stepped back into the hallway and waited.

"Sofia, look at me, tell me what's wrong," Sherman said in a paternal tone, as he took a seat alongside her, pondering the possibilities of her predicament. "You know I'll do whatever I can to help."

"I can't, I can't," Sofia mumbled, her head bowed and her lips trembling, then in a whisper, almost inaudible, she continued:

"Mr. Sherman, the shooting in Prospect Park?"

"My God. Sofia, did you see or hear something? It's alright. You know what you say here is completely confidential. I'm only asking to best protect you."

Sherman was about to let slip that he knew Sylvester but caught himself.

"No, that's not it. It's much worse."

With her head buried in her lap, Sofia haltingly stuttered: "The woman, the woman at the scene in the costume… the woman in the costume who ran from the tree, the one they're looking for."

After seconds of agonizing silence, Sofia raised her head, and looked through Sherman, seeking, beseeching someone far beyond the room.

"I'm the woman."

Sofia Hushemi

One

January 1996
JFK International Arrivals Terminal

Snaking her way around the passport control line at JFK International, Sofia anxiously relived her last night at home with her parents. "I don't want to go to America. Please don't make me."

"Sofia," her father sighed, as he pulled off his Windsor glasses and eyeballed her, "we know of only one way to take care of a daughter—finding the best possible husband to have a good home and make a family."

"No… no… no."

"But Edward can do that for you. We made sure of that *this* time," her father said. Haunting images of domestic abuse flashed before Sofia's eyes. Her older sister, Ajola, had often been brutally beaten by her husband. Sofia cringed as she remembered the last time and the sight of her beloved sister eating through a straw.

"You must trust your father," her mother Galina implored her, handing Sofia a tissue as she choked back tears. "He never could have known your sister's marriage would turn so sour."

Sofia and her mom looked very similar; both had hair as dark as night and chocolate eyes, a sharply defined uniquely Albanian nose and a playful mouth with the same distinctive gap between their teeth. It gave them a look that attracted men like bees to honey. But their characters were poles apart: Sofia was flighty, with a troubling desire to dance to her own drummer, while her mom was grounded and steadfastly obedient. Galina embraced the male dominance of her world while Sofia was raised to adhere but dreamed to transcend. Yet, there was no denying that Sofia, despite all her whimsy and ambition, would make a good wife.

"I'm not going," Sofia repeated.

"We've already been sent the dowry for your hand. We cannot afford to return it," said her father before he stalked out of the room in uncharacteristic anger.

"Your father and I… I don't know how we'll survive without your help from America."

Sofia realized sobs were futile. Even before the age of menstruation, like all her girlfriends in their run-down village in the mountains of Northern Albania, she knew her fate was an arranged marriage.

"Your husband-to-be is not like Ajola's. Edward is a very brave man, an army veteran who served in the war in Iraq. He is the brother of the man we have told you about ever since you were a little girl. Edward's the younger brother of Victor Hushemi, who we hid from the Communists until he escaped to America. He is a successful businessman in America."

"But Edward's old."

"Old! He's only thirty," Galina said laughing.

"But I'm still a teenager."

"I was a teenager when I married your father. Take another look at him. He's very handsome," said her mother, handing Sofia a 5x7 black and white photograph of Edward in his combat gear.

This time Sofia gave the photograph more than a perfunctory glance. Edward was about five foot eleven with broad shoulders, dark hair, and a soft, almost feminine smile. He had pronounced jet-black eyebrows. He was heavily muscled, yet still lacked the gaze of a fighter. That night, Sofia took the photograph into her bedroom, lay on her back, and unexpectedly found herself in a fit of giggles.

She snapped back to the present when reaching the front of the line at JFK. She was being told to step forward. Walking up to the raised desk of a Latino immigration officer, she presented her passport. The officer kept waving his fingers at her mouth, urging Sofia to respond to the simplest of questions in her broken English. Before every answer, Sofia hesitated, straining for the right word. She continuously reminded herself to heed her parents' warning not to breathe a word about her real scandalous purpose – a minor about to marry a much older stranger. But it was the Albanian way. What's wrong with it? Sofia assured herself.

"I see it's your first time overseas, young lady. And traveling alone. Who are you staying with?" he asked very slowly.

"Sir, I have family here. I stay with them, yes," Sofia replied in her rehearsed answer, calmly masking her terror, somehow ignoring the panic cascading through her veins. The officer had heard enough and motioned Sofia to move on through. Rushing to the nearest restroom, she locked herself inside a stall. Buckets of tears spilled down into the toilet. Sofia calmed herself and sat down to pee with not a second to spare. *Don't be scared. Your brave soldier will be here. It's going to be all right*, Sofia told herself, as she readied herself to meet her groom and his family a day before their arranged marriage, her blissful destiny.

Once back out in the arrival hall, she heard a raspy voice call out her name. Sofia spun around, frightened by the sight of a gaunt, pale man gingerly approaching her. He was holding a bunch of roses.

"Hi, Sofia. You look nice, just like your pictures."

Could this really be Edward? *My war hero?* He was a shell of a man compared to his photos. He also looked years older thanks to his five o'clock shadow and the streaks of gray in his sideburns. His bushy eyebrows looked like they'd never been trimmed. Smiling self-consciously, Edward was dressed in an oversized denim shirt and a woolen black tie, fastened in a clumsy knot. It appeared as if he had been ordered at the last minute to dress up for the occasion and had forgotten to shave.

Sofia glanced at Edward's brother Tomas standing alongside him. He smiled sympathetically at her. Tomas had a kind face and wore a stylish navy-blue suit but looked almost as uncomfortable in his attire as Edward did in his. Prodded by Tomas, Edward timidly moved forward to hug his bride. Sofia reflexively recoiled. He smelled of excessive cologne and tropical shampoo.

"I'm going to try and take good care of you," Edward whispered, as he handed her the flowers.

"Thank you," Sofia replied, smelling them.

"I hope we'll have a happy family. When I am up to it, I work hard, Sofia. As the super of our building, I can repair anything. All you must do is take care of our apartment, talk to tenants if they have a problem, and be a good wife. We'll have a great marriage."

Sofia's eyes widened. *Up to it?* What did that mean?

Tomas helped Sofia retrieve her luggage and crammed it into the cargo area of his Ford Explorer, along with all the tools and work clothes. He took the wheel while Edward hesitated, before electing to sit alongside his brother. Sofia sat alone in the rear staring out the side window. She found herself awed and confused by the majesty of the high-rise buildings. They cast long shadows, alongside the grittiness of the urban landscape that adjoined the highway. As much as she tried not to, Sofia could not stop dwelling on Edward's words. Indeed, the harder she tried, the worse it got. What was he talking about? Was Edward physically disabled or mentally disabled? Or both? Could she be facing a situation even worse than Ajola's?

"Sofia, you all right back there? You're breathing so hard and fast. Are you feeling unwell?" Tomas inquired glancing in his rear-view mirror.

"Must be the long trip," Sofia fibbed, "it made me a bit nauseous. I'll be fine."

It took almost two hours of crawling in mid-week traffic on the Parkway and maneuvering through side streets to finally arrive at Tomas's Brooklyn apartment. Sofia cast her eyes over the modest six-story red brick building on Cortelyou Road. Her new home was very basic, and a far cry from Sofia's head-in-the-clouds fantasy of palatial splendor. She was to live with Tomas and his wife Karina, and their two daughters, ages nine and eleven, until her marriage.

There being no elevator, Tomas lugged Sofia's luggage up two flights of stairs to their two-bedroom residence. He put her suitcase in the smaller bedroom she would share with his children. Sofia made a beeline for the bedroom, went to her suitcase and opened it up on the floor. She lifted piles of clothes and turned over several sheets and pillowcases lining the bottom, finding the silver bullet safe and sound in its leather pouch, exactly where her mother had placed it. "Yes, daddy dearest," Sofia whispered to herself, "Edward's dowry is safe and secure."

A loud knock startled her.

"Time for the family Inquisition," Thomas said through the door.

Sofia laughed, even though she didn't understand.

"Everybody is in the living room and dying to meet you," he added.

Along with Edward, Tomas, his wife Karina, and their daughters, Sofia was greeted by two of Karina's cousins, their wives, and children. Their stares made Sofia intensely uncomfortable. but their kisses and hugs were warm. Tomas told the children to run along and play with their cousins in their bedroom while the adults went over to the dining room. Tomas poured drinks from a bottle of vodka without spilling a drop. He raised his glass.

"Today couldn't be a more perfect day," he toasted. "Not only are we welcoming Edward's new bride into our family, but Victor will be returning home any second."

Tomas, a powerfully built man who stood a full foot taller than his wife, turned to Karina. "What has it been? Six months since we last saw him?"

"You know your brother. He disappears and comes and goes as he wants, and don't anyone dare ask any questions," Karina said in a sharp, deep voice; an unlikely match for her diminutive frame.

"Certainly not you," Tomas snapped back. "Why don't you just go check on how the meat is coming along?"

Karina stood and returned to the kitchen. The sharp exchange silenced the table, and everyone sat, simply sipping their drinks. Everyone except Sofia and Edward. After one gulp, the vodka was too powerful for Sofia's fifteen-year-old frame. Edward just sat there with a blank stare, his hands limp in his lap. Suddenly, there was a harsh buzz from the lobby intercom.

"He's here," Tomas said, as he bolted out of his chair to open the front door and led Victor into the small dining room.

Victor was solid as steel. Sofia liked his immaculately groomed gray hair and ruggedly compelling features. Everyone at the table was transfixed by his heterochromatic eyes.

"This is my brother Victor," Thomas boasted.

Victor embraced Tomas and kissed him on the cheek.

"Tomas, you look overworked and underpaid," he said, laughing. "Now, take your brother's jacket," Victor said, handing his cashmere winter overcoat to his brother who carefully hung it up in the hallway closet.

Victor was dressed in a bespoke brown, woolen three-piece suit. He was significantly older than Tomas and Edward, but fitter than both put together. Looking at Victor, Sofia thought he could easily break her father in two with a snap of his fingers. Victor's eyes went in one direction.

"Aha, I need no introduction to this young beauty," he said, while walking over to Sofia.

He knelt, took her hand, and softly kissed her fingers. Victor's touch was purposely gentle. "Edward is the luckiest man on the earth. I promised I would find a dream bride for our youngest brother and, if I do say so myself, I have made a masterpiece of an arrangement."

Victor draped his arm over Sofia's shoulder. "He'll treasure you my dear, and I know you will take great care of him," he emphatically whispered. Something in his manner frightened the teenager.

Victor stood up and, not a second too soon, he walked to the seat reserved for him at the head of the table. If he had stayed alongside Sofia for even another second, she would have passed out. As it was, her head was spinning. She had yet to digest Edward's words at the airport and now she had Victor's comments ringing in her ears which felt far more like commands than praise.

"Now, where is my other sister-in-law? Victor called out. "In the kitchen, I hope, ready to serve her guests."

Karina walked into the dining room with a huge piece of venison, the bounty of the cousins' hunting expedition upstate earlier in the week. As she placed the roast on the table, Karina said, "I'm here, Victor, to serve as always. You and everybody else."

Her words dripped with as much sarcasm as the juices on the slab of meat. Thomas couldn't believe his ears. He glared at his wife, a woman whose face reflected her years of never-ending sacrifice for her family, but before he could open his mouth, Victor laughed it off and turned to Tomas.

"A little too much Brooklyn is beginning to grow in that wife of yours, Tomas. But she is such a skillful cook, I guess we can stomach her words." He laughed again. "As long as she knows her place, and you do know your place, don't you, my dear sister-in-law?"

Karina glanced at Tomas before answering: "Yes, Victor, I didn't mean to offend you. It's been a long day for me. I'm sorry if I spoke out of turn."

Sofia gripped her hands together so tightly she could see blood filling her fingernails. She was struggling to keep her trembling body unnoticeable.

"No worries," Victor said, licking his lips and rubbing the palms of his hands together. "Now let's enjoy our dinner and celebrate Sofia's arrival and her upcoming wedding to our Edward."

Karina had prepared a wonderful meal. In addition to the scrumptious roast, there were all sorts of chargrilled vegetables and potatoes, and three different types of bread, all sourced from the motherland. As everyone ate, Victor once again dominated the conversation.

"In celebration of our newlyweds, I have additional great news. The building I purchased last month near the Manhattan Bridge, the neighborhood they're now calling Dumbo as a way to raise the prices to all the young Wall Streeters… you recall Tomas, I told you all about it?"

Tomas nodded as Victor continued, "There's a glut of commercial property on the market and the answer was staring me in the face. I can convert the building into residential units and you and Edward can be the supers and have your choice of apartments." Slapping Tomas on the back and grinning, Victor boasted, "My sisters-in-law will live like Queens in my new luxury apartments in downtown Brooklyn."

Tomas, always respectful, but never intimidated by his older brother, shook his head. "Don't get me wrong, it's a tempting and wonderful offer, but you know what my answer is going to be. I'm not interested. I like my quiet and peaceful life here in my apartment on Cortelyou Road, and Edward is nowhere near ready for such a move. I haven't even been able to convince him to move upstairs from his basement flat after the wedding. How many times have we spoken about this? The last thing our brother needs is upheaval. With all due respect, can we talk about other things?"

Sofia listened in stunned silence, while Karina shot Tomas a sharp look of disapproval for speaking with such loose lips on Sofia's first night at the dinner table. Karina jumped in and shifted the conversation as fast as she could to life in Brooklyn. She waxed lyrical about all the different places to eat and shop in the locality.

Victor then took his turn trying to ease the anxiety so clearly etched on Sofia's face. "It must all seem a bit too much right now, Sofia. But don't worry. You are going to have the most wonderful marriage to the most wonderful man. And there are many people here from our culture. You'll have many friends. And others are nice too, lots of Italians and Jews we do business with, as long as you buy food and clothes from the Italians and pay the Jews all the rest of your money," he chortled.

"They'll all love you," he continued, "But this city can be dangerous, you must be careful around *zezaks,* especially the young black boys. They all carry guns and just wait for a chance to sneak up on you and steal whatever you have. You are lucky to have such a brave soldier for a husband. Right, brothers?"

Tomas sighed while Edward averted his eyes from Victor's gaze and bowed his head.

"You are doing a wonderful job of scaring poor Sofia into catching the first flight back to Albania," Tomas said. "Why don't you try telling her about the presents you'll be bringing to the wedding this weekend? Let's change the subject to something more pleasant, Victor."

"But I'm certain Sofia is as smart and brave as she is pretty. She is not frightened by my advice. And I bet she's curious about the world in which she'll be living. Am I not right, Sofia?"

"I know you just want me to be safe," she replied. "Thank you."

Victor broke into a wide grin and raised his glass. Sofia, crying on the inside, stoically smiled.

"Sofia, you're a welcome princess to our family. A storybook bride for my brother!"

Two

January 1996
Brooklyn

The following morning, Sofia stared for ages at her reflection in the full-length mirror, as she auditioned her long white wedding dress.

She had never looked more beautiful. Under the veil, her auburn hair was framed by wisps of curls. Sofia turned slowly, watching her dress gently sway with her body. It fit perfectly, neither too loose to hide her tiny waist nor too tight to be immodest. Even her large bottom and muscular legs were safely concealed beneath the long, flowing fabric.

Yet, there was one feature of her anatomy that Sofia watched carefully. At fifteen, she still barely had breasts. How could she get married without a proper bosom? The thought made her queasy.

The day before an Albanian wedding is a separate day for the bride's family to celebrate the couple being joined in matrimony. But Sofia's parents were weighed down by the needs of the farm and far too anxious about flying overseas to make the trip. It meant that only a few of Tomas's friends and their children had come over for Sunday breakfast. There was a great buzz in the air. Everyone sat around the kitchen table enjoying eggs and a variety of home baked Albanian breads and pastry.

Alarm bells rang louder than ever in Sofia's head when she noticed the absence of anyone there to support Edward. She watched the way he acted at dinner; he didn't speak a word. And the way he walked, as if something was causing him pain. Yet, she saw no visible deformities. And then there was Tomas and Victor's conversation at dinner. Rather than marrying a military hero, Sofia was discovering that Edward was a victim of warfare.

Seeing Sofia sullenly poking at her food disturbed Tomas; he attempted to lift her spirits. "Sofia, it's a glorious day for your family," he said. "It's terrible that they cannot be here. But this is a day to celebrate your new life. What do you think your girlfriends' lives will be like back in Albania? Certainly, not like life in America. And as for your parents, Edward will send them money whenever he can. You should rejoice."

Sofia forced a wan smile as she looked around at her new family. They had all been strangers only twenty-four hours earlier, but now they were all she had. Struggling to maintain her composure, Sofia quietly excused herself to bathe and dress for her imminent nuptials.

Sofia went down the hallway and closed the door of the children's bedroom, the room where she had slept squeezed alongside her small cousins. She sat at the foot of the bed, weeping, desperately praying for her parents to come to her rescue, craving for the embrace of Ajola, whose warm hugs had seen her through all the dark times of her childhood.

Sofia was startled by a knock on her door, "Sofia, may I come in?" It sounded like Tomas.

"Of course."

To her surprise, it was not Tomas, but Victor. Seeing her bloodshot eyes and sorry state, Victor took Sofia into his arms "There, there little one. Dry those tears. Everything is going to be fine. I promise you are going to be the happiest of brides. You must trust your brother-in-law, Victor."

"Oh. I'm sorry, Victor. I'll be fine. It's just a lot to get used to."

Victor withdrew his arms, continued sitting alongside Sofia on the bed, and tenderly patted her knee. "Sofia, I know it's been only a few days, but would you mind if we talked privately?"

"Oh, oh," Sofia momentarily hesitated, then nodded her head.

"You're going to find that, as the oldest brother, the family depends on me. Our father left his boys in my hands. Sofia, I didn't arrange your marriage to Edward carelessly. You are going to discover that there is nothing I plan carelessly. And all my plans succeed... failure is never an outcome for me," he said.

"But am I really the right girl for your brother, I fear I am too young to be the right bride for him?"

"My dear, I know your family. They took me in and protected me before I came to America. I made sure to learn everything I could about you, Sofia. You see, I know that you're not just beautiful. I know how intelligent and mature you are as well. The only girl in your school district to learn to speak and read English."

Sofia didn't bother correcting Victor about her real level of English. Victor smiled at Sofia's puzzled look.

"It's my business to know every detail of things that involve my family." Victor took Sofia's hands. "My brother is a wonderful and courageous man," he continued. "He sacrificed so much by going to war for America. And now, he suffers pain from having watched so many horrible things. He had to be paired with a special woman to help him heal. Fate brought you to us." Sofia was frozen by Victor's words. She robotically nodded.

"Trust me, Sofia. Your commitment to Edward and our family will bring you happiness beyond your wildest dreams. You will never want for things. You will always have what you need. And your children and family will be envied by all."

Victor again opened his arms. Sofia cautiously embraced him, as he patted her on the back. "You will see, you will be so happy my dear." Victor let go of Sofia and then reached into his pocket and took out a small jewellery case.

"Sofia, I have a confession to make. I have had only one love in my life. Shpresa, my wife, I married her in my first year in America. We never had any children, and when she turned twenty, she was hit with cancer. She suffered for years. I have never looked at another woman. But I must say, you remind me of her. That crooked smile of yours, a little bit devilish, and those eyes... full of understanding. I saw it in your pictures, and I knew you were the one for Edward."

Victor opened the box to reveal a worn brass ring with a ruby heart attached. "Before I brought the band from Albania when I left. I had the rubies added for Shpresa. Edward's wife will now adorn her finger with the family's only heirloom and the rubies will be envied by every bride."

Sofia struggled to gather her wits about her.

"I cannot take this gift, Victor. It's too dear to you," she said. Hot tears again started trickling down her cheeks. Victor took Sofia's hands, holding them uncomfortably tightly.

"You don't have to be concerned, my dear brother-in-law," she continued. I will be the wife you expect for Edward. But this gift, I can't accept it."

"My dear," he said, dabbing away her tears with the corner of his handkerchief. "I want you to have it. You will not reject such a request from your brother-in-law?"

Sofia felt uneasy with the idea and responsibility of wearing such an extravagant ring, but she knew it was futile to argue. "If it's your request, I will, of course, wear it and pray to be worthy of such a gift."

Victor placed the ring on Sofia's finger. It fit loosely but felt sufficiently firm. "You are the only other woman who is worthy of having it grace her finger. Letting Karina even look at it on your hand is more than she deserves."

An hour later, Sofia and Edward were both whisked off to the civil court for the wedding. They rode in a limo that Victor had ordered for the occasion. It was lucky Sofia didn't recall it was bad luck to see the groom before tying the knot, seeing as she grew up immersed in superstition. After Victor placed Shpresa's wedding ring on her finger, the moment he left the room, she took it off and blew on the inside for an hour petrified of catching Shprepa's cancer. Growing up, after seeing a dead mouse she always held her hair to stop it from falling out. Yet here she was unwittingly ignoring one of the biggest old wives' tales. But would she be an old wife with Edward? she asked herself on that last journey as a single woman. Correction: single young girl, she thought.

The wedding ceremony itself was an embarrassing bathos. Victor, who had filled in all the forms, using a fake ID for Sofia's age, insisted on her keeping on the veil at all times. But it was all unnecessary because the judge, dressed in a rumpled suit, had already been brought on board by Victor's attorney. He didn't look at her once during the short ceremony. He reeled off the words of their union without any real feeling, and in a soft, halting voice, Sofia blurted out a yes to her wedding vows. Edward affirmed his in an even shakier tone.

"You may kiss the bride," the judge said dryly. Edward smiled weakly, pulled up Sofia's veil as he pecked her on the lips.

Sofia spent the remainder of her wedding day in a fog. At the reception, she made sure to show a happy face to the crowd of more than two hundred guests. The men, a dozen relatives, the rest employees, and associates of Victor, were dressed in white and black tuxedos. Their wives wore long gowns of every color other than white. "Out of respect for the bride," Victor explained to her.

The meal was a royal banquet. Lentil and fish soups, casseroles filled with cabbage, leeks, onions, and feta cheese. Lamb, beef, squash, and spinach pies. Veal, chicken, and rabbit stew, as well. Dolma, a stuffed dish of cabbage, green peppers, and vine leaves filled with rice and bread. Victor had also made sure there were Italian dishes like lasagne, veal, and chicken parmesan. And, as for the proverbial and figurative icing on the cake, there were seven tiers on the gigantic Italian wedding cheesecake; this was accompanied by Albanian baklava with nuts, sugar, and cinnamon. Expensive wine, vodka, and champagne were in abundance from the free bar.

Having learned her lesson the night before, Sofia only took a few sips of red wine in order to calm her nerves. Edward sat next to her at the head table reserved for them, along with Victor, Tomas, and Karina. He attempted to drink a glass of white wine while having a few bites of rabbit stew. Sofia filled her plate with Albanian dishes she had not tasted in years but ate only slightly more than her husband.

After the meal, the band requested Sofia and Edward take to the dance floor for their first waltz as man and wife. Looking at Victor, as if he were faintly hoping to be relieved of this burden, Edward half-heartedly offered Sofia his hand. As they slowly made their way to the dance floor to applause, Sofia moved ever so slowly to the music, discretely leading her husband through the few steps he could manage. Guests kept walking over to the newlyweds, handing Edward an envelope with money, or stuffing it into his pocket. When their dance mercifully finished, Victor rushed over and triumphantly held his brother's hand up in the air. He proceeded to shower Sofia and Edward with hundred-dollar bills. Everyone loved the traditional gesture. There was a standing ovation. The guests clapped and cheered for a long time after it finished.

As the evening wore on, the time came for Edward and Sofia to depart. They climbed into the back of a limousine. The doors slammed shut, muting the noise of the party. For the first time since they met, Sofia and Edward were alone. They nervously looked straight ahead, with their hands in their laps on opposite sides of the backseat. There was an uncomfortable silence as their car drove away. A full minute passed before Edward could even look at his bride. Finally, he turned and managed a nervous grin. Sofia returned the compliment. She could tell Edward was desperately trying to think of something to say, but the words would not come.

"It was a wonderful ceremony," Sofia offered as if she were commenting on someone else's nuptials. "You have a wonderful family."

Edward offered a slight nod. At that moment, Sofia noticed their limousine was being followed by a caravan of cars honking their horns and cheering.

"Why do they have to do this?" Edward whined. He gritted his teeth, started to shake and descended into a full-blown panic attack.

"I can't do this," Edward hollered. He leaned forward and repeatedly hammered the partition window, startling the limousine driver, and causing Sofia to shriek. "Pull over right now," he shouted at the top of his lungs. The limo came to a sudden halt on the side of the road, but the honking continued unabated. Sofia debated fleeing, while Edward rocked and kept taking staggered breaths. Having never witnessed anything remotely like it, Sophia was terrified by Edward's behavior. "Can't they stop!" he screamed. Edward saw the wretched look on Sofia's face and tried to gather himself.

"I'm sorry," he gasped, reaching into his pocket and throwing several pills down his throat. Their limo driver rolled down the partition and offered some soothing words.

"Hey Eddie, it's only a panic attack. I suffered from PTSD myself. Trust me, everythin' is gonna to be just fine and dandy. It will soon pass. Breathe in and out," he said in a strong Bronx accent.

A few moments later, the honking grew dimmer, and Edward began to relax.

"I'm sorry, I'm OK now," he said.

As the driver pulled back out onto the road, Sofia vacantly stared out the window, feeling on the verge of her own panic attack. Edward, now recomposed, held the door to the lobby open for Sofia and the couple made their way down the one flight of stairs to Edward's apartment. Sofia's heart pounded out of her chest at the sound of his key turning the lock. When Edward picked Sofia up and carried her over the threshold, she was completely taken by surprise, the gesture momentarily lifted her spirits only to be erased mere seconds later when she scanned her new home.

There was a stained couch, a 22-inch TV, and a couple of cheap wooden chairs. Unwashed clothes that smelled like onions lay on the grimy floor. Sofia could smell dust in the air. The two windows looking out on the sidewalk had off-putting grates on them to prevent burglary and were decorated with soiled curtains. There were no working bulbs in the overhead lights. The only illumination was provided by the dim bulb of a tattered standing fixture with a gray shade. It may have been winter in Brooklyn, but with the radiators fully unleashed, the cold wasn't the problem. It felt hotter and more humid than the most uncomfortable summer day in Albania.

Edward walked to the closet, shuffled through a pile of unfolded blankets and bedding, and found a relatively clean white sheet which he draped over the couch. He tentatively took Sofia's hand and led her to sit on the middle cushion, as he placed himself on the far end making sure not to be uncomfortably close to his bride. Edward just sat, slouching, looking down at the floor.

Sophia went to the bedroom, opened her suitcase, and took out the black pouch with the silver bullet. Returning to the living room, she opened her hand and placed the pouch in her husband's lap. Hard as she tried, Sofia could not hide the tears streaming down her cheeks.

Edward untied the pouch, took hold of the bullet with his thumb and index finger and sighed. "Please Sofia, don't cry, it's such a stupid custom. Pay no mind, if not for Victor, I would throw it out the window." Edward delicately wiped the tears from Sofia's cheeks. The bullet, however, was not the reason for Sofia's tears.

"Edward, I know we are husband and wife and will be lovers forever," she nervously began. "But, please, I am a little scared." Sofia paused, half-expecting her husband to say, "Scared! Scared of what?" But he just sat and listened.

She pressed on. "We just met, and you know, I still have not yet turned sixteen. I know what is expected of me. But please, please can I just sleep on the couch tonight?"

After what seemed an eternity, Edward replied, "Sofia, you do not want to sleep with me? Tonight, of all nights?" Edward lifted his head and mysteriously looked up at the ceiling.

"Wait a minute," he said. Edward went to the front door and peered into the hallway, then exited the apartment and made his way towards the stairs. Sofia followed and watched him look up towards Tomas' apartment. He stood there for several more minutes, staring and mumbling to himself. Sofia tried to make sense of yet more eccentric behavior from her husband. Finally, he walked back to the apartment, rubbing his forehead.

"I think it will be OK," Edward said. "Victor must have left for the evening. Maybe he even went back to his home in Westchester County. I doubt he will return by tomorrow morning. The earliest will be tomorrow afternoon. You sleep in the bedroom; I'll sleep on the couch."

"Thank you, Edward. Thank you. Just give me a little time. I will be a good wife, you'll see." Sofia was too relieved to dwell on Edward's bizarre conduct. She did not bother to ask what Victor had to do with anything. Sofia started towards the bedroom when Edward called out.

"Sofia? Please, there is one thing you can do for me. Can you look in the bathroom for my pills, the blue ones?"

Without forewarning, Edward collapsed. He lay groaning on the coach, with his arm wrapped around his head. Sofia rushed to the bathroom and opened the medicine cabinet, gasping at the sight of more than a dozen pill bottles with names she could barely pronounce: Ibuprofen, Tramadol, Prozac, Zoloft, and a small liquid bottle with bold letters "for intravenous injection only" labelled meperidine. Only one bottle contained blue tablets—Oxycontin. Sofia grabbed the bottle and washed out a dirty plastic cup from the kitchen sink and filled it with tepid tap water. Then she put her hands on the overhead cabinets and hung her head. *Could the night get any worse?*

Sofia gathered herself and walked over to Edward. "Here are your pills."

He grabbed the pills from her hand and swallowed them without a sip of water.

"Thank you, Sofia. Goodnight."

Sofia watched Edward fall into a deep sleep, closed the door to the bedroom, slowly took off her dress, and put on her nightgown, sick to her stomach. Sofia pulled the covers over her head, no longer fearful but overwhelmed. She had begun her evening petrified of being molested by a husband she hardly knew, but instead had discovered that her parents had sent her to wed a man who couldn't even care for himself and couldn't be saved by anyone, let alone his child bride.

Three

January 1996
Brooklyn

Sofia rolled over in bed. Half-dreaming, she reached out for Ajola and muttered her beloved older sister's name in her sleep. Sofia felt deflated when she awakened to find herself all alone in her marriage bed on her first morning as a newlywed. As Sofia tiptoed along the darkened corridor to the bathroom, she peered into the sitting room through the half-ajar door. Edward was passed out on the sofa. Sofia was relieved, she didn't want him to see her like *this*, with bloodshot eyes and her hair all pins and needles.

She soaked herself in the shower until the bathroom was so filled with steam it was impossible to see. When she limped out and grabbed a towel. Sofia's skin was still on fire from the boiling bath, but she felt calmer. Towelling off, she heard Victor and Tomas. Sofia carefully cracked open the door and was shocked to find Victor in *her* bedroom ripping off the blankets and studying the sheets, which he then thrust into Tomas's hands. Sofia secured the towel around her body and timidly walked on the balls of her feet into the room.

"Is everything OK?" she asked, hoping her presence in nothing but a skimpy towel would encourage them to leave the room for her to get dressed in private. Victor was still studying every inch of the sheets.

"No blood, Sofia," he uttered in the tone of a judge handing down a death sentence. "Look!" Victor tossed the covers to Thomas, who then dropped them in apparent disbelief. Victor's demonic bloodshot eyes would not leave them as they fell to the ground.

"Did your parents send a whore to marry my brother?" Moments passed, nobody moved. The paternalistic brother-in-law of the day before raised his right hand, and a mere second before he delivered his palm to Sofia's face, Edward ran into the room and cried out:

"Stop! Don't you raise a hand to my wife. And don't you dare accuse her like that. Call her a whore! What are you thinking?"

Victor turned and tilted his head towards Edward, a sarcastic smile etched on his face.

"My youngest brother has some balls after all. What would you call your bride then, brother?"

Edward with great effort stood straight and took a deep breath. "My wife is the angel you arranged for me to wed; she is the woman I am blessed to have in my life. And she is a virgin bride. Not that our marriage is your concern, but I was not in the mood for relations last night. I slept on the sofa, and Sofia was alone in the bedroom."

Sofia stood against the wall and backed up Edward's words. "Victor, I'm only fifteen. I would die before I would disobey the Kanun. You know all about me. You told me yourself. Even if you beat me, my answer won't change… because I'm telling you the truth."

"There will be no beating," Edward cried out, "isn't that right, brother?"

Victor looked at Edward and sniggered. "I know you, Edward. You're so trusting and easy to take advantage of. Don't think I won't be back tomorrow or the next day, until there is blood on these sheets," Victor said, jabbing his finger at the bed.

"Victor, you'll do no such thing," Edward said.

"Are you disrespecting me?"

"You know how I respect you. But this is my marriage, and what happens in our bedroom will not be your business."

Victor put his face right up in Sofia's personal space, in the same way someone might do when squaring up for a fight. Terrified, Sofia could smell expresso and brandy on his breath. He thrust his index finger inches from her nose. He's either drunk or mad… *or both*! she feared.

"You're lucky, Sofia. But hear my words, if you have deceived my brother or ever deceive him, even Edward won't be able to save you from the silver bullet."

"I am a virgin," she screamed again and again, until she collapsed down on the bed in a flood of tears. Victor stormed out. Edward sat on the bed beside her, his head bowed, still staring at the sheets. Victor's tirade more than terrified and humiliated Sofia: it made her feel ashamed, unworthy of her parents' arrangement and even somehow guilty.

"Don't worry, Sofia," Edward said, looking up at his wife with tears in his eyes and a heartfelt smile on his face. "I cannot predict my brother. You don't know him. We must do everything right. But I promise you, he will never hurt you."

Edward stared at the sheets, as if he was hoping a blood stain would appear like magic. Even when Sofia inadvertently dropped her towel and embraced her husband it failed to distract him. Her bare breasts pressing against his upper chest, inches from his mouth, produced no response. *What kind of man is this?* Sofia pondered. Edward unwrapped Sofia's slender arms from around his neck, slowly stood and made his way to the kitchen mumbling to himself. Rummaging through several kitchen drawers, he removed the sharpest knife he could lay his hands on. Edward clenched his teeth and cut his forearm. With blood dripping from the gash, he grabbed a bathroom towel and tightly wrapped it around his arm. Edward then went over to Sofia and muffled her hysterics with his uninjured arm.

"Shhh! Don't let my brother hear you. Please. Young lady, please." Keeping hold of Sofia with his right arm, he stood over the sheets and squeezed enough blood onto it to fill half a shot glass.

"Be careful, Edward," he said, addressing himself, "not to put too much blood. We don't want it to look like a cow was being slaughtered here." Edward stepped away from the bed only when he was satisfied that the sheets looked like someone's virginity had been lost on them. Releasing his grip on Sofia, he gently wrapped his arm around her, walked her to the couch and sat her down.

"Sofia, are you feeling better?" he said. "I'm sorry but this had to be done. You shower, put on the prettiest dress you can find and sit with me in the living room. I will call my brother back down; show him the sheets and prove your virginity. I will remind him that I always feel my worst at night."

Sofia stared at her husband unable to respond, paralyzed by the madness of her new life.

Four

March 2001
Brooklyn

As an Albanian child bride, Sofia accepted her plight and over time, she even developed deep feelings for Edward. Compared to Ajola's sadistic husband and her relatives and other neighbors, she was living with a saint. Edward wouldn't hurt a fly and suffered unimaginable pain in silence. By the age of twenty, however, more than ever her mind and body yearned for fulfillment. To make matters worse, whenever she and Edward attempted intercourse, it heightened his anxiety.

Sofia began dreaming of a better life. But until that day came, she vowed to make the best of her lot; no matter how difficult, she would fulfill her responsibilities and keep her counsel. In the meantime, she played the part of the perfect Albanian wife to Edward and the grateful sister-in-law to Victor. Sofia devoted herself to household chores while covering for Edward when tenant after tenant would knock on their door complaining of long overdue repairs. She bore the brunt of Tomas' endless complaining about Edward's inability to help. He was always implying to Victor that she was somehow responsible.

As much as she resented and feared Victor, her emotions towards him were evolving. "She's the best thing to ever happen to our brother," Sofia once overheard Victor say when she eavesdropped on them at the end of one of their regular Sunday afternoon visits for expresso and cake.

It must've been a heartfelt compliment because Victor was a callous man who rarely sang praises. Sofia had heard whispers about the unspeakable things Victor did to those who double crossed him and foolishly disrespected him. But, in his defense, he met his brother's condition with astonishing kindness and concern. Victor frowned on the free care his brother was eligible to receive at the VA and instead spared no expense for Edward's treatment. Edward's team of professionals were the best in their field: doctors, psychologists, physical therapists; they were always the finest money could buy. Despite everything, Edward remained mired in depression and pain. True to form, Victor had to be repeatedly told by Edward's doctors that Sofia's failure to become pregnant was not her fault, it was Edward's condition and medication which rendered him unable to perform. Edward was trapped in a vicious Catch-22 circle; he needed the meds to survive, but these lifesavers robbed him of the opportunity to live a full life.

Sofia used to hate how often Victor would unexpectedly appear at the apartment. He would fly off the handle if it wasn't spotless, and a special meal had to be prepared in his honor. Yet, after the first few years, Sofia surprisingly learned not to mind the intrusions; at least it broke up the monotony. Besides, the wolf in sheep's clothing often came bearing gifts.

Three weeks after that compliment, Victor sent word that he was on his way and Sofia immediately went to work cooking a slow roasted chicken. She then fiercely mopped the kitchen floor and ran around the apartment making sure everything was perfect, Sofia shook her head, smiling in disbelief at how much she was looking forward to Victor's visit. She was scrubbing the last of the utensils in the sink when Victor knocked on the door. He walked in and gave Sofia a big bear hug, as Edward struggled to get up off the sofa.

"My dear, you look as pretty as ever, but perhaps a bit worn down," Victor said, inspecting Sofia in her sweaty state.

"Thank you, Victor. There is no rest for the wicked," Sofia replied, using one of the latest idioms she'd just learned. She had a thick book of them and would memorize one a day.

Victor turned to Edward. "What have you been doing to wear out our Sofia?" Victor winked at his brother. But the innuendo went over Edward's head.

"Nothing, Victor. Nothing. Sofia does everything. I do nothing. I'd be lost without her."

"Don't be so hard on yourself, brother. We all know you're doing your best. Right, Sofia?"

"Of course, he does. We're fine, Victor. I hope you'll stay for dinner."

"I'm afraid I'll have to take a rain check, with a heavy heart, because your cooking is beyond compare. I have a business meeting I must get to. Do you need anything? I bet you could use a new spring coat."

"I'm fine, Victor. We both are. We'll let you know if we run into any problems. But thank you for asking."

"Oh, I almost forgot. I do have something for you. The postman gave me your mail. I think it's a letter from your sister."

Sofia froze. Her heart almost leapt out of her mouth. "Ajola?" Sofia had not heard from Ajola in months and had grown more worried by the day. Her husband Rinor frowned upon her having contact with anyone in her family, but she somehow still managed to sneak out hand-scribbled notes to Sofia. The sisters communicated by forwarding mail to their cousin Alexandra and she, in turn, would put it in the hands of a man who would discretely deliver Sofia's letters to Ajola when Rinor wasn't home.

Sofia resisted opening the letter immediately, wanting to savor it in private after Victor left. Following a quick hug goodbye, and trying not to be the least bit obvious, Sofia hurried Victor out the door and dashed to the bedroom, leaving Edward on the couch where he was likely to remain without ever bothering to eat dinner. She tore open the envelope like a child excitedly does with a birthday present and hungrily drank in every word:

Dear Sofia,

I'm so sorry not to have written sooner. But my bastard husband watches me like a hawk, waiting to pounce if I make one wrong move. I can't risk angering him... again. These past few weeks, he has thankfully not hurt me. I have been his perfect slave. I speak only when spoken to and do everything I am ordered to... in both the kitchen and the bedroom. He no longer cares about my not becoming pregnant. Thank God. But he comes home smelling like other women.

How are you Sofia? You're so lucky to live in New York with a decent man. I dream every day of joining you. Rinor would never divorce me, he'd kill me first. But don't worry I think I might have figured out a way to escape and he'll never find me. I'll run away and never look back.

I have to go now. I hear him at the front door. Write back the way we always do.

Love,
Ajola

Sofia was both elated and gravely worried by her sister's letter. Sofia had never told Ajola the truth about Edward—that he was physically incapable of doing much more than laying around on the couch. The last thing she wanted was to add to Ajola's concerns. She already had the weight of the world on her slender shoulders.

Two weeks passed before Victor's next visit on a rainy Sunday. He stayed for a hearty dinner of fried liver and onions with gravy and oven baked potatoes. Even Edward managed to eat some supper and grunt noises of satisfaction. Sofia had decided to approach Victor about Ajola's situation and was waiting for just the right moment to talk about it all. After helping clear the dishes, and assisting Edward back to the living room couch, Victor started talking to Sofia about Edward's care over a mug of Indian tea and honey.

"Doctors! They boast of being the best and fill their pockets with tens of thousands and do what? The only thing they're expert at is stealing my money." Victor grimaced.

"They try, Victor. Trust me. No matter how busy they are, they always take my phone calls. There's no effort spared to help him."

"Don't think I'm blaming you. You're the best wife a man could want or dream of."

"We can't give up," she replied. "And there are some good days. It's not all darkness. I believe Edward will one day turn the corner. He'll surprise us. Sooner than you think."

"Let's hope so," Victor said before abruptly standing. "I have a gift for you."

Victor presented Sofia with a beautiful wine-colored raincoat. Sofia wondered if it had *fallen off the back of a truck*, which was one of the favorite expressions she had underlined in her book of idioms. Still, she kept quiet.

"Victor, you shouldn't be spending your hard-earned money on me all the time," Sofia gushed, putting on the most grateful smile, even risking a flirtatious look, to draw Victor in.

"You are Edward's guardian angel. It's the least I can do," he said, gently caressing her cheek with the back of his hand.

Sofia wrapped herself in the coat and did a 360-degree twirl in slow motion just to make sure the fit met with Victor's approval.

"Victor," Sofia began, changing her tone. "I don't know where else to turn." Sofia paused for dramatic effect, just like she had done when practicing her spiel in the steamed-up bathroom mirror.

"My sister Ajola," she continued, "her life is in danger."

"Oh! How? Tell me everything."

"Her husband is a sick man. He cheats and beats her. He has even put her in the hospital. I believe he'll kill her one day. Just because he is tired of her. Please, I beg for your help."

Sofia fully realized the risk she was taking with such a plea. In her culture the husband was the supreme king of his castle, and it was disrespectful for a woman to be critical of someone else's marriage. She took a step back, trying to prepare herself for the worst.

Victor sat silently for a moment, debating what he just heard. "Sofia," he responded in a surprisingly soothing and kind tone. "Of course, I'll help. If you tell me your sister is in danger of physical harm, I'll check on things and if a talk or even more is needed with her husband it will be done. Your sister is family. No more harm will come to her."

Victor's reply had pumped up her deflated heart. If anyone could help Ajola it was Victor. Even from Brooklyn, she knew he could protect Ajola and help someday unite them. She rushed to Victor and, for the first time in her life, sincerely kissed his cheek and embraced him.

"Thank you, thank you," Sofia sobbed; her hot tears splashing onto his shirt. "There is nobody like you. What would Edward and I do without you?"

Victor walked over to the couch where Edward was moaning in a barely audible voice in his deep sleep. Victor stood over him. He delicately patted his brother and sighed before turning to say goodbye.

After walking Victor to the hallway and softly closing the door, Sofia gazed briefly at her husband before making her way to the bedroom and praying before going to sleep. There were sincere prayers uttered for both Edward and Ajola. When the time was right, Sofia planned on telling Victor that Ajola would be such a great help in caring for Edward, because his needs were becoming more and more difficult to handle alone. And that Ajola couldn't remain in the same house as Rinor. Coming to America was the perfect solution.

Sunday dinner at Karina's was Victor's next scheduled visit to Brooklyn. Sofia insisted on doing all the cooking without telling Victor beforehand. She wanted to surprise him with all his favorite dishes. He arrived in a jovial mood shortly after the sun went down and sat in the living room talking with Tomas. Karina went back and forth serving drinks and Sofia's pre-meal appetizers of meatballs, yogurt, and feta cheese wrapped in fried bread and a salad of romaine, onions, and boiled eggs.

"I know you had to have these delivered, they're wonderful," Victor joked to Karina. When she admitted she had not prepared them, he sarcastically replied, "It would be a crime against good taste to waste Sofia's many talents in the kitchen."

He and Tomas shared Sofia's creations with large glasses of chilled vodka. Victor could never understand how Americans drank vodka at room temperature on the rocks. Good vodka needed to be ice-cold from the freezer. He drank a Polish brand that would have a hidden logo appear on the back label just like magic once it was at the right subzero temperature.

"Where is our Sofia?" Victor asked.

At that very moment, Sofia was secreting herself in the kitchen. With the veal dumplings sizzling and their aroma tantalizing, she scooped them up and placed them on a tray and readied herself to surprise her brother-in-law. A second before pushing the swinging door into the living room, Sofia hesitated at the sound of Victor's raised and agitated voice. He banged the table with his fist, and the cutlery jumped to attention.

"Slow down and tell me again what the fuck you're talking about," he said in a surprisingly loud voice. "I should end your pathetic existence. You promised me everything was taken care of."

Victor wasn't talking to Tomas; he was on his cell phone, pacing back and forth on the hardwood floor to the rhythm of fury. Making sure not to intrude on Victor's private business, Sofia quickly turned around and went back into the kitchen where she placed the plate back on the top of the stove and tended to her other cooking. As Sofia opened the oven door and hot steam hit her in the face, forcing her to jump back, she checked on her veal and slow roasting potatoes.

Victor's voice grew so loud, it could be heard throughout the apartment. "You and your crew will need to make amends in the next six months," he threatened. "How? I have yet to decide. Hear me. You fucking guaranteed me that you would not let him disturb a hair on her head and you couldn't prevent that piece of shit… from murdering her."

Sofia violently slammed the oven shut and placed both her hands on the side of the stove for support. She began to tremble and couldn't breathe properly. Shock mode had kicked in. The lights of the kitchen started to spin; Sofia struggled to remain standing when she heard the next words out of Victor's mouth:

"With all poor Sofia has suffered dealing with my brother… now I have to dump this shit on her!" He stopped to listen and then roared: "That fucking Rinor butchered Ajola. That you hesitated to take his life until after it was too late. I swear if I wasn't in Brooklyn, you'd be joining him."

Suddenly, Sofia's whimpers turned into an unsettling howl. Victor and Karina came running into the kitchen. Before she lost consciousness, Sofia's head crashed against the tile floor.

Five

January 2002
Brooklyn

The bullet, made entirely of silver, is precious. The laws of the Kanun command that every woman present a silver bullet to her husband on their wedding day as part of her dowry. It is to be used to take her life if she's ever unfaithful.

The bullet must not be found. So, she hides it inside her vagina wrapped in a tampon.

She has just arrived in America. The airport building is eerily white with sheer glass walls and ceilings stretching as far as the eye could see. There are a multitude of travelers, yet not a sound can be heard. Trapped in a speeding current of nameless faces, she yells for her mother and father before being stopped, pulled aside, and ordered by a homeland security officer to walk through an enormous metal detector.

The silver bullet sets off the metal detector.

"Më fai!, it's not my fault, she desperately tries to explain..

She is 15 years old. She is speaking Albanian. They don't understand.

She is 35 years old. She has lived in Brooklyn for twenty years. She speaks perfect English. Why don't they understand?

She looks into the different colored eyes of the officer and freezes.

"Victor!"

Sofia screamed and bolted out of bed. After Ajola's killing, this recurring nightmare haunted her. Edward was popping his pills like candy. Whenever he attempted to cut back, the pain and depression increased tenfold. He was unable to sleep, and when he did finally nod off, Edward would wake in the middle of the night screaming down the house from the terrors. Sofia's indifference didn't help. The wind had gone out of her sails after Ajola's brutal murder at the hands of the very man who had promised to be different but turned out to be even worse than all the rest from their neck of the woods. Part of Sofia was buried in the cold ground beside her sister, who went to her grave with a disfigured face and broken body parts. The only reason Sofia didn't attend the funeral was because her parents urged her not to waste her energy making the ten-hour flight back home only to look at a closed casket.

Even in the throes of despair, Sofia could not escape the grind of daily life. The washing machine had broken, forcing her to pile a week's worth of filthy clothes into a large suitcase with worn-out wheels on the bottom. Those wheels constantly got stuck. She had to trudge up the basement stairs with two weeks' worth of smelly clothes, and then slowly make her way through the icy streets to the laundromat. At the entrance, Sofia was dragging her heavy boatload of wash up the stoop with both hands, when an attractive young black woman, holding a baby in her right arm, rushed over and pushed open the door with her free hand.

"Girl, you sure look like you could use a hand... or should I say three!"

The young mother giggled and smiled in the sweetest way, revealing symmetrical dimples on either cheek. The woman wore an oversized, dark blue hooded college sweatshirt and a pair of jeans, and bounced the baby on her wide hip. Her hair was cut short, showing off her gorgeous face and distinctively dark skin. If she had been taller, and a few pounds lighter, she could have been a model.

After shyly thanking the woman, Sofia began unloading her clothes into the nearest empty machine. Unsolicited, the woman joined her, standing uncomfortably close. She was full of laughter.

"Are you new to the area, Ms. Hands-full? I haven't seen you around."

"I live around the corner," Sofia said, looking down out of shyness. "Our washing machine is broken."

"Oh." She giggled again. "You're one of those rich white folks moving into the area." She directed her speech to her baby, who was standing in her lap watching her mom's mouth move. "Not only a washer, I bet she's got a dryer and a dishwasher," she cooed, before turning back to Sofia.

"I'm far from rich," Sofia protested.

"But I bet you live in a bigger place than us. We just moved around the corner into an apartment so tiny my ass barely makes it through the door."

Sofia was the one now giggling. It crossed her mind that it was the first time she had even smiled since losing Ajola.

"But, what the hell, I wanted a better/safer place for me and my daughter," she heard the woman continue in her radio friendly voice. "Who would have thought there'd be so many of you rich, white folks here on Cortelyou Road opening restaurants and health food stores? You all turning this place into another Park Slope! Thought my daughter and I deserved a taste."

"I said, I'm not rich."

"That fine suitcase sure does tell a different story, honey."

Sofia tried to hide how uncomfortable this stranger made her feel, with her unfiltered mouth. God, Victor would have shut it down in a heartbeat with just one of his *don't fuck with me* faces.

"I wish we were rich," Sofia said. "My husband's the super of the building. So, hooking up a second-hand washer-dryer wasn't difficult, or too expensive. But it broke just when I needed it most. Murphy's Law, right." Sofia stood awkwardly next to her now-empty suitcase.

A buzzer went off, and the woman pushed her cart one-handed towards the dryer to unload her clothes, while still cradling her child.

"Maybe I can help," Sofia offered.

Sofia became startled when the woman suddenly swung her baby-bearing hip in her direction and asked, "Do you want to hold her?"

"What...?"

"I mean, could you?" She giggled again. "I could fold a lot faster with two hands."

"Oh, sure." Sofia's heart raced, but she was too scared to refuse. Sofia walked over and nervously put her hands out to take the child.

"I'm Angela, by the way. And this is Sonia," she said, as she plopped her baby into Sofia's arms.

Sonia stared deeply into Sofia's eyes. "She likes you," Angela added, as she returned to her dryer. "You got any?"

"Any what?" Sofia said, wishing she could find a way to put an end to the interrogation.

"Any kids?" Angela said, with her face in the dryer, coming up with a handful of baby socks.

"Oh, not yet."

Angela started folding with expert hands. Sofia felt a little weird holding a baby and asked herself why? Then it hit her—she had never cradled an infant before in her arms.

She liked smelling the baby's head, and was soon in her own little world, imagining Sonia was her own flesh and blood.

Angela snapped her out of it with another question: "Well, how old are you? Twenty-two? Twenty-three?"

"I'm only twenty, actually," Sofia's cheeks blushed. She asked herself, *Should I have lied and said I was older? When will she stop?*

Angela waved it off. "Oh, sorry. No offence, but it can be hard to tell how old you white girls are. Isn't that what you all say about us?" she giggled again.

"None taken. But you must be near menopause age, right?" Sofia blurted out tongue-in-cheek. *Where did that come from?* There was a moment of uncomfortable silence, as Angela's mind computed what Sofia had just said. Perhaps I should apologize? Sofia thought. But before she uttered the first syllable, Angela beat her to the punch line with a throaty laugh.

"I wish! It would mean no more fear of popping out any more of these little energy-draining creatures every time my man comes home with one too many and gets all frisky in bed. You know what I'm saying, girl, right?"

Sofia played along and nodded. She could feel herself coming out of her shell in the presence of this woman, but there was still no way in hell she would even tell a therapist, never mind a total stranger, the truth about her sad sex life.

"So, no babies, huh. Girl, you got plenty of time. I had Sonia when I was nineteen, not that I regret it, but it would've been nice to celebrate my twenty-first birthday in a bar like everyone else does, you know what I mean?"

Sofia nodded yet again; she was starting to feel like a puppet. Angela put all her laundry in a cart and walked up to Sofia, smiling at Sonia, who was sucking her thumb with her head still on Sofia's shoulder.

"Thanks for your help. We should get coffee sometime. It's hard to explore the hottest spots by myself with a baby."

"Oh my, I wish I could, but I..."

"What! You don't drink coffee?"

"I just... I don't really go out much." But Angela was stubborn as a mule about almost everything in life, even the little things.

"Well, how about right now? You got twenty minutes before you got to move to the dryers."

Sofia wondered what Angela would think if she spoke the truth: that she had lived in the neighborhood for close to five years and had no friends outside of Edward's family of bigots and racists. This was the first time Sofia had even had a proper conversation with a black person. Suddenly, Sonia giggled into Sofia's ear. Sofia couldn't help but laugh back.

Angela went on: "I'll go grab us some coffee from across the street. How do you take it?"

"Just plain is fine," Sofia said, not wanting to use the word "black" in front of her.

"Black coffee, huh. You got it, girlfriend. Be right back." Angela pulled on her coat and headed towards the door. "Oh, what's your name, by the way?"

Angela was an irresistible force. Sofia felt the wall she always put up start to crumble.

"Sofia."

"What a wonderful name. Nice to meet you, Sofia. Be right back!"

Angela ran out the door and across the street, while Sofia looked at Sonia and whispered, "You're the cutest thing I've ever seen. Maybe I shouldn't be so scared of your loud-mouthed mother?"

Long after they finished their coffee and their clothes were dried and folded, Sofia and Angela continued talking, while taking turns holding Sonia. For the first time since her sister's passing, Sofia didn't feel a dark cloud hanging over her head. Suddenly, she looked up at the clock on the wall and saw it was after 2 pm.

"Oh my, I'm sorry I have to go," Sofia said, quickly handing Sonia back to Angela. She now felt guilt-ridden about leaving Edward alone for so long. "It was nice meeting you!" Sofia grabbed her suitcase and started lugging it towards the door. "You and Sonia really lifted my spirits."

"Girlfriend, you're not going anywhere without agreeing to meet next week for coffee and breakfast at Corteleine's. You'll die figuring out what to pick from their menu."

"Corteleine's?"

"The I where I got the coffee. Is it a date, girlfriend?"

"Sure, it's a date," Sofia lied.

"How's nine-thirty next Saturday? Don't you dare be late, or I'll track your behind down and be knocking on your door," Angela said with a giggle.

Dashing home, Sofia could not believe what she had done. Despite the spark ignited by Angela, even her name made Sofia feel their meeting was preordained and a bond destined, Sofia was still deeply anguished by the prospect of seeing her again. She may not have harbored the prejudices of her in-laws towards *zezaks,* but whenever Sofia walked to the store, the sight of a group of African American teenagers gathered on the corner frightened her. After dark, she never walked the streets alone.

As the weekend approached, Edward was sitting at the dining room table, his spirits up for a change, enjoying dinner. "Edward, Sofia began with a worried look on her face, "I've made a new friend, and was wondering what you thought about it."

Taking care of me all day, you need to get out and make friends. What are you concerned about, Edward laughed, "is he a man?"

"No, of course not," Sofia replied with a flushed face, touched by Edward's words, and comforted by how well he was looking on this particular evening, "We met at the laundromat, she's a young mother, and so easy to talk to, it's just," Sofia paused, "she's black."

Edward stood. "I am not Tomas and Victor, and I don't judge people by the color of their skin. My closest friend in Iraq was Jamaican, Chris was his name. He lived ten minutes from here, in Fort Greene." Sofia was startled not by her husband's words but by the tone of his voice. Never before had she heard him speak in such a firm and self-assured manner.

With trepidation, Sofia asked, "What happened to Chris, do you still see him?"

"That's a story for another day. You keep this date with Angela on Saturday, you hear me Sofia?"

Sofia leapt from her from chair, wrapped her arms around her husband and kissed his cheek. And so, after losing Ajola to unspeakable brutality, Sofia's budding friendship with a beautiful self-assured black mom became her new source of emotional support.

Six

July 2002
Brooklyn

On a hot and oppressive humid New York city summer evening, Angela invited Sofia over to share Chinese takeout at her apartment. Angela lived on the second floor of an old two-family Victorian brownstone in the smallest but cutest one bedroom apartment in tree-lined Ditmas Park.

The old home was never re-wired for air conditioning, so the two women took turns sitting close to the one big fan which provided marginal relief from the suffocating heat. After Sofia eagerly tasted General Tso's chicken for the first time in her life, the two women sat alongside each other on a small couch, both using the few napkins that were not stained with Chinese sauces and wiping away the perspiration from their faces.

While Sonia slept in a tiny adjacent bedroom, Sofia opened up to Angela. Thanks to some Dutch courage she spoke about her past, her family, her arranged marriage, Edward's illness. Everything. Except Victor.

Angela finally reacted after listening in near silence to Sofia pour her heart out for almost an hour. Angela stared at Sofia. Shaking her head in disbelief, she reached out and touched Sofia's arm.

"I'm sorry, Sofia, but you're living in the dark ages," she continued. "A woman is not a package, an item shipped overseas to be inspected and tried out, with the right to return if dissatisfied. That shit went out centuries ago, Sofia. Dark ages... your people are live in the fucking dark ages."

As much as she hated what was done to her, it was not the place for an outsider, even Angela, to judge, Sofia thought. Angela's words pierced her heart and pissed her off in equal measure. She didn't hold back:

"Look who's talking. You think a *zezak* man would throw a fifteen-year-old girl out of his bed?"

Angela's eyes widened. "I have no idea what *zezak* means, but it sounds disturbingly racist." Before Sofia could respond, Angela held up her hand, equally angry. "Look, little girl this is not two hundred years ago, the land of sheiks. It's America and your husband has been here for decades. He knows you don't fuck children —only paedos fuck minors."

Sofia slapped Angela's hands away.

"Edward's a good man," Sofia's voice shook. "You have no idea how much worse it could be for me. The Kanun, the law, it's followed like the Bible where I grew up. It says that a woman is a sack, made to do nothing more than to endure in her husband's house." There was a long pause.

"My sister Ajola lost her life at the hands of her husband," Sofia continued after Angela failed to take up the invisible verbal baton. "Who the fuck are you to talk to me about things you don't know anything about?" Sofia dropped her rage-filled eyes to the ground. It was all too much to handle. She broke down in tears. Almost heartbroken herself, Angela reached down with her left hand and stroked Sofia's face. But the peace offering was slapped away.

"I'm so sorry for your sister. I was only trying to comfort you."

Sofia grunted. "I never talk about my shit," Angela went on, "which may sound like nothing compared to yours. Sonia's father would come home high and drunk every night and beat me. I was nineteen when I got pregnant. One night, just after she was born, while he slept dead to the world, I wrapped Sonia in a blanket and fled. A shelter took me in. I got counseling, and social workers got me legal services that made sure he was going to stay away."

Angela paused to gather her thoughts. "Eventually, I found the inner strength required to both get a job and return to school while relatives helped to take care of Sonia. If you insist Edward's a good man, I'm sorry Sofia. God, I'm so sorry, please forgive me. I love you Sofia, I would never hurt you," Angela concluded.

Sofia slowly looked up as Angela wiped away her tears with two fingers.

"I'm sorry for what I said about *zez-*... I mean, African American men."

Angela and Sofia embraced, silently holding each other for several minutes. Sofia sheepishly looked into Angela's eyes afraid of what she was feeling. She buried her head in Angela's ample bosom. Angela's hands slowly dropped down and stroked Sofia's backside before carefully working their way all over her firm torso. Suddenly they were kissing: first, tenderly with closed quivering lips, then passionately with open mouths. Angela started to work her tongue inside Sofia's mouth.

As if struck by summer lightning, Sofia suddenly jumped up and back. "What are we doing? NO! NO! We must stop," she shouted. Lesbian sex was blasphemous, back home even a whisper of a woman being gay would result in exile from the family home... or far worse.

Seeing the terrified look on Sofia's face, the moment was lost for Angela as well. She smiled and reached out her hand.

"Shush, shush, Sofia, don't worry, we're sisters not lovers, we both just got a little tipsy." Giggling to reassure Sofia she reached out her hand, Sofia still kept her distance.

"Please honey, I'm not going to bite you. Anywhere." She laughed some more.

Sofia tentatively stepped towards Angela, they hugged and fell back on the couch. Angela held Sofia sniveling in her arms, until feeling the weight of her drinking, Sofia nodded off.

Sofia jolted awake. It had just gone the witching hour and she left Edward alone. *Had he woken up? Had he told Victor that she was gone? My God, Sophia told herself, I have to get home.*

Without making a sound, not wanting to wake Angela who had also passed out alongside her, Sofia tiptoed to the front door, holding her breath out of fear any creak on the old wood living room floor would awaken Sonia or Angela. Carefully making her way down the darkened narrow staircase, she stepped out onto the front porch and sighed in relief. Before reaching the sidewalk, Sofia froze, locking eyes with a tall muscular black male in his late thirties, wearing a starched white shirt and a navy-blue suit.

"Hold it. Who are you, what are you doing here?

Caught completely off guard, Sofia was terrified about what to say and decided to respond in broken English. "Me no understand... me going home."

"Wait a second, you're the friend Angela keeps talking about. Fuck, she swore you were just friends, that she was done fooling around. Goddamn, you're just her type too."

Sofia screamed, "Me no understand?"

And with that, Sofia fled. Racing home barefoot with a mini-heel sandal clutched under each arm. Sofia was mightily relieved when she found Edward passed out on the couch in the dark. She kissed his cheek and then tiptoed to her bedroom and collapsed onto the hard mattress, thanking God for what she had not done, yet unable to prevent dreaming of what she might have done.

Seven

Ten Days Later
Manhattan

Angela was not answering her phone. Heartbroken, Sofia feared she had been ghosted, that despite what Angela said, she wanted nothing to do with Sofia for rejecting her advances. Not hearing a peep from Angela was driving Sofia crazy. Sofia desperately needed Angela's assurance that they were both intoxicated and were truly sisters not frustrated lovers.

Even through his morning daze of medication Edward knew something was wrong.

"You're not ok," said Edward, pressing Sofia, as he munched on a sandwich of cheap cheese and cold cuts. "What's wrong? Maybe, for once, I can help."

Sofia managed a smile. "To be honest, I'm only worried about us," she lied.

"Oh!"

"Are we going to start trying to have a family?"

Edward lowered his head in shame.

"Maybe you could find a way to cut back on your medication?"

The look of dread on Edward's face ended the conversation. Sofia patted Edward's arm, stood up from the kitchen table, and threw several dishes in the kitchen sink. She grabbed her pocketbook, glanced at herself in the mirror, and told Edward she was running out to take care of a few errands. She was going to track down Angela.

As soon as she hit the hot summer sidewalk, her phone beeped with a text. Her heart skipped a beat. She knew it had to be from Angela. It read: *Meet me at the library on the third floor reading room in the back. It's important. A*

Sofia ran the few blocks to the Cortelyou Road subway station. Angela had introduced Sofia to the library in mid-town Manhattan near where she worked days as a paralegal. Whenever Angela was able to arrange for a babysitter, it had become one of their favorite weekday meeting places. Putting her paranoia on hold, Sofia stopped thinking about anything other than the fastest subway route to 42nd street. Arriving at Time Square, she bolted off the train, rushed up the stairs and into the library at Fifth Avenue.

Sofia moved into the enormous open area of the reading room; she then stopped and noticed that she was drenched in sweat. Sofia took a moment to find the nearest restroom to wash and dry her blouse and short summer skirt as best she could with a paper towel.

After passing an endless number of long oak tables, she found Angela seated at the end of the last one with her head down. Despite the summer heat, she wore a thin tan trench coat and dark sunglasses. She was pretending to be reading a book. Angela looked up the second she heard Sofia's footsteps. She knew the walk.

Angela remained seated. She dropped her sunglasses to the bridge of her nose and looked at Sofia with bloodshot, tear-filled eyes.

"Angela... where the hell....?" Sofia snapped; she could not hide the hurt in her voice.

Angela immediately cut her off, saying: "Something happened, a few days after the night you came over, on my way to work. I was waiting on the subway platform, and a man in a black leather jacket came up to me. He was fucking huge and scary as shit. I was going to yell but he had a gun inside his jacket."

"Oh my god!" Sofia gasped.

"It all happened in the middle of the goddamn rush hour. I was so fucking scared. I didn't know what to think. When the train arrived, he held my arm and walked me into the car and told me to get off with him at Court Street. Then he walked me into a Starbucks, sat me down and the bastard tells me he knows all about me and you."

"Me?"

"Says, I'm probably a nice girl, but he has been sent to tell me our relationship has to end, that I'm putting crazy thoughts into your head, that you're starting to ignore your responsibilities and forget your place."

Sofia's head was spinning. "Forget my place? Sent by whom?" she asked.

Angela's voice grew to a loud whisper. "When I asked, he said, 'That's not your business.'" The penny finally dropped, but Sofia kept playing dumb.

"My God, Sofia what if he spied on us the other night?" Angela continued. "I swear, Sofia, could you imagine! Spying on us through the half-opened curtain, the sick creep! Gun or no gun I told him to fuck off."

"What did you do?"

"I was getting ready to scream for him to be arrested. But a second before I was about to yell, he asked about Sonia. Tells me he's heard she's an angel. And that's not all. He starts talking about my boyfriend, Daniel. Talks about USC and how Daniel used to play football. He knew everything about my personal life, Sofia." Angela was shaking now.

"I can only imagine how scared you must have been..." Sofia said.

"We both know who's behind this. Who the fuck dug up all this information about me? Which sick bastard told him to threaten me and my loved ones? It had to be your brother-in-law, Victor."

Sofia was ashamed because she was feeling greatly relieved that all this was about Victor and had nothing to do with Angela ghosting her.

"I'll take care of it. I'll talk to Victor. Don't you be worrying. Trust me, his bark is far worse than his bite. Especially when it involves me," Sofia said, hoping to calm Angela.

"You're going to take care of it! My God, Sofia. You can't be serious," Angela's voice grew steadily louder.

"You're overreacting," Sofia said, trying to quiet her, as she looked around nervously. "I told you that I'll deal with Victor."

"Overreact! Are you fucking kidding me?" Angela shook her head. "You know what I did the night after I was threatened? I spent two hours googling Victor. You've always insisted he's a good man who at times has been unfairly targeted by the government and the media; insisting that black men aren't the only ones falsely accused of things they never did. I never paid any attention because I trusted you, Sofia. But what I didn't know is, he was put on trial a decade ago for the murder of a federal agent."

Sofia shook her head. "That's not true. That can't be true."

"See for yourself. It's all there in black and white." Angela reached into her bag and pulled out a stack of papers, and printouts from her research on Victor's dark past. Sofia flipped through the headlines. She wanted the ground to swallow her up.

"All the things he's been suspected of," Angela continued, "it scared me just to read about it. Maybe you can hide your head in the sand. But I sure can't afford to. I'm scared out of my mind. I'm thinking of going to the police for protection. Or maybe even moving away."

"I'm telling you Angela, you're overreacting."

"Daniel, my fiancé—"

"He's your fiancé?" Sofia flinched, realizing that it was Daniel she ran into the morning she fled Angela's apartment and, without fully understanding why, feeling hurt by the revelation.

Angela continued without answering the question. "Daniel has been offered a new position in Chicago. I think it's best if we all relocate."

Sofia put Angela's damning research face down on the table. "Okay, so let's assume you're right and Victor's behind this and everything you've read is true—"

Angela rolled her eyes. "It would be insane to go to the authorities and risk retribution," Sofia warned her. "It would only put you and your family in far more danger. And after all you've overcome in life, you can't allow something like this to force you to permanently leave your family and friends to move to a place you've never been. Come on, Angela. There's only one thing to do. Let me talk to Victor. I can make him listen. I'll make certain he backs off."

"Sofia, no matter what he says, how can I ever feel safe? This is my daughter and future husband we're talking about. You'd be on a plane out of the country if it was one of your family threatened, right?"

Sofia's voice cracked with emotion: "I beg you, Angela."

"I've made up my mind, girl."

Sofia reached across the table and took hold of both of Angela's hands.

"Give me a week. Just a week. We'll have no contact and I'll report back to you," Sofia pleaded.

Angela shook her head. "I'm sorry," Angela answered in a broken voice. "I love you; you know that. But I can't. I just can't."

Angela withdrew her hands and abruptly stood up. Sofia was shushed by readers as she pleaded with Angela. Both women had tears in their eyes. Then, Sofia watched helplessly as Angela literally turned her back on her and walked out of her life.

Eight

May 2003
Brooklyn

On a rare evening when Edward was coherent on the coach, a broody Sofia stood at the doorframe of their small sitting room and took the plunge.

"Edward, I want a child," she began with butterflies in her stomach, as the theme tune for M*A*S*H played on their overused TV in the background. "I know it will be difficult, but, please, we can adjust your medication and we can try? Please Edward, will you do that for me?" What Sofia didn't say was at times she felt so down she preferred being the target of the silver bullet to another year locked in loneliness.

Edward's face tightened, his eyes closed, and he put both hands on his head. Without any further prompting, he finally responded: "If you want a child, I'll try. I care for you, Sofia. I hate myself for not being able to show it. Maybe I can do one thing right for you."

A teary-eyed Sofia ran over to Edward and hugged him. "Don't say such things. You're so strong to have lived through a war. I'm lucky to be your wife."

A week after adjusting his medication and adding Viagra to his regimen, Edward was able to perform. They managed to have intercourse the same way three times the next week. Sofia was relieved that it no longer hurt by the third time, it even started to become pleasurable for her. Each time when he had fallen asleep, again with a huge grin on his face, Sofia would lay beside Edward, staring at her husband feeling contented for the first time in memory. After all they had endured, could she be falling in love?

Less than a month later, Sofia was expecting. Within that time, Edward had started to finally turn his life around. He cut back on his daily dosage of pills and was working a full schedule. Even the prior mood swings from the reduced drugs were almost non-existent, albeit with the help of some nightly beers that took the edge off. He put on fifteen pounds. Edward came to bed most nights and fell asleep, holding Sofia in his arms.

After one such tender-hearted night, Tomas arrived at their door early the next morning because he urgently needed to get a leak fixed in a fifth-floor apartment. Edward was in the bathroom showering at the time. While Tomas waited in the living room, he said to Sofia, "Whatever you're doing for my brother, keep doing it."

Nine

September 2003
Brooklyn

It was a beautiful autumn day. Awkwardly walking with two shopping bags to match her huge pregnant belly, Sofia was careful not to slip on the dozens of multi-covered leaves scattered all over the sidewalk. She unloaded her groceries in the kitchen and found Edward sitting on the couch. He looked up with red and watery eyes.

"Edward?"

Sofia lowered herself onto the couch next to her husband. Edward looked paler than he had in months. He took a shaky breath.

"Sofia, I want to tell you about my time in Iraq."

Sofia clenched her teeth. She thought, *What! Not now, of all times, when you're finally feeling better, and things are going so well.* But perhaps it would be best to get it over and done with, like ripping off a band-aid. She reasoned with herself that it would be best to let him get it all off his chest. Tactfully, Sofia took Edward's hand. "Please tell me. We're husband and wife and bringing a life in this world. We must share our pain, not just our joy."

Edward withdrew his hand from Sofia's grasp and rubbed it back and forth across his forehead. Then he swept his fingers up and down the length of his face. With a tremor in his voice, he began:

"After living in the States for almost five years, I still didn't really know anybody besides Victor and Tomas. I only needed a green card to enlist. I thought it would be my way to get out on my own, out from under my brothers. But most of the guys in my training group were Southern white boys. I never made it a week without someone making fun of my accent, even questioning me, trying to fight me, calling me Saddam." Edward looked at her with a pained smile. "Chris wasn't just my best friend; he was my only friend in the Army.

"Chris and I shipped out to Iraq together. There was little fighting. It was just days on end in the desert. Chris and I kicked a soccer ball around more than anything else. After ten months of waiting, we received notice we were going home. We were counting the days. We talked about getting a place together back in Brooklyn."

As he wiped his face on his shirt collar, tears started to fall. "The day before we were supposed to get shipped out, something happened. There was concern that a group of Saddam's soldiers had returned to a village five miles away.

"Once we got within half a mile, I closed my eyes and covered them with both hands. God, the smell I can't forget the goddamn smell! And the air, it was so hard to breathe. You smell and breathe death before you see it."

Edward was deteriorating before her eyes. *Do something Sofia, hold your husband's hand, go to him.* But Sofia remained silent, her hands helplessly frozen in her lap.

"Walking side by side with Chris, I can still hear him telling me, Eddie, just remember whatever happens, always keep your guard up. If we keep our guards up nothing'll happen." Images of the horror reappeared before Edward's eyes. "Oh God. There were dead children, dead babies. There were tiny, little limbs scattered all over the place." With a trembling hand, Edward took several pills out of his pocket and dry swallowed them.

He buried his head, wept, and moaned until falling silent. Several minutes passed, his breathing slowed, and not a muscle in his body moved. Sofia was traumatized herself but managed to take Edward's legs and raise them on the couch. Ever the loving wife, she went and got a pillow for his head. After tucking it under him and covering him with a blanket, Edward suddenly opened his eyes.

"There's more," he said in a sluggish voice with a vacant look. Sofia wished to God there wasn't, but nodded.

"Yes, my dear tell me please, I want to help," she whispered.

"I stood there with my hands down staring at the carnage. I fucking didn't listen to Chris, I dropped my guard. And then… I got ambushed. Two Iraqi commandos surprised me and fired."

"My God!" Sofia struggled to compose herself.

"The doctors have never been able to remove all the bullet fragments. It's too close to my spine," he said matter-of-factly.

"No wonder you're always in so much pain," Sofia said, selfishly praying there was nothing left to tell.

"That first shot levelled me, the pain slicing through every inch of my body. Then I was hit again. I screamed in agony, ready and hoping for death to put an end to my suffering. Without giving a shit about himself, Chris jumped out from behind a corner, returned fire and took out one of the men. I killed the other one, but Chris was hit by several bullets. One cost him his right arm. We were both given medals for our heroism at the village. Whatever I did, I have no idea. Chris was the hero, not me."

"Oh my God, Edward! I'm so sorry. How is Chris? Do you see him from time to time or are the memories too painful?"

"Painful?" Edward's voice started to rise.

Sofia trembled; afraid she had ignited a new fire.

"I loved Chris, more than my own family. After we came home, I'd go see him because I didn't want to deal with Victor or Tomas' nonsense about Chris being Black. One year before Victor arranged our marriage, Chris was found dead in his bed from an overdose of painkillers and fentanyl."

Sofia's eyes bulged out of her head.

"I often wonder if he found the only way to put our memories and suffering behind us."

Without waiting for his wife's reply, Edward left the couch, walked to the bedroom and shut the door.

Ten

March 2008
Brooklyn

The morning Ilka was born, Sofia was re-born. There was much pain during the delivery, the type of pain she never imagined possible, but, thankfully, there were no complications when the doctor delivered her perfect princess. Sadly, the exhilaration was short-lived. Even the pure joy of motherhood could not stop the re-emergence of an undeniable restlessness inside Sofia. Victor's attempts to convince Edward to move into a brighter and more spacious apartment would bring on a panic attack until the subject was dropped. Suggestions of simply taking over a vacant storage room to build a second bedroom brought on increased bouts of depression.

Edward's stark regression following the night he relived his time in Iraq, saddled Sofia with *two* children. Edward took more pills than ever just to get through the day. It meant Tomas had long returned to grudgingly covering for him. When Edward was coherent and pain-free, which was as rare as hen's teeth, he would apologize and promise to do better. Every single time Edward held Ilka he would remark on the way her looks were so reminiscent of his deceased mother, Sarah—especially her big brown eyes and cupid's bow mouth. It was almost as if he didn't recall holding their precious baby on any of the previous occasions.

Victor also changed after Ilka's birth. From a man who had always been so indifferent to Tomas's daughters, and so full of machismo, he showed a side of himself nobody knew existed. When Victor noticed Edward curled up on the sofa, he would softly tell Sofia she looked like she could use a rest and then he would take Ilka out in her carriage and stroll to Prospect Park. Come summer, it would be hours before he returned to the apartment. Victor would pick Ilka up, kiss, and cuddle her before placing her back in her mom's arms. He loved doting on the little girl, and, in a way, he became her real father figure.

By the time Ilka started school, she was a carbon copy of her grandmother, with her cute dimples and moon-shaped face. Ilka once picked up a photograph of her granny at the same age and said, "I don't remember this photo being taken of me." Sofia reckoned this uncanny resemblance was one of the reasons why Victor's attachment kept growing and growing. He would visit more frequently and walk her to class. She would always wear one of numerous new outfits he lavished on his niece. The traditional Albanian dresses may have been out of place in contrast to the jeans worn by her peers, but Ilka happily wore her uncle's gifts.

One day, when Ilka was five, Sofia overheard Victor lecturing her about the responsibilities and duties of an Albanian woman while she obediently listened. Too obediently.

"A woman must always be loyal to a man and do whatever he says," Sofia heard Ilka repeat back to her uncle. Her blood boiled. *There's no way in hell that she'll end up like me. I'm not allowing Victor to brainwash my daughter.* After hearing Victor's words, she vowed to return to school to get a GED. She would go to the library the next day to sign up for online classes. With Ilka in kindergarten, Sofia could now start dreaming for herself as well.

Early the next morning before the sun had come out, Sofia awakened and cleaned every inch of the apartment while waiting impatiently for the right time to wake Ilka and drag her to the shower to get ready for school. As her princess munched on buttered toast and cornflakes, Sofia put Edward's breakfast of eggs and potatoes on a plate ready for the microwave and wrapped a lunch sandwich in plastic before putting it in the refrigerator. She left a note on the coffee table next to the couch for Edward when he awakened and hoped he might be up to eating at least one of the meals.

Sofia dropped Ilka off at the bus stop for school and raced six blocks to the local library. The poorly maintained gray brick building was utilized more as a way station for the homeless than by anyone looking for a good book. But there were laptops and manuals available for Sofia's purposes. She quickly signed on to an online GED course and spent the rest of the day hitting the books in an effort to brush up. Feeling as if she had rekindled a long-lost love, Sofia spent the day buried in work, seeking to capture a year's worth of learning in one day.

In the middle of an algebra problem, Sofia looked up, searching her mind for the correct formula, and noticed it was already four in the afternoon. She had not had a bite to eat and a moment before panicking, she recalled that she had arranged for Karina to pick Ilka up at school. Still, she needed to get back to Edward.

"Edward, I'm home," Sofia half-whispered, unlocking the door, not wanting to disturb him if he was asleep. Sofia switched on the light. He wasn't on the couch.

"Edward?" Sofia raised her voice.

She looked down the hallway, terrified at the sight of Edwards' legs extending halfway out the bathroom door. Sofia's heart stopped.

"Edward!" Sofia's screams still met with no response.

Sofia dropped her books, rushed into the bathroom, and saw the front mirror of the medicine cabinet shattered and shards of glass scattered over the floor. Blood streamed down Edward's cheeks as he lay face up on the ground unconscious. Sofia pulled out her cell phone and dialed 911, but for some reason, she couldn't get through. She tossed her phone into the hallway and started pounding on Edward's chest. Having heard Sofia's screams, Tomas and Karina, holding Ilka by the hand, ran downstairs. Tomas pulled Sofia back by her shoulders and took over giving Edward CPR. Ilka's screams bounced off the apartment walls.

"Please, please," Sofia chanted.

Thomas rang for an ambulance, getting through on the first go. Sofia figured she must have dialed the wrong numbers when she had tried to call for help. A young-looking EMS worker stormed into the apartment.

"Everyone, please, stand back," he ordered. "Please, wait in the other room."

Sofia picked Ilka up and cradled her like she was half her age. After what seemed like an eternity, another EMS worker, this one much older, emerged from the bathroom.

"We were able to revive him," he reported, as everyone let out a collective sigh of relief. "They may need to pump his stomach at the hospital," he continued. "But the immediate danger has passed. Thank God you called when you did."

Sofia carried Ilka to the couch, brushed the tears off her cheeks, looked up at the ceiling and thanked the heavens.

"You hear that, sweetie? Everything's going to be ok. Daddy is awake."

Tomas and Karina were watching, judging. Looking down at Ilka, Sofia vowed to never again forget her place.

Sylvester Stanley

Eleven

February 2016
Federal Correctional Institution Otisville
Medium Security
Otisville, New York

Even after all his appeals had been denied, Sylvester Stanley refused to accept that he'd never come home. Nobody was going to be more ready than Sylvester when the racist crack laws were finally overturned. Prison had robbed him of decades he would never get back, but he was going to have a future that more than made up for it. When not spending his earned free time sketching and painting with worn out brushes and pencils in the prison's tiny art studio, Sylvester could be found in the prison library engaged in his own legal research and writing. Compared to the maximum-security prison he had been housed in for the first five years of his sentence, Otisville was heaven. Having been a model prisoner from the day he arrived, Sylvester earned the privilege of extra library time after dinner.

There were few people he cared to see. As far as family went, there was only his mom. His younger brother, Marco, had moved to California after college and he hadn't seen him in more than a decade. His girlfriend Jennifer's visits were a distant memory. He desperately looked forward to his mom, Lorraine's visits, although they often left him feeling worse rather than better. The visits almost always ended with her breaking into tears, with him using the same words to try to console her: "Don't worry, Ma, I'll be coming home."

The years of forced optimism rose almost to the level of expectation in 2016. Instead of having to constantly pump himself up, Sylvester now had to make sure he didn't get too carried away. President Obama was in his last year of office and was freeing many non-violent drug offenders. With the assistance of attorneys and students at the New York University Law School Mercy Project, Sylvester filed a clemency petition which was under review. The odds were still stacked against him, but for the first time, he *really* felt he would be one of the lucky ones. God knows he'd worked too hard not to be.

On this particular night, no matter how hard he tried, he could not focus. He had been in the library for almost three hours but read fewer than five pages. All he could think about was clemency.

"Sylvester, time to get back to your cell for the count!" The unmistakable voice of Officer Freddie Daniels interrupted his thoughts. "Come on," Daniels commanded. "I swear nothing makes you people move, not even a letter you've been dying to receive."

"What letter?" Sylvester said, looking up and slamming the book closed. *My clemency.*

"Some mail came for you. I laid it on your bed."

"Did you see if it was from the Mercy Project or the Department of Justice?"

"Oh, Sylvester, you know I wouldn't look at your personal mail," he said mockingly. "That wouldn't be right."

It seemed like Freddie Daniels had been a federal corrections officer his entire life. His retirement was only two years away. He talked about it all the time. There was not one other officer in the prison that Sylvester didn't get along with. But with Daniels, almost every day he struggled to hold himself back from responding to his taunts and tactics. Dozens of officers had signed Sylvester's mercy petition and were rooting for him to beat the odds. Not Daniels.

"What you think Sylvester? You going home, my friend?" Daniels called out.

Sylvester's heart was racing too fast for him to respond.

"Oh, come on Sylvester. You too educated now from all those hours in the library to talk to me?"

As usual, Sylvester ignored Daniels. What would he do if it was a denial? I won't be able to handle it, he thought. He hustled back to his cell as fast as Daniels allowed. Daniels was uncomfortably close behind, banging a stick on the floor in rhythm to every one of Sylvester's strides, intentionally doing everything he could to heighten Sylvester's anxiety.

Sylvester walked to the end of the hallway and bounded up the steep steps to the second floor of cells where he was housed. He stood and waited for Daniels, who had now decided to move in slow motion and was taking forever to unlock the cell door. A brown envelope lay on the narrow steel frame of the bed beside the mattress. Sylvester ripped it open without even looking at the address of the sender. Inside was a smaller white envelope and a card. He reached inside and pulled out a birthday card.

What the fuck is this? he thought, my birthday's not for six months.

Daniels looked at him and started laughing uncontrollably.

"Read it," he snickered.

Sylvester opened the card. The word "Birthday" was scratched out and the word "Anniversary" was written in blue ink in its place. Inside an additional small yellow note read:

Happy 22nd Anniversary of your time in our prisons.
Here's hoping, many more to come.

Your number one caretaker,
Freddie Daniels

Sylvester dropped the card on the floor and stared at Daniels.

"Hey bud, I thought you needed something to take the pressure off your waiting every day for the fucking decision on that petition of yours. So, I wanted to lighten things up for you. I know you boys have a great sense of humor. That's how you survive, right? And come on brother, we both know you have as much chance of getting clemency as I do of having a monkey jump out my ass!"

Daniels dropped his head and started laughing uncontrollably to the point of tears. A second before reaching through the bars, grabbing Daniels and snapping his head off, Sylvester held back and watched in silent rage until the correction officer finally composed himself.

"Thanks for the sentiment, Daniels," Sylvester responded. "Good to know what I'll be missing if clemency is granted."

Twelve

March 1989
Bushwick, Brooklyn

Sylvester was nine the first time a gun was stuck in his face.

It happened late one evening when he was returning home from the store, his mom trailing behind, holding his younger brother Marco with her right hand, a bag of groceries in her left. While Bushwick was plagued by crime over the decades, the crack epidemic brought new levels of armed violence to the neighborhood. The family's Linden Street brownstone, the beautiful historical artistic row house purchased by Sylvester's grandfather in the late '60s, was the only home on the block owned by a Black family. The street was protected by a private block association. Out of nowhere, a young red-haired white man, wearing a blue windbreaker and a neighborhood security baseball cap, brazenly displayed his revolver. Lorraine dropped her bag on the sidewalk and immediately grabbed the collar of Sylvester's shirt and pulled him back behind her.

"Where do you think you're going?" he barked.

Lorraine bravely smiled and put her hands together as if in prayer, terrified any second Marco's ear-shattering screams would trigger bullets raining down on her boys. Pee ran down Sylvester's leg.

"Good evening, sir, we live here, everybody knows us. If you would give me a moment, I'll reach into my bag and provide proof." When Lorraine cautiously displayed several pieces of identification proving she lived down the street, the man holstered his pistol.

"My first week here. I'm usually assigned to Seaview Estates, sorry, can't be too careful in this neighborhood." Despite his apology, the guard still had a skeptical look on his face.

Loraine quickly gathered her groceries. "I understand, sir. Thank you for keeping our neighborhood safe." Nudging Sylvester, she commanded her sons, "Say 'thank you,' boys."

Sylvester glared rather than comply, holding his bag so tightly all the groceries were crushed. Marco's weeping quieted to a whimper.

After unlocking the front door, Sylvester's mom turned to her shaken children. "So many of our young boys are nothing but hoodlums, gangsters, dealers and addicts. What do we expect? We've brought this on ourselves. I don't blame that man."

It was at times like this that Sylvester wished his old man was still on the scene. But Lorraine was raising her two boys as a single mom, brown-nosing every white face. Much as she needed her husband—a jazz musician with an unpredictable income and an insatiable desire for young women—his departure two years earlier to New Orleans had been a relief.

Marco wept long into the night. Sylvester climbed into his brother's bed and wrapped his arms around him until he dozed off. Sylvester tossed and turned until finally falling asleep. But soon after he jumped awake at the sight of the unforgettable red-haired man pointing his gun. Insanely suspicious of his family solely for the color of their skin.

The next morning, he begged his mom to move to a safer neighborhood, but she was a stubborn woman. Nothing would make her sell her parents' home.

Thirteen

June 1992
Brooklyn

From an early age, art was Sylvester's salvation. It provided his escape from the neighborhood trenches and eased the pain of his father's departure. Drawings and paintings, mostly tropical landscapes, took up every nook and cranny of the teenager's room. Everybody was impressed by his talent and technique—they far exceeded his age. By the end of middle school, the best institutions in the city were knocking at his door—literally. The head of the art department at the exclusive Manhattan High School of Performing Arts turned up unannounced at his home, dispensed with the rigid intensely competitive requirement of a formal evaluation of his portfolio and surprisingly offered him admission, right then and there. Her son, Lorraine, liked to crow, was destined for the Ivy League.

On his sixteenth birthday, Loraine surprised Sylvester with tickets to the Summer Reggae Festival in Jamaica. Maxing out her credit card, she tried not to think of how she would cover the exorbitant monthly interest fees. She also arranged for Sylvester's older cousin Pete to chaperone him, paying full room and board for both as well as the festival tickets. Lorraine felt Pete could use the trip as much as her son. Pete, who everybody said could pass for Syl's older brother, had lost his father one year earlier, a tragic unintended victim of a stray bullet in a neighborhood shoot-out.

After settling into their hotel room, Pete, getting into the party mood, pulled a huge joint out of his shirt pocket.

"I brought this from home to get us started," Pete said, smiling at the shocked look on Sylvester's face.

"Oh, I'm not that into drugs, cuz."

"Not into drugs. It's only a joint… for Pete's sake!"

They both chuckled.

"Look, I know your mom has your ass on lock down," Pete continued, "but come on Syl, spare me the simpleton act. It's me. And we got to get us some real deal ganga down here."

Eyeballing Sylvester, Pete lit the joint, took a long drag, and then held the smoke. He blew out perfect smoke rings, each one smaller than the last, as they merged into one another. Then he offered his younger cousin a toke.

Reluctantly, Sylvester took the joint. Sylvester felt he had already embarrassed himself enough and there was no way in hell he was going to let his cousin know he had never smoked. Sylvester took a short puff, felt his throat burn, and was unable to stop coughing.

Pete erupted in laughter.

"Look at you, the only brother in Brooklyn clueless about how to smoke weed."

"You know my mom. She would kill me and Marco if she caught us smoking. You'd be one dead bro' if she knew what you were up to down here."

"Aunt Lorraine's too much. Ganja never hurt nobody."

Pete and Sylvester would sleep late and spend the afternoons on the beach getting high. The captivating reggae rhythms enveloped their nights. Sylvester also discovered weed helped his drawings become much more uninhibited. He drew a portrait of Pete that was more abstract than anything he had ever attempted; his face on a unicorn galloping across the Caribbean.

It was the happiest week of Sylvester's young life. On their last night, Pete danced into the room with the evening's music still in his head and dropped two pounds of Ganja on Sylvester's bed.

"Let's get this tucked away in your luggage. I've already got mine safely stored for passage," he said with a chuckle.

"You're fucking nuts, cuz. I like this shit, but no way I'm getting locked up for it. Or having Mom discover it."

"Give me a break. Aunt Lorraine will never find out. Stop the paranoia and get your black ass over here and help me figure out how to get this into your suitcase."

Fear gripped Sylvester from head to toe, but he couldn't bring himself to stand up to his older cousin, who had shown him the time of his life. While Sylvester watched in silence, Pete neatly packed a dozen half-ounce packets of ganga into the zippered lining at the bottom of his suitcase. Sylvester could barely keep his footing as he passed through customs. He was still stressed out afterwards and incessantly bounced his legs up and down while seated in both the subway and bus back to Bushwick. He barely kissed his mother when he got home, wanting to rush up to his bedroom and hide the drugs.

"One peck on the cheek! That's all I get as a thank you," she said.

"Sorry mom. I need to use the bathroom," he lied.

"Is something wrong? You look upset," she observed.

"I'll tell you all about the trip later. But first, I really need to go..."

"Ok, go."

After rushing up to his bedroom, he took the drugs out of his luggage and hid them in a corner of his closet. He had dodged a bullet.

During the first few days after returning home, Sylvester would regale Loraine with selective stories of his trip and return to his bedroom every evening too scared to touch his stash. As the weekend approached, he would lie on his back staring at the ceiling, unable to sleep through the night. *Fuck it, I'm being ridiculous*, he silently muttered to himself, making up his mind to indulge with a few friends. First thing in the morning, he called his buddies to share some of his treasure with them—without charge. He picked a secluded area in the Pratt sculpture park where they could smoke without fear of the cops. For the rest of June, until starting his new school, Syl and his pals would meet to get high.

Sylvester loved the newfound respect his boys had for him. Even better, come September, his stash eased his freshman path among so many artistically talented classmates. Especially with Grayson Donald Roberts III. Donnie was the spoiled son of Grayson Roberts who had just left a Wall Street bank to manage his own spectacularly successful hedge fund. Insisting on being called Donnie was one of his never-ending attempts to show he was just one of the guys. Donnie did three things well: acting, basketball and bull shit. Sylvester had never met anyone like him. Hanging around Donnie, Sylvester couldn't quite put his finger on why, but he ended up liking him. Maybe it was the contrast, his more than six-foot frame, blonde hair, absurdly white teeth and perpetual smile.

Shooting hoops with Sylvester one afternoon after classes, Donnie pushed him to play varsity. "Syl, man, I want you feeding me for a j when I come off the wing. Be showtime if you're running the squad. I'm sick of doing it all myself. Nobody else on the team has any game," he said.

Sylvester cracked up. "Man, will you ever stop with your BS. Only reason you made the team is coach needed a token white guy. Anyway, that's enough balling for me. I'm too into my latest work to spend any more time."

"More your loss than mine," he said, with a laugh. As they were getting ready to leave, Donnie said, "I'm throwing a big party this weekend at my house. My folks are away. What you can bring, what you better bring, is that weed you brought back from Jamaica. I'll even give you five hundred bucks for four ounces."

"I'll bring some, D. But I'm not going to sell it to you. It'll be my gift, from time to time."

Donnie came over and put Sylvester in a loose headlock.

"I insist. Ha, or should I say demand."

"No, it's a gift."

"Charity is the one thing I don't need bro."

Sylvester gave Donne a playful shove in return, and he staggered back. "Alright, *paleface bro,*" Sylvester replied, "I won't leave you hanging. I'll be there and I'll bring the goods."

Early Saturday evening, Sylvester waited until his mother and Marco were out buying groceries to pull the black canvas bag from its hiding place and grab enough of his stash to please Donnie. There was an inner voice warning him about what a BS artist Donnie was and he shouldn't be trusted, but Sylvester shook it off. *Don't be paranoid like mom*, he told himself.

Sylvester threw on his best navy blue jacket and headed out to catch the subway uptown to Manhattan.

Crawling along in a typically crowded and slow-moving weekend subway car, Sylvester despite his self-admonition, fretted about the stash hidden in the lining of his jacket. He could've sworn the transit cops gave him a funny look. He wondered if he looked like a pot dealer.

It was almost eight when he finally got off the train at 86th Street and scampered to his friend's new four-story brownstone near the 90th street entrance to the Central Park reservoir. Before walking up the steps and ringing the bell, Sylvester stopped in his tracks, staring at the stunning residence owned for generations by Donnie's family.

"My man Stallion. Donnie greeted Sylvester, proudly flashing his porcelain smile, impressing himself with knowing Sylvester's neighborhood nickname.

Sylvester walked into the big, high-ceilinged living room. There must have been more than one hundred people. It was the first time he had ever been in the company of so many classmates outside of school.

"Let me get you a drink," said Donnie, as he grabbed a bottle of Heineken from a nearby cooler and tossed it to Sylvester, catching him unaware. Sylvester bobbled the bottle, but somehow managed to save it. "Sly, I hope you brought that weed?"

Sylvester nodded.

"Good, I'll be back in a minute." With that, Donnie vanished. Sylvester scanned the room. His underage classmates were talking and sipping liquor or guzzling beer as if it was New Year's Eve 1999. A few were dancing in a small open area in the middle of the room.

In the far corner, there were two pretty girls he had never laid eyes on before. One was tall, the other curvy and very pretty, with a dimpled smile that captivated Sylvester. After exchanging greetings with a few classmates, Sylvester found a sidewall to lean on where he finished his beer and, inconspicuously (he hoped), continued to admire the two girls.

Sylvester was startled by the sudden impact and chill of a fresh beer thrust into his chest.

"Don't drop this one," said Kevin, one of Sylvester's childhood friends whose mellow voice earned him a place at Performing Arts. "Glad you made it, Syl."

"Hey, who's that?" Sylvester motioned with his head towards the girl. "She go to Performing Arts?"

"Nah. "She goes to Bronx Science. Wanna meet her?" Before he could say anything, Kevin grabbed his arm and pulled him over to the girls.

"Jennifer, meet the only person on the planet shyer than you," he said.

Sylvester blushed but managed to engage in polite conversation. He'd never had a girlfriend, never had the time or the confidence. He was sometimes so shy around females his age that he wondered if there was something wrong with him. Donnie suddenly re-appeared.

"Hey, ladies," Donnie said. "Syl and I got some business to take care of."

"I'll let you go, Sylvester. It was nice talking to you," Jennifer said.

The timing of Donnie's message could not have been worse. But it was said in a way that left Sylvester feeling he had little choice. He followed Donnie up a wide, curving carpeted stairwell near the front entrance. Inside his bedroom, Donnie smirked and held out his hands. Sylvester handed him the two packages of weed inside his jacket.

"One for the party and one for you to keep," Sylvester said.

"How much?" Donnie asked.

"I told you, no charge. Enjoy."

Donnie hesitated for a moment. "How many times do I have to tell you, no way a child of Grayson Roberts takes handouts. I'm paying you."

Donnie nervously laughed while reaching into the drawer of his computer desk and took out an envelope, showing five-hundred-dollar bills.

"That's too much, man."

"I won't take no for an answer." He practically forced the envelope into Sylvester's hand, wrapping his fingers around it. Then he sniffed the grass. "Awesome! Jamaica's finest ganga!" Donnie shouted.

"Come on, man. Let's party," Sylvester said, worried that by now some other guy might be talking to Jennifer.

Donnie slowly opened the door, ushering Sylvester out before him. From out of nowhere, a much older black male in a baseball cap and a windbreaker blocked his way. Another white man in the same getup forcibly grabbed Sylvester under his arm and pulled it behind his back. Sylvester gasped at the sharp pain of handcuffs locking around his wrists.

"Stay calm and quiet, son. I don't want to embarrass you. I'll walk you out of here," the officer said.

Sylvester locked eyes with Donnie.

"Sorry, man," he said, suddenly looking awfully sober.

"You spoiled white piece of shit. You stitched me up."

"I had no choice."

Fourteen

Manhattan

On the ride to the 32nd Precinct, Sylvester could think of nothing other than his mother's anguished screams. The promising son was now just another teenage drug-dealing thug. *My future's down the toilet.* He knew it was his mom's worst nightmare come true.

Sylvester was relieved when the tight cuffs were loosened after he was processed. They had been so tight he was worried they would leave a permanent scar on his left wrist. He was permitted one phone call. Luckily, Marco answered. Sylvester had a kaleidoscope of butterflies in his chest and stomach.

"Where the fuck are you, bro? It's the middle of the night. Mom is going to kill you."

"Listen," Sylvester said, cupping his right hand over the receiver, while his left almost strangled the phone handle grip, "I called because I ended up sleeping over. No big deal. Tell her everything's okay."

"Are you sure?"

"Yeah, ok. You're still gonna get your ass kicked. I'm going back to bed," Marco said, yawning.

"See you tomorrow, bro," Sylvester hung up, praying it was the truth. Officer Stubbs, a middle-aged black cop with a moustache and a short Kodak hairstyle, marched Sylvester over from the hallway and cuffed him to a wooden chair at his desk. There was a mountain of paperwork that reflected the number of unsolved crimes Stubbs had on his hands.

Officers roamed around the thirty-foot rectangular office, filled with a dozen desks and chairs, piles of files, and wanted posters adorning the walls.

"Why's a kid like you selling? Talk to me, maybe I can help."

"I have nothing to say. Just do what you're gonna do," Sylvester replied, dubious of anyone who wore a uniform, regardless of their color. Stubbs muttered something under his breath, got up and left. Sylvester sat there in silence for more than a half hour. The streetlights filtered in through the broken blinds on the small window above Stubbs' desk and formed shadows on Sylvester's face.

Stubbs eventually reappeared, wearing a sourpuss expression. The shadows might have made Sylvester look as shady as Nixon with his infamous five o'clock shadow, but Stubbs could see a naïve kid under the façade. "You changed your mind about talking yet?" Stubbs asked.

"No, sir."

Stubbs shrugged. "There's one born every minute; I suppose."

He uncuffed Sylvester and took him to a holding cell. Sylvester went to the back corner of the eight by ten cage and sat silently on a wooden bench. In no time, his untucked shirt was soaked with sweat. Having not eaten or had a cup of water since his arrest, Sylvester was dishevelled and exhausted. He badly needed to defecate but recoiled every time he walked over to the silver toilet stuffed with days old excrement. It made him so nauseous he thought he would puke.

Sylvester lost track of time. He couldn't tell if it was night or day when Stubbs returned, and frog marched him outside to a cop car. With the patrol lights flashing but the siren off, it took less than twenty minutes to speed down to lower Manhattan to central booking. Going through the system was surreal. He felt like crying when an officer rolled his thumb in ink to memorialize his rap sheet. But he somehow stopped the tears when the cop eyeballed him and warned him, "Son, don't you cry."

Afterwards, Sylvester was interviewed by a woman. She told him she needed to verify his ties to the community. But he just shrugged.

"Look, it's important in the judge's consideration whether to set bail," she explained. Even then, a stubborn and frightened Sylvester refused to give her any phone numbers.

"Sylvester, the judges want us to verify where you live and, given your age, speak to a parent before they will release you. It would help even more if your mother or father came to court."

"Sorry, I'd rather rot in jail than have anyone tell my mom I got locked up. No way I'm giving numbers."

She suddenly felt sorry for the kid. "Nobody can force you," she began in a sympathetic tone, "but you'll think differently when you're riding the bus to Rikers Island. You get my drift?"

Sylvester just shrugged again. He was put in a cell. Two or three cons wouldn't leave Sylvester alone, peppering him with questions and taunting him. He feared they might start swinging at him. Just in time, he was taken upstairs and locked in a cell adjacent to the courtroom. A dozen inmates in this pen, sick of the wait, took turns shouting for a lawyer and yelling, mostly things like: *Why the fuck was it taking so long to see the judge?*

On the far wall, opposite the holding cell, were four doors with small glass windows.

"Sylvester Stanley. Booth three," a loud voice called out from one of the interview booths. Sylvester turned the handle on the door to the third locked cubicle and was buzzed in by a good-looking man in a sharp suit. The guy looked more like he had just stepped out of a photo shoot for a cologne or a designer label than an attorney. *He's far too young to be a lawyer!* Sylvester thought.

"Have a seat, Sylvester," he said while glancing down at a file. "My name is Walt Ruiz. I'm going to represent you. Give me a second to look over this paperwork, and we'll talk."

"You're a lawyer?"

"All lawyers don't have a paunch and granny glasses, you know?" Walt snapped.

Ruiz's words frightened his teenage client far more than they impressed him. "Sorry if I offended. I have no clue what a lawyer is supposed to look like. I've never been in trouble before. All I know is I'm scared shitless."

Ruiz looked up from his papers. "Sorry, man. I see now you've got no record and you're just a kid. I didn't mean to be so abrupt. Don't worry, Syl. I hope you don't mind if I call you Syl? Sylvester sounds too fucking formal. I'll take good care of you. As good as your mama." There was something about Ruiz's braggadocio that was irresistible. For the first time since his arrest, Sylvester had some hope.

"Thank God it's marijuana. And you go to the Manhattan High School of Performing Arts. Excellent stuff. So, tell me what happened here, Syl? How did a nice guy like you end up in a place like this?"

Unable to suppress the anxious shake in his voice, Sylvester began: "I was invited to a party. This kid Donnie asked me to bring some marijuana. I brought some pot with me. He offered to buy it, but I told him he could have it as a friend. Next thing I know he's shoving money in my hand and before I know it, a cop arrests me."

"Obviously, that's not all of it, but that's all I need to know today."

"How much more do you need to know? Just ask me. I'm not looking to hide anything."

"Why the fuck is a cop at a party, knowing you're there to *sell* grass?"

"That I can't tell you. All I can add, if it means anything, is that Donnie said sorry when I was arrested."

"Hmm, no matter how much of an asshole this kid Donnie is, he wouldn't just set you up, nor would the cops be interested if it's just some idea of his that you're selling. There's something more, but we won't get that info today. Today is only about getting you home."

Sylvester was irked by hearing there was something more sinister about his arrest, but there was no point in dwelling on it. *For now, at least*, he thought.

"And I know that's not going to happen. The lady who interviewed me said I needed to provide my mom's address and phone number to be released, and there's no way I'm doing that. My mom will flip out. I won't put her through that. So, I guess I'm sleeping at Rikers."

"I'll put your head on your pillow tonight. I guarantee it. I'll go to Rikers with you if I don't. How's that?"

As he stepped out of the booth, Sylvester's optimism suddenly faded. Sure, Ruiz had eased his mind, but how could he really trust anything he said? He skulked back to the corner of his holding cell.

A few minutes later, Sylvester was cuffed again and taken into the courtroom. It was a large, run-down, sad excuse for one. There were high ceilings, large oval-shaped windows on one wall, and scratched wooden benches in the seating section. The area in front of the judge's bench had tables on both sides for defense counsel and the prosecutor. Sylvester was told to sit down beside four other prisoners on a side bench a few feet in front of the defense table. Uncuffed, Sylvester placed his right hand under the bench and was grossed out when he came across a nasty surprise: a used piece of gum that stuck to three of his fingers. As discreetly as possible, he rubbed his hands together to scrape it off before appearing before the court.

Everybody was ordered to rise when Judge Frederick Gruden walked in. He was a middle-aged white man with a well-groomed goatee and a surprisingly warm face. Sylvester was shaken when a court officer called his name out first. He was taken over to stand next to Ruiz in front of the judge's raised bench. Ruiz winked at him.

"What the fuck?" an overweight officer muttered when the sticky remains of old gum touched his hand when re-cuffing Sylvester, who whispered an apology. But the tightness of the grip around his arm suggested it was not accepted. Sylvester's charges were read out. The prosecutor requested that the judge set a thousand-dollar bail, given that Sylvester was selling and his assertion of living at home with his mom could not be verified.

"Your Honor," Ruiz responded. "There's no reason to hold Mr. Stanley. His failure to provide a phone number is solely a product of his pride and bravery. He's a gifted student at the Manhattan High School of Performing Arts, has never previously been arrested, and is so embarrassed to be here that he simply cannot bear to let his mother know that he's been arrested. He needs to be home to be able to sit down and break the news to her. He's only charged with selling a small amount of marijuana."

"Mr. Ruiz, with your permission, I would like to address your client," Judge Gruden responded, nodding reassuringly towards Ruiz.

"Sure, Judge," Ruiz agreed.

"Mr. Stanley, is what your counsel said true, that you refuse to provide your mother's number because you are ashamed of the arrest and for no other reason?"

"Yes, your Honor. I swear that's the truth."

"I promise you that nobody will speak to your mother. What's your number?" Sylvester reluctantly provided it.

"Dial the number and hand me the receiver," he directed one of his male clerks.

"Judge!" Ruiz shouted.

Judge Gruden held up his hand and said, "Relax, Mr. Ruiz." The clerk dialled the number. Sylvester's pulse raced. The phone rang and was answered.

"Oh, ma'am. I'm sorry. I must have dialed the wrong number." The judge quickly put the receiver down as he addressed the courtroom.

"Let the record reflect I dialled the number provided by Mr. Stanley, and the voice of a middle-aged woman could be heard on the other end. She answered the phone, 'Sylvester, is that you?' It is clearly the defendant's mother's voice. Over the objection of the Assistant District Attorney, Mr. Stanley is released on his own recognizance to appear in this court on August fourteenth, at ten in the morning."

Relieved far beyond expectations, Sylvester shook hands with Ruiz and began to rush out of the courtroom. Judge Gruden called out to him. Sylvester's heart sank.

"Mr. Stanley, phone your mother immediately. I can tell the poor woman is going through hell worrying about you."

By the end of July, Sylvester had lost fifteen pounds and still hadn't said one word to his mother about his arrest. Lorraine continually barraged him with questions and concerns over why he wasn't eating and was spending so much time locked in his room. However, Sylvester provided her with even fewer clues than he had to the cops while in jail.

Sylvester's only salvation turned out to be the girl he met at the party on that ill-fated night. He was able to get Jennifer's number from Kevin and, after apologizing to a fault with a feigned excuse about rushing off because he started to feel unwell, he summoned the courage to ask her out and they began dating. Sylvester entered his relationship with newfound confidence. After a month, he secretly felt like a real man now that he wasn't a virgin and had a rap sheet. Fortunately, Sylvester was able to hide his arrest from Jennifer and did not even have to worry about her learning about his case because her family was planning a trip to South Carolina at the end of the summer.

With his court date approaching, Sylvester was exasperated by not having any contact with Ruiz, despite leaving countless messages. Finally, late one afternoon, on the tenth ring, Ruiz answered a mere millisecond before Sylvester was about to slam the phone down in frustration.

"Hey, Sylvester, how are you? Ruiz responded breathlessly, "Sorry," he continued without missing a beat, "I've been swamped. But, trust me, if there was something to worry about, I would have called you immediately. Let's just see where we're at when we're back in court."

"What do you mean? Are we going to trial?" Sylvester was incredulous, his voice angry.

"Of course not. It takes forever to have a trial. The best way to get what we want is for you to be patient. The older the case gets, the better. The District Attorney's office has so many more serious cases to deal with. Chances are, after six months, yours will be dismissed."

"So, all this time, you've done nothing?"

"Didn't I get you out? Didn't I tell you I'd take care of things? Relax, Syl. Let me do my thing. I assure you I'm not going to let you get hurt. I have to get going. I'll see you in a week."

Before Sylvester could get in another word, Ruiz hung up. Sylvester stared at his bedroom wall, feeling as let down as when his father walked out. Boiling, Sylvester punched the plaster over his headboard so forcefully that he ended up with a nasty gash on his knuckles.

Two days before his appearance, Lorraine burst into Sylvester's room and woke him up. She was waving a letter, screaming. *Oh shit!* he thought.

"What is this? You've been arrested for selling drugs and you never said a word about it?"

"What are you talking about?" Sylvester answered with feigned surprise, raising himself off his bed.

"Don't play stupid with me, boy!" she shouted, smacking her son on the head with the paper in her hand. "It's a letter from your school, filling in all the details and notifying me of your possible suspension. Or even permanent expulsion! "Lorraine threw the letter on the floor, repeatedly slapping Sylvester's head and shoulders.

"Mom, stop,"

"How could you, Sylvester? All I've done? All we've worked for? And you've thrown it away! For what? To get high?"

Loraine's hands flailed wildly. Sylvester grabbed both her wrists and pulled her downwards. She collapsed, burying her head in his chest, sobbing uncontrollably. Sylvester wrapped his arms around her. He could not hold back tears himself.

"I'm so, so sorry, Mom. I don't know what I was thinking. But I swear I'll fix it. It will never happen again."

Slowly, Lorraine composed herself. She reached for a tissue from the nightstand and wiped her face. "We have to get you a lawyer. There is a man, David Sherman. I've heard so many great things about him. I don't know how much he costs, but whatever it is, we'll pay it. You can't trust a free lawyer. You always get what you pay for in this life. He'll sell you out. We have to hire Mr. Sherman."

Sylvester had to agree. His life was on the line, and he no longer had confidence in Ruiz, who had been ducking his calls for weeks. That guy was too busy with other cases and hadn't yet lifted a finger to get him off the hook. After several minutes of hugging his mom and softly chanting *mea culpas*, Sylvester got up and showered. Deep down, he was relieved that his mother finally knew how badly he fucked up and, even more importantly, he was glad she was in his corner. Her forgiveness meant the world to him.

Sherman's small office was on the fourteenth floor of a building near the Brooklyn courthouse. The moment Sylvester and Lorraine walked into the reception area, Sherman immediately came out to greet them and warmly invited them into his office. The middle-aged man wore a dark gray suit and a navy-blue tie that was knotted tightly around his neck. He had wire-rimmed glasses perched awkwardly on his nose.

"Sylvester, your mom has told me a little bit about the case, but more importantly, I'd like to hear about you," Sherman said.

Sylvester was sceptical of Sherman's sincerity. "What would you like to hear?"

"How you grew up? How are you doing in school? Your likes and dislikes. I never agree to represent someone until I get to know them." Sylvester nodded, impressed with this line of thinking.

"And if you have questions about me," Sherman continued, "I will be glad to answer them as well. You should not want me to be your lawyer unless we are both familiar and comfortable with each other."

An hour later, Sylvester and his mother left the lawyer's office with a bounce in their steps. They unhesitatingly retained him. Outside, Lorraine warmly embraced her son.

"We're going to beat this with Sherman in our corner, I can feel it in my bones, son."

"I'm really glad you persuaded me to get this guy in my corner."

Two days later, Sherman called Sylvester out of the blue and asked him to drop by the office. Stepping into Sherman's reception area, his new attorney gently put his arm around Sylvester's shoulder. As sincere, as the gesture felt, it seemed unprofessional to the young man and made him uncomfortable.

"Let me fill you in on the case and tell you what I've found out," Sherman said, as he led Sylvester into his office. Once inside, he continued, "Just as I suspected, there's more to it. Apparently, Donnie's habits are not restricted to marijuana. He's been into cocaine for at least the past year and has even tried crack."

Sylvester's mouth dropped. "Not possible...coming from his family?'

Sherman waved away his disbelief. "Substance abuse knows no class or race."

"Wow!" Sylvester shook his head.

"My sources told me Donnie was too afraid to ask his folks for the money his habit was costing so he started selling. Donnie was arrested, his father took control, retained the biggest name white collar firm he could find. Donnie's lawyer enrolled him in a ritzy residential treatment program and got him a plea bargain to have the charges dropped if he successfully completed treatment. Part of the deal was that Donnie had to tell everything he knew and even be willing to help."

Sylvester was stunned. "Did he set me up?"

Sherman nodded. "Likely he was reluctant but had no choice. His information on his source of crack which was what the District Attorney's office was really after turned out to be useless. The cops settled for Donnie setting you up."

"So, he's a crack dealer and I get fucked for marijuana! What kind of justice is that?"

Sherman sighed and took off his glasses, laying them down on an open law book on his desk. "I would love to tell you justice is blind, young man, but like too many things in our society, it favors the rich and crushes the poor. I assure you and your mom, however, in your case, justice will be served."

"I just can't go to jail Mr. Sherman and mom will never forgive me if I end up with a record."

"I understand and that's why I 've convinced the prosecutors to permit you to plead to the marijuana sale to Donnie, and to agree to your getting youthful offender treatment, which, same as with Donnie, will vacate and seal the conviction. And of course, no jail time."

Sylvester punched the air with joy, his eyes lit up lit up like a Christmas tree.

"But there's just one more thing, Sylvester," Sherman cautioned. "I discovered that the authorities were also looking into your selling marijuana to your friend Kevin."

Sylvester shook his head in disbelief, "I knew this was all too good to be true."

"Relax son and let me explain," Sherman responded holding his hand out. "I'm guessing Donnie talked about Kevin too and I'm sure no harm will come to him for smoking a little marijuana. But the last thing we wanted was a new case to blindside you. So, I took the bull by the horns and demanded things get set up so immediately after we take care of your case in Manhattan, we run over to criminal court in Brooklyn and have you enter the same plea with the promise of Y.O. wiping out this case as well. We must do it on the very same day under the law for it to be sealed too. It's a technicality that many lawyers miss."

"What about school?"

"Of course, your schooling is of paramount importance. I have gotten the school to agree they will not hold it against you as long as you have no other disciplinary infractions at school in the future or any new arrests."

"Mr. Sherman, this sounds too good to be true. There's gotta be a catch. The way you make it sound, it's like I was never even arrested."

"Sylvester, you're a young man with so much talent and potential. You made one silly mistake. This is the kind of misjudgement we all make at a young age. I'm sure it will be your last. You deserve a second chance. I know someday you will make your family and everyone who knows you proud."

Sylvester walked over to Sherman intending to shake his hand, but instead, before he could stop himself, he gave him a big bear hug. Sherman reciprocated.

The following week, Sherman led Sylvester through a plea in Manhattan; then they jumped into a cab with Loraine and quickly made their way to criminal court in Brooklyn. Sylvester was promised youthful offender treatment in both cases, and the records were sealed.

On the ride home, Sylvester kept thinking that nothing could go wrong now.

Fifteen

October 1994
Brooklyn

Two years after Sylvester's arrest, the tenant who rented their ground floor apartment vanished, and Lorraine lost her job as an administrative secretary at a mid-Manhattan commercial law firm. In desperation, Lorraine and Sylvester went to see their family banker Bill Bradley, a lifelong friend of the family who had arranged the original mortgage on the house for her father. Lorraine was sure he could arrange for a re-financing that would enable the family to weather the storm.

Lorraine put on her Sunday best, making sure not a hair was out of place, and meticulously applied her make-up for the meeting with Bradley, who warmly hugged her and offered Sylvester a two-handed handshake, as he walked them into the conference room. After engaging in frivolous conversation for as long as possible, he dropped the hammer:

"The housing market in New York has been down for a few years and your neighborhood has really been hit hard. The value of your home dramatically plummeted during the 1991 recession. Unfortunately, you still do not have a new job, Lorraine. My bosses deem the risk too high."

Lorraine was left speechless.

"I'm so sorry, Lorraine. I did all I could," he added in the same way a doctor would inform family members that their loved one didn't survive the operation.

"I know you tried your best. We'll make do somehow. We always do," she said, as Bradley held the door open for them.

Outside Sylvester could not contain his anger. "Tried his best? Give me a fucking break. All these years I've seen you breaking your ass to never miss a mortgage payment. Now we come looking for help and where the fuck is everyone who cashed in on us all these years? Bet if we were one of their white clients, it'd be a different story."

"Please son, stop. We'll figure out a way. I'll get back to work and we'll find another tenant it's just a matter of time."

Sylvester hugged Lorraine tightly without saying a word, but he knew time had already run out. One week after the meeting, without telling his mother, Sylvester took a leave of absence from school and put college applications on hold. Both maddened and saddened, he felt he had little choice. Bagging groceries for eighty hours a week, even when supplemented by his part-time employment in the Soho art studio, still barely covered the family's heating costs. Sylvester rarely had time to see Jennifer. Foreclosure loomed.

Despite vowing he would rather lose an arm than ever again commit a crime, Sylvester was *not going to let his mother lose her home*. Looking out his bedroom window late on a Friday evening, exhausted, bitter and broken, Sylvester cursed his fate: a harsh reality he and his mom had always refused to believe. Ultimately, there was only one solution for black kids like him from Brooklyn. Jim Burton. Sylvester had known Burton, who was a few years older, ever since grade school, before their lives took different paths. They became fast friends, as only young boys do, when JB, picked a fight with Sylvester only to discover that Sylvester had been taught to box by his Uncle Hinton and despite being five inches shorter and twenty pounds lighter beat the crap out of him. Laughing it off the next day, Burton called Sylvester "Stallion" after Rocky, and the nickname stuck.

JB was still only twenty and already had his own apartment in Fort Greene. Walking down the steps to Burton's basement residence on the ground floor of a four-story Classen Avenue brownstone, Sylvester looked cool as ice in contrast to his racing pulse when he rang the bell and was buzzed up.

"I want to speak to JB if he has a minute. Is he here?" he said to some tight-faced dude who looked vaguely familiar.

"Wait, I know you. You're Marco's brother, Sylvester, right? You live a few blocks from me."

"You got it Einstein. Now let me see JB."

"Yo, JB, there's someone here to see you. Sylvester Stanley."

"Stallion, you shitting me!" JB yelled out from the living room. "Let the brother in."

Sylvester was led into a room that was decked out in cheap IKEA furniture and dark oak floors. JB was half-asleep, lounging on a red plastic-covered couch watching MTV. There was a strong stench of marijuana.

"What's up, Stallion?" he said rubbing his eyes. "How'd you know where to find me?"

"Not difficult. Just asked around. Listen, I'm not here to waste your time or mine. You once offered work, I'm here to accept," he replied.

JB's eyes lit up like a carnival.

"Just a couple of conditions," Syl continued.

"I like your style, treating this like a business because it is a business. Shoot, bro."

"One, I won't carry a piece. Two, this is just between me and you. I don't want to know shit about anyone or anything else you do and couldn't care less. And one last thing, I heard about Marco helping carry for you. You ever have my little brother work for you again, I'll fucking kill you."

JB snarled. "Whoa, slow the fuck down, Stallion. It's always best to hear both sides of the story before you go around threatening drug dealers who carry guns," JB said, sitting up and whipping out his shooter.

Syl didn't blink, which had now gained him even more respect in JB's eyes, as he returned the gun down the back of his trousers.

"Two weeks ago," JB continued, "I gave five grams to Trevor Johnson to deliver to one of my sellers in Bed-Stuy. He was with someone else, another young nigga he told me was coming along for back up. I had never seen him before. Didn't give Johnson an extra dollar, what's it to me if your brother tags along? Had no idea that was your brother, until Johnson vouched for him. Don't fucking blame me. Blame the company your brother keeps. I never recruited him."

He sat forward, reaching for a joint on the low coffee table. Syl kept his cool but underneath it all he was tense as hell.

"Why am I even explaining this shit to you? You come here asking for work and you threaten me. Fuck you, Stallion. Why you really here? I'm not buying this sudden change of heart. You wearing a wire? If you are, you're a dead man."

Before saying another word, Sylvester ripped off his shirt, dropped his pants and stood in front of Burton with his drawers around his ankles, naked except for his socks and shoes.

"You want to check if I have a wire stuck down my big cock too?" Syl said as seriously as a dead man.

JB broke out laughing.

"I need the money. It's personal. It's my business. You got something for me or not?" Sylvester had no difficulty holding his nerve; he couldn't, however, shut off the voice in his head pleading for him to walk out the door before he embarked on something he'd forever regret.

"I swear, Stallion. You've always been one crazy motherfucker. That's why I like you." He took a long drag. "Tell you what, get dressed and get the fuck out of here. Meet me tomorrow at Junior's for breakfast. We'll talk business. Just the two of us."

The next day, Sylvester and JB met at ten-thirty at Junior's, on the corner of Flatbush and Myrtle Avenue. Sylvester found JB at a back booth, with the long-curved mirror for a wall behind him, sipping coffee and devouring a piece of cheesecake.

"Sit, Stallion," JB pointed to one of the comfy orange, low-back leather chairs opposite his table. "Junior's cheesecake. Gotta be a sister who bakes it. It's the shit."

The waitress came over. Looking at himself in the mirror, Sylvester ordered only a cup of coffee. "Stallion, you gonna fade away man. I know you're a starving artist, but come on, eat. It's on me."

"I'm good, JB. Not a breakfast man."

After the waitress brought Syl his coffee and was out of earshot JB got down to brass tacks. "Alright, nigga, let's talk turkey. I've been thinking. Came up with something perfect, something that will work for both of us. I need a mule to Charlotte. But I need someone I can trust. I'm not talking small quantity. You're going to pack serious weight in your suitcase. I got a bunch of them with false bottoms. You take the train down there and deliver to an address I give you and leave it in the hallway. There won't be anyone there when you arrive or leave. You won't see anyone, and they won't see you."

"I don't know, JB. A homeboy on Amtrak with a suitcase? It's an advertisement for an arrest."

"Listen, man. I got it all figured for you. There's an art museum downtown nearby that holds a seminar every Saturday. You purchase a ticket in advance and have it with you. With that and your old school ID who's going to question you? If anyone does, you just say you're there for the seminar and staying with your aunt for the weekend. I'll even give you an address."

Sylvester stroked his chin, impressed by the plan. He underestimated JB, he knew he had street smarts, but never thought him capable of so quickly devising a scheme this clever and well thought out. JB even made it sound less risky than bringing the weed he carried back from Jamaica.

"I'll give you twenty-five hundred dollars the day before the trip and another twenty-five hundred when you return. Sound good, Stallion?"

With his family on the brink, Sylvester was in no position to bargain. He slapped hands with Burton.

"Deal, JB. Deal. You got yourself a mule you can trust."

"Not a mule," JB laughed. "A stallion."

Sixteen

September 1995
Charlotte, North Carolina

The first time he caught the Amtrack to Charlotte, Sylvester was beside himself. No matter how many times he told himself there was nothing to worry about, it was as simple as when he carried the ganga from Jamaica, he could not take his eyes off his suitcase half expecting the crack to jump out. But repetition turns even the illicit routine. He made the trip once every few weeks, picking up the suitcase with the false bottom from JB's apartment the night before each delivery. The fifty to sixty grams of crack never weighed more than a couple of ounces. Sylvester packed the suitcase with several outfits, and toiletries, and, on top, placed brushes, sketch pads, and a partially painted canvas.

After nine trips to Charlotte that year, Sylvester had accumulated a nice nest egg. Loraine relentlessly interrogated Sylvester about his newly discovered income and was skeptical of his explanation that several of his paintings were purchased by an individual for his private collection. When Sylvester insisted his buyer wanted to remain anonymous, she reluctantly sat on her fears only after Sylvester insisted that keeping the money and identity of the buyer hidden would enable him to remain eligible for securing the college scholarship she dreamed about. With the drug money he had earned and Lorraine close to returning to work, he was more than ready to re-enroll in school and get his life back.

On the tenth trip, his luck ran out. Peering out from the side of the window blind, he saw several uniformed policemen and other plainclothes officers waiting to board. He saw that several were wearing FBI insignias, and in that second, his heart stopped.

Don't fucking panic, Sylvester told myself. Carrying his suitcase in his right hand, he walked as casually as possible to the end of the train car and stepped down to the platform. Breathing a sigh of relief, Sylvester made his way down the platform towards the main concourse. As he walked out into the open area of the station, another FBI agent suddenly appeared.... with a leash holding his drug-sniffing canine.

Two minutes later, Sylvester was arrested, charged, and detained without bail for trafficking more than fifty grams of crack.

Seventeen

FourHours Later
United States District Court
Charlotte, North Carolina

After being processed in a downtown DEA office, Sylvester was taken one block to the courthouse to be arraigned. Sylvester was no virgin suspect, so he knew to keep his mouth shut. Having prepared himself for the filth and snail's pace of the state system, the clean efficiency of the feds left his head spinning, and with barely enough time to fully assess the gravity of his situation.

Shackled, Sylvester felt strangely numb when he was taken in front of a young male Magistrate in his mid-thirties with a trim goatee, a slight Southern twang and a matching gentlemanly demeanor. He was informed that he had been charged with conspiracy to possess with intent to distribute more than fifty grams of crack/cocaine and one count of possession with intent to distribute. Asked if he wanted the assignment of a public defender, Sylvester suddenly revived himself. Hell, no, he thought, I have to get Sherman here.

"No, your Honor, I have an attorney, but he is in New York."

The Magistrate entered a not guilty plea to the charges and adjourned the case for 48 hours. "You will be remanded to the County Jail until then."

Federal inmates at Mecklenburg were held in a separate area and allowed only two calls of no more than twenty minutes per day. Sylvester's first call was to

Lorraine, but he stood with the receiver in his hand unable to bring himself to dial. He picked the phone up again and called Sherman.

On the third ring, Sylvester heard Sherman's always harried voice.

"Mr. Sherman, it's Sylvester, Sylvester Stanley..."

Sylvester's voice was interrupted by a prison recording. "This is a call from a federal inmate, if you agree to accept the call, press 1 to reject the call press 2." Sylvester heard a beep followed by a loud sigh.

"Dear God, Sylvester, where are you, what happened?"

Trying to sound unshaken, Sylvester provided Sherman with the abridged version. Before Sherman could respond, he dropped his guard, pleading:

"Mr. Sherman you've gotta get me out of here. We'll pay you whatever it takes."

"It's not about the money. You know that. But I can't come down there. I'm not admitted in federal court in North Carolina and even if I could figure out a way, I'm about to start a trial."

Devastated, Sylvester was able to make one request. "My mom, she doesn't even know I'm here. I told her I was going to attend an event at an Art Museum in the area. I'm too ashamed to call her. She must be losing her mind, please you must call her before she sends out the National Guard looking for me."

"I'll take care of it, son. You and your mom are special to me."

"God bless you, Mr. Sherman." Before Sylvester could say another word, a portly white corrections officer grabbed the phone from his hand. "Time's up bud."

Three hours later, with only an hour left before the prison would lock down for an inmate count, Sylvester was summoned for a counsel visit. *Who the hell could it be?* He wondered. Walking in cuffs, flanked by two guards, Sylvester was taken down a long corridor to the area reserved for attorney conferences. He was led into a small room with a gray plastic desk and two chairs. Unshackled, he peered out the door trying to guess which of the half dozen counsel in the waiting area was his.

Scott Corbin, carrying a slender tan leather briefcase, looked more like he belonged on a California beach with a surfboard than indoors wearing a suit and tie. The look on Sylvester's face when Corbin walked in and introduced himself told it all. "Sylvester, I know we don't know each other but I'm not stupid. You didn't choose or pay me to represent you and it's natural for you to be skeptical. But all I do is defend people and my reputation for doing everything possible for my clients is the way I make my living. I know you're not from around here, but you'll find out."

Any kernel of hope Sylvester still held, had evaporated at his surprisingly brief court appearance the following morning. After Corbin entered a not guilty plea for Sylvester, the court refused to re-consider his remand, and the case was put over one week for a preliminary hearing to be held in the event an indictment had not yet been voted.

After only five minutes in Court, Sylvester wanted a new lawyer. "What the fuck, I should have represented myself," Sylvester shouted between the bars, when Corbin came to see him in the holding cell adjacent to the courtroom. "You didn't do a goddamn thing in there. I fucking knew you were more beach bum than lawyer the second I saw you."

Corbin didn't raise an eyebrow. "Look, bro, this is federal court, if you think you're walking out the door after you're found carrying a suitcase with a shit load of crack in it, you're not as smart as I thought you were. We've got a long road. There're no short-term fixes. It's not how long you're in before the case is taken care of, it's how long you're in after. You have to wrap your mind around that and let me do my job. I'm the right lawyer for you. Trust me."

The following morning Sylvester finally summoned the courage to call his mother.

"Mom?" Sylvester's voice cracked at the sound of her voice, tears immediately welling up in his eyes.

"Mr. Sherman has already filled me in," her voice was cold as ice. "What else is there to say?"

"Mom, I'm so sorry."

"Stop. Not again with sorry. Don't play your mother, boy. Just tell me why you're calling? What do you want?"

Feeling as hurt and abandoned as a five-year-old, but not wanting to add pain to his mom's wounds, Sylvester spoke optimistically.

"I called to tell you I have a good lawyer here. He spent a lot of time with me today before we went to court. He's going to do his best. Listen, Mom, these calls are all recorded. I can't really say more. I just wanted to tell you that I'm alright."

A stonewalled silence followed; Sylvester thought the phone had gone dead.

"Mom? You still there?"

A second before hanging up, he heard her sobs.

"Sylvester," she said between tears, "Sylvester, how could you?"

"Mom, listen. It'll be ok."

"We have to find a lawyer. Sherman told me he can't take the case."

"No, no we're not doing that. For a fed case, it's a fortune. And if it's not Sherman, who can we get? We don't have the money. And the lawyer the court gave me knows what he's doing. He has a great rep. He told me he even gets paid good because it's a federal case."

"Oh please, Sylvester. Don't be naive."

"I'm not. I heard from other inmates' that private lawyers can be worse. Take as much money as they can and end the case as fast as possible. Talk you into a bad plea."

"I don't know."

"Mom, I won't let you lose everything trying to pay a lawyer."

"Well, you're the expert. What do I know about drugs and drug cases?"

His mother's sarcasm pierced his heart.

"Mom, I love you. I don't want you to travel down here either. I'm locked up in the middle of nowhere. I'll keep you posted."

"Okay, son," her voice a strange mixture of disappointment, hurt and love that could only come from a mother's mouth. "Be good boy. Your brother misses you. I'll talk to you soon." And with that Sylvester was left alone to grapple with his demons.

Eighteen

December 1995
United States District Court
Charlotte, North Carolina

"Sylvester, God, I don't know how to tell you, other than to give it to you straight. You're facing a life sentence." Corbin's devastating words blasted Sylvester. They couldn't be true.

Sylvester sat opposite Corbin in a small conference room he was taken to following a status conference of his case after his third appearance in court. Two Court officers stood outside monitoring his behavior.

"Mr. Corbin, I have no idea what you're talking about," Sylvester refused to take in the reality of his prognosis. "I know the crack in my trunk was worth serious cash. But come on, how much time am I really looking at?"

"Sylvester, as much as I wish it wasn't true, you're looking at life."

Sylvester felt dizzy, momentarily unable to harness his thoughts and emotions. He quickly regrouped.

"Bullshit. Stop scaring me with the max possible time. I want to know the real deal. What kind of time we're talking about if I cop a deal?"

"I know it's hard to believe Sylvester, but your crime and past record have you looking at a life sentence. Carrying for sale more than fifty grams of crack carries a ten-year minimum sentence in federal court. For powder, five thousand grams. One hundred times more. I know it makes no sense but thank Clinton and his crime bill. If you have one prior conviction for a drug felony it's a twenty-year minimum and two priors it's life."

For a moment Sylvester felt slightly relieved. Even ten years didn't sound so bad compared to the rest of his life.

"I don't have any priors Mr. Corbin. I got youthful offender on both my cases. They were dismissed and sealed. My lawyer promised me I'd have no convictions on my record."

"I know it's hard to believe. Maybe your lawyer didn't even catch it. But in the fucking federal system, even a Y.O. can be used as a past felony conviction. It was vacated, yes, but that doesn't mean it's not a prior conviction as far as the federal courts are concerned. You have two prior drug convictions, man. You're looking at life."

"If you were arrested in Brooklyn, the federal prosecutors would likely never enhance your sentence based on two minor marijuana convictions. But down here and given that the assistant United States attorney assigned to your case is Cliff Lessons, you're getting fucked. Lessons is the worst. I wish I had a hundred dollars for every time I've heard him preach that marijuana is a gateway crime that must be punished as harshly as heroin or crack. He's an asshole, a heartless cracker."

The young man didn't know whether to cry or burst out laughing. He banged the table with a clenched fist.

The guards turned to look at them. Corbin apologetically showed them the palm of his hand, as if it had written on it: *Please give the kid a break. He's just been given a raw deal.* Corbin breathed a sigh of relief when they turned away. He'd had client conferences, especially with black prisoners, broken up for much less.

"Shush. Keep your voice down. They'll call time if you keep causing a ruckus. Take a deep breath... please."

A part of Sylvester was more than ready to start a fight after hearing his plight. Instead, he directed his ire at Corbin. "Come on, Corbin. I've been trusting you, but I think I better get me a retained lawyer." Beads of sweat rolled down his face. "This is complete bullshit. I need to pay someone. If I pay a lawyer enough, I bet he'll beat this case at trial."

"And how is that going to happen?" Corbin replied. "Tell me how and I'll be glad to take you to trial. I'll get paid way more by the courts too. You were seen by at least six federal agents in possession of the crack found in your luggage. Yeah, you can argue that you had no idea how it got there and knew nothing about the false bottom of the suitcase. Good luck with that."

"So, what are you saying? Plead guilty and spend the rest of my God damn life in prison?"

"No, I believe there's a way you can avoid it. Cooperation. It's the name of the game in the federal system. If you provide what's called substantial assistance in the prosecution of someone they want more, the government will give you a letter which allows the judge to avoid the legally required sentence. In your case, as you've told me, it's obviously Jim Burton. Cooperate against Burton and the judge can give you whatever she feels is right. Once you cooperate the judge will have the power to consider all the reasons you deserve leniency. The reality of your two minor marijuana cases, your promise as an art student, and your family's desperate economic situation, are powerful reasons for a compassionate sentence. And your case has been assigned to one of the really good judges, Elizabeth Parsons. She'll listen."

"So bottom line turn rat or get blown out the water as a sitting duck," Sylvester quipped. Both men laughed, considerably easing the unbearable tension between them.

"That's the spirit, Sylvester."

"So, if I cooperate, what are we looking at?"

"I can't predict, Sylvester. You have a lot of things going for you. Lots of reasons for mitigation. But it's the south, not Brooklyn. I'm hoping with cooperation you might get close to or maybe even less than ten."

Sylvester slowly shook his head, a tear rolled down his cheek. He had no reason to cooperate against his old friend JB. The prospect of cooperation disgusted Sylvester. But spending the rest of his life in prison. How could he refuse?

Nineteen

Two Weeks Later
Mecklenburg County Detention Center
North Carolina

Before Sylvester could even turn rat, JB was arrested in Brooklyn for being a leader of a crack cocaine conspiracy which extended far beyond Sylvester's train trips. Corbin hoped it was a game changer. He expected Lessons would transfer Sylvester's case to join Burton's in the Eastern District of New York. Cooperating in Carolina was one thing, cooperating against JB in Brooklyn and having the right Judge sentence him might even get him home.

The Brooklyn assistant United States attorney reached out to Lessons seeking to add Sylvester to his indictment and requested Lessons dismiss his. He refused. To make matters worse, time was of the essence. Co-defendants in the Brooklyn case were lining up and falling all over themselves to testify against JB in the hopes of avoiding decades in prison. First one in the door is the name of the federal game. Within fewer than two weeks, Sylvester's cooperation would be useless.

Lessons wouldn't budge; he steadfastly refused to follow protocol and agree to the transfer of Sylvester's case to join a much larger conspiracy indictment. Barely over five feet tall, with carefully groomed gray hair and a thick Southern drawl, Lessons relished having Sylvester's fate in his hands. Nothing turned him on more than telling someone from the North, even a fellow federal prosecutor, to fuck off.

With his hopes of cooperation in the wind and the possibility of leaving his Carolina dungeon for a cell in his hometown erased, Sylvester descended into darkness. When Corbin came to see him late one evening after a busy day in the courtroom, Sylvester was disheveled as a homeless beggar. Corbin threw out one last life preserver. He explained that the law provides one other way besides cooperation where a defendant can avoid the mandatory minimum in a drug case referred to as the safety valve. "Few defendants qualify but I think you're eligible. And best of all, if you qualify, the court can grant it even over Lesson's objections," he informed Sylvester.

Sylvester's pulse quickened with a hopeful jolt he had not felt in weeks.

"So, what do I have to do to get this safety valve?"

"There are four basic requirements. First, you have to be unarmed, which fortunately you were. Second, you cannot be a major player in the crime and, since you were just a courier, I think you're also fine. Third, you have to have almost no prior criminal history and, for once, you got lucky. You were convicted the same day for both your marijuana cases which means you receive only one point instead of two in terms of a criminal history calculation. More than one point and you wouldn't be eligible."

Sylvester was incredulous.

Corbin continued, "The last requirement is that you tell the government everything you did and know about the crime. You cannot hold anything back. You have to tell Lessons all you know about Burton's operation and every person involved, no matter how little or how much they may have done."

Sylvester knew better than to relinquish skepticism. "Come on, stop playing me, you know better than I do that

Lessons will tell the judge I'm lying no matter what I say, so I'm still fucked."

"Not true, Sylvester. The Judge decides it, not Lessons. But, whatever you do, you can't hold back. It's your only hope. You just gotta believe that if you do your part the Judge will do hers."

Corbin's speech went on too long. The what ifs and buts sapping Sylvester's initial spurt of optimism.

"And what part is that she'll give me forty or fifty instead of life."

"You can't think like that. In terms of your sentence, it will be just like I told you the situation was with cooperation. Once you qualify for the safety valve the Judge will have the power to consider all the reasons you deserve leniency. Of course, Lessons will have a pissy fit. That would be a big problem if it was a different prosecutor, but like I told you Parsons, and most of the other Judges, are no fans of Lessons. No way she'll be his rubber stamp."

Sylvester pulled up his pants and swept his hands through his unruly hair and beard. For the first time in weeks the cloud over his head lifted slightly. But Corbin's speech was too much to digest in one sitting. Sylvester banged on the door of the conference room, ready to return to his cell.

"I'll think on it," he told Corbin.

Twenty

January 1996
United States District Court
Charlotte, North Carolina

After deciding to bare his soul to Lessons and subsequently entering his guilty plea, Sylvester was back in Court anxiously awaiting the arrival of Judge Parsons to determine his eligibility for the safety valve. The judge entered from a back door and quickly stepped up to the bench with an irritated look on her face. Judge Parsons was surprisingly young, no older than her mid-forties, with light brown hair, a tall and slender frame, and a small face that was overwhelmed by the size of her dark brown glasses. Her courtroom was elegant and spacious, with natural wood-paneled walls, a white-painted ceiling, and wall-to-wall carpeting. The judge excused herself for being late due to dealing with other matters and got right to the point.

"Mr. Lessons, Mr. Stanley has met with your office after his plea and fully admitted his crime, so why are we meeting prior to his day of sentence? What is the problem?"

"Your Honor, ma'am, the issue is I do not believe Mr. Stanley qualifies for the safety valve. I am not challenging his proffer. In fact, it is the truth of what he said which makes him not qualified."

"The point, Mr. Lessons. Get to the point."

"Your Honor, Mr. Stanley admitted to making many additional trips besides the one which resulted in his arrest.

The government was not aware he was repeatedly paid to deliver vast amounts of crack to our community. He was paid far more money than the government ever knew. Therefore, he indisputably occupied a higher position in this conspiracy and is not eligible for the safety valve."

Sylvester and Corbin had endlessly debated whether to disclose his multiple trips and agreed that the risk of their being discovered was simply too great. Corbin was more than ready for Session's argument.

"Your Honor, the law is clear," Corbin responded. "The safety valve requires that you not be a leader or organizer or have a supervisory role in the offense. My client was a courier only. The fact that he made several trips before he was apprehended does not change that. The fact that he was well paid does not change that. And it must be stressed that Mr. Stanley's family circumstances were desperate. The loss of his mother's home was imminent."

Judge Parsons called her law clerk up to the bench to speak to him privately for a few minutes while Sylvester clenched both hands and held his breath. After what seemed like a lifetime, Judge Parsons looked down at everyone and directed her focus on Lessons.

"Normally, I would take written submissions from counsel before rendering a decision. But, Mr. Lessons, your argument does not require an in-depth analysis. You have argued loudly but cited no legal authority for your position. There is nothing in the law that says the safety valve is precluded if a courier is well compensated rather than poorly compensated. And you have presented no facts at all to suggest that the defendant ever occupied any higher role. I find that the defendant qualifies for the safety valve. Sentencing is scheduled for one month from today and I welcome submissions from both sides on whether any departures from the sentencing guidelines are warranted."

Before any court officers could intervene to prevent prohibited contact, Sylvester tightly embraced Corbin. "The best from the west, Corbin, you're the man," Sylvester flashed a smile for the first time since the start of his ordeal.

"Thanks, Syl, let's just keep our fingers crossed," he whispered in his ear.

Twenty-One

February 1996
United States District Court
Charlotte, North Carolina

When dawn broke, well before a corrections officer unlocked Sylvester's cell and put on his handcuffs and shackles, he was up and dressed. Sylvester could barely maintain his sanity. In the weeks leading up to his sentencing, he spent his days endlessly drawing nonsense on a sketchpad, obsessively looking at pictures and photographs of his family and staring at the cement crevices of his cell. Nothing worked. This last night Sylvester felt like the smallest, creepiest insect was ceaselessly inching its way up and around every pore of his skin. He prayed he would see the outdoors again without walls and restraints. He desperately tried to focus on how nice it would be when he would one day again play basketball in the park on the first warm day of spring. But that diversion failed.

After being led to the basement, Sylvester was placed on a bus with a dozen other inmates who were also due in court. It was a two-hour ride to the downtown federal courthouse and a three-hour wait in the holding cell. Sylvester was on the verge of banging his head against the bars a second before he heard his name called.

He entered from a side door of the courtroom, cuffed and in the middle of two guards, elated at the sight of his mom and Jennifer sitting in the first row. Sylvester had bravely insisted he did not want them there, but deeply yearned for their presence. They were seated together in formal attire just behind the defense table. Sylvester exchanged heartfelt looks with both.

The moment he took his seat beside Corbin, he knew from the look on his counsel's face that something was wrong. "Lessons called Chambers early this morning and told the Judge that there was a change of circumstances that needed to be addressed. I'm sure it's more of his desperate bull shit, nothing to worry about."

Corbin patted Sylvester on the back, but the gesture failed to reassure him. Judge Parsons took the bench, making no attempt to disguise her annoyance.

"This better be something different, Mr. Lessons," she announced in a loud voice.

"Yes, your Honor, it very much is. My office learned that, in the past few days, the man responsible for filling Mr. Stanley's suitcase with crack, Jim Burton, has decided not to proceed to trial and has entered into a cooperation agreement with the United States Attorney's office in Brooklyn."

"The relevance, Mr. Lessons?"

"Give me a chance, your Honor."

Sylvester, his pulse racing, looked on in frightened silence. "Mr. Burton has proffered to the authorities in Brooklyn and has informed them that Mr. Stanley is not the only member of his family to act as a courier for him. The defendant's brother Marco also carried crack for him. Now it may be possible, although highly doubtful, that Sylvester didn't know that his younger brother was part of the conspiracy, but we have definite proof to the contrary. As part of his debriefing, Mr. Burton told agents that Mr. Stanley warned Mr. Burton to stop using his brother as a worker and even threatened him if he did it again. So, your Honor, Mr. Stanley did not provide a complete proffer as to everything he knows and is therefore not entitled to the safety valve."

"Mr. Corbin?" Judge Parsons inquired.

"Your Honor, what can I say?" Corbin's mind raced, searching for the best response. "This is the first I'm learning about this proffer session. I have no idea as to the credibility of Mr. Burton. He has countless motives to fabricate and to minimize things he did and exaggerate what others said or did."

Not bad, at least I can postpone this mess, Judge Parsons thought to herself before replying, "It's obvious that the sentencing of Mr. Stanley cannot take place today. I am adjourning the matter one last time and I expect everybody to be ready. Any additional submissions must be made within two weeks, and we will reschedule for six weeks from today."

Before walking out of the courtroom, Parsons felt compelled to try to prepare Sylvester for the worst. "Mr. Corbin, you have a very sympathetic client. I had thought he was a compelling candidate for a downward departure, but there is no circumventing the law in this courtroom. Do I make myself clear?"

"Absolutely, your Honor. I understand."

"See everyone in six weeks. Check with my clerk for the exact day."

Lorraine's sobs reverberated throughout the courtroom.

Twenty-Two

March 28, 1996
United States District Court
Charlotte, North Carolina
Judgment Day

Sylvester was convinced he was walking the Green Mile when he entered the Courtroom. Corbin rose, cleared his throat and spoke first.

"It's understandable why Mr. Stanley left his brother out of his proffer your Honor," he argued. "It was such a marginal piece of evidence which, at most, established that Marco Stanley was present when his friend made a delivery for Burton. The court has the discretion to overlook it and still find the defendant made a comprehensive rendition of his involvement and knowledge of the crime."

Lessons smugly responded, "Your Honor, the law is the law, and the facts are the facts. This court cannot possibly believe Mr. Stanley satisfied his legal duty to tell all he knew if he was to escape the statutorily required sentence of life imprisonment."

As all Jurists do, Judge Parsons had made her decision days before the arguments of counsel. Nevertheless, with Sylvester's life in her hands, she feigned attentiveness and concern at the attorney's words and allowed several minutes to pass. Judge Parsons took off her glasses and placed them on the small, tilted table attached to her bench, as tension consumed the courtroom. She paused, uncharacteristically needing a moment to find her voice and wiped her eyes with a Kleenex. They were noticeably red.

"Mr. Stanley, if I had the power, I would grant you a downward departure to a much shorter time in prison. You are a young man with great potential and there are compelling mitigating reasons for your crime. And the only information you left out of your proffer to Mr. Lessons was the involvement of your younger brother. And protecting a family member, particularly a younger sibling is in some sense admirable, but not more admirable than what is required under the law. The law has no ambiguities, and no flexibility in this regard. To have qualified for the safety valve, you were required to tell everything you knew and there are no exceptions for family. So, while I feel significant, indeed more than significant, substantial compassion for your circumstances, there is nothing this court can do. My hands are tied. You failed to qualify for the safety valve. I have no choice but to sentence you to a life term."

"No, no, no," Loraine screamed from the first row, "Please, your Honor!"

"I can only add," the judge concluded, while looking sympathetically at Lorraine, "that your son should use his time productively and never give up hope. Things change in life, and the law as well, and he must put himself in a position to take advantage of such a possibility."

Lorraine collapsed. Sylvester bolted out of his chair and launched himself over the railing separating himself from his mom, only to be tackled and thrown to the floor by a court officer. None of it seemed real. Except for the satisfied look on Lessons' face.

Twenty-Three

July 1997
United States Penitentiary Canaan
High Security Institution
Waymart, Pennsylvania

Sylvester's life sentence mandated a designation to a high security prison. It meant guards barking orders every hour of the day, and a population of inmates with little to lose; creating a toxic environment and a constant specter of violence.

Sylvester would go through the motions of any work assignment, complying without a word to every command. He barely slept. Every night, he stared at the walls, trying not to believe that this was his eternal home. He also refused to back down to other inmates, his frequent fights earning him more than his share of time in lockdown. A particularly brutal altercation, five years into his sentence, resulted in Sylvester being sentenced to two weeks in solitary confinement.

Following his stay in a dungeon, Sylvester was summoned to a meeting with his counselor, Frank Donaldson, a middle-aged salt-and-pepper haired white man, who always did his best to come off as a decent guy. His handcuffs removed; Sylvester was directed to sit in a chair opposite Donaldson's veneer desk in his tiny office. He looked sympathetically at Sylvester's diminished condition and spoke:

"Sylvester, I know you think this is bullshit, but not everyone in here is out to get you. What would make things here easier for you?"

Sylvester gave Donaldson a skeptical look.

"Tell you what, you commit to doing the right thing from now on, I'll do everything I can, when you're eligible, to support your transfer to a medium security facility. Deal?"

Sylvester vowed during his endless hours in solitary to strengthen, not lose, his mind. And reminded himself that prison could warehouse his body but not his spirit. And there was no way he was going to be there forever. If he had to be a model prisoner to get it done, then so be it. Sylvester stood erect, shook Donaldson's hand and returned to his cell. Time for self-pity was over.

Twenty-Four

December 2016
Federal Correctional Institution Otisville
Medium Security
Otisville, New York

Professor Conrad Marvel arrived for his weekly visit. He taught political science and was the chairman of African American studies at New York University. A nationally recognized voice on civil rights issues, he had a sardonic wit and made regular appearances on news and talks shows. Such was his profile that the Professor often considered a run for office as a third-party candidate. After hearing of Sylvester's plight from one of his colleagues at the Law School, the Professor not only became one of the major contributors to Sylvester's clemency petition, the two men became close friends.

A steel door was unlocked to allow Sylvester to enter the meeting area reserved for counsel visits and other authorized professionals. He had to be frisked a second time before being allowed into a private room to speak with a visitor. The walls were gray, the doors black, and the four conference rooms transparent. At all times inmates had to be within sight.

"Hi, Syl. How are you holding up?"

Sylvester shrugged, held up his hands and wiggled his fingers, trying to feign optimism. The imminence of Obama leaving office without having addressed Sylvester's petition was taking a heavy toll on Sylvester. If Obama was turning his back, his years of faith felt little more than a cruel hoax.

"Any updates for me?"

Stroking his beard, his signature bushy gray afro adorning his head, the professor, having just turned sixty, wearing a gray suit and vest, which disguised his paunch, sighed. "Sorry man, still no word. You have to somehow remain patient. I know it's easy for me to say, brother. But Obama is in office another month. There are thousands of deserving petitions still being reviewed by the lawyers. Your turn has not come up yet. But it will, Syl, it will. You have to keep believing."

"Let's be real here, any clemency Obama's giving has already been granted. He's not spending his final days worrying about whether one more drug-dealing boy from the hood got too much time. He already did more than expected. It's like that mother fucker cracker Guard Freddie Daniels says, I have as much chance of getting clemency as seeing a monkey jump out his ass."

"Syl, you can't predict these things. Until the day he leaves, there's no telling. Given the Satan who won the election, I think he wants to grant more. He knows what's coming."

Tears welled up in Sylvester's tired bloodshot eyes. His voice cracked, "Professor, I'm closing in on forty-five years old, been locked up over twenty years. I don't want to die in prison."

Marvel struggled for a consoling response, but nothing came. Then:

"Try and stay optimistic, Syl. There's reason to still believe. I'm not just saying that."

"I'll try," Sylvester said, composing himself. "Guess I better get back to my job. Can't keep the Man waiting. My employers like me so much, don't think they'll ever fire me."

After the two men clasped hands, Sylvester rose to get back to his duties in the prison kitchen.

The professor smiled and said, "Queen to H5."

"What?"

"My final move in our chess by correspondence. Checkmate!"

"Fuck you, Professor," Sylvester chuckled, grateful to have his somber mood interrupted.

After returning to the elevator, Sylvester was dropped off at the fourth-floor cafeteria. A moment before entering the kitchen, a correction officer yelled out, "Stanley, the warden wants to see you."

"What now?"

"No idea. He said to bring you right away."

As Sylvester waited outside the warden's office, he wondered if Daniels fabricated a complaint against him for not kissing his ass enough. He sat alongside a guard on a brown bench. Ten minutes passed before the warden came out. The guard stood.

"Should I come in too, Warden?" he asked.

"That won't be necessary," the warden replied.

Warden Arthur Stone, with silver hair and blue eyes, was in his late forties. The stresses of getting to the top of his profession wore on his face in the form of crows' feet around his eyes and a furrowed brow. The two men stood only a few inches apart when the Warden surprisingly extended his hand. Sylvester shook it tentatively, a quizzical look on his face.

"I'll not keep you in suspense," Stone said. "It's my pleasure to tell you, you're going home. Clemency was granted an hour ago. I got a call from D.C., the Department of Justice. The assistant Attorney General Mark Jacobs called. The President has granted you clemency. He didn't just reduce your sentence, he granted you time served. Of course, you'll be on supervised release but you're going home. Just waiting for the paperwork. Tomorrow evening you'll be sleeping in your own bed."

Sylvester dropped to his knees, brought his hands to his face, and wept.

As he lay on his cot, looking up at the ceiling, smiling almost in disbelief, trying to collect his thoughts, Sylvester could hear the tap tap tap of Officer Freddie Daniel's baton against the concrete floor and steel bars as he made his nightly rounds. Placing his face between the bars of Sylvester's cell, he called out, "What's up homeboy, for once, you seem like you're in a decent mood. Not moping as usual about your stupid petition."

"Oh, the hell with that," Sylvester replied. "But, Officer Daniels, I do have one thing on my mind, that is if you have the time, could you maybe answer one question for me."

"Sure Syl, why not, What's up?"

"Where's the monkey? Wait there it is! Coming right out your ass! As we speak!"

Victor Hushemi

Twenty-Five

June 1987
New Jersey

Arriving two and a half hours early, while there was still sunlight, Victor Hushemi lay perched on a heavily wooded hill behind the last row of the diner's parking spots. The restaurant was located ten miles off the Vince Lombardi exit of the New Jersey Turnpike. Customers were impatient commuters who couldn't wait another fifteen or twenty minutes to eat before arriving home.

From age ten, in the mountain forests of Albania, with one shot, Victor could take out a rabbit darting between trees five hundred yards away. Fatal blood feuds between families were a fact of life in Northern Albania and Victor's father made sure his son was well prepared.

Bosi I mafias Elseid Selimi had arranged a sit down with Anthony Martini, a captain of the Lucchese crime family. The meeting was supposed to be an attempt to resolve a dispute over whether Albanians or Italians were going to control gambling and narcotics operations on Arthur Avenue in the Bronx. In the days leading up to the meeting, Selimi decided to deliver a different message.

Holding his Austrian Steyr SSG 69 sniper rifle in a crossed-arm position, Victor rested the barrel on a pack. During the long wait for the two mob leaders to arrive, Victor's impatience gave way to anger. Taking Martini's life would unquestionably strengthen Victor's position in the organization. Everyone already referred to him as

Pjesa e madhe [the big Margin] but he was no mindless executioner grateful to earn his livelihood by carrying out his master's death sentences. And hits, unless they were a last resort, were the hallmark of morons. Back home the life he had taken was more than justified, it had been required to preserve the family honor. But here in New Jersey, with the passing of each minute, Victor became increasingly agitated by the looming prospect and stupidity of killing a man he had never met. His only comfort was his certainty that it was just a matter of time before he, not Selimi, would be giving the orders.

Surrounded by heavily leafed trees that blocked out the sky and trapped the ventilation, the late-night summer New Jersey heat was suffocating. Crickets' shrill chirping pinged in his ears while mosquitoes munched on every inch of exposed skin. By the time Selimi and Martini arrived, Victor was drenched in five times more perspiration than was normal even for an evening in late June. The two mob bosses were each accompanied by five associates. As planned, Selimi made sure to place everyone at a long four-foot rectangular table situated between two picture windows on the east side of the restaurant.

Selimi and Martini sat at opposite ends of the table. The two men were shorter than everyone else. Selimi with his small eyes and long thick nose could not have been more than five-and-a half feet, and Martini with his greased black hair, distinctive curly eyelashes, and pockmarked face was even shorter. Selimi wore a black shirt and matching trousers while Martini had on a tan, waist-length summer jacket which was zipped tight up to the middle of his basketball-shaped belly. A gold chain hung from his neck in front of his unbuttoned shirt.

Despite the hour, ten additional tables in the dining room were occupied but none of them interfered with Victor's view of his target. Peering through his scope, Victor waited for the group of men to order their food and drinks to avoid an unanticipated waiter being the recipient of his bullet. Blinking his eyes to keep the sweat away, Victor's arms ached from holding the rifle dead set on Martini's every move. Finally, Selimi stood and raised his glass, the moment for execution.

Shaking away all the tension in his trigger finger, ready to fire, Victor froze at the sound of screeching tires. He turned his head and saw a black SUV racing through the parking lot, hurtling the curb, and slamming the brakes inches from the front steps of the diner. Two men jumped out, Victor redirected his rifle thinking it must be Martini's men seeking to beat Selimi to the punch. The man closest to the entrance door reached into his front breast pocket, and Victor fired a fatal bullet into his back.

The object he was reaching for fell to the ground. He wasn't reaching for his gun. He was reaching for his badge.

Twenty-Six

July 1987
Brooklyn

After the shooting, federal agents took Selimi and his men into custody under a racketeering indictment that had been years in the making. The crimes and killings of the Selimi organization crossed several state lines making the defendants subject to an Eastern District of New York federal prosecution in Brooklyn. In the days following the shooting, the feds knocked down the door of a dozen additional members of Selimi's organization. The youthful lead prosecutor, Allen Troutman, had meticulously built his case on wires, videos and witnesses both inside and outside the gang that would leave no doubt of their role in a wide range of violent offenses.

Yet, when it came to Victor, the prosecutor was maddingly frustrated. Only Victor, forever mindful of being recorded, never had loose lips. In meetings witnessed by confidential informants, Victor rarely uttered a word or even made an incriminating gesture. He subjected anyone in the gang who met with him to a search before speaking. Troutman told colleagues he would bet his career on Victor having fired the fatal shot at the diner, and he wouldn't rest until Victor paid the price. Convicting Victor for committing a murder in the course of a racketeering conspiracy meant he would face the possibility of a death sentence.

It was August 1987. After a month in captivity at the Metropolitan Correction Center in lower Manhattan,

Pietro Prifti, a/k/a Brumbullak [Albanian for chubby] let his attorney, Ashton Fried, know that he would sell his soul rather than spend another day in prison. Fried secured a cooperation agreement allowing him to be released on bail in exchange for Prifti's testimony before a Grand Jury. Following trial, he was to be recommended for placement in the witness protection program.

Suspecting that at any moment Brumbullak might turn, Victor kept track of the whereabouts of his family. When Adem Hadjari, an uncharged low-level member of the gang, informed Victor that Prifti's wife and kids had been relocated and were nowhere to be found, Victor presumed Brumbullak had ratted him out and been released on bail. Victor also realized that at any moment he would be arrested and added to the indictment and assumed that at most, he had one last weekend to act before being taken into custody.

Despite figuring the feds had Prifti tucked away in an unknown location, Victor was still certain their star informant would find an opportunity to slip away. Brumbullak may have told the government all his crimes, but there was one piece of information he would keep secret. His eight-year-old son with an Italian woman in Bay Ridge. Instead of being eternally faithful to his loyal Albanian wife, he had cheated. His wife's brothers would kill him for such infidelity. Victor knew that Brumbullak loved the boy. The combination of dark Italian features and Albanian heritage made for one handsome child. Brumbullak saw him for a few hours every weekend.

On Saturday afternoon, Victor parked his car down the block from the apartment of Brumbullak's goomah and waited. By two o'clock Brumbullak emerged walking as fast as his chubby legs could take him, bundled up in a cheap winter ski jacket with the hood hiding his face, continuously glancing behind to make sure nobody tailed him. He entered the outside vestibule, rang the bell, and disappeared into the lobby. Brumbullak's ten-year-old navy blue Camaro was parked halfway down the block. Victor walked over, jimmied the lock, and climbed into the backseat, then laid low and out of sight. Four hours passed, as the temperature dropped in the growing darkness, Victor shivered with the engine off in the unheated vehicle. *Where the fuck was Brumbullak?*

Finally, Brumbullak stuck his key in the door and squeezed into the front seat. As he turned the engine on, Victor raised up and slapped the back of his head.

"Fuck, Victor," Brumbullak gasped, "Oh my God, how did you know where to find me?"

"Mr. Brumbullak, my dear comrade, your whereabouts may be unknown to the feds but not to me. How is that pretty young bastard of yours?"

Brumbullak couldn't stop shaking. "Victor, kill me if you must, but please not the boy. I had no fucking choice. You have no idea the pressure I was under. I am not like you and the others. I can't survive prison."

"Let's go for a drive and talk."

"Where are we going?"

"Drive to the Belt Parkway. Go past the exit under the bridge. Don't stop there, it's not secluded enough. Go one more exit, then get off and make a right and park on one of the streets by the woods."

"I'm a dead man!" Brumbullak started crying. He couldn't even drive properly, the car kept making fitful starts and stops. His leg was trembling so much he could not keep his foot on the accelerator.

"My God, man. Pull over. I'll drive. And fucking compose yourself. I'm not going to kill you. Not that I don't want to."

Brumbullack pulled over, gave Victor the keys and exchanged places. Victor drove in silence while Brumbullak wept like a baby. Pulling over and turning the car off, in an area with no streetlights and only an occasional passing car, the two men sat in complete darkness. "Brumbullack, get a hold of yourself," Victor commanded. "I told you I'm not going to kill you."

Brumbullack replied in a voice so shaky it was almost a stutter, "Victor, I'm not stupid. Somehow you figured out that I've agreed to cooperate and you know what I'm going to say. Just get it over with. But please don't torture me. Just shoot me. I'm begging you."

Victor looked at him and thought, there is nothing more pitiful than watching a fat man's body jiggle with fear. "Listen and stop crying for God's sake. You know what is going to happen if I take you out. You know what those fed motherfuckers will do? I saw it happen to one of Martini's captains when one of his men turned on him, signed on with the feds and they made sure he disappeared from the face of the earth before trial. Your ratting me out in the grand jury will be read to the jury at my trial and I'm fucked. My lawyer won't be able to do shit about it. No cross-examination. No nothing. Just your words in the Grand Jury saying I shot the fucking agent. So, you see, my chubby friend, I cannot kill you. No matter how much you deserve it and no matter how much I want to."

Brumbullack finally regained some composure and managed to speak in a normal voice. "Then why are you here? What's the plan? You always have a plan."

"That you are right about. Yes, I do. This is what you're going to do. You'll continue to be the government's ass-kisser. Do everything they say and act like you can't wait to testify and get things over with. When the time finally comes, you'll take the stand and tell the jury about Selimi and how you've been working for him all these years and about everyone else. Except me. You will testify about all the drug dealing and the gambling and the killings and you'll send everyone away forever. Except me."

"Victor, I can't do that. They'll send me to prison. And I'll be with the others. And they'll kill me. What you're saying, I can't do. I'm sorry."

"Ha. You can and you will. This is not a negotiable offer, my friend. And just to show my appreciation, I have twenty grand in my pocket for you and your illegitimate family. After you do this there'll be fifty more."

"I don't know, Victor."

"Listen to me, fat man. You will be responsible for putting Selimi and the others away. That won't be forgotten. Yeah, you'll get a few years for changing your testimony. But not too many. Not more than you can deal with. And you do it right. Be fucking sincere. They'll have no reason to think anything other than that you are telling the truth and lied before to make them happy." Victor knew his words were bullshit, that Troutman would never forgive Brumbullak for exculpating Victor. What wasn't bullshit was that Selimi's conviction would fast track Victor's rise to the throne.

"I don't know, Victor. I have to think about it."

Victor took the money out of his right back pocket and with his left hand squeezed Brumbullack's Adam's apple so tight he couldn't breathe.

"This is not a debate, Brumbullak! This is what you will do! You love that little half-breed of yours? You want to be here to see him grow up? Do you? You think after I'm busted you got nothing to worry about?"

Gasping for air, Brumbullak succumbed. I know what you're capable of Victor and being in prison won't stop you. I'll do everything you say. Just promise you won't hurt my boy."

"Do you think I'm a monster? I should slit your fucking throat for even suggesting that I would harm a hair on your little half-breed's head. Take the fucking wheel and the twenty. You've said enough for one night. Keep your stupid mouth shut and drive me back to my car."

Three months later, Brumbullak took the witness stand with Troutman directing his testimony. Cool as a cucumber, Brumbullak testified about Selimi and his co-defendants, even Victor. Seven defense attorneys, one for each defendant took turns trying to rip him apart and he never budged. Until it was Sherman's turn.

Rising from the large, long desk provided to counsel and their clients, Sherman stood at the lectern and in a voice not a decibel too loud or too low, and in an even tone, asked a few preliminary questions and then inquired,"Mr. Prifti you want this jury to believe you are a truthful witness when you cannot even be truthful to your wife?"

Slowly but surely Brumbullak unraveled. "Mr. Prifti," Sherman finally asked. "Look around this courtroom and tell me if it is still your testimony that Victor Hushemi is the man who fired the shot that struck the man with the badge, FBI Agent Steve Schwartz?"

Brumbullak remained silent for a minute.

"Do you need me to repeat the question, Mr. Prifti?"

Shifting uncomfortably in the witness chair, directing his gaze at the prosecutor, with tears in his eyes, the large man responded, "I'm sorry, Mr. Troutman," Brumbullak began. "I have cooperated with you all the way. But I cannot continue when it comes to Mr. Hushemi. He wasn't even there. I know you wanted me to identify him as the one who killed Agent Schwartz. But, the truth is, he wasn't the one. It was Azem Gashi. He was a member of the Selimi organization for only a short time. As far as I know, he's no longer in the country. He returned to Albania a week after the shooting at the diner. Victor wasn't even there that day. I'm sorry, I can't live with this lie any longer. May God forgive me."

Sherman looked compassionately first at Brumbullak and then at the jury. "Thank you, I know this has been difficult. I have no further questions."

Troutman tried everything. He reminded Brumbullak that he signed a cooperation agreement where he swore to tell the truth and was aware that if he lied he could be prosecuted for perjury and that the government would withdraw any possible support for a reduction of his sentence.

"And knowing all this," Troutman asked, "do you, Mr. Prifti, stand by your testimony that Victor Hushemi was not even present at the diner?"

"Mr. Troutman, I am well aware that it would be much better for me to continue my lies about Mr. Hushemi. But I could not live with myself if I did that. What I said about everyone else is the truth. It was the truth when I signed the cooperation agreement, and it was the truth when I said it again at this trial. But as for Victor, it was a lie when I said it to you and what I have said now at this trial is the truth. Victor Hushemi is innocent!"

Fried stood up a half dozen times and attempted to stop the proceedings to speak with his client. Each time, Brumbullak waved him away and told the judge he didn't need to speak with his lawyer. The judge even halted the proceedings and excused the jury while Fried spoke to him privately for a half hour, but it made no difference. The trial resumed and Brumbullak never budged.

Troutman, the other defense counsel, and even the Judge could barely disguise their disbelief. Victor, arrested and detained two days after his car ride with Brumbullak, wearing the three-piece gray pin striped suit he was permitted to exchange for his prison garb during the trial, maintained an intentionally subdued demeanor. Agent Dan Ford, lean, around five foot ten inches, with eyes almost as distinctive as Victor's, stood with his back against the side wall nearest to the defense table, a slight smile on his face. A smile like he knew something that nobody else did.

"Who is that?" Victor whispered to Sherman.

"Ford," he replied. "That's Dan Ford. We've known and respected each other for a long time. He's one of the bureau's top men. I used to have some cases he was involved in, but not recently. I've no idea what he's up to but he still hangs around and can be seen observing a few high-profile trials like yours."

It took less than an hour for the jury to acquit Victor and convict Selimi and six additional co-defendants. Selimi was sentenced to life, the rest of the crew received thirty-year sentences, except for Brumbullak who was sent away for twenty.

As Selimi and his crew were handcuffed and taken out of the courtroom, and Victor was congratulating Sherman,

Dan Ford made his way through the chaotic conclusion of the trial and also offered his hand.

"Great job, David, very impressive." He locked eyes with Victor. "Hope you know how fortunate you are to have Mr. Sherman as counsel, but even with the best, next time you might not be so lucky."

"There will never be a next time, Agent Ford, take that to the bank."

The Crime

Twenty-Seven

April 7, 2018
Brooklyn

For a convicted con, even if the bars come down, confinement remains. Add two decades in prison and being black to the mix, playing the lottery was a better bet than finding a decent job. But for Sylvester defying odds was old hat. Finally free, nothing was going to stop him. With the help of the Professor, he made some connections at art museums and galleries and was even getting some nibbles regarding several sketches and paintings he produced with overused brushes during his incarceration. Although the minimum wage he received as a part-time tour guide at the Brooklyn Museum during the day was laughable, he supplemented that income by staying up all night delivering for Uber Eats. Despite the increasing value of their home justifying significant rents for lodgers, with Lorraine having recently retired, Sylvester's contribution was vital.

After a hard day's night delivering packages, it was almost noon when Sylvester dragged himself out of bed. While Lorraine was beating a bowl of pancake mix for her long-lost son, Sylvester showered, threw on some clothes, and sat down at the kitchen table. With Marco having moved to the West Coast ten years earlier, Lorraine felt reborn having her older son home.

"You gotta stop working these overnights, you're no teenager."

"Prison's a preservative, ma didn't you know?"

"Not amused, I've waited too long for you to come home to watch you kill yourself working like this."

Sylvester walked over and squeezed his mom tightly around her waist. "I'm not going anywhere, you're stuck with me."

Sylvester opened his laptop and started listening to the news. He heard a politician condemning mass incarceration. "Liberal white people," Sylvester mumbled. "You gotta love 'em. Always thinking of us collectively never individually. Same as the racist right."

Lorraine just shook her head.

Sylvester devoured his pancakes in record time, gulped two cups of coffee, gave Lorraine a smooch and hurried off to throw on his running clothes. During his incarceration Sylvester had discovered running as a panacea. Compared to endless laps around the prison yard, Prospect Park was paradise. Every Saturday, he ran three laps around the three-mile perimeter, sometimes even four.

He slipped on his favorite dark blue hoodie and headed to the train for the subway ride from Bushwick to the park. Finding a seat for a change on a Saturday train, Sylvester leaned back, his mind drifting to Jennifer. The first year after his sentence she visited religiously, vowing to stand by him. Then slowly but surely, reality set in. Her visits dwindled until she broke the news that her family was moving south. Sylvester doubted that was the reason. He felt angry but resigned to the idea she had more than likely found someone new.

Sylvester snapped out of his trance a second before the doors closed on him at the 15th Street station to the park. Bounding up the stairs to the street, he glanced at his cell phone and could not believe it was already a little past three. He would have to keep a good pace to finish his run and still have time for dinner with the Professor.

Sylvester hurried across the outer grass and trees to the road which encircled the entire perimeter of the park. The humidity was a bit uncomfortable, but Syl always liked to start jogging with his hoodie draped over his head until he was fully loose and had worked up a sweat. With smooth steady strides, Sylvester jogged down the west side of the park, around Prospect Park lake, circling past Coney Island Avenue. He then made his way up a slight incline and descended to the bottom of a steep hill which led up to Grand Army Plaza.

A throng of pedestrians were walking down the hill towards him wearing what looked like costumes from a cultural event. His adrenaline pumping and endorphins starting to soar, in gleeful anticipation of his workout, Sylvester smiled.

Twenty-Eight

April 7, 2018
Brooklyn

The first Albanian celebration of its kind ever held in Prospect Park was scheduled to start at ten and it was already half past noon. Sofia was dressed in a traditional Albanian outfit: a long white dress with gold stitching and a beautifully embroidered, sleeveless, red outer jacket. She looked stunning. The jacket stopped at her slim waist while the dress ran down to her ankles. She wore red stockings, gold and red-bordered shoes with red tassels at the end, all topped off with a hanging red headdress. The dress was made of fine wool and velvet. The downside of the outfit was that it was sure to be uncomfortable on this unusually warm spring day. Ilka, always the contrarian, was only willing to wear the headdress which she wrapped around her curly hair.

Ilka scoffed at the matching outfit Sofia placed on her bed for the event.

"No way! I'll go, but I'm not wearing that stupid costume."

"Ilka, don't s start with me. Uncle Victor got these specially made for us to wear to the festival and you said you'd wear it."

"Uncle Victor will let me have my way. He always does."

Sofia didn't know what worried her more; Ilka's beauty or her obstinance. Her father's looks softened Sofia's sharp features to produce a young athletic face and figure that was captivating in an All-American girl kind of way. Sofia's looks drew discriminating eyes, Ilka's attracted everyone's.

Ilka prided herself on being unconcerned with what she called "superficial fashion and grooming," flaunting, unless Victor was present, her wild, frazzled hair and ripped clothing. Whenever Sofia expressed concern about Ilka becoming involved with a boy, she would laugh at her mother.

"You think I'm you? No boy is going to get in my way." Sofia prayed her strong-willed daughter was right. But she knew the girl was naïve, especially when it came to her uncle.

As disappointed as Sofia was that Ilka refused to wear their mother/daughter dresses, she wearily relented when Ilka agreed to fold hers in her backpack saying that if Victor insisted, she would immediately change. Ilka and her Uncle were deeply bonded, but any thoughts Ilka had of Victor "letting her have her way," were a teenage fantasy. God only knew how Victor would erupt when he saw his niece with her hair flying in all directions, squeezed into her tight jeans and lowcut top that showed off her belly button. Of course, Sofia knew she, rather than Ilka, would be held to blame.

The only way Sofia could convince Edward to attend was in his wheelchair. It was impossible to know whether it was pain or depression behind his regression and all-too-frequent refusals to walk. Whenever Sofia pushed Edward to exercise his legs, his mood ultimately lightened, but time was way too tight to undertake the half-hour pep talk it would take to motivate him to make the effort.

Realizing she was about to walk out the apartment without putting on her wedding ring, Sofia let out a sigh of relief. The ring fit so loosely that she only wore it on special occasions and of course whenever Victor was around. Today was both. She also feared Victor's reaction if she adjusted the band. The look on Victor's face the day he placed it on her finger so terrified Sofia that she wouldn't dare do anything to alter it. Yet whenever she wore it, she was obsessed with securing it. Ilka would even make fun of how often Sofia would check her finger whenever she had it on.

"Yeah, ma you're still married," she would mock her mother. Sofia retrieved the ring from her jewelry box in the bedroom dresser, placed it on her finger and did her ritual turning of the heirloom in the futile hope of making it fit tighter.

"All right let's go everyone," Sofia ushered Ilka out the door, pushing Edward behind her. "Victor is probably wondering where we are. As the family made the twenty-minute walk to the park, Sofia quickly became damp with perspiration. Ilka did not make matters any better by galloping in front of her parents. After acting completely indifferent about the festival, she was suddenly in a big rush to get there. Edward had dozed off and was slouched over in his seat, making it even more of a struggle for Sofia to push him.

Entering the park, before she could think twice, the name, never far from her thoughts, even after all these years, escaped, in a shout, "Angela!"

Angela was older and heavier, but her bright irresistible face, even from more than one hundred feet away, was unmistakable. Angela stiffened when she heard Sofia, looked up and their eyes met. She flashed her uniquely dimpled smile.

Sofia waved and approached with caution; afraid she might scare Angela off if she ran towards her with too much enthusiasm. The closer they got, the less tentative

Sofia became, and once within arm's reach, Sofia didn't hold back. Neither did Angela, who came to the Park, after hearing about the Festival, harboring a hope that Sofia would be there even if she had no clue how they would meet. They grabbed and tightly hugged, gleefully taking each other into their arms. Letting go, they stood inches apart, silently gazing at each other, smiling, both with tear filled eyes.

"It's been a while," Angela said softly.

Sofia shook her head, as if to negate the reality of her reply,

"Coming up on two decades."

Angela's presence surprisingly stirred Edward, he started to rise from his wheelchair,

"This is Edward," Sofia gestured. "I've always hoped for you to meet him."

Angela reached her hand down. "Please, no need to stand, you mustn't hurt yourself. It's wonderful to meet you. Your wife was a special and dear friend."

"Special, that's putting it mildly," Edward's response surprised Sofia.

Angela couldn't hold back a giggle, long lost music to Sofia's ears.

"You'll get no argument from me there, sir," she said, smiling warmly. "None whatsoever. She's quite a girl."

Ilka suddenly appeared next to Sofia.

"You coming or what?"

Angela gasped, "Oh my lord, your daughter?"

Angela quickly gathered herself and inquired, "Are there any other family members on their way?"

"No," Sofia anxiously responded , hoping Victor was already at the festival.

Angela kept glancing around awkwardly, worried Sofia's reply was merely wishful thinking.

"We're going to the Albanian festival. You should come with us!" Ilka offered, trying to move things along.

"Oh sweetie, I would love to, but I have to meet my daughter in Manhattan. Another time."

"Do you live nearby? You two should hang out. Mom needs more friends," Ilka said, sarcastically.

"Coffee sounds nice," Angela said.

Sofia and Angela's eyes locked again. Sofia felt a lump in her throat.

"Yes! I'll call you," Sofia said, thinking of the countless times she had pondered doing so over the years.

"Sounds like a plan, hard as it is to believe, my number's the same," Angela said as she started to walk away. "Nice meeting you, Edward."

"Okay, everyone. Let's go!" Ilka urged, walking ahead again.

For the ten additional minutes or so it took to get to the festival, Sofia found herself lost in thought. Seeing Angela felt like fate. Not her passionate moment of youthful indiscretion, a rabbit hole she would die before permitting herself to ever go down again, but the sisterly love. There was a glimmer of hope for its resurrection.

Twenty-Nine

Prospect Park

Entering the park at the south end by Coney Island and Parkside Avenue, Sofia found herself surrounded by cyclists and joggers heading in the same direction while she struggled with Edward's chair. When she got to the bottom of a steep hill, Sofia pleaded with Ilka to help. Reluctantly Ilka turned back to take turns pushing her father's chair. After struggling three quarters of the way up the difficult incline, cursing under her breath a few times as to why she had even bothered to bring Edward, Sofia breathed a huge sigh of relief at the site of the flat grassy field reserved for the festival.

Dozens of picnic tables occupied the grounds. Beautiful women in distinctive Albanian costumes and men dressed in traditional white kilts, red vests, and colorful hats in all sorts of shapes and designs happily mingled. A wide grin replaced Sofa's distress as Ilka raced off with some friends. Sofia couldn't wait to see what Victor was wearing. She pushed Edward over to a picnic table, and surveyed the grills, steaming pots and tables of ethnic food, all products of months of planning. Sofia turned to Edward before going to fill their plates.

"Do you see your brother?"

Tomas and Karina were upstate with their family for the week. Victor, who was responsible for the entire event, was nowhere in sight. Searching the grounds, two heavily muscled young men approached. They were in their early twenties, one barely taller than Sofia, the other overas tall as a basketball player, both with shaved heads, sleeveless black t-shirts, and multicolored tattoos covering their arms and backs.

They lived in the Bronx but were at Victor's beck and call. One time when Sofia was in Tomas' apartment, she overheard Victor talking to Tomas about them.

"If I told Novack and Mikhail to walk down Fifth Avenue and shoot a man in the head in front of a thousand people, they wouldn't hesitate. They're ambitious. Not too bright but, damn, they're so hungry to impress. Which is exactly what I need; soldiers, far more than generals."

"Good afternoon, Mrs. Hushemi, Victor has been unexpectedly delayed," Novack said reading Sofia's mind.

Sofia frowned, making little attempt to disguise her displeasure.

"He sent the two of you instead? Seriously when will he be here?"

"Victor asked for us to keep an eye on things," Mikhail chimed in.

Sofia knew better than to ask any more questions. "Enjoy the festival, gentlemen."

Edward sat waiting for Sofia at one of the picnic tables with several neighbors engaged in a rare conversation. Edward for once seemed to be enjoying himself, eating the entire plate of food Sofia prepared for him. He was offered some wine but refused, knowing all too well not to mix booze with his current regimen of pain pills.

Sofia was euphoric at seeing her husband so alert. Enjoying her plate of Fergus, a cold summer stew of tomato sauce, green peppers and garlic, as well as a small piece of watermelon and souvlaki, Sofia was taking a sip of red wine, when her neighbor Arlinda called her onto the elevated temporary outdoor stage for a traditional dance. Sofia tried waving her away, but she was not to be deterred. Arlinda came over to Sofia and gently pulled her arm until she relented and joined a dozen of her neighbors.

Sofia started timidly at first, melting to the back row of dancers, spinning, and skipping around to the music. As the pulsing drumbeat and traditional rhythms rang out from the sound system, childhood memories took hold. For the first time in America, Sofia felt the happy and carefree emotions just as she had as a child dancing with Ajola and her father at family get togethers.

From out of nowhere, shocking her mother, Ilka joined Sofia on stage. Victor had made sure Ilka was taught all the traditional dances growing up, but Sophia couldn't remember the last time Ilka had danced a single step. Grabbing Sofia's hand, she pulled her mom from the pack of female dancers and moved to center stage. Prancing around together, mother and daughter had the crowd riveted. Everyone pulled out their phones to take videos.

Suddenly, Ilka pushed Sofia away, left all the traditional steps behind, and twisted her body in perfect rhythm to the music in the seductive manner of hip-hop. Sofia wanted to run off the stage in embarrassment, but, to her astonishment, everyone roared in approval. Even Edward had the biggest grin painted on his face and clapped his hands above his head in approval. Sofia feigned a smile at her daughter's far too provocative gyrations.

Despite loud collective shouts of disapproval, Park officials intruded on the festivities, insisting it was time to start cleaning up because the permit expired at four. Ilka was about to disappear back into the woods with her friends when Sofia called out for her to come over and help.

Throwing the headdress in the back of Edward's wheelchair, Ilka remarked, "I guess I didn't need to wear this after all. Uncle Victor didn't even show!" She stuck her lip out for added effect.

"Well, thanks for wearing it," Sofia responded, resisting her desire to comment on her daughter's unseemly dance moves. "And thanks for dancing with me. I'm so proud of you." Sofia pulled Ilka into a hug. "I love you so much."

"I love you too, Mom."

Sofia froze at the unmistakable smell on her daughter's breath. "Have you been drinking?"

"Oh my God! You're so ridiculous. Why would you say that?"

"Why? Because your breath reeks of alcohol young lady."

"Oh my God!" Ilka shouted. "I had a sip of wine, that's all!"

"Come to think of it, what were you and your friends up to sneaking off into the woods? Did you smoke drugs too? No wonder why you danced like a gypsy slut on that stage."

With tears in her eyes, Ilka angrily shouted, "Next, you'll be accusing me of being a junkie."

"Please, girls," Edward pleaded.

Suddenly, Ilka grabbed Edward's wheelchair. "Come on, Dad, I'll take you home."

Ilka tightly gripped the back of the chair and started sprinting down the hill towards Coney Island Avenue, ignoring the packed crowd of pedestrians, joggers, and cyclists.

"Ilka, stop! Ilka!"

With Sofia shouting at the top of her lungs, Ilka ran even faster. Petrified, Sofia raced after them with the bottom of both her dress and jacket trailing behind her, getting tangled between her feet. Already struggling not to stumble, the tassels of Sofia's shoes started tripping her. As she rounded a curve just past the exit to Empire Boulevard, she lost her footing. A moment before crashing to the pavement, she collided headfirst into the chest of a jogger.

Sofia tumbled sideways while the runner was thrown backwards, knocked completely off the road, landing headfirst on the grass, only the softer turf saving him from a serious concussion. "What the fuck! Watch where you're going woman!" the man yelled as he lay on the grass. His face was wrapped inside a blue hoodie, hiding all but his chin and mouth covered by a light goatee.

"Oh my God. I'm so sorry. I was running after my daughter and my husband, and I tripped. I'm so sorry. Are you alright?"

"I'm good," he answered, as he raised himself from the ground. He pushed his hood back revealing the rest of his handsome face and his dark, bald brown scalp glistening with sweat. He grabbed his knees and sprang to his feet. His lanky figure towered over Sofia as he held his hand out to help her.

"I've survived worse. How you doing?"

Sofia looked down and saw her dress was ripped and her knee was scratched, but otherwise, she was unscathed. "Other than embarrassed, I'm ok. Thank you,"

The stranger looked down at Sofia's dress. "Better to damage your clothes than your body. At least that's my take on it." He laughed, with an innocent shrug. Sofia blushed slightly when he slowly walked completely around her.

"I just want to make sure there were no injuries we overlooked. Yes, you look fine. More than fine," he chuckled. "And all dressed up as well. It's a sin to have ripped such a nice-looking outfit."

Ilka rushed up with Edward. "What happened?" she said. Edward looked dumbfounded. "I'm all right. I just had a slight collision. Nobody was hurt."

Sofia turned back to the jogger. "My family and I were at the Albanian Festival in the park. I never should have tried to run in such an outfit. It's all my fault. So stupid of me. I'm so, so sorry."

"No worries at all, Miss Albania. Let me get back to my run, you guys should try walking the rest of the way."

The man reached out his left hand and shook Sofia's hand, sandwiching it gently with his right hand momentarily resting on top indicating there were no hard feelings. "Try and be a bit more careful and you all get home safe. Maybe we'll bump into each other in the park again sometime without crashing," he said smiling, as he turned away and resumed jogging.

Sofia turned on Ilka, "I hope you're happy. What gets into you, I have no idea. Now give me this." Sofia grabbed the wheelchair, "let's get home without any more fuss."

"I'll take him. You're the one who fell, not me. I'm not the klutz."

"Give your father to me!" Sofia shouted as she tussled the chair back and forth with her daughter.

Edward called out, his voice trembling, "Girls! I'm tired. I need to get home."

Storming away, screaming "I hate you," Ilka relinquished the wheelchair.

Thirty

Prospect Park

Getting back into stride, Sylvester shook his head. *Albania?* During his decades of incarceration, he encountered every ethnicity. Serb, Croatian, Bosnian, Ukrainian. He watched his back around them. Clearly no friends to his kind. He knew Albanians had a fierce rep, they were not to be messed with, but he had never run into any. Bet anyone who looked twice at her hot ass wouldn't live to talk about it, he snickered to himself.

After making his way up the hill and circling past Grand Army Plaza for the second time, he was drenched in sweat and needed to get rid of his hoodie. Fortunately, Professor Marvel was nearby, immersed in one of his chess games at a table below the bandstand. Veering off the road, Sylvester called out while pulling his Nike sweatshirt over his head without coming to a complete halt, "Professor, grab this before I pass out."

The professor looked up just in time to catch the hoodie. "Don't kill yourself, too hot to run your usual three and I'll be done real soon."Sylvester raised his right arm, waving back. Despite the heat, Sylvester had no intention of curtailing his run. His workouts were an obsession.

"Hey, Syl, what's up?" a chubby middle-aged man with a bald head, shouted.

"How you doin' Chuck?" Sylvester momentarily paused. Chuck Barksdale, one of the professor's regular chess competitors, was standing under the shade of a tree in the fading sunlight, in a baggy Knicks basketball t-shirt with a blunt in his hand. "I don't know how you do those runs of yours, man. At least take a hit and make it easier on yourself."

Sylvester hesitated, then took the blunt thinking it couldn't hurt after his collision. After one deep inhale, he tossed it back and coughed.

"Young lungs," Chuck responded, amused.

"That's my limit," Sylvester laughed. "Now back to my real turn on. Catch you later, Chuck!"

Sylvester waved, returned to the roadway and, sticking to his routine, reversed directions for his final lap.

Thirty-One

Prospect Park

Exiting the park with Edward, Sofia couldn't stop thinking and smiling at how nice the jogger was and so cute!

Suddenly looking down, *My ring! Gone!* Anxiety blanketed Sofia's body. Again and again, Sofia ran her hands over every stitch of her clothing searching for the ring: pockets, creases, even inside her stockings and shoes.

"Sofia, I have to get home and lie down," Edward groaned.

For once, Sofia paid no attention. "Ilka, stop," Sofia screamed. "Did you see my wedding ring?" Ilka was two blocks away, if she heard she ignored Sofia.

"You'll find it," Edward said. "Please just get me home."

Sofia bit her tongue a second before telling Edward to shut up.

"Ilka! Get back here, NOW!"

Ilka finally stopped, stamped her feet and still red-faced and tearful from her mother's accusations, walked back.

"Take your father home," Sofia commanded, before turning around oblivious to both husband and daughter.

Sofia's desperation grew by the second. Her heart racing, her body shaking, staggering back and forth, she could barely remain upright, fearing her chances of survival were better running into onrushing traffic than losing Victor's ring. With onlookers staring, wondering if Sofia was in her right mind, she abruptly stopped in the middle of the sidewalk, took a deep breath and tried to compose herself.

"I can find it. Doesn't help to get hysterical, Sofia," she whispered. After the pep talk, Sofia sprinted back to the park, and retraced her steps, constantly looking at the ground to see if the ring was anywhere to be found. She prayed nobody had picked it up.

"I'll find it, I'll find it, I'll find it," she chanted, with every step. She went over to the trees and lawn on both sides, even separating each blade of grass, then returned to the road. Walkers and joggers were yelling at Sofia to get out of the way as she blocked the track, trying to recall exactly where she had collided with the jogger.

The jogger!

The jogger of course, it dawned on her. How could she have been so naïve? He purposely collided with me! No wonder he was so nice, sizing her up for the theft, the second he got up from the ground and saw the ring. The way he twirled her around and shook hands at the end. And he reached out his left hand to shake her left hand. Why do that? Everyone reaches out their right hand. And the way he put his hand on top of her hand. The bastard must have been an expert at it. He even dresses up to look like a jogger. How could she have been so stupid?

How many times had Victor warned her to be careful around Zezak men. After meeting Angela, Sofia questioned the things he and Tomas would say about them, things Edward would never say. But what else could have happened to the ring? Sofia's mind raced as she recalled the man had a pocket on his jogging shorts, thinking she actually did notice there was something stuffed inside when she watched him depart.

After frantically looking in the vicinity where they had collided, she returned to the festival grounds. Reluctantly she realized it was futile. How could the ring be found when it was stolen? By the Black man!

The blood chilling look of rage and contempt on Victor's face from her first morning as Edward's wife flashed before Sofia's eyes leaving her sick to her stomach. She staggered to a sidewalk trash can and threw up.

Arriving home, overwhelmed with despair, Sofia met Novack and Mikhail coming down the steps of her building.

"Hello, Mrs. Hushemi," Novack said. "We were hoping Victor might have made it back by now. Have you heard from him?"

After waiting for a response and receiving none, he shrugged.

"I guess we'll try again next week."

Mikhail asked, "Are you all right? Look at you, your clothes are ripped."

Utterly desperate, Sofia blurted out, "I need your help. Can you help me?"

"What's the problem?"

Explaining her collision in the park and the theft of the priceless heirloom by the Zezak runner, Sofia enlisted Privates Novack and Mikhail. They knowingly nodded at each other.

"Don't worry, we'll get it back."

"We'll take care of it. And him," Mikhail chimed in.

Sofia's heart skipped a beat, but it was too late to reconsider.

Novack tossed his keys to Mikhail and told Sofia to hop into his green second-hand Mustang. The car had tinted windows and a large picture of an Albanian flag displayed on the back window.

"You drive," he told Mikhail.

Sitting in the back seat, Sofia realized recruiting these boys was a prescription for disaster. Vainly attempting to justify her reckless plea, Sofia reminded herself of one of the sayings in her night table book, *desperate times call for desperate measures.*

"Fucking *zezak*," Novack said. "First, he knocks you to the ground without giving a shit and then he steals your wedding ring. Animals, fucking *gabel* animals."

"Every fucking one of them," Mikhail chimed in.

"Please, boys," Sofia pleaded, "let's just try and recover my ring."

"Don't worry, Mrs. Hushemi. We know what we're doing."

As they neared the park, Sofia knew nothing was farther from the truth.

"I think maybe we should forget this," she said. "No way he'll still be in the park. We should just go home."

"Nah, we'll find that dirty low life gabel. Don't worry."

When they arrived at the southern entrance of the park, Mikhail drove right onto the perimeter road and darted north up the east side of the park in blatant disregard of the park's restriction to vehicles with proper authorization for the delivery of food and supplies to the festival. With their Albanian flag emblazoned across the back windshield and no entry sticker on the front, Novak advised Mikhail to drive slowly, believing their car might pass for an official vehicle.

My God. Any second the police will show up and we'll be the ones arrested, Sofia thought.

Mikhail turned the first corner, slowly drove past the zoo on the right, and started to head up the hill leading to Grand Army Plaza. He drove directly behind three Black joggers:

two males and a woman. He drove the car within a foot of them, turned his head, and peered down at Sofia, who was so stressed she crouched in the back seat despite the tinted windows making it impossible for anyone to see her.

"You see him?"

"Get that car off our asses!" one of the male joggers yelled.

Growing more frightened by the second, Sofia replied, "I have no idea. Their backs are to me, and I'm crouched down here."

Mikhail pulled out and veered alongside them.

"Look up," Novack demanded in a low voice. "No way they can see."

All three joggers cursed as Mikhail idled next to them. Neither of the two men had a goatee.

"It's not him. Neither one. Now, please, take me home before the police come."

Mikhail passed the trio. Then, when rounding the corner another man jogged towards them. Sofia thought he looked like the man she had run into, but he was not wearing a sweat jacket and he was running in the opposite direction.

Mikhail pulled the car over.

"Is that him?" Novack asked.

"I'm not sure, please let's just go."

Mikhail turned the car around and trailed behind the jogger.

"Sofia, is that him?" Novack demanded.

"I can't tell from behind."

Mikhail pulled alongside the jogger and, for thirty seconds, the car remained right by his side. The windows remained up.

"Is he the one? Is he the one?" Their words exploded in Sofia's ears. Over and over again.

"I don't know! I want to go home to my daughter!" she screamed.

Mikhail finally pulled ahead while Novack kept insisting that Sofia look out the back window. "Come on, Sofia," he said in a low consoling voice. "Is that the fucker who stole your ring?"

They circled past Coney Island Avenue and stopped. The man spit on the ground, lifted his head, stuck his middle finger up at the car, and smiled.

Once he grinned, Sofia knew.

"For the last time," Novack's tone grew more and more agitated, "is he the one?"

Sofia wanted to say no.

She was also sick of Novak's unrelenting interrogation.

She was also desperate to get her ring back.

"He's the one. He's the one. He's the one. He's the one!"

Thirty-Two

Prospect Park

Assholes, Sylvester spit and gave whoever it was inside the car the finger, thinking it was beneath him to react further. He walked off the road, over to the professor who looked up from his chess game.

"About time, Syl. How many brothers do I have to vanquish before we can get something to eat? How was your run?"

"You have no idea. Wait till I tell you. Let me go stretch and we'll get the fuck out of here."

"Ten minutes if he's lucky," the professor said, referring to his opponent.

Sylvester ambled over to the nearby woods and found one of his go-to trees for post-run stretching. Placing his hands on its thick trunk, he lifted his right and left leg almost as high as his shoulder. Fatigued, yet exhilarated by his run, he was lifting his right leg for a final rep, when Novak and Mikhail approached.

"Aren't you one nimble motherfucker," Novack said.

Sylvester tensed, in anticipation of having to defend myself. "I thought you clowns were finished having your fun."

Mikhail let out a condescending laugh. "Clowns! This ain't no fucking circus, boy. A zoo maybe, you monkey. You have no idea who you're dealing with. Give back the ring and maybe we'll let you keep a few fingers to put the next one you steal on."

Sylvester already knew this wasn't going to end well but still held back from unduly escalating things.

"What the fuck are you assholes talking about?"

"Don't play stupid," Novack said, as he and Mikhail moved closer, surrounding him.

"The ring you ripped off the woman's finger when you crashed into her."

"Are you serious? What are you guys smoking? That woman ran into me!"

"Listen, *zezak*. Give us the ring or you're going to get hurt," Novack threatened.

Sylvester coiled his body, ready to spring.

"Maybe you didn't understand me," Novack continued. "Give me the fucking ring you dumb ass nigger or I'll rip your tiny *gabel* brains out of your head. You get me now?"

"I don't want trouble. I'll forget the words I just heard. You boys said what you had to say. I don't have shit. Now, turn, and get the fuck out of here before something you don't want to happen, happens."

As a crowd of bystanders looked on, Professor Marvel left his chess game and rushed over to see what the commotion was all about. Two black men and two white couples moved close, listening and watching, debating whether to intervene.

"The *zezak* says he doesn't have it. Says he didn't do nothing. What you think, Mikhail? You believe him?"

"A nigger? Not for a fucking second," Mikhail said menacingly.

Sylvester had enough. He moved forward with clenched fists while the two onlookers stepped forward as well.

Novack pulled out a gun, stopping them in their tracks. Shrieks rang out from every direction.

Thirty-Three

Prospect Park

A gun! Sofia's heart stopped.

A second later, Mikhail also whipped out a small pistol from the middle of his waistband. Several onlookers ran for cover, while all others fled. Sofia tried to scream but had no voice.

Novack aimed his gun at Sylvester. Mikhail wheeled and pointed his weapon directly at the two men coming to his defense. Enjoying the moment, Novack and Mikhail flashed wide grins, saluting each other with raised clenched left fists. Cocking his gun at Sylvester, Novack mocked his targets.

"The only thing that's going to happen is that we're going to teach all three of you motherfuckers a lesson. This *zezak* for stealing the ring, and you *zezaks* for not minding your own business. And all three of you pieces of shit for being disrespectful niggers who don't know their place."

Frozen in fear, Sofia forced her body to move, ran to Sylvester, looking right into his eyes hoping he would see she was not a part of what was happening, wildly flailing her arms at both boys attempting to end the madness.

"HE'S NOT THE ONE! HE'S NOT THE ONE! HE'S NOT THE ONE!" Sofia shouted over and over, amidst the turmoil of an erupting cacophony.

Novack hesitated, quizzically looked at Sofia, turned back to Sylvester, shrugged, and fired.

"NO! GOD, NO!" Sofia screamed.

Sylvester collapsed, landing face down, blood soaking through the back of his shirt.

Shaken by the sight, Mikhail, dropped his gun. Sylvester's two defenders rushed forward, tackled him and started pummeling Mikhail about the face and arms. The taller man picked up a thick tree branch, raised it above his head, and a moment before unleashing it, Novack fired another shot that barely missed his face. Mikhail pulled himself up, joined Novack, and with sirens blasting the air, jumped into their Mustang and sped out the Park.

Sofia rushed to Sylvester, almost falling on top of him as she leaned over his lifeless body.

Seeing no signs of breathing, her mind racing, her thoughts and emotions cascading, Sofia grappled with how to respond.

Should I place my hands on his chest? Try to give him CPR? Put my white mouth on his black mouth? Is he already dead? Oh God what should I do? Suddenly, three or four police vehicles as well as an EMS van drove off the road and onto the grass. Panicked, Sofia fled in the opposite direction. Once she made it to the street, she slowed down, hoping to avoid attention despite still being in costume. With every step, she said another prayer.

Before entering the apartment, her mind still in disarray, Sofia took a tissue out of her pocket, and dried her tears. Edward and Ilka were sitting on the couch.

"Where have you been? We were starting to worry." Edward asked.

Ilka jumped up and wrapped her arms around Sofia's neck.

"Listen, Mom. I just want to say, I'm sorry. But sometimes you just make me so angry. I had one sip of wine at the festival and next thing I know you're calling me a drunk!"

"I'm sorry too," Sofia answered, barely aware of her words, her heart still racing, all thoughts with Sylvester, "Let's just forget about it."

She sat down next to Edward, avoiding his gaze. *What would they think if they knew what I had done, what I brought about, the man I may have killed?*

Suddenly, Edward turned to Sofia with a smile. "Here," he said, holding up Sofia's wedding ring.

Sofia gasped. "I've been looking... Where did you..." she stammered.

"It was in the back of my wheelchair," Edward said quietly.

Sofia put it on her finger and gripped her hands tightly together to keep them from shaking.

"We should really get that resized."

"Wow, that's so lucky it fell into the chair," Ilka plopped on the couch next to Sofia, "Uncle Victor would never have forgiven you if you lost his wife's wedding ring."

"Ilka, what are you talking about?" Edward said. "That's my mother's wedding ring."

"Your mother?" Now Sofia was certain she was mad.

"I told you this before, haven't I?" Edward said. "She gave it to Victor for good luck and to keep the Communists from stealing it when he fled to America. Victor's never been married."

Thirty-Four

April 10, 2018
Manhattan

The doctors who operated on Sylvester at the Columbia University Irving Medical Center of New York Presbyterian Hospital on the upper west side, discovered that the bullet fired by Novack had struck Sylvester in the chest and exited his back on a downward trajectory. Following surgery, Sylvester was placed in a medically induced coma to assist his breathing and reduce inflammation. Ten days later the doctors determined that his breathing was sufficiently stable to allow him to be brought out of the coma.

As he regained consciousness and the ability to speak, Sylvester realized that he could not make his legs move. When asked, his nurse declined to discuss his diagnosis, insisting that he would have to talk to his doctor. Hours later, a grim-faced middle-aged surgeon, Dr. James Lin, explained to Sylvester that the bullet had struck his spinal cord, doing considerable damage. Months of physical therapy lay ahead. Regrettably, in all likelihood, Dr. Lin told Sylvester he would not be able to walk again.

Sylvester was devastated. Wracked with pain, haunted by the shooting, he began to entertain suicidal thoughts. Freed from the penitentiary, only to be condemned to a worse fate.

Almost two weeks later, Sylvester was unexpectedly visited by Detectives Fred Burns, paunchy with a pale, heavily lined face who looked burnt-out from his years of carrying too high a caseload, and Detective Eduardo Rodriguez, tan, clean-cut and handsome, who wore an immaculate suit that looked far beyond the pay scale of New York City's finest. A young man looking to make a name for himself.

After expressing insincere words of sympathy, they asked if Sylvester could recall the events leading up to his shooting. Whenever Sylvester tried talking to the Professor about his recollection, Conrad told him that his doctors did not want him to do anything to agitate his condition. Yet here they were, insisting time was of the essence. Sylvester agreed.

Do you recall what anyone looked like? Faces, can you provide any descriptions?"

Sylvester closed his eyes, shook his head, reopened them and sighed.

"I keep trying. Every second I'm awake. Every second I sleep."

"Do you recall any words that were spoken?"

"God, in my dreams, I feel myself being surrounded and all of a sudden crumbling to the ground. But, other than that, my mind's blank."

The detectives exchanged looks.

"Mr. Stanley, we don't want to tell you anything that will plant false ideas in your memory. But here's a few things we know for sure. That day in the park, you were confronted by two men. You exchanged words. A crowd gathered. A woman was also present. Possibly someone you know?"

"What? What are you talking about?"

Sylvester could feel his agitation growing.

"Did you know that there was a festival in the park that day you were shot?"

"No..." Sylvester's head was starting to throb worse than his body.

"Did you go to the park with anyone?"

"I was supposed to meet Professor Marvel for dinner. That I recall."

The two Detectives flipped through their memo books. The drumbeat of pain in Sylvester's head was visible. He squeezed his eyes together tightly and took his left forearm and rubbed it across his temple. His blood pressure monitors loudly beeped.

Rodriguez rushed out into the hallway, loudly calling for a nurse. Burns rose from his chair and patted the foot of Sylvester's bed.

"Don't worry, Mr. Stanley. We're working on this around the clock. We'll be back in a few days. Hopefully your memory will improve. Meanwhile, sooner or later, eyewitnesses will come forward."

Two male nurses rushed into the room. After checking the monitor, they gave Sylvester two blood pressure pills and placed an additional pillow behind his head. Sylvester leaned his neck back, trying to calm himself. Now, he was a forever prisoner not behind bars, but in his own body. When Sylvester was sent away, at least he had known why. Now he didn't have a clue as to who was responsible. His anguish was as unbearable as his physical torment. Both defied description and threatened his sanity.

Thirty-Five

April 10, 2018
Brooklyn

The bullet, made entirely of silver, is precious. The laws of the Kanun command that every woman present a silver bullet to her husband on their wedding day as part of her dowry. It is to be used to take her life if she's ever unfaithful.

The bullet must not be found. So, she hides it inside her vagina wrapped in a tampon.

She has just arrived in America. The airport building is eerily white with sheer glass walls and ceilings stretching as far as the eye could see. There are a multitude of travelers, yet not a sound can be heard. Trapped in a speeding current of nameless faces, she yells for her mother and father before being stopped, pulled aside, and ordered by a homeland security officer to walk through an enormous metal detector.

The silver bullet sets off the metal detector.

"Më fai!, it's not my fault, she desperately tries to explain.

She is 15 years old. She is speaking Albanian. They don't understand.

She is 35 years old. She has lived in Brooklyn for twenty years. She speaks perfect English. Why don't they understand?

She looks into the different colored eyes of the officer and freezes.

"Victor!"

Her blood curdling screams bounce off the walls of her bedroom. Sofia awakens.

Yet another silver bullet nightmare. After the shooting, whenever Sofia managed a few hours of sleep, her dream had become a nightly horror show. The dream so terrified Sofia that she could not talk about it. Disclosing the details somehow felt as if it might bring her nightmare to life. When pressed, she would tell Edward and Ilka that she could not stop having bad dreams which ended only after she cried out for Uncle Victor to save her.

As she bathed, Sofia relived for the hundredth time the tragic events of the past weekend. She was dying to confess but couldn't handle the thought of prison and losing Ilka. Also, she feared what her two deranged "helpers" might do if she sang like a bird.

While Ilka slept, and Edward groaned, half-awake on the couch, Sofia made herself a cup of coffee and sat in the kitchen staring into space. Rarely indulging in such a thought, Sofia longed for a mother and father to lean on. Yet, there was one person in the world to whom she could turn. Even after all these years.

Angela was seated at a table in the back corner of Corteleine's wearing a baggy gray sweater over a pair of jeans. A cup of coffee was waiting for Sofia at the table. Before Angela could even stand to greet her, Sofia rushed over, bent down, and hugged Angela. She laid her face on her friend's shoulder while Angela patted the back of her head, both of them repeatedly exchanging "I'm so sorry."

Sitting opposite each other at their tiny table, sipping their coffee, Sofia slowly worked up the courage to confess.

"Angela, I have something I need to tell you."

Angela cut her off. "Wait, I need to say something first. I know I walked out on you all those years ago. And I still think there's a lot about your brother-in-law that you refuse to see. He's a dangerous man. But maybe there was a better way. And it's been such a long time, it can't matter to him anymore."

Angela paused, wiping her eyes and small nose with her napkin, struggling to find the words. "When I saw Ilka and poor Edward in a wheelchair... now... I was your friend. And I wasn't there for you. And I'm sorry." She reached across the table and held Sofia's hand. "I never stopped thinking about you for a second."

Sofia teared up and looked away. She had longed to hear those words for so long, only to risk losing her friend again. Sofia's head dropped; a torrent of tears hitting the floor.

Angela stroked her back. "It's ok, Sofia. It's ok."

"You don't understand. It's so awful. I'm so ashamed. That poor man. That poor man."

"What man?"

Sofia shook her head, unable to respond.

"Just tell me, honey," Angela whispered.

Sofia straightened up, trying to regain some semblance of composure. "I was there when the man was shot in the park the other day."

"Oh my God! How awful. No wonder you're a mess. It never ends. Another brother shot. And the racist animals nowhere to be found. I can't believe you were in the park when it happened. My God, you must have been terrified!"

In a shaky and halting voice, without interruption, Sofia told Angela everything. The festival. The jogger. The ring. Novack and Mikhail.

With each passing sentence, the warmth drained out of Angela's face. Her eyes widened; her nostrils flared, the long red nails of her delicate fingers scratched against the wooden table.

Sofia concluded, "That poor man, it never should have happened. God, if only I knew what those boys were capable of."

Angela had heard more than enough. "That poor man, that's all you have to say! How could you, Sofia?" she screamed, the volume of her voice reaching beyond the café to the sidewalk. "What were you thinking asking those Nazi pigs for help?"

"Please understand," Sofia begged. "You of all people should understand how scared I was to lose Victor's ring. There was no predicting his reaction."

"And, of course, it was the nigger who stole it. And you hire two of your brother-in-law's butchers to get the ring back and lynch the nigger," her voice was beyond sarcastic.

"Who else? I thought it was the *zezak*..." Sofia blurted out before she could take it back, "I mean the Black man. I mean who else could it have been?"

"Fucking, fucking leopards never change their spots. Zezak. I may not understand a syllable of Albanian, but I know Nigger when I hear it from a white mouth."

Before Sofia could say another word, Angela stood up, and pointed her finger. "How in God's name could you target that man the way you did? You're all the same. No better than your brother-in-law. You're just like the rest of your family, just like every fucking white bastard. When push comes to shove, you may hide it, maybe even convince yourself it's not there, but down deep you think we're all animals."

"Oh my God, Angela. You can't mean that."

"I'm not nearly as mad at you as I am at myself," Angela continued, her voice so loud, several customers were ready to intrude. "For believing in you. For loving you. For trusting you. You disgust me. I have to go."

Sofia shivered in shame.

"Sylvester Stanley!" Angela shouted from the door before leaving,

"What?"

"That's his name. Sylvester Stanley! That's his name!"

Thirty-Six

April 13, 2018
Brooklyn

The city was a cauldron, more on edge than after the Florida killing of Trayvon Martin. Because Sylvester's shooting was in New York's own backyard, without an arrest soon, the urban volcano was sure to erupt. Tense demonstrations clogged streets in every neighborhood.

"Not here, not now, not anymore. Not Sylvester!" was a chorus heard day and night in all five boroughs.

The repulsive racist epithets hurled at Sylvester Stanley were attributed to two people with Slavic sounding accents. Even Trump people were joining in to shout about how the shooting was another example of what happens when bad people invade America.

While Novak and Mikhail remained hidden in a basement apartment off Pelham Parkway in the Bronx, a joint task force of federal, state and local law enforcement agencies searched everywhere for the shooters. The license plate seen on Novack's Mustang had been traced to an Albanian man in Fort Lauderdale in his sixties who had his car stolen years ago when he lived in Brighton Beach. It was also reported that a confidential witness had identified two of Victor's men as the shooters but documentary proof established they were visiting family in Albania on the day of the festival. Several witnesses said there was a woman in a traditional ethnic costume at the scene.

After Angela's hostile rejection, Sofia lay all day in bed, fully clothed, her eyes bloodshot from sleepless nights and never-ending tears. Ilka pounded on her door to the point of exhaustion trying to rouse her mother. Fearing her mood stemmed from their fight in the park, she implored her father to find Victor to settle things. Edward had seen Sofia devastated by Ajola's death but she was in an even worse state now. His Sofia lived to be there for Edward and Ilka, now she couldn't even care for herself. Edward knew all too well the signs of PTSD.

Ignoring his own pain, and the comfort of his medication, Edward stayed by his wife's bedside. Stroking Sofia's hand, he would tell her whatever the problem was they would find a solution. His words unavailing, he desperately awaited Victor's return from his unexpected trip to Albania.

Flying back to New York, as he reclined in his first-class seat, free from disturbances by adjacent passengers, Victor reflected. Fucking Novack and Mikhail. Was there no end to their stupidity? Shooting a zezak in plain view with Sofia there. Calling him after it's too late. He hoped they at least listened to him and ditched their goddamn cell phones and guns along with their car.

Less than an hour after arriving at JFK, Victor walked into Sofia's apartment, shocked to find Edward clean-shaven and more alert than he had been in months. Ilka came out of her bedroom rubbing her eyes, looking exhausted but to her uncle as beautiful as ever.

"Uncle Victor, thank God you're here. Mom's losing it. She won't speak to anyone. Just mopes around and even cries during the day for no reason. Nobody can get through to her. She just keeps asking for you."

Victor gently knocked on Sofia's bedroom door and stepped inside. Before closing the door, he told Edward it would be best if he first spoke to Sofia alone to try and figure out what was going on. His younger brother deferred.

Sofia sobbed, sitting up and pulling the covers down below her neck. "I'm so sorry. I'm so scared, Victor. I don't know what to do."

Victor sat by the side of the bed with a comforting smile. "Tell Uncle Victor what's going on."

Cracking the door open, Ilka said from the doorway, "We're all dying to hear what's eating you up."

"Why don't you make your mother and me some coffee," Victor said.

Ilka initially resisted, then obeying her uncle, turned, and briskly walked to the kitchen.

"I'm so ashamed, I'm such a horrible person," Sofia said, in anguish, "How could I do something like this?"

"Start from the beginning. Tell me everything, Leave out no details."

Sofia spoke for a half hour; her recitation interrupted only by her sobs when reliving the shooting. After she finished, Victor feigned ignorance and even thought it wise to display annoyance.

"Let me get this straight, you sought help from Novack and Mikhail without my permission? Two half-wit half-breeds? I don't understand, Sofia, how you could be so reckless? It's so unlike you."

"Victor, please understand. I thought I lost the ring. I was hysterical and you were nowhere to be found. Before I even knew what I was doing, I asked for help. And I was so scared to have you see me without the ring. All I could think of was getting the ring back and your boys were right there before my eyes eager to help."

"Those two trigger happy punks!"

"I didn't know they were armed. When they confronted him, I did everything I could to prevent things from getting out of control. But it was too late. How was I to know those boys are crazy?"

Victor stood up and stroked his chin, pivoting back to a consoling tone. "I don't think we should do anything rash. I heard some news reports about this on the ride over to the apartment. They say the *zezak* cannot remember anything. So, at most, the police know nothing beyond your being at the festival. Difficult as it is, for now at least, you should remain quiet."

"Victor, why, why would Novack shoot someone in cold blood? He shot a defenseless man like he was an animal. Like he wasn't even human. Who does something so hateful?"

Victor was cautious not to reveal too much. "Novack and Mikhail are members of a gang in the Bronx that calls themselves the Albanian Bad Boys. Even though they're only Albanian wannabes with Serb fathers. The Albanian gang is always at war with other local black gangs. I've given them odd jobs but would never trust them to do anything important."

Sofia interrupted, "Victor, this never would have happened if it wasn't for me. But I can't go to prison. I can't lose Ilka. Oh God help me, Victor." Sofia plaintively clasped her hands together. "Help me. God help me. I can't live with myself if I don't confess."

Victor remained momentarily silent, carefully weighing the options, reconsidering his advice, realizing

Sofia could never stay the course of keeping her mouth shut. Knowing that even if the police were morons, with the feds involved, it was only a matter of time before they'd connect the dots. And it was a case that demanded a solution. And these days, he figured they'd react twice as fast when it's a zezak. The boys were going to be locked up within at most a day or two. And whether the imbeciles talked or the *zezak* remembered or other witnesses came forward, or simply because she was his sister-in-law, it was stupid to entertain the possibility that Sofia wouldn't join them.

"Sofia, there's only one thing for us to do." In an effort to minimize the emotional impact of what he was about to say, Victor addressed Sofia in the calmest of tones, "We have to get you an attorney. I'm getting you the best. My lawyer. David Sherman."

Thirty-Seven

April 16, 2018
Brooklyn

The Monday evening after Sofia bared her soul, Sherman called Victor into his office to explain his strategy. He knew it would be a difficult sell.

"Victor, we can make this all go away, I truly believe it. The city is on fire; Sylvester is paralyzed in a hospital fighting for his life and nobody is charged. Let me take Sofia to the District Attorney's office to tell them what happened. What she did. What the boys did. And where the boys can be found. Hold nothing back. I'm confident I can make sure she won't be prosecuted. But she can't wait another second. Especially after what I've heard. Not from what I've learned."

"What are you talking about counselor?"

"Victor, my friend, you think I've been doing nothing but nosh at my desk. Your sister-in-law's a prime suspect. Big surprise. My sources informed me Sofia's been under twenty-four-seven surveillance. The cops are hoping that Sofia will lead them to Novack and Mikhail. We're lucky they haven't already charged her and locked her up."

Sherman paused, making sure not to disclose any privileged conversations he had with Sofia the prior evening.

"Let's get her to the DA's office. I'll set everything up. I'll get her to the person I most trust in their office. In exchange for them bringing no charges against her, I'm hopeful she'll do exactly what they've been hoping. Lead them to the shooters."

Victor took a minute to digest Sherman's words before responding. "I can't believe I'm saying this, only fools talk to cops or prosecutors, but you may be right, she doesn't really have a choice."

Victor stared at Sherman, his heterochromatic pupils piercing his attorney.

"But, Counselor, you sure as shit better be right about this."

Sherman's insides always burned when Victor was involved. Advising his brother's wife, he needed a fire extinguisher. He nervously smiled at his number one client.

"Sure as shit, as you so aptly put it Mr. Hushemi. Sure as shit."

Thirty-Eight

May 2018
Manhattan

Sylvester was out of the woods. The danger of life-threatening complications had passed, he had regained some color, his pain meds were reduced, he looked far stronger and slept less. Yet, he still had no memory of the shooting.

After three weeks in acute care at New York Presbyterian, Sylvester was transferred to its inpatient rehabilitation center. Every physical therapist who walked into his room was welcomed; every psychiatrist, psychologist or social worker who offered counseling rejected. I don't need their help, Sylvester thought, *to remember*.

Lorraine and Professor Marvel provided the only support he desired and trusted. Both insisted that it was best for him not to get agitated talking about the case. When pushed, the Professor told Sylvester he had been instructed by prosecutors not to discuss the shooting because they feared if Sylvester recovered his memory defense attorneys would argue the Professor suggestively influenced him. For the same reason, the DA's office insisted it would be best if he did not watch or listen to any news reports about the case. Sylvester begrudgingly accepted being kept in the dark only because it fueled his motivation to remember.

An hour after another tasteless lunch, Sylvester was unexpectedly visited by Chief Assistant District Attorney,

James Bridges, a stocky African American who had been head of the Hate Crimes Unit for more than a decade, and one of his colleagues who was also assigned to Sylvester's case.

"How are you feeling Mr. Stanley?" Bridges asked. "I hear you are making progress."

"Better thank you, but not better enough. Still can't remember. Still can't walk."

"I understand. Although I can only imagine what you' re going through. You have to be patient with yourself, hopefully things will improve." Bridges paused for a moment. "I've got some news, hopefully it will make you feel a bit better."

"Really?" Sylvester responded, pushing his tray of barely eaten food away. "Progress on the case?"

"More than progress, Mr. Stanley. Not only have we caught the two shooters, but we also have every expectation they will plead guilty, and you will not be put through the burden of a trial."

Sylvester was shocked.

"A witness to the shooting came forward," Bridges continued, "She knew the two Serbian men who shot you and told us where we could find them. They've been arrested and confessed."

Sylvester held up his right hand. "Whoa, wait a minute, run this by me again. Who is this woman?"

Without missing a beat, Bridges replied in an even tone, "She's Albanian. She was at the festival in the park the day of the shooting with her family. She saw the two men confront you and tried to stop them. We've exhaustively examined and investigated what she told us and reached a conclusion that she was telling the truth and had nothing to do with the shooting. These two men acted alone."

This rankled Sylvester, and his voice rose. "I don't understand. How can you possibly know that? Who else have you spoken to? What other investigations have you done?"

"We've spoken to dozens of people who were at the scene who were willing to speak to us. Everyone we spoke to corroborates the woman's account. We even obtained videos of the shooters pointing their guns. We have seen no evidence which incriminates the woman."

"I don't know Mr. Bridges, it doesn't feel right to me. I just wish I could remember."

"Mr. Stanley, look at me, this is a hate crime bad as they come, do you have any question in your mind of *my* desire to hold accountable everyone involved? If I had any doubt of the woman's story, any evidence of her involvement she would have been charged and prosecuted."

"I wish I felt the same way, but I'm sorry I don't, I just don't," Sylvester said, ending their meeting, buzzing for a nurse to help turn him to his left side to get some rest,

July 15, 2018

"STOP! I DIDN'T FUCKING TAKE ANYTHING! GOD, I'M SHOT!"

A matronly black Jamaican nurse in her sixties, rushed into Sylvester's room.

"Oh Lord. Mr. Stanley, calm yourself, you're having a nightmare."

"*His eyes! Shoot his eyes! Shoot his eyes!* She fucking ordered it. She's an assassin!" Sylvester screamed, pushing himself up from his hospital bed, he collapsed to the floor.

"Shit," he pressed his arms on the ground, straining to raise himself, frightening Nurse Rebecca Thompson.

A second before Sylvester keeled over on his left side, she placed her arms under his shoulders and managed to raise him back up to his mattress. Sylvester's right forearm was bleeding badly, but he paid no attention.

"Finally, God! I fucking remember! Please call Professor Marvel. He can get to the DA before it's too late."

"Ok Mr. Stanley but please calm down, you're going to seriously hurt yourself."

"Ha, I thought I already was hurt. Please just get him here."

"You lie back Mr. Stanley and let me clean this blood off you and I'll hand you your phone. A deal, sir?"

"Deal."

Nurse Thompson handed Sylvester his cell. He called the Professor and notwithstanding any prior admonitions about not discussing the case with him or other potential witnesses, he provided every detail of his resurrected memory.

The Professor also replied without holding back, "You know I heard that woman Sofia yell something as well. Just was never sure. This is the game changer we've been hoping for. Let me get a hold of Gibson and I'll check in with you this afternoon. Always felt those Serb boys didn't act on their own."

Waiting for the Professor, Sylvester's mind was off to the races, even if the Serb motherfuckers had already pled guilty, he was sure he could still go after their accomplice. Shit, their boss not their accomplice. That Albanian bitch was more responsible than her butcher lackeys, her hired animals. Once Bridges heard he remembered, it would be a slam dunk to convict her.

Later that night, Conrad Marvel walked into Sylvester's room without a trace of his usual exuberance. Sylvester was shocked.

"You don't look right Professor, what's wrong?"

"I went to the DA's office, Bridges was tied up, so I spoke with one of the other prosecutors in the Hate Crime Unit and laid out everything you told me. They asked me to come back in two hours while he ran things by his superiors. When I returned they keep me waiting another two hours to see Bridges until I told them there would be twenty people sitting with me if they kept me waiting any longer. Bridges finally showed up along with the District Attorney himself, Tom Whalen. They told me they had been discussing the case all day and regrettably there's nothing they can do that it's too late, the case is closed and can't be reopened."

"What the fuck, you're shitting me."

"He says 'I'm sorry.' We heard what the Albanian woman had to say, and everyone believed she was sincere. She gave up the shooters, Novack and Mikhail, and they've pled and are going to receive lengthy sentences. It was the right thing to do."

"But that was when I had no memory."

Professor Marvel shook his head in disgust. "Brother, I kept on them. So, what do they do? What the establishment always does. Even the brothers. They patronize me. Tell me I must understand that they have a very high burden, your recovered memory months after being shot and seriously injured is nowhere near enough. Find them additional evidence to corroborate your hearing Sofia yell shoot his eyes and they can't make any promises, but they'll see what they can do."

Sylvester's eyes filled with tears. He banged the bars of his bed so hard he bruised the knuckles of his right hand.

"So that's it then? She goes scott-free for reducing me to half a man, whose only working body parts cause him far more pain than pleasure. Never ends does it. Emmit Till, Sylvester Stanley. Now or then. White bitches exterminate brothers. White man gives the stamp of approval."

Professor Marvel came over to Sylvester and wrapped his arms around him. "Can't give up the fight brother. Black lives matter. We will overcome!"

Thirty-Nine

September 2018
Brooklyn

Special Agent Dan Ford and AUSA Alan Troutman, sat alone in the chief prosecutor's top floor office at Cadman Plaza East in Brooklyn. Troutman wanted to hear Ford's thoughts on his prosecuting the shooting of Sylvester Stanley as a federal hate crime and charging Sofia as well as Novak and Mikhail.

"I disagree," Ford told Troutman, "the DA's office got it right. Sofia tried to stop the shooting, she cooperated, the shooter and his accomplice are locked away. Who more than I would want a federal prosecution if the evidence showed otherwise?"

Troutman rose from behind his glass desk adorned with half a dozen plaques he had been awarded for a long line of convictions of America's most wanted. The head of the criminal division for the past fifteen years, his hair almost entirely gray, opaque glasses accentuated his handsome face, he wore a navy blue Brooks Brothers jacket over tan trousers and matching loafers. He was as thin as he'd been in law school. Despite being the most accomplished and self-assured of federal prosecutors, voicing a different take to Dan Ford left him uneasy,

"After the DA closed the State's case, Sylvester recovered his memory. He's certain he heard Sofia give the order the to shoot him. And Agent Gabriel found a witness who had been reluctant to come forward whose cell phone not only showed the video of the shooting but captured Sofia running from the tree. Unfortunately, the video's inaudible and she also couldn't hear anything with all the chaos surrounding the shooting. I had the recording sent to the lab at Quantico trying to extract what Sofia said but no luck. Even without sound, the video's consistent with Sylvester's recollection. And we've shown it to Professor Conrad Marvel, a friend of Stanley's who was a witness to the shooting, and seeing Sofia's lips move on the video refreshed his recollection that he heard the word shoot even though he couldn't swear to anything else that was spoken. It's no slam dunk, Dan, but I believe she ordered a hate crime and we have an obligation to pursue it after the State dropped the ball."

Dan knew all about Sylvester's post traumatic recall. He believed Sylvester's hearing "shoot his eyes" and the Professor's fortuitously refreshed memory was an emotional creation rather than a reality.

"Isn't that for a jury to decide?" Troutman responded. "You're not telling me that Sylvester Stanley doesn't deserve his day in court. And there's a clear way out for Sofia. Victor's likely walked into her apartment dripping in blood. Or counting stacks of money. Or looking to hide kilos of cocaine or heroin. She cooperates and I'll give her a letter that'll keep her from serving a day in prison."

Ford responded, his voice not a decibel louder, despite his growing agitation, "I know how bad you want Victor. You think I don't? He killed one of my own. And then despite the overwhelming evidence you presented at trial, Sherman pulls a rabbit out of a hat somehow getting Brumbullak to recant. But using Sofia to get to Victor is a bad play."

Troutman rubbed his chin. A moment before embellishing his position, Ford held up his hand, ending the debate.

"Alan, if that's the way you want to see it, I said my piece."

"You know I'll take your position under advisement Agent Ford; everyone always does."

Forty

October 2018
Brooklyn

Dawn had barely arrived when a dozen FBI agents descended upon Cortelyou Road. Despite being armed with a no-knock warrant for the arrest of the sister-in-law of Victor Hushemi, knowing there was a child in the home, lead agent Gabriel elected to forewarn.

"Mrs. Hushemi, open the door," followed the thunderous knocking by her team, "or we will be required to enter by force. We have a federal warrant for your arrest."

Edward, sleeping alongside his wife ever since the shooting, grabbed Sofia's arm in reaction to her shrieking, trying to calm her. Ilka rushed into the room, shaking in fear, squeezing her arms around Sofia, burying her head in her bosom, the chaos reducing her to childhood.

"Mom, make them stop!" she wept.

Edward rose from the bed, and shouted that they were coming, as Sofia held Ilka.

Cracking open the door, Edward was brushed aside by an Agent half a foot taller, as four more rushed into the apartment. Sofia stood by her bedroom door in her nightgown, still holding Ilka in her arms when two agents pulled her hands away and handcuffed her.

"Let go of my wife!"

Only when an agent's gun was held inches from his face did Edward halt.

"Stay right there, sir. Let's not create any problems. Your wife must come with us."

A strikingly athletic African American woman with auburn hair, entered. She was wearing a blue FBI jacket pulled neatly over a bullet proof vest and was the last to enter the room. She spoke sharply and clearly: "Mrs. Hushemi, my name is Desiree Gabriel. I'm the agent in charge. I need you to stay calm. Nobody is here to hurt you."

Crumbling inside, yet somehow mustering her composure, Sofia said, "I don't understand, why are you here?"

"You are being charged with a federal hate crime, acting in concert with Novack Lukic and Mikhail Markovic in the attempted murder and assault of Sylvester Stanley."

"That's not possible. The case is over. I already explained everything to the District Attorney's office and the police. Please call my lawyer, he will confirm it."

"Everything will be explained in due course," Agent Gabriel said in a soft, yet firm voice. "Even though the state never charged you, the federal government has chosen to prosecute."

A second later, Victor's voice boomed from the hallway.

"Stop! All of you. Drop your fucking weapons!" Victor shouted, standing in the doorway in a black leather jacket, his hands ominously close to his zippered side pockets.

Agent Gabriel commanded the stage. "Let's everyone calm down." She turned to Victor. "Mr. Hushemi, let us frisk everyone, and we'll give you all a moment of private time. You can even accompany Sofia to our vehicle before we take over and bring her in for processing."

A second female agent came over to Sofia, who having been frisked, removed her handcuffs and said, "It's all right Sofia. I have a daughter Ilka's age. Let's go to your bedroom.

I will stand by the door, and you can take as much time with your daughter as you need while you gather a few personal belongings."

"Stop them Uncle Victor, make them leave," Ilka cried.

Agent Gabriel turned to the agents patting and fingering Victor from head to toe, and said, "Let Mr. Hushemi speak to his niece." She turned to Edward. "You can come, too, Mr. Hushemi."

With two Agents keeping a close eye on everyone, Edward slowly walked into the bedroom with his brother.

"Victor, what's the story?" Edward inquired.

"Hard as this is, we must stay calm," Victor replied, overlooking his brother's insinuation, keeping his voice as low as possible, trying to prevent being overheard, "These are the feds. We have to let them have their way. Nobody will hurt Sofia, and we'll get this straightened out. And this won't be forgotten, they'll pay for what they're doing."

"You can't let them lock Mom up."

"Nobody's locking your mom up, trust me. She'll be home in a few hours."

"Promise?" Ilka asked, her voice shaking.

"Promise, sweetheart, I promise."

Edward whispered to Victor, "You know you can't promise that."

"I promise, brother."

"We have to leave, Mrs. Hushemi," Agent Gabriel commanded. "My team will remain, we have a search warrant as well for the apartment."

Victor clenched and unclenched his fists, watching tears fill Sofia's eyes. Ilka's sobs returned as she was gently separated from her mother. The outfit Sofia wore the day of the shooting was found behind a mountain of clothes in the back of her closet. Two male agents, each lightly holding one of Sofia's arms, led her out of the apartment while Victor trailed at a permissible distance.

As they walked down the hallway, Victor had reached his limit, he let go. "I know who's behind this. You tell that motherfucker Troutman coming after my family is a line he should never have crossed."

"What did you say, Mr. Hushemi?" Agent Gabriel asked as she rushed up from behind. "Was that a threat?"

Victor smiled, sarcastically. "Not at all, I'm just concerned for my sister-in-law and urging you to take proper care of her. What did you say your name was again?" His eyes narrowed.

"Special Agent Desiree Gabriel. If you have anyone you need to speak to, Mr. Hushemi, it's me." Gabriel's and Victor's eyes locked.

Despite the early hour, the street was packed with onlookers. Sofia was placed in the back of Agent Gabriel's car, sandwiched between the other female Agent and her partner.

My case is over, this can't be, Sofia kept telling herself, her head bowed, staring into her lap. David Sherman promised me.

The Trial

Forty-One

October 2018
Brooklyn

Victor assured Sofia there was nobody better than Sherman. Sherman promised, absolutely promised there would be no charges after she confessed so long as she spoke the truth. And here she was, in FBI custody on her way to federal court. Sherman had betrayed her faith. She would never be free from her own prison of guilt over Sylvester's shooting, but she would not lose Ilka. Sherman had promised her that.

Gabriel broke the rules by not handcuffing Sofia. Gently touching her arm, she spoke. "Listen, Sofia. I'm not here to hurt you. I will respect all your rights. I know all about you and how difficult your life has been. You just lost control for a second. Talk to me, trust me, and I will be in your corner. As I advised you before, you have the right to remain silent, but the sooner you cooperate, the sooner I can do my best to try and improve your situation. There is a path for you." After a pause, Gabriel continued. "AUSA Troutman is eager to work out a cooperation agreement with you. Tell us what happened, tell all you know about your brother-in-law and you might even avoid a prison sentence."

Agent Gabriel's compassionate tone made Sofia forget Victor and Sherman's admonitions to never speak to law enforcement without an attorney. "I don't understand, I've already explained everything. Novack and Mikhail are in jail.

I tried to stop the shooting." Gabriel replied without words, instead offering a smile and a slight shake of her head.

When Sherman appeared, Sofia could barely look at him between the bars of her holding cell. He tried to explain that the State's promises did not prevent a federal prosecution. Exasperated and contrite, he sighed, softly telling Sofia that he was going to do everything possible to secure her release.

With a federal marshal holding each arm, Sofia grimaced as she was handcuffed, taken out of her cell and led into a surprisingly small Magistrate's courtroom, packed with reporters, who had been tipped off about her federal hate crime arrest. For the first time, but far from the last, shouts of "Albanian Assassin" rained down upon her. Shaking, Sofia desperately searched for a family face. Sherman whispered that Victor and Edward were waiting at home for his call.

Rising above the tumult, Magistrate Karen Broderick, petite, surprisingly young with long red hair spilling down her robe, quieted the din. "We are here for an arraignment on the charges, a bail determination, and the setting for a preliminary hearing date if an indictment has not been voted. Nothing more. I expect quiet or you will be immediately removed from my courtroom."

The charges, of conspiring to violate the civil rights of Sylvester Stanley by an assault with a deadly weapon were read. After Sherman entered a not guilty plea, Troutman rose requesting Sofia be remanded pending trial, stressing Sofia was being charged with a heinous crime, targeting a man simply because of the color of his skin. With Victor as her brother-in-law, Troutman claimed Sofia was certain to flee.

Sherman's response restored Sofia's faith. Not simply the strength of his words but the passion in his voice. "Your Honor, what is reprehensible is Mrs. Hushemi's arrest and Mr. Troutman's innuendo. Are we determining Mrs. Hushemi's culpability and risk of flight based on guilt by association? Mrs. Hushemi has lived in this country since she was fifteen and has a teenage daughter and an ailing husband, a decorated war veteran, she would never abandon. And proof that Mrs. Hushemi had knowledge that the shooters were armed is highly questionable. Indeed, the State declined to bring any charges against Mrs. Hushemi. The federal government has mischaracterized a brazen shooting Ms. Husemi tried to prevent as a federal hate crime."

Sherman's argument convinced the Magistrate to release Sofia, but she ruled that the seriousness of the case compelled intensive pre-trial supervision. Looking Sofia directly in the eye, she sternly warned that there would be grave consequences if she made her regret her decision. Once Sofia heard she was being released, the conditions were irrelevant. Her only thought was going home to Ilka and Edward. As her cuffs were removed and she was led out the courtroom, her reservations about Sherman lifted. Suddenly, Sofia glanced to her left and gasped. From the opposite side of the courtroom, a new buzz erupted. There in handcuffs and leg irons, stood Novack and Mikhail.

On the ride home, sitting next to Sherman in his Honda, Sofia sniffled non-stop and stared out the side window. Sherman pulled over, shut off the engine and turned to Sofia. "My dear, I wish I could take your pain and make it mine. I wish I could erase your fear."

Before he could stop himself, Sherman continued to speak from his heart instead of his head. "Sofia, I will not allow you to go to jail. You will not be convicted. You will be there for Edward and Ilka. Always. You have my word."

Sherman fully realized these were words a lawyer should never utter, yet for the first time in his life, he had lost control. Whether it was his years of fealty to Victor or seeing Sofia as he saw his own daughter, he was overcome with emotion.

Sofia tightly grabbed Sherman's hand, her eyes filled with tears,

"Promise?"

"I promise."

When they arrived at Cortelyou Road, Sofia buried her head in Shermans' arms. He stroked her back, consoled her with a few additional words, and watched her make her way up the front steps of her building. He had called Victor and informed him of Sofia's release and expected he would be waiting with Edward and Ilka. Sherman banged the steering well and slapped himself for his unprofessional guarantees. Before driving away, the gray-haired counsel broke down in tears.

Forty-Two

One week later
Brooklyn, NY

In 1991, four short years after his stunning acquittal, Victor Hushemi saved David Sherman's law practice. Victor had started a successful limousine service and had purchased a profitable trucking company. He was also investing in commercial and residential real estate in Brooklyn. His growing business interests required continuous legal representation. So, he contacted Sherman and offered him an extravagant annual retainer to serve as his counsel.

Although Victor was not facing any pending criminal charges, Sherman hesitated. With Elseid Selimi serving a life term, and Victor the only one acquitted in the racketeering case, Sherman assumed the feds had targeted Victor as his successor and placed Victor's every move under a microscope. Even Victor's new businesses, Sherman figured would be suspected to be serving as a front which laundered money for both the Italian and Albanian mafia. Representing Victor as corporate counsel would require an enormous commitment.

Nonetheless, Sherman accepted Victor's offer without hesitation. The recession of the early '90s had left too many of Sherman's clients unable to afford his modest fees. The retainer would allow him to maintain his life's work, representing those in his community who needed his help the most. Sherman also recalled his father's stories of Albanian families risking their lives hiding his cousins from the Nazis. Besa, the promise to grant refuge to all who knock on your door, distinguished Albania from all other countries in Europe. Representing Albanian businesses, Sherman thought, "might just be my of repaying our family's debt."

Over the following years, Victor became extremely wealthy, and he regularly increased Sherman's retainer. Sherman no longer worried about the financial viability of his community-based law practice. The retainer, however, did present an ethical quandary that he was never able to resolve.

When Sherman was called upon to represent employees of Victor who had been charged with criminal offenses, he realized that an independent defense attorney would try to negotiate plea deals in exchange for incriminating information about Victor. As Victor's attorney, Sherman could not do so. He ruefully wondered whether this was the real reason Victor kept him on retainer. However, Victor's men all insisted that they had no interest in talking to prosecutors about Victor, let alone paying for their own lawyer. So, Sherman buried his doubts and represented them as best he could.

But representing Sofia? That posed a problem of far greater dimension. Sylvester Stanley's life haunted Sherman. Despite meticulously orchestrating youthful offender sentences for Sylvester's two marijuana offenses, he exposed him in federal court. He did not cover all the bases, all the possibilities. No lawyer can look into the future, countless colleagues consoled him, but he still felt he should have done something different, protected him from subsequently being subjected to a Draconian life sentence in the South. When he heard the news, Sherman, as only Sherman would, felt as if it was his own son or nephew who was granted clemency. And when he said his prayers in his customary pew in his neighborhood synagogue, he felt he had been pardoned as well.

Sitting in Sofia's apartment, the night she poured her heart out to him, Sherman was sickened to learn of her involvement in Sylvester's shooting, even feeling personally responsible for her predicament. Despite recoiling at the sight of judges signing off on the marriage of Hasidic girls barely beyond puberty, when Victor needed Sherman to find the right judge to make an exception for Sofia's parents to sign a deposition of approval rather than requiring their appearance at the ceremony, Sherman turned a blind eye. He couldn't even bring himself to attend the reception.

Sherman felt no less compassion for Sylvester by representing Sofia. He didn't doubt her innocence, but he still realized he was emotionally compromised. Cross-examining Sylvester would be impossible. Imagining looking into Sylvester's eyes, rendered Sherman queasy, the thought of questioning his recollection of events, of impugning his credibility and character would be impossible. Yet Sherman wanted, needed to be there for Sofia.

Sherman couldn't help but chuckle. Defending Sofia was mishegoss of Biblical dimension. Walking home from schul the Friday night after securing Sofia's release, the star filled sky interrupting the darkness, he realized that, the answer was staring him in the face. *Sharron! Sharron!* But would she take the case?

Forty-Three

Late October 2018
Brooklyn Heights Promenade

Having just turned 40, Sharron Bernstein, Sherman's favorite niece stood as tall as a runway model; she had the darkest of eyes, jet-black hair interspersed with faint streaks of gray. Her marriage to Eric, three years after they met at Columbia, where she starred as point guard on the basketball team while he occupied the bench on the men's varsity, unsettled the family. Choosing a Black woman was not nearly as objectionable as marrying out of faith, but the birth of their irresistibly cute daughter Samantha calmed the seas. Her grandparents adored her.

Other than being criminal defense attorneys and obsessively committed to their craft, Sherman and Sharron could not have been less alike. Sharron, twenty-five years younger, wore costly, tailored outfits, and performed with incomparable swagger. Sherman struggled to keep his suits unwrinkled and, appearing deferential, won jurors' hearts and minds. Sherman gained a measure of notoriety throughout his career; Sharron was a social media icon. While Eric earned seven figures on Wall Street, Sharron clerked for a Federal Judge followed by a two-year stint as an Assistant United States attorney. Shortly after being hired by a white-collar criminal defense firm, she launched her spectacular career defending high profile clients, from corporate executives to rock stars and, of course, politicians. Bernstein was the name attached to front page arrests with stunning regularity. Sharron only frowned upon defending famous men against charges of sexual misconduct.

Sharron worshiped her uncle. But Alan Troutman had been her mentor during her time at the US Attorney's Office. So, Victor was never a comfortable topic for discussion with Uncle David. The tension was unbearable the few times she and Victor occupied the same room. Despite all that, Sherman decided Sofia had to be represented by Sharron. Making it happen was a different story.

The following week, on a bright Spring morning, Sherman persuaded Sharron to drop by for an alfresco lunch on the Brooklyn Promenade. Although Sharron was a sounding board for Sherman prior to Sofia's federal arrest, she bit her tongue about her doubts concerning the innocence of anyone named Hushemi, and only warned her uncle to think twice about taking her in to confess. If the strategy backfired, they both knew Sharron's real concern was Victor. Taking their sandwiches out to the Promenade, enjoying the view of New York Harbor, Sharron was wearing a conservative tan suit with a pale blue blouse, Sherman his well-worn black suit, white shirt, and thin black tie.

After talking family matters the entire lunch and seeing the latest dozen cell phone pics of his grandniece, Sherman cleared his throat. Slowly working his way to the punchline, Sharron, better than anyone at reading her beloved Uncle, interrupted.

"Oh God, Uncle David," she said, eyes closed, shaking her head, "You know I can't? Don't. Please don't ask? I barely understand your taking her case. You talk about Sylvester all the time. I can't even count the number of times I've heard about his case and how we all celebrated the Sabbath after he was granted clemency."

Sherman bowed his head, remaining silent, almost in prayer. Sharron brushed away a few flakes of dandruff from the collar of his suit and stroked his back.

"Oh, Uncle David, only you can get yourself into these kinds of situations. I've told you countless times, I'll get work referred to you, just get away from Victor Hushemi, break it off once and for all."

Sherman raised up. "My dear, you're still so young. Life's not that simple. Please honey, do me this one favor. Meet Sofia. Just meet her. Then if you can't represent her, it's ok, I'll never bring it up again. I promise."

"I'll meet her, of course I'll meet her," Sharron sighed, hugging her uncle. She kissed his cheek, and smiled. "I'm her lawyer, I can't properly represent her, without meeting her, now, can I?"

Sherman feared Victor's reaction to bringing Sharron into the case. Sitting back in an armchair opposite Sherman's desk, Victor caught himself before responding. Always savvy, never allowing emotion to outweigh reason, Victor surprised Sherman.

"Counselor, maybe you're on to something. Who better to cross examine the zezak than Bernstein? Take the color out of the situation. Bring the woman into it, too." Overlooking the fact that she was Sherman's niece, he continued, "If she can tone down that fucking ego of hers it could just work."

Sharron instantly won Sofia over. Without hesitation, the moment Sofia walked into Sherman's office, alone, with Victor out of town, Sharron embraced her.

"David has told me so much about you," she said. "What a devoted wife and mother you are. I feel I already know you. The shooting of Sylvester Stanley is so tragic.

And now the government is compounding it all by charging you. Don't worry. You're in the best of hands. The injustice of it all makes my blood boil."

"Thank you," Sofia whispered, looking down at her shoes, clearly embarrassed.

Sharron graciously sat next to Sofia on the small couch pressed against the right wall of Sherman's office while he sat in a side chair less than a foot away. After talking to Sofia extensively about her life and even confiding a few details about her own marriage into a Jewish family, Sharron, waited until just the right moment, and then launched into the case.

"David and I are confident the Government won't be able to prove the charges against you. Convincing a jury that you had racist intent at trial is a far cry from what's needed to obtain and uphold an indictment. But we can't be blind here. Your trial will turn on emotion just as much as facts. We have to show the jury that your heart is pure, that Novack and Mikhail were loose cannons who acted completely on their own. Right, Uncle David?"

Sherman was concerned that Sharron was moving too fast for the first meeting. Perhaps she was a little too used to clients well versed in having their ass in the frying pan. Sherman smiled at Sofia and responded, "I don't want you to worry, my dear. When Sharron cross-examines Sylvester and the other government witnesses, she'll make sure they know you never had anything to do with the shooting. And we'll point out that you already told the police and Brooklyn DA everything and they believed you. If you have to do it again with this jury, we'll prepare you. The result will be no different. They'll believe you."

Sharron took Sofia's hand. "Not only are we going to win the case, we'll embarrass the federal government for ever bringing a case against you."

Sharron's supreme self-confidence stood in stark contrast to Sherman's style. From the look on Sofia's face, seeing and hearing such confidence concerning her fate from a woman she had never previously met was a bit overwhelming. Yet when Sharron walked Sofia to the elevator, neither doubted she was the right woman, indeed the best person for the job.

Forty-Four

November 2018
Brooklyn

The bullet, made entirely of silver, is precious. The laws of the Kanun command that every woman present a silver bullet to her husband on their wedding day as part of her dowry. It is to be used to take her life if she's ever unfaithful.

The bullet must not be found. So, she hides it inside her vagina wrapped in a tampon.

She has just arrived in America. The airport building is eerily white with sheer glass walls and ceilings stretching far as the eye could see. There are a multitude of travelers, yet not a sound can be heard. Trapped in a speeding current of nameless faces, she yells for her mother and father before being stopped, pulled aside, and ordered by a homeland security officer to walk through an enormous metal detector.

The silver bullet sets off the metal detector.

"Më fai! It's not my fault," she desperately tries to explain.

She is 15 years old. She is speaking Albanian. They don't understand.

She is 35 years old. She has lived in Brooklyn for twenty years. She speaks perfect English. Why don't they understand?

She looks into the different colored eyes of the officer and freezes.

"Victor!"

Sofia screamed before awakening from her ritual nightmare. Edward, lying alongside his wife, remained in a deep sleep. Ilka was not awakened, either. Sofia's morning eruption had become no more annoying than an alarm clock.

Pulling the covers off her shivering body, Sofia pushed herself out of bed and moaned in pain. She staggered to the bathroom, showered for as long as it took to regain a measure of composure, put on the first blouse, dress, and sweater she found in her closet and quickly prepared breakfast for the family. Edward, having awakened, sat with Ilka at the dining room table. Sofia did her best to assure husband and daughter for the umpteenth time that everything was going to be fine. Edward and Ilka tried to hide the doubt from their faces.

Glancing at her phone, Sofia realized she was late to meet Sharron and Sherman at his niece's office. She quickly picked up everyone's dishes, put them in the sink, rushed over to the hallway closet, called her pre-trial officer to inform him of the meeting, grabbed her red jacket and said her goodbyes. After making her way to the subway, she luckily found a seat, and heard her heartbeat pounding through her blouse for the entire half hour ride.

Exiting the elevator of Sharon's midtown office on the 42nd floor, Sofia could never get used to the stark contrast with Sherman's place of business. The reception area was larger than Sherman's entire suite and when Sharron came out to meet Sofia, she walked her down a long corridor with floor to ceiling windows providing views of surrounding skyscrapers. Sherman was seated at a small conference table opposite Sharron's large semi-circular glass desk. The office looked out on the East River.

The moment Sofia took a chair alongside Sherman, Sharron assured Sofia that she had informed her pre-trial services officer she would call him when Sofia was on her way back home. He was a hard ass that had to be kept abreast of Sofia's movements by the minute.

Sherman turned to Sofia. "My dear, Sharron and I have been discussing a new development in the case. I've been on the phone with Sal Sussman and Leonard Meizel, Novack and Mikhail's lawyers, trying to arrange a joint counsel meeting where we can exchange information and discuss the extent to which our defenses might be consistent. And both lawyers said they could not attend."

"I'm not supposed to know any of this and clearly you're not either, but Novack and Mikhail are being taken out of state prison to attend a meeting with the federal prosecutor. They must be exploring pleading guilty and cooperating. There won't even be a light at the end of their twenty-five year tunnel if federal time is tacked on to their sentence."

Sofia stared at Sherman, at a loss to understand the significance of his words. Sharron walked over from her desk and draped her arm around Sofia. "Honey," [Sherman unnoticeably, did a quick double take, he could never recall his uber professional niece addressing a client in such a manner] "we don't know all the things the government will ask them at a meeting, but as I have told you many times, you're not the real target. Troutman has been obsessed with your brother-in-law for a long time. Ever since he lost a trial to David where Victor was acquitted for the murder of a federal agent."

Sofia gasped. She recalled Angela mentioning the case but had never put two and two together.

"You're just a pawn. Novack and Mikhail are pawns too."

Sofia, held her head, struggling to order her thoughts, "Ms. Bernstein, what if they lie and make it look like I was behind the shooting?"

Now it was Sherman's turn. "What you must realize, Sofia, is that it's very dangerous to lie when you have one of these meetings with the government. The slightest fabrication and anything they agree to do for you gets thrown out the window. You have the truth on your side, Sofia, and believe it or not, that wins out in the end. Allen Troutman can be an ass, although Ms. Bernstein has a different opinion," he chuckled, "and he's never gotten over losing Victor's trial to me, but in the end, he does things by the book. And even if the boys sell him a story, pointing a finger at you, we will destroy them on the witness stand. Having them corroborate Sylvester's story that you were behind the shooting will end up doing more harm than good. And anything they have to say about Victor has nothing to do with you and if and when the time comes, I'll deal with it."

Sofia was terrified with where the conversation was heading. Protecting Victor was no less a priority than her own freedom. She blinked back tears, feeling hopeless.

Sherman rose from his chair, "Sofia, I'm not worried. Novack and Mikhail will not be able to get away with deflecting blame and trying to lessen their guilt. And they know nothing that can hurt Victor. Nothing I can't handle. Trust me."

Sharron looked at Sofia. "One last thing. You absolutely must not say anything about this to anyone. Not even to your husband. And especially not to Victor. No one. Leave all of this to us. Understand, Sofia?"

"Of course, I won't say anything to anybody."

"Well, it's been quite a meeting. Let's get you home to Ilka and make sure to keep that pretrial officer from barking."

After tossing and turning the entire night worrying about what Novak and Mikhail might tell the prosecutor,

Sofia jumped up, wide awake, panicked at the sound of Ilka shouting,

"Mom, come look at this fast. Hurry!"

Sofia made her way to the kitchen as quickly as possible. Ilka held up cell phone for both to view and hear a CNN reporter standing outside an upstate prison wall. There were photos of the faces of Novack and Mikhail in the top corner of the screen. Sofia cringed.

"Another dramatic turn in a case that has captivated the city," announced a middle-aged reporter in a black ski jacket. "An hour before sunrise, Novack Lukic and Mikhail Markovic, the two men serving state time for the shooting of Sylvester Stanley, and now facing federal hate crime charges along with the sister-in-law of Victor Hushemi, were found dead in their cells with their throats slashed. Whether it was an act of retaliation by another inmate is under investigation."

Forty-Five

March 11, 2019
United States Eastern District Court
Brooklyn

Senior United States Judge Eugene Nicholsby of the Eastern District of New York was assigned to preside over Sofia's case. After months of intense pre-trial litigation concerning discovery and evidentiary issues, the trial was finally ready to begin. His top-floor courtroom located at Cadman Plaza had magnificent views of the Manhattan skyline, the Brooklyn Bridge, the harbor, and the Statue of Liberty.

Judge Nicholsby took the bench from a private back door and addressed the panel of prospective jurors seated in the jury box of the courtroom. Even the most experienced and self-assured judge would have found the madness and chaos surrounding Sofia's trial difficult to control. Not Judge Nicholsby.

Despite constant warnings from officers, "Albanian Assassin," chants from the rows of spectators filled the courtroom. Sofia sat expressionless, wearing the mask, hoping it would provide a shield.

Judge Nicholsby, with his deep booming voice, turned the room silent. No federal judge looked more patrician nor better commanded a stage than Judge Nicholsby. Lean, seventy-years-old, six feet two with silver hair, he looked the part of a Shakespearean actor.

"All are welcome to attend any proceeding in my courtroom. But with respect and decorum," he cautioned.

"The failure to behave in such a manner will result in immediate banishment and permanent expulsion. Does everyone understand?"

The entire courtroom respectfully nodded their heads.

Sharron, Sofia, and Sherman were a striking trio seated at the defense table. Sharron was wearing a perfectly tailored long black dress which accentuated her tall athletic frame along with an ivory necklace and a matching black vest. Sofia wore a blue blazer over a white blouse and matching skirt with a thin gold necklace with a small silver charm with the letter "I" dangling around her neck. Sherman wore his ritual uniform, changed only with a gray tie.

Troutman, wearing a gray pinstriped suit was joined by Agent Gabriel and a handsome young male agent who was as skilled at being his paralegal as he was at making arrests. Four thick document filled notebooks were stacked in a rolling cart on top of a host of DVDs and CDs. Regardless of the case, the federal government came armed to the teeth. Sherman joked that the feds used nuclear weapons to kill an insect.

Sherman was lucky Judge Nicholsby allowed him to sit at counsel's table. He was deeply troubled by his prior representation of Sylvester and worried even if his niece were compromised. No jurist, not even Judge Nicholsby intimidated Sharron.

"Your Honor, I had hoped my reputation would precede me. As well as my uncle's. Rest assured my representation of Mrs. Hushemi will be zealous, limited only by the rulings of the Court. And as for being in possession of privileged information from my uncle's prior representation of Mr. Stanley and exploiting it, I need not dignify that with a response. I am stunned the Court would even entertain such a thought.

Judge Nicholsby ruminated a moment, before speaking,

"I am going to take a half-hour recess before beginning jury selection. Mr. Troutman, I want you to meet with Mr. Stanley and advise him not to mention anything about his prior relationship with Mr. Sherman. Mr. Sherman, the only reason I am permitting you to continue even as passive counsel is that Mrs. Hushemi with full awareness of the conflict wants you to remain as her co-counsel."

Finding people to sit as jurors who had not heard about the case and already formed an opinion posed a huge problem. Time and time again, for a variety of reasons, feigned and real, people were disqualified. When Judge Nicholsby inquired whether a juror would have difficulty sitting because the case involved an accusation of the victim's race being the reason he was targeted, Sharron strained to gauge the expressions on their faces and body language. As always, the jurors she and Sherman feared the most were not the honest ones, some of whom were more than willing to admit their prejudices, but the ones who kept hidden what they really felt.

Finally, by the end of the day, twelve jurors and four alternates were selected. Six of the twelve jurors were African American, four women and two men and a Black male and a white female as alternates. A few of the jurors were under thirty, two were over sixty, the rest middle aged.

Walking to the parking lot, the vile screams of spectators pierced Sofia, her body twitching in anguish as she made her way to Sharron's car. Cameras loomed and microphones were shoved at her from all directions. Hundreds of hands held their cell phones aloft taking videos. Sherman parted the way with both arms and protected Sofia and Sharron as best he could.

"Please, let Mrs. Hushemi breathe. Show some common courtesy," Sharron yelled at the throng of reporters and protestors. "We have nothing to say. You'll have to hear it all in the courtroom."

"Show some humanity," Sherman yelled. "You're suffocating the poor woman."

"Black lives are humanity! Try telling that to your bitch client, Bernstein!" After Sherman helped Sofia get into the front seat of Sharron's sky-blue Jaguar XF P300 and brushed aside two camera men to squeeze into the back seat, Sharron sped past the mob and out of the garage.

Forty-Six

March 12, 2019
United States Eastern District Court
Brooklyn

At six thirty a.m., the madness escalated. Stretching farther than the eye could see was a line of people hoping to grab one of the two hundred and fifty available spectator seats in Judge Nicholsby's courtroom. A police escort was needed to clear a path into the garage.

After opening statements, Troutman decided to go for the jugular by calling Sylvester as his first witness. Dressed in a tie and newly pressed suit that overwhelmed his diminished frame, Sylvester was wheeled up to the witness stand by an attendant. Sofia and Sherman thought they were ready for the moment. Nothing could have been further from the truth. Sofia squeezed the defense table with her hands, suppressing her desire to rush to the witness stand and beg forgiveness. For Sherman, seeing the man he protected as a young boy rendered a paraplegic sickened him. He was able to regroup only after Sharron patted his left arm.

Holding Sylvester on each side, two court officers helped lift him into the witness chair adjacent to Judge Nicholsby. Struggling to catch his breath, Sylvester finally was able to get comfortable and placed his hand on the Bible and took the oath to tell the truth. The jury looked ready to convict before a word came out of his mouth.

Sylvester threw Sherman a contemptuous glance before quickly shifting the look to Sofia and then focusing on Troutman as he began his direct examination. Troutman set the stage by asking Sylvester about the responsible life he was leading since his release from prison and then moved to the shooting.

"I want to direct your attention to this past April, the twenty-seventh to be exact. Do you recall where you were and what you were doing on that day?"

"I'm an avid runner. Or I was an avid runner. I ran often in Prospect Park. I was on my usual Saturday run, several laps around the perimeter."

"Did anything happen while you were running?"

Sylvester paused, and cleared his voice, while several jurors leaned forward in their seats. Sofia's hands clenched the defense table, as her face grew pale.

"I was on my first lap, running down the west side of the park and up the east side. All of a sudden, a woman who was running in the opposite direction, she looked like she was chasing after someone, stumbled and crashed into me. We were both knocked to the ground."

Sylvester, looking anguished, directed his eyes at Sofia. "Seated at the table right there, in between her lawyers, that is the woman who crashed into me."

Sylvester slowly shifted his waist in the chair while his eyes reddened. "I just need a moment," he paused before continuing. "The first thing I did was check to see if the woman was ok. I helped her up and made sure she was all right.

"Then her husband and daughter came from somewhere in front of us. The daughter was pushing her father in a wheelchair. She told me she was coming from the Albanian Festival in the park. We shook hands and went our separate ways."

"Did there come a time when you saw Mrs. Hushemi again?"

You could feel everyone in the courtroom growing anxious, sensing the horror of what they were about to hear.

"After the accident, I was finishing my last lap, a car passed by me, turned around, and started following behind me. Cars were not permitted in the park, so I found its presence disturbing."

Sylvester's voice grew edgy and agitated. Sofia looked close to breaking down, Sharron motioned for her to stay strong.

"The car then pulled up alongside me. The car had tinted windows so I could not see inside. When the vehicle pulled up, the window came down and I was able to catch a glimpse of the driver and the guy next to him. I tried to ignore them, finished my run, and then went over to the bandstand area on the southwest side of the park. I walked over to some nearby trees and started stretching and…" At this point, Sylvester's voice broke. "And then it happened,"

"What happened?"

"The two guys came over to me. I'm sure they were the ones in the car."

After identifying photographs of Novack and Mikhail, Sylvester testified:

"They were calling me names of some sort, I had never heard the words before. They kept on accusing me of stealing a ring. I told them I didn't do anything and they better be on their way. A crowd gathered and two young Black men who were to the left of me started coming at Novack and Mikhail as well."

Sofia sat with her hands in her lap, sick to her stomach. She never said a word that Edward had found the ring. What was the point? She had to live with the guilt of her unforgivable presumption. It was too painful and shameful to share it with anyone. It never mattered. Until now.

"They kept accusing me of taking the ring. Suddenly they pulled out guns. Small black pistols. Novack aimed his directly at me and kept ordering me to hand over the ring. And threatening to shoot if I didn't. Mikhail pointed his gun at the two men who had gotten close to him and froze them in their tracks."

"Do you remember exactly what was said?"

"I will never forget the words. Novack said he didn't know if he should shoot me for taking the ring. Or for talking back to him. Or because I was a nigger. I could take my pick."

Gasps could be heard throughout the courtroom. Court officers rushed over and were about to grab a man who cried out, but Judge Nicholsby stopped them. "Sir, remain seated, and not another word. I'll let you stay."

Sylvester's eyes widened in anger, his voice rose, "Suddenly, Mrs. Hushemi came running towards us pointing at me. Novack and Mikhail turned and looked at her. They lowered their guns, placed them by their sides. Mrs. Hushemi looked at me, looked me straight in the eyes, and yelled, shouted words I will never forget. *'Eyes. Shoot his eyes,'* she screamed. *'Eyes. Shoot his eyes!'* She has an accent, a strong one. But those words were clear. After hearing her, Novack turned back to me, raised his gun, and fired. The bastard wanted to kill me."

Sylvester went silent as tears filled his eyes.

"Albanian Assassin" was followed by a rising chant of "Black Lives Matter." The judge rose from the bench and put his hands out to calm the seas. Suddenly, Edward, who was seated in the first row of spectators, groaned and doubled over, holding his stomach, and staggered out of the courtroom.

"It's been a difficult morning for everyone," Judge Nicholsby spoke over the chant. "We will take a two-hour break for lunch and that should give everyone time to calm down. If Mr. Stanley is up to it, we will resume with his testimony. I also am striking from the record the last sentence spoken by Mr. Stanley, he cannot know the intent of another person. That is for you the jury to determine."

Sharron sat alone with Sofia in the basement cafeteria. Sherman remained in the courtroom perusing FBI 302 reports while eating a tuna sandwich from his briefcase and sipping coffee from a thermos. Sofia stared straight ahead expressionless, eating and drinking nothing, with tear-stained eyes. Sharron, sipping an herbal tea after eating a small lunch, placed her arm around Sofia, fearful she might be on the verge of a complete collapse.

Following the lunch break, Sharron ushered Sofia back into her seat at the defense table, but as Sylvester returned to testify, Sofia looked completely lost. Sharron debated whether to request a recess but leaving Sylvester's direct testimony untested overnight would be catastrophic. He had already said far too much.

"How are you holding up, Mr. Stanley?" Troutman began.

"I'm feeling better. It's so difficult to relive things."

"It's understood. Mr. Stanley," Judge Nicholsby replied.

"Mr. Stanley, it's terrible for me to even ask," Troutman said, vastly experienced in the theater of the courtroom, conveyed a sympathetic tone to the jury, "but if somehow you can summon the strength, it would help this jury so much, if you can take us through the video of the incident."

"Yes, I think I can do it," Sylvester replied, his voice firm but his face quivering.

Troutman introduced the video of the shooting into evidence, playing and stopping at poignant moments. The video was slowed and stopped several times so that Sylvester could testify step-by-step as to Sofia's behavior and the moment she shouted. Darting out from the trees, Sofia could be seen looking directly at Sylvester and then her mouth could be seen open as she raced towards Novack.

"What is she saying here, Mr. Stanley?"

"She is yelling, '*Eyes, Shoot his eyes.*'"

"Are you certain?"

"Listen, it was chaos. People were screaming all over the place, but those were her words. One hundred percent I heard them. Did she literally mean that? Was it her Albanian way of saying take him out? Did she mean to say shoot him in the eyes? That I can't tell you. But those were her words."

Sylvester's testimony chilled Sofia causing her to shiver and stare forlornly into her lap. How could he have heard such vile words, when she screamed at the top of her lungs trying to save him? Yet witnessing Sylvester relive the horror of the shooting, she also felt deserving of words that condemned rather than exonerated her.

"Can you take us through what we are seeing next on the video?

"After her words, you can see Novack raise his gun again, and point it right at my eyes. I made a move, he ended up pulling the trigger and hitting me lower, in the middle of the chest."

Almost in a whisper, Sylvester said, "Pain all over. I felt weak. My chest was burning, and my head was thumping. But most of all I remember looking down at my legs and feeling nothing. The bullet shattered my spinal cord. I'll never walk again. I have the use of my hands, but I don't have the dexterity I had before the shooting. I'll never be able to paint or draw again."

Sylvester started to tear up but was able to continue testifying.

Troutman concluded Sylvester's testimony by addressing several issues he feared could undermine his credibility.

"Mr. Stanley, the day of the shooting. Did you have any marijuana in your system?"

"Yes, I ran into a friend at the park who was smoking a blunt. We spoke for a few minutes, and he offered me a drag. I took one hit and kept on running."

"Mr. Stanley, I also need to ask you about other things in your life."

Sylvester provided the details of both his first arrest and federal conviction.

"Thank you, Mr. Stanley, I have no more questions." Troutman turned and looked at Sharron.

"Your witness."

Before he rose, Judge Nicholsby informed everyone that it had been a long and difficult enough day for Sylvester and recessed the trial until the following morning.

Forty-Seven

March 13, 2019
United States Eastern District Court
Brooklyn

Even if Sherman and Sylvester were strangers, cross examining him would not have been an easy task. Sherman was not the cold-blooded professional his niece embodied. His emotions did not possess an on/off switch. Standing up to interrogate a Black victim of a horrific crime of hate, even believing in Sofia's innocence, was never going to feel right. Sharron received seven figure retainers for a reason. This was far from the first case where her client was white and the victim black. But her unexpected bond with Sofia, that was an exception to the rule. When she rose from the defense table to begin her interrogation of Sylvester, Sherman wondered how it was going to play out.

Wearing a dark blue three gold button vest over a white blouse and a matching dress that went down just past her knees, a perfect match for her delicate features and tall torso, Sharron captivated the jury before a single question was asked. When Sylvester, with his piercing dark pupils, delicate and wounded body, tensed his mouth as if he was confronting a traitor, you could hear a pin drop.

"Good morning, Mr. Stanley." Sylvester remained silent.

"Mr. Stanley, when you observed Mrs. Hushemi for the first time, she was running in the opposite direction from you?"

"Yes."

"And you testified that she was wearing a costume of some sort?"

"I don't know if it was a costume. She told me she was dressed for the Albanian Festival in the park."

Sharron cleared her throat and cool as ice, subtly adjusted her tone, adding a dose of innuendo. "Did you see any jewelry she was wearing?"

"Absolutely not."

Troutman stood. "Your Honor. There is no basis for questioning him in this manner."

"Overruled, I will allow some leeway," Judge Nicholsby ordered. "It's a cross-examination. But I will not allow too many questions of this nature."

"Thank you, your Honor. Specifically, Mr. Stanley, did you observe Mrs. Hushemi wearing a ring when she collided with you?"

"No, I did not."

Sherman looked down, understanding, but clearly uncomfortable with where Sharron's questioning was heading. Sofia tightly gripped the defense table and started to perspire, wondering what to do: Disrupt the proceedings? Shout at Sharron? Whisper to Sherman? Terrified, she looked around the courtroom, at the jury, at the Marshalls, at Judge Nicholsby, but remained silent.

"And afterward? You reached out your hand and helped her up?"

"Yes."

"You noticed her tights were torn?"

"Yes."

"You looked carefully enough to see that?"

"Yes."

"But you did not see a ring on her finger?"

"No."

"And isn't it correct you twirled Mrs. Hushemi around and examined her from the back as well as the front?"

Sylvester angrily sneered back. "What are you trying to say? Twirled her! I don't know what you're hinting at. I politely turned her around to see whether she had any other injuries."

"So, you were being attentive?"

"Yes."

"But you were not examining her to see if she was wearing any jewelry?"

"You can ask the question a million times. I never saw any jewelry or any ring."

"I must object," Troutman exclaimed. "This questioning is irrelevant and designed solely to badger and harass Mr. Stanley."

Judge Nicholsby directed the jury to step out of the courtroom. The second they exited; he turned on Sharron. "What is the good faith basis for this line of questioning?"

Sharron raised her dark eyebrows, "Your Honor, it's undisputed that Mrs. Hushemi's wedding ring was gone right after the collision. Mr. Stanley just testified that he was accused of taking it by Novack and Mikhail. I have every right to cross-examine as to whether their suspicions were well-founded."

Sofia was sick to her stomach. Paralyzed worse than when she was behind the tree watching the boys pull out their guns. She never told Sharron or Sherman she had found the ring. What was the point? She never thought Sharron would do this to Sylvester.

"No, you don't," Judge Nicholsby replied noticeably louder, "unless you have some better proof than that to support an inference that he stole the ring."

Sofia breathed a sigh of relief.

In a different setting Sharron would have detested her next words.

"He has a criminal history, your Honor. The ring was obviously stolen from my client. It was never recovered. That's my good faith basis."

"Her argument is absurd, your Honor," Troutman replied. "Ms. Bernstein is appealing to sheer prejudice and hoping to divert the jury's attention from the crime and the person who this trial is all about."

"I agree. But you know what, upon reflection, given the seriousness of the charges in this case, I am going to permit a wider latitude of cross-examination than I might otherwise, but do not go overboard, Ms. Bernstein. Understood?"

Sofia closed her eyes, praying for Sharron to stop. Instead, Sharron was determined to press the limits of her line of questioning. Raise the specter that Sylvester was and always will be a hoodlum. A sickening racist portrayal, of a paralyzed, forty plus-year-old, black man. No matter how uncomfortable, she was committed to her task.

"Now, after examining Mrs. Hushemi, didn't you shake hands before leaving?"

"Yes."

"And you shook her hand with your left hand? Left to left. Unusual wouldn't you agree, Mr. Stanley?"

"Not if you're a lefty like I am, or should I say was. Before I was butchered and lost the dexterity in both hands."

Sharron bit her lip, incredulous at herself for being so sloppy not to have at least checked with Sherman whether Sylvester was right-handed. She quickly pivoted. "Sir, isn't it correct that your right hand wrapped around both of your left hands when you were shaking hands?"

"You may be right, Counselor. I may have used my right hand and momentarily placed it on top both our hands to show that there were no hard feelings."

"Do you normally use both hands to shake another person's hand?"

"Normally? What do you mean?"

Sharron slightly raised her voice, raising her level of skepticism. "Mr. Stanley, isn't it fair to say that using both of your hands for a handshake is not the way you typically shake hands with a stranger?"

"I guess you can say it's not typical, but I just explained my reasons for using both hands."

Sharron smiled sarcastically and dropped the hammer. "Isn't the real reason you used your right hand was to disguise your surreptitious removal of Mrs. Hushemi's priceless wedding ring from her finger?"

"Objection, your Honor!"

"Sustained. No more questions about the ring, Ms. Bernstein. Move on," Judge Nicholsby said sternly.

Sofia exhaled so loudly that both Sherman and Sharron momentarily gave her a look.

Sharron switched gears. "After your collision with Mrs. Hushemi, you testified that you bumped into a friend and smoked marijuana with him."

"I took a puff after I took a quick break to toss my hoodie to Professor Marvel and then got back to my run."

"So, you were impaired?"

"What do you mean?"

"I'm sure you know exactly what I mean Mr. Stanley."

"Stop the speeches Ms. Bernstein," Judge Nicholsby interjected.

"What do I mean? Your sense of perception was diminished by inhaling an illegal substance."

"Absolutely not. Ms. Bern Steeen!" Sylvester sarcastically emphasized Sharron's last name.

Jurors leaned forward, the crowded courtroom stirred, Judge Nicholsby debated whether to order a recess to lower the tension but elected to allow Sharron to press on.

"Now, you said that you were stretching your legs by a tree near the bandstand when you first saw Novack and Mikhail."

"And Novack accused you of stealing her ring?"

"Yes."

"Did you?"

"No!"

"Your Honor," Troutman cried out.

"Ms. Bernstein, I hear the word 'ring' again and I will hold you in contempt of this court. The jury is to completely disregard any additional questions about Mrs. Hushemi's ring."

Sherman shot Sharron a what are you doing glance, suddenly Sofia bolted out of her chair, screaming "Stop, already! Sylvester didn't take the ring. Nobody did!"

The entire courtroom was nonplussed. At first there was not a sound to be heard, and then seconds later there was chaos. Sofia collapsed in her chair sobbing, cursing, vile shouts came from every direction, Sherman draped his arm around Sofia, both Sharron and Troutman couldn't believe their ears.

Sylvester exclaimed, "There you have it, straight from the bitch's mouth."

"Clear the courtroom, the jury is excused, Court is recessed!" Judge Nicholson banged his gavel and quickly exited his courtroom out the back door, leaving the circus to his court personnel.

With Sofia's head buried in her hands on the table of an adjacent conference room, Sharron was in no mood for kid's gloves. "You knew the ring was never stolen and all this time you never said anything to me or David. How could you hide this? You just made your lawyer look like a heartless fool."

Sofia, hurt by Sharron's words, thought she wasn't the only one with dirty hands, raising her head, wiping her face, surprisingly loud, she responded, "I hate myself for everything that happened to Sylvester. I was too ashamed to admit it was in Edward's wheelchair. And what was the point? It has nothing to do with this trial. He's not on trial for taking it. I had no idea you would bring it up. No idea you would question him like this."

"Sharron, I love you, you know that," Sherman interjected. "But there was no need for racial innuendo, there is never a place for it, by the defense as well as the prosecution."

Sharron glared at her uncle. "You think I did this on impulse Uncle David! Like some rookie. Like I, more than anyone in this room doesn't understand why it's wrong! This was a cross that had to be conducted. I had Sylvester on edge. My approach was working, how could I have expected anything like this?"

There was a bang on the door. "The judge wants everyone back in fifteen minutes."

Sharron looked at Sofia and sat down next to her. "It's all right Sofia, I'm sorry if I snapped, We can fix this, it's all right, these things happen. It's not your fault.".

Sherman sighed, walked over to his niece and patted her shoulder. "Let's take a step back, you may have to tell

Nicholsby this is the first time you ever heard Sofia say Sylvester did not take the ring. We could request a mistrial, but since it was an outburst by the defendant, I doubt he would grant it."

Sharron gathered her thoughts. "We may be overreacting. The only damage is a few jurors feeling I was beating up on Sylvester for no reason. I'll take care of it in summation."

Returning to the courtroom, it was clear from the look on his face that Judge Nicholsby had already decided what was to be done. Before Troutman or Sharron said a word, the Judge spoke.

"I am going to instruct the jury not to consider anything that Mrs. Hushemi shouted; that the only testimony from anyone, including the defendant, comes from the witness stand. If any juror cannot do that, they should tell me now and they will be excused and replaced by an alternate. As for you, Ms. Bernstein, we will address the ethics of your cross examination at the conclusion of the trial."

"Anything else from either counsel?"

Sharron and Sherman exchanged looks acknowledging that there was no need for a response. Sharron simply nodded that she understood. After weighing the possible impact of Sofia's outburst, Troutman concluded that Sofia's shouting that Sylvester never took the ring would only help the government's case. He was pleased to let it hang in the air.

The jury returned, not one juror admitted having difficulty following the instruction to ignore Sofia's outburst. Sharron continue, her cross examination of Sylvester. "You said Novack and Mikhail called you names. And then threatened you?"

"Yes."

"Did you see Sofia at this point?"

"No."

"Or hear her?"

"No."

"So, isn't it correct you have no idea if Mrs. Hushemi could see or hear anything that was being said or happening at this point?"

"Obviously, I could not," Sylvester answered, fighting hard to maintain composure.

"And you testified Novack pointed his weapon at you and Mikhail pointed his at the other two men?"

"Correct."

"Before you ever saw or heard Sofia?"

"Correct."

"Now, you said Sofia came running from the trees after Novack's gun was pointed at you."

"Correct."

"And isn't it correct that his gun remained pointed at you?"

"No, that's not correct. He turned and put the gun down at his side and looked at Sofia."

"But isn't it correct she was trying to prevent them from hurting you and screaming for them to put their weapons down?"

"Wrong!"

Sylvester's voice rose, "She looked at me, looked right at me, into my face, and yelled, 'Eyes. Shoot his eyes.'"

"With an accent that you never heard before, isn't that fair to say?"

"She had an unfamiliar accent."

"So, you can't be sure what she really said."

"I'm sure. Those words *I'll never forget.*"

Never forget. Sharron loved hearing Sylvester say those precise words.

"Mr. Stanley, unfortunately, the shooting caused you to lose consciousness for a few days."

"Correct."

"The pain and trauma must have been overwhelming. Correct?"

"Not just my physical suffering, but the mental trauma as well."

"Of course. I am sorry to have to ask you, Mr. Stanley, but I need to pose a few questions about what happened after you regained consciousness."

"Do your job, counselor, just don't look in the mirror."

Shouts of approval rang from the back of the courtroom.

"Quiet everyone, Mr. Stanley, please I know it's difficult, but you must just answer her questions without comment," Judge Nicholsby admonished.

Sharron paused for a few moments, for the first time momentarily stung by Sylvester's unexpected retort. She glanced down at her papers, which included Sylvester's prior statements to law enforcement. Looking up she embarked on a rhythmic succession of point scoring questions:

"Mr. Stanley, do you recall being visited by two detectives from the 77th Precinct, Detectives Rodriguez and Burns?"

"Yes."

"And that was a short time after you first awakened from the shooting?"

"Yes."

"And they asked if you could recall what happened and you said, I believe your exact words were, 'My mind is blank'?"

"Yes, at that time it was."

"And you were asked if you could recall faces: if you could recall what anyone looked like, and you said that you could not."

"Yes, at that time."

"And even more precisely, you were asked if you could recall any words that were spoken. Words. Any words?"

"They asked me that. Yes."

"And isn't it correct that you could not recall any words, not one word, that was spoken?"

"At that time, I couldn't."

"You forgot?"

"Yes, at that time."

"Now, Mr. Stanley, weren't you also visited three weeks later by Assistant District Attorney James Bridges?"

"Yes."

"And isn't it correct that at that meeting he told you the case was solved and that two men had been arrested and confessed?"

"Yes."

"And that the case was solved?"

"He said that, yes."

"And didn't he also tell you that an Albanian woman had come forward with information about what happened? And you were upset that she was not being investigated for wrongdoing?"

"I was. I wondered if she might have been involved."

"But that wasn't because you recalled her doing anything."

"No, not at that time."

"Or because you heard her say anything."

"Not yet."

"But it was the first time you heard anything about an Albanian woman, and it was knowledge that was given to you not anything you had a recollection of. Correct?"

"Not yet."

"In other words, it planted a seed."

"Objection," Troutman cried out. "That's an improper question about the motives of others."

"I will allow it," Judge Nicholsby ruled.

"I don't know what you mean. I felt it was a premature conclusion."

"Now, let's talk about when your memory returned. Isn't it correct that it was months after the shooting?"

"Yes."

"One morning at the rehabilitation center where you had been transferred you awakened from a dream and cried out. Correct?"

"Yes."

"It was a memory you believed after a dream."

"It's what I know happened."

"But you never had this memory before this dream, did you?"

"It was all the trauma I guess had finally lifted and I recalled everything."

"It was a memory you believed after a dream."

Sylvester's face tightened. "It's what I know happened. My memory came back."

"Was this recollection before or after Assistant District Attorney Bridges told you there was an Albanian woman who had information about your shooting?"

"You know it was after. I was upset, I thought the DA might have acted too soon."

"Isn't your new memory a memory restored with the help of the prosecutors and agents who have brought these charges against Mrs. Hushemi?"

"Objection!"

"Overruled, Mr. Troutman," the judge said.

"I remembered before I ever saw a federal agent or prosecutor. They came to see me."

"That is your memory after being shot, and, unfortunately, paralyzed, and Mrs. Hushemi is the only person on trial for shooting you?"

Sylvester had had enough. "It's more than a memory, Sharron, it's what fucking happened!"

"Mr. Stanley!"

"I'm sorry your Honor. She's just too much."

Sharron made sure to look wounded as she turned towards the jury. "Do you need a break, Mr. Stanley?"

Sylvester lowered his voice, stroked his beard and declined. "Your client looked into my eyes and ordered Novack to shoot them out of my head."

"But you never really heard or saw anything. You are speculating. Isn't that what is going on here?"

Sherman almost banged the defense table in frustration. He knew it, Sharron posed an open-ended question, that was certain to be met with a devastating response.

"I saw and I heard it," Sylvester replied. "Do I wish there was audio as well as video on the recording so we can all be one thousand percent sure that's what I heard? Of course. But that's the vile racist command that came out of Sofia's mouth. *Eyes. Shoot his eyes.* You can keep asking the same question and you won't change my answer."

Troutman looked elated. But Sharron wasn't finished. Not by a long shot. "Mr. Stanley, you testified on direct that Mrs. Hushemi yelling those words were words you would never forget. Correct?"

"Absolutely."

"But you forgot them when Detective Burns and Rodriguez questioned you shortly after the shooting?"

"I had lost my memory."

"You forgot them?"

"Temporarily."

"And you forgot them when Senior Assistant District Attorney Bridges came to see you and informed you that two Serbian men had confessed to the crime. And that an Albanian woman had come forward and helped the police find them. Correct?"

"My memory still had not returned, but I felt there was something not right."

"But you didn't recall her words or her doing anything wrong, isn't that correct? Her running out from the trees?"

"Not at that time. I still had not."

"Mrs. Hushemi looking into your eyes?"

"No."

"Mrs. Hushemi doing anything wrong? Doing anything wrong whatsoever?"

"No. I did not at that time."

"Mr. Stanley, you admitted that you ingested marijuana even though you were on supervised release at the time."

"Admitted, ha. Yes, I stated that I inhaled a tiny amount."

"You risked going back to prison for a couple of drags of marijuana?"

"Objection," Troutman cried out.

"Sustained. The jury is to disregard that question. Do not appeal to prejudice rather than reason in my courtroom, Ms. Bernstein."

"I have no further questions for Mr. Stanley."

Judge Nicholsby called for a ten-minute break. Sharron had regrouped masterfully. For Sofia, it barely mattered. No questioning or verdict would change the fact that if not for her, Sylvester would not be paralyzed.

"Any redirect?" Judge Nicholsby asked Troutman.

Once again, the video was shown to Sylvester Stanley. Sylvester reinforced that Novack and Mikhail lowered their weapons and looked at Sofia before she ran towards him while pointing and yelling to "shoot his eyes."

"And then and only then did Novack point his gun at your eyes, and fire the shot that paralyzed you? After Sofia issued the command?"

"Objection," Sharron cried out.

"Sustained. Do not have the witness give opinions or characterizations, Mr. Troutman."

"Did Novack shoot you before or after you heard Sofia point and say, 'Shoot'?"

"After."

"No further questions," Troutman announced with satisfaction and sat down.

The court recessed for the day. Sylvester wheeled himself to the end of the hallway, waiting for Lorraine and his aide to return from the restroom. Staring out the window at the Brooklyn Bridge and lower Manhattan, Sylvester was surprised by an all too familiar face.

"Sylvester, I just wanted to check on you and see how you were holding up," Sherman said in a soft voice. "I need you to know that I'm just doing my job. Same as I did for you, the same as I do for every client."

Sylvester's eyes widened as his arms tightened on his wheelchair. "Just doing your job? You motherfucker. You discard people like yesterday's garbage. You and your niece painting me as some piece of shit nigger out to steal a ring. You're the man, Sherman! Don't let the jury spend too much time thinking about how your immigrant bitch set me up to be slaughtered by her goddamn Albanian henchmen. All your phony bullshit years ago, all the time you're thinking of yourself as some white savior, nobly trying to save another thug from the hood. Try your guilt-ridden rationalizations on some other ignorant victim."

After stripping Sherman of all his armor, Sylvester sped past him to the elevators.

Forty-Eight

March 14, 2019
United States Eastern District Court
Brooklyn

Taking the witness stand as the Government's second witness the following morning, Professor Conrad Marvel's self-confidence was unmistakable. His afro rising to the sky, his intentionally unkept gray beard jumping off his face, he was attired in a brown tweed suit. After being sworn in, Professor Marvel informed the jury of his impressive academic and professional credentials and related that he was the only non-lawyer member of the team that prepared Sylvester's clemency petition.

"Professor Marvel, when did you first meet Sylvester Stanley?"

"I met Mr. Stanley after he was incarcerated and serving his Draconian lifetime sentence."

"Objection, your Honor!" Sharron shouted.

"I know you know better, Professor. Please eliminate the hyperbole."

"Hyperbole to some is stone-cold observation to others."

"Let's save that debate for another time in another forum, Professor. Please stick to the facts in my courtroom."

"Hmm, yes, your Honor. I will try to conform," the professor sarcastically replied.

"I learned about Mr. Stanley during his incarceration, befriended him and wrote a fifty-page supplement to his clemency petition which painted a complete picture of the extraordinary and righteous man Mr. Stanley had become during his oppression."

"Professor!"

"Sorry, your Honor, I meant to say incarceration," Professor Marvel met Judge Nicholsby's gaze with a smile.

"Continue Mr. Troutman," the judge sighed.

"Can you describe your relationship after the petition was granted?"

"I rushed to see Mr. Stanley immediately after he received clemency. I have helped Mr. Stanley find employment and have found people who've invested in his artwork. I've also spend time with him socially despite our fifteen-year age difference."

"Professor Marvel, were you present in Prospect Park on the afternoon of April seventh?"

"I sure was."

"Did anything out of the ordinary happen that day?"

"Well sir, I wouldn't necessarily call seeing two white men pull out guns and point them at three innocent Black men… then shooting one of them 'out of the ordinary.' But if that's what you are talking about, that's what I saw."

"Objection, your Honor!" Sharron exclaimed. "This must stop!"

Judge Nicholsby rose from his chair, "Professor, for the last time, confine your testimony to what you observed. Your inflammatory characterizations are not welcome in my courtroom."

Judge Nicholsby turned to the jury. "The jury is to ignore any and all characterizations and opinions offered by the witness."

"Tell us what happened, Professor," Troutman asked.

"I was vanquishing yet another opponent in a chess match. After his run, Sylvester went to stretch by some trees when out of the corner of my eye, I saw two men surround him. I rushed over to see if he needed my help. I couldn't make out what these two white men were saying but things looked tense."

The Professor identified pictures of Novack and Mikhail and continued. "They were involved in some kind of argument with Sylvester. Then clear as day, I heard the N word. Novack called Sylvester a nigger. Several times. Two brothers far younger than I, rushed to help Sylvester. Suddenly, the white men drew small guns from their waistbands."

"What happened next?" Troutman asked.

"A woman darted from the trees, almost staring at Sylvester, with her hand pointed at him. Novack turned and looked at her with his gun down at his side. She yelled, with her hand still pointing. 'Shoot! Shoot!' I couldn't make out all she said, but I absolutely heard the word shoot. Novack then turned back to Sylvester and pulled the trigger. I could not make out the other words she said. She spoke with an accent. An accent I was not familiar with despite my speaking several foreign languages," the Professor proudly testified. "On her command, I saw Novack turn and fire."

"Objection to the word, 'command.' It's his subjective and distorted opinion," Sharron claimed.

"Do not give opinions Professor, just tell us what happened."

"Yes sir, Sylvester was shot in the middle of the chest and collapsed. Two men who tried to prevent the shooting were able to subdue Mikhail. Police arrived, instead of coming to Sylvester's aid, or trying to apprehend the animals, they seemed far more interested in arresting two heroic good Samaritans."

"What do you expect?" one African American man shouted from the audience. Several other spectators throughout the courtroom yelled out as well.

Judge Nicholsby asked the jury to leave the courtroom for a few minutes so that he could address some matters with counsel. After the attorneys assembled in his back office, Judge Nicholsby furiously turned on Troutman, who looked shaken.

"How many years have you been trying cases before me, Mr. Troutman? How can you allow your witness to testify in this manner? I have half a mind to excuse him and strike his entire testimony from the record."

"Your Honor, I have tried to control my witness," Troutman replied. "I have cautioned Professor Marvel more than once not to turn the proceedings into a theater for his beliefs."

"You may have tried but you have completely failed. I think I will excuse the witness and strike his testimony."

"Your Honor," Troutman pleaded, "He is an eyewitness to the shooting, an essential witness. You will fatally undermine the government's case."

Sharron and Sherman remained quiet, hopeful that the judge would deprive the government of its only unequivocal eyewitness. However, in less than a minute, the judge reconsidered and instead advised Troutman that if the professor had one more slip there would be no need for cross-examination.

Returning to the courtroom, before recalling the jury, Judge Nicholsby glared at the Professor. "Professor Marvel, the court has great respect for your standing as one of this country's most talented teachers and writers. This court expects such respect to be returned."

"Your Honor?" Professor Marvel inquired despite knowing precisely what Judge Nicholsby meant.

"Professor Marvel, you are not an attorney, but I have no doubt that you have prior experience in a courtroom and full awareness of the rules. Yet you testify with total disregard of what is permissible and continuously voice your social opinions rather than confine yourself to what you observed as a witness. This is not a forum for political oratory."

Professor Marvel realized he was on thin ice when the jury returned, and Troutman resumed questioning.

"Professor, can you tell us in more detail what the gunmen did after Novack shot Mr. Stanley?"

"They jumped into a car, a green Mustang, and sped away. Then EMS arrived and tended to Sylvester."

"And did you see where the woman went?"

"No, I looked everywhere but, she must have escaped."

"Objection!"

"No opinions, Professor," the judge said.

"Sorry, your Honor. No, I did not see where she went."

"Professor Marvel, I have just a few more questions. Do you see the woman who said, 'Shoot,' anywhere in the courtroom?"

"Yes, I do. She is seated at the defense table."

"Are you certain, she pointed and said the word shoot?"

"Yes."

"And when did Novack shoot Mr. Stanley?"

"I am positive it was only after Sofia pointed and said, 'Shoot.'"

"Thank you, Professor Marvel."

Sharron rose, jurors leaned forward, eagerly anticipating fireworks. "Professor Marvel, good afternoon, it's an honor to see you sir."

"Defense counsel extraordinaire, the honor is mine."

"Ms. Bernstein," the judge interjected, "this is not a mutual admiration society, please cross-examine the witness or be seated."

"Professor Marvel, you testified that you met Mr. Stanley several years ago while he was incarcerated and at that time you became involved in his clemency petition."

"Correct."

"You believed his life sentence was unduly harsh."

"Without question. Every rational person with a heart came to the same conclusion."

"But your interest in Mr. Stanley became something more than professional. You developed a close friendship not only with Mr. Stanley but with his family as well. Is this correct?"

"Let me answer your question this way. Mr. Stanley is a real-life hero. In the face of the gravest injustice, he refused to be bitter. He had the superhuman strength and will to rise above the decades he lost during his unjust incarceration. Yes, so despite the difference in our years, we developed a close friendship."

"Wouldn't it be fair to say, Professor, if ever there was a person who deserved a reversal of fortune and a future that would make up for the past, it would be Mr. Stanley?"

"Objection, your Honor," Troutman interrupted. "The court has previously ruled that the professor's opinions are not relevant."

"I will allow a few questions on cross-examination on the issue of potential bias. Your objection is overruled."

"Professor, isn't Mr. Stanley one of the last people in the world you would have ever wanted to see hurt again?"

"Hmm, nice try, Counselor. I see where this is going. You may be one of those sisters who have had the luxury to forget, but there are far too many of our people who have unfairly suffered, and who are victims of a system that remains plagued by prejudice. So, no, I cannot say that."

Rather than objecting, Sharron ignored the Professor's slight and pressed on. "But, after all Mr. Stanley has been through? If someone attempted to hurt Mr. Stanley, physically hurt him, wouldn't you do everything in your power to prevent it?"

"Not just Mr. Stanley. I would hope every person of good conscience would come to the aid of an innocent victim."

Sharron had the stage set. "You testified that Novack pulled the trigger and fired the bullet that paralyzed Mr. Stanley?"

"He is the one."

"And, according to you, it was at the direction of Mrs. Hushemi?"

"She ordered his execution. Novack carried it out."

Sharron looked up at the Judge, who scowled at the Professor.

"She ordered his shooting," Marvel amended.

"Now, Professor, in testifying here today, isn't it correct that you are doing everything possible to bring about the conviction and punishment of the only person still living that you believe, rightly or wrongly, played a part in the shooting of Mr. Stanley?"

"Objection," Troutman cried out.

"Sustained, said Judge Nicolsby. "The question is completely improper and struck from the record. The jury is reminded again not to speculate as to the availability of Novack and Mikhail or anything else about them. Rephrase your question Ms. Bernstein."

"Isn't it correct, sir, that you want to do everything possible to bring about the conviction of the only person on trial in this courtroom who has been charged with the shooting of Mr. Stanley?"

Professor Marvel smiled and then took his right hand to the top of his balloon-shaped afro and doffed his hand as if he was tipping a hat.

"So clever. Like the fox you are!"

"Professor, answer the question, nothing more!"

"Sorry Judge, I would do everything I could within the law to assist in their punishment. But if you are insinuating, which of course you are, that I would not tell the truth when testifying at trial, I would never do that. My life, my career is built on integrity, my sister. I would never perjure myself on a witness stand. Sofia ordered the hit and Novack obeyed. Am I clear or would you like to ask the question another way for this honorable jury?"

The professor was pleased and proud of his answer. Little did he know Sharron loved his smug, condescending response. She walked back to the counsel's table, gave her uncle and Sofia a discrete sly smile, and pulled out several police reports. She laid them on the raised lectern from where she was conducting her questioning, took a long, slow drink of water, and looked up.

"Professor Marvel, Assistant United States Attorney Troutman was not the first prosecutor you spoke to about the shooting. Isn't that correct?"

"Of course, he wasn't."

"And at that time nobody had even yet been arrested for the shooting of Mr. Stanley?"

"Correct."

"And, of course, you wanted to help as much as possible to see all persons responsible for the shooting taken into custody and prosecuted."

Professor Marvel smiled, eager to fence with Sharron. "Of course."

"And it was a time shortly after the incident, so your memory of what took place was, if anything, fresher than today?"

"I wouldn't necessarily say that."

"Professor Marvel, I am sure you will concede memory fades rather than improves over time?"

"Ha. I've been waiting for this. Ask away."

"Please, Professor Marvel, why do you keep doing things a man of your professional background knows are improper? Just answer the questions," Judge Nicholsby scolded.

"Ask your question again, Sister Bernstein."

"You knew how important it was to provide your sharpest recollection of what you saw and heard when you spoke to the police and the local district attorney the first week of the shooting?"

"Which was exactly what I did."

Sharron looked down directly at her paperwork to be sure the jury sensed she was getting ready to reel the Professor in.

"To be precise. That was what you did when you spoke to Detectives Rodriguez and Burns at the seventy-seventh precinct on April twenty-ninth, two days after the shooting?"

"Yes."

"And when you spoke to Assistant District Attorney Bridges just days after the shooting, you told the police and prosecutors you were not certain what Mrs. Hushemi yelled. That you saw a woman run out from behind the trees waving her arms, that she may have been pointing at Sylvester, but you could not hear what she was saying? And she spoke with an accent. Isn't that what you reported?"

"I told them Sofia pointed."

"But not her words."

"At that time, I did not."

"And it was not until months had passed after the federal authorities took over the case that for the first time, you magically became certain that you had heard the word 'Shoot?' 'Shoot,' and no other word. Somehow as to that one word you suddenly had super hearing?"

The professor shifted uncomfortably in his seat before responding, "Let me explain so not only you can understand, but all the members of the jury can as well. I cannot tell you why, but neither the police nor DA Bridges ever showed me the video of the shooting. Thank God, when Mr. Troutman did take over the case, he showed me the video, and I knew she had yelled shoot."

"Let me get this straight, Professor. You were unable to hear her words at all at the very moment of the incident itself? And unable to recall what she said only two and three days following the incident when you talked to Detective Rodriguez and Assistant District Attorney Bridges? And subsequent to seeing the video, many months later, you now claim there is one word Mrs. Hushemi spoke that you can recall?"

"Seeing her lips move on the video made all the difference."

"The video in which Mrs. Hushemi's voice could not be heard?"

"Our senses are remarkable that way. Sight can impact sound."

"*Your* senses, perhaps," Sharron, clearly incredulous, emphasized. "And the voice you heard was with an accent, an accent you were not familiar with?"

"I conceded that."

"And your remarkable senses even after seeing the video still could not even make out the other words she said."

"I was one thousand percent sure I heard shoot, my sister."

"Perhaps the truth is the sight of the video inspired your imagination?"

"Ha, it inspired my hearing. My imagination never needs inspiration."

"Or perhaps, you wanted to hear it?"

"I heard her words. I heard Mrs. Hushemi's order clear as day."

"You heard her words, or Mr. Troutman wanted you to hear them?"

"Objection, your Honor! That's sanctionable!"

"Sustained, the question is completely improper. The jury is to totally disregard it."

"Heard it with your ears? Or thought it with your mind because you believed it was needed to right a wrong?"

"Objection, your Honor! This entire line of questioning is improper and disgraceful!"

Judge Nicholsby stood, weary of everyone's theatrics, and turned on Troutman, "What is improper are your comments following the objection. Register your objection without hyperbole, Mr. Troutman. Overruled."

"Political oratory is one thing," Professor Marvel continued. "But no matter what, when it comes to an individual being accused by the state, any individual, regardless of the complexion of their skin, I would never stray from the truth. Mrs. Hushemi yelled 'Shoot.' That is the unvarnished reality."

"Your unvarnished reality. I have no further questions."

On redirect, Troutman had Professor Marvel reiterate all over again in precise detail how and at what moment he heard Sofia yell, "Shoot!"

Several jurors looked skeptical.

Forty-Nine

March 14, 2019
Brooklyn

After Sharron's surgical cross-examination of Professor Marvel, during a late-night meeting at Sherman's office, Victor was seated alongside Sofia receiving an optimistic update on the case. All that remained of the Government's case was window dressing. No other witnesses could shed light on Sofia's words or actions. Victor agreed he should stay away from the courtroom, realizing his presence at the trial risked prejudicing the jury against Sofia.

Sharron held up her hand, momentarily interrupting the discussion. She needed to answer her cell phone. She was surprised by Troutman's cold voice on the other end, informing her of the name of his next witness. He added he had made a last-minute decision to call this woman, and was in the process of e-mailing all her prior statements.

Ever since she'd agreed to represent Sofia, Sharron's relationship with Troutman had turned from friendly to icy professional.

"If you want to know anything about her, ask your client," were Troutman's parting words.

Sharron turned to Sofia. "Who is Angela Styles?"

Sofia's small eyes widened, and her mouth trembled, but she didn't say a word. She looked at Victor, seated in an armchair closest to Sherman's desk, and he shrugged.

"Terrific," Sharron snapped, "neither one of you can tell me anything and she's the government's next witness.

How can I cross-examine her if I have no idea who she is and what she's going to say?"

"I can't help you, Counselor," Victor replied, annoying Sharron. "Sofia?"

"Looks like she's African American. Works in law," Sharron said, googling on her phone.

Sofia was avoiding eye contact with everyone in the room.

"Sofia?" Sharron asked again.

With her legs crossed on Sherman's couch and her back straight up, Sofia stared at the opposite wall. "Whatever Angela wants to tell you, whatever she wants to say about me, you'll have to hear it from her."

"Please honey," Sharron rose from her seat and clasped Sofia's hands, "you must tell me."

"I'm sorry," Sofia responded, "I will not talk about my relationship with Angela. It's sacred."

"Sacred? She's testifying against you. She's your enemy. Whatever she might have once been to you, she's trying to get you sent to prison."

"I have nothing to say," Sofia said, withdrawing her hands from Sharron, and looking at the floor.

"Take the cotton out of your ears, Bernstein, she has nothing to say," Victor barked.

Sherman stood. Victor's agreeing to Sharron's representation was limited to the courtroom, their being in the same room remained toxic. When it came to Victor's trash talk, Sharron kept the cotton in her ears.

"Mr. Hushemi, why don't you take Sofia home?" Sherman said, jumping in. "Tomorrow's going to be a long and difficult day."

After they left, Sharron took a deep breath, started looking at the e-mail Troutman had sent detailing Angela's prior statements, and said to her Uncle, "Well, let's see what Troutman's bringing to the party."

Fifty

March 15, 2019
United States Eastern District Court
Brooklyn

Wearing a loose-fitting black jacket and a white blouse, Angela Styles looked noticeably uncomfortable as she took the oath and delicately sat down on the witness stand.

After leading Angela through all stages of her close friendship with Sofia, Troutman quickly got to the point. "Ms. Styles, how would you describe Sofia Hushemi's feelings towards people of color?"

"Objection, how can any witness know a person's inner feelings and in addition their relationship was far too long ago to be relevant."

"Normally I would agree," the Judge responded, "feelings are not normally relevant in a criminal case, intentions and actions are what matters. But this is a trial for a hate crime and the defendant's feelings are an element of the offense. So, I am going to allow it, but I strongly caution that it is up to you as members of the jury to determine whether Ms. Styles' testimony is at all probative on the issue and the weight and significance if any it has."

Before answering Angela took a long look at Sofia with her eyes frighteningly forlorn. "When I first met Sofia, she was very guarded, and she told me that we had to keep our relationship private; that we could not be seen together."

"Was that also the reason your relationship ended?'

"Yes, it was because...."

"Objection," Sharron shouted a second before it was too late, "Can we approach, your Honor?"

"I am going to ask the jury to leave."

Everyone else remained in their seats as the jury exited.

"Mr. Troutman," Judge Nicholsby began. "As much as you want to bring Victor Hushemi into this trial and prejudice Mrs. Hushemi, he is not here, and this is not a racketeering trial. Sofia Hushemi is charged with acting in concert in a hate crime involving attempted murder. And Victor Hushemi is not one of her co-defendants, as much as you wish he was."

Troutman, looking unhappy, replied, "I understand, your Honor."

The jury returned.

"Ms. Styles, without getting into any of the reasons, did there come a time when you and Sofia stopped seeing each other?"

"Yes, I had not seen her for more than ten years when I bumped into her at the park on the same day of the shooting."

"And did you see her after that?"

"Yes, a few days later, Sofia called and pleaded with me to meet her at Corteleine's coffee shop, which was our old haunt."

"And can you describe what happened or anything Sofia said when you met?"

Angela looked at Troutman and then directly at Sofia. She bowed her head. "Can I have a minute?" she asked the judge tearfully. She took a tissue from her purse and dabbed her eyes.

"What happened at Corteleine's?" Troutman asked again once Angela composed herself.

"Sofia admitted she was with the men who shot Sylvester Stanley."

Angela lowered her head. Sharron could feel Sofia shaking in the chair next to her.

"What exactly did Mrs. Hushemi say?" Troutman inquired.

Angela measured her words carefully, "She said that she believed Mr. Stanley took her ring. I asked her how she knew."

"And her reply?"

"I will never forget her words because they were so hurtful."

Sharron didn't object because doing so would only serve to further highlight the moment.

"Sofia said, 'Who else could have done it? It had to be the *zezak*."

Several jurors gasped.

"Had you ever heard that word before?"

"*Zezak*? Yes, I heard Sofia use it before. I looked it up. It's Albanian. It's as vile as the N-word. It's just as racist."

Several jurors noticeably cringed.

"Objection!"

"Overruled."

"Did Sofia say anything else?"

"I couldn't listen to another word. I stood up and stormed out of the restaurant."

"Thank you, Ms. Styles. I have no further questions."

Sharron requested a ten-minute recess to allow the tension in the courtroom to dissipate before beginning her cross-examination. As she and Sherman sat with Sofia in the conference room while Sharron again poured over the reports Troutman had e-mailed the night before, Sofia, drowning in despair, suddenly mumbled from her chair:

"She came to see me. Why do that if she hates me so?"

"What are you saying, Sofia?" Sharron gently inquired, trying to draw her out of her trance.

"Oh, God. Please forgive me, Angela," Sofia said, beginning to weep. "She came to see me, right before your uncle took me to speak to the Brooklyn district attorney. Edward called her and asked her to see me."

"My God, really?" Sherman was dumbfounded. "What did Angela say?"

"She sat with me. She told me she's never stopped thinking about me. That she would never want to see me harm myself. That she prayed for me."

"Anything else?"

"I was so happy to see her. Thinking that she might understand. Her visit gave me the strength to keep that meeting with the DA."

Sherman turned to Sharron. "Why didn't Troutman bring it up on direct? Why didn't he have Angela explain this subsequent meeting with Sofia? Even if he didn't like it he would want to explain it, not let me bring it up for the first time."

"Maybe Angela never told him," Sharron said. "Maybe she hid it. She was afraid of being reprimanded or something worse. What does she know about how he would have reacted?"

"I think you're right," Sherman glanced at his phone. "We better head back into the courtroom."

As Sharron rose to begin her cross-examination, she looked at Angela carefully. The way Angela returned her gaze, it almost seemed she could not determine whether Sharron was friend or foe. After recovering her composure for the remainder of Troutman's questioning, Angela's face was tight as a drum and her legs were locked around each other.

Sharron readied herself to embark on a cross-examination that was anathema to a defense attorney. Sofia had left her no choice but to shoot in the dark, embark on questions which she could only gamble would produce the right answers.

"Ms. Styles, you said you and Sofia were close for several years. Is that correct?"

"Yes. We had a very strong bond."

"Even shared confidences?"

"Yes."

"And provided emotional support for each other?"

"Yes, you can say that?"

"And Sofia told you how sheltered a life she led, correct?"

"Yes."

"And that she was married at a very young age?"

"Yes."

"An arranged marriage where she had no choice?"

"Yes."

"And her opinions and desires were not relevant?"

"Yes."

"Objection!" Troutman cried out. "There is no relevance to this line of questioning."

"I will allow it, but start getting to the point, Ms. Bernstein."

"Did Sofia also tell you she had to follow many rules and that her family, particularly her in-laws, wanted her to interact only with her own people and she asked to keep your friendship hidden from her family?"

"Yes, she did, more than once."

Sharron paused before posing a more treacherous question. "And you did that not only because you respected Sofia's concerns, but you also believed she did not share in those feelings, those prejudices?"

"Yes."

"In fact, all the time you and Sofia were so close, when you spent as much time together as possible for several years, isn't it correct that you never thought Sofia shared those prejudices?"

"Yes. It's why it was so hurtful to learn how wrong I was."

Troutman smiled at Angela's response.

Sharron furiously attempted to compute the plusses and minuses of her next series of questions.

"Ms. Styles, you testified that you and Sofia stopped seeing each other more than a decade ago?"

"Yes."

"And was that because of anything Sofia said or did?"

"No, absolutely not."

Angela's eyes clouded over, and Sofia's did as well.

"I loved Sofia, and I believed she loved me."

Sharron had struck oil.

"And you did not separate because you believed Sofia was prejudiced."

"Of course not."

"Ms. Styles, isn't it correct that it is only those things that transpired in Corteleine's after the shooting of Mr. Stanley that made you think differently?"

"*Only what transpired at Corteleine's?* It was the shooting! The crippling of Sylvester Stanley that made me think differently!"

Sharron bit her lip, disgusted with herself for undoing the progress she had made with such a loose question. She attempted to regroup. "I'm sorry, Ms. Styles. Of course, it was the shooting. The terrible shooting of Mr. Stanley. Sofia said she thought Mr. Stanley stole her ring. but isn't it correct that she only told you she was there? You never even gave her the chance to tell you what she did or exactly what happened?"

"She did not get into details."

"Or what the actions were of the other two men?"

"No."

"Or if she knew the two men were armed?"

"No."

"Or that she tried to stop the shooting?"

"No. Like I told you, we never got into details. After she said she was part of it, I refused to hear any more."

It was time to shock Troutman.

"Ms. Styles, a few days after you stormed out of Corteleine's, you went to see Sofia didn't you?"

"I did."

Troutman moved to the edge of his seat. Seeing his reaction, Sharron knew she hit paydirt, that Angela had never mentioned it to him.

"Did you tell Mr. Troutman you had gone to see Sofia?"

Angela nervously glanced at Troutman.

"I never told him."

"Because you thought it might have angered him?"

"I don't know what I thought. I received a phone call from Sofia's husband. In all the time I have known Sofia, he never called me before. He told me he was worried about Sofia, that she was in a bad state. And I thought maybe I could help."

"And you wanted to help her, correct?"

"Yes."

"You still cared for her?"

"Yes."

Sharron readied herself for Angela's unpredictable response to one more dangerously precarious question. "Ms. Styles, if you thought in your heart that Sofia was prejudiced, that she had hate for Black men, would you still have cared about her?"

"Objection, that's not an appropriate question." Troutman was desperate to slow Sharron's momentum.

"Overruled."

Angela lowered her head in her lap.

"Do you need a minute, Ms. Styles?" Judge Nicholsby asked.

Without responding to the Judge, Angela raised her head. "I have gone over that day in Corteleine's in my head a million times. I was so angry. I could not believe Sofia's words. I could not believe my ears when she admitted to being part of a shooting of another one of us for no other reason than the color of our skin. So, I don't know. I just don't know. Why did I go to see her? Why?" Angela's eyes filled with tears. "I guess, no matter what, despite it all, whatever she's done and even for whatever reason she did it, I love Sofia. I love Sofia. She needed me. I had to go. That's what I know."

"Thank you. I have no further questions."

Troutman bounded up.

"Ms. Styles, I want to ask you again about when you stopped seeing Sofia ten years ago. Can you tell us now, what was the reason for it?"

"Objection! This is outrageous, your Honor!" Sharron cried out.

Judge Nicholsby ordered counsel to approach the bench. Once out of earshot of the jury, the Judge continued in a hushed, stern voice: "What do you have to say for yourself, Mr. Troutman?"

"Ms. Bernstein opened the door, your Honor," Troutman said. "Her questioning of Ms. Styles about the break in their friendship having nothing to do with Sofia being prejudiced requires explanation. And Victor Hushemi is the explanation."

"That certainly raised my eyebrows when she embarked on that line of cross. You clearly opened the door, Ms. Bernstein."

Sharron was not oblivious to the risk but felt compelled to take it.

Before attempting an explanation, Judge Nicholsby cut her off. "I'm still not going to allow it. I don't want the possible reaction of the jury to the name of Victor Hushemi being the reason a conviction is reversed if Mrs. Hushemi is found guilty. If you request before summations that I instruct the jury not to speculate on the reason Angela and Sofia separated, I will do that. But my ruling stands. Move on to something else, Mr. Troutman."

Noticeably unhappy, Troutman walked back to the lectern. Sharron, having dodged the bullet, sat down, quicky flashing a smile at Sherman.

"At Corteleine's, only a few days after Sylvester Stanley was shot, did Sofia Hushemi tell you she was the reason he was attacked?"

"I guess so," Angela replied in a low monotone voice.

"And that it happened because she lost her ring, correct?"

"Yes."

"And that the Black man stole it, did she level that accusation?"

After a few seconds of silence, Angela answered, "She said words to that effect."

"And did she say, 'The *zezak* took it. Who else?'"

Angela once again bowed her head and sighed deeply before responding, "I'm afraid she did. She used those words."

"Did Sofia ever tell you she tried to stop it?"

It was the same question Sharron asked Angela to show she never gave Sofia a chance to explain that she'd tried to prevent the shooting, but Troutman's implication and tone were the exact opposite.

"Objection! Mrs. Hushemi was not even provided an opportunity to tell Ms. Styles she tried to prevent the shooting. The question is misleading the jury."

"Given your cross-examination, I am going to allow it."

"She never mentioned trying to stop it. Or that the two men acted on their own. But I never really gave her the chance. I was too angry."

"But Sofia admitted she was responsible for the shooting."

"Well, yes, she blamed herself, if that's what you mean."

"Are you a mind reader, Ms. Styles?"

"Excuse me?"

"Are you a mind reader, Ms. Styles?"

"Objection!"

"I will withdraw the question," Troutman responded. "Can you look into a person's mind, Ms. Styles?"

"No."

"A person's heart?"

Before Sharron could object, Angela replied, "How can anyone know someone's innermost feelings? You can only judge a person by their behavior. Their words and actions."

"Exactly. Thank you, Ms. Styles. I have no more questions."

Angela stepped down from the witness stand. As she passed between the prosecution and defense tables, her eyes locked with Sophia's for a fleeting moment. With tear-filled eyes, and in clear view of the jury, Sofia mouthed the words, "I'm sorry. I love you."

The sincerity of Sofia's gesture achieved far more than any lawyer's questions.

Fifty-One

March 24, 2019
Manhattan

Following a parade of police and expert witnesses who added little if anything to their case, the prosecution rested. Staring out her office windows at the East River, the Sunday before beginning the defense case, Sharron listened to her favorite investigator confirm her suspicions. Given that Sofia refused to provide any details about her relationship with Angela, Sharron knew Leroy Martin would uncover the truth.

Leroy had opened his own agency after 18 years with the FBI and there was nobody like him. Only five six, slightly paunchy, gray hair sprinkling the top of his scalp and white, red face, he loved seeing people's expressions when they met him for the first time. Everyone assumed Leroy was black. With large, oversized glasses adorning his elementary school teacher's face, he hardly looked the part of a veteran Federal law enforcement agent. Yet, Leroy had contacts in the darkest corners of organized crime and people of every ethnicity trusted that what they confided in him would not come back to haunt them.

Leroy learned all about Angela being terrorized by one of Victor's men from the horse's mouth. Troutman either violated his discovery obligations by never turning over any prior statements from Angela which mentioned it, or she kept silent on her own. The reasons were of no immediate concern. Sharron was instead hell-bent on calling Victor as a surprise defense witness. The move would not simply catch Troutman completely off guard, it could assure Sofia's acquittal. She wanted to call Victor to explain why Angela stopped seeing Sofia and to admit that he had sent someone to tell her the relationship had to end. That when he saw Sofia becoming too close to Angela, he felt he had to put his foot down.

Sharron called Sherman shortly after Leroy left and arranged for her uncle to immediately come to the office and to have Sofia and Victor arrive an hour later. The moment Sherman stepped off the elevator, despite the kiss on his cheek, he knew something was amiss. Sharron remained silent as they walked the corridor to her spacious office. Instead of sitting behind her glass desk, she sat closely alongside Sherman on a leather couch. After explaining her strategy, she insisted that having Victor testify would mean that Sherman needed to get off the case.

"Uncle David, I should have taken it over completely from the start. It was stupidly short-sighted of both of us not to realize it. I'm calling Victor, let him take the fifth if he has to, but I'm calling him."

Sherman sighed. "You're right, but Victor is more of a problem than I am. And Judge Nicholsby will be none too pleased when we tell him."

"The Judge is the least of our problems. Let's just handle your client when he gets here. If you need time with him alone, there are plenty of empty offices."

Chaperoning Sofia into the office, Victor dropped his right arm from her side to direct her to sit on a chair at the conference table while he took the office armchair. Sofia tried to look brave in Victor's company, but she was obviously worn down by all the stress. Victor looked as regal as ever, showing no signs of worry over the fate of his sister-in-law.

Sharron wasted no time confronting Victor.

Victor glared at Sherman. "Have you both lost your fucking minds? We all agreed that I shouldn't step foot anywhere near the courthouse. We even agreed that Tomas and Karina should stay away from the trial to do everything possible to keep my name out of the minds of the jury."

Without raising her tone, Sharron continued, "Things have changed Mr. Hushemi. The jury must hear from you. Despite my cross-examination, there's no telling the impact of Angela's testimony on the jury. It could prove fatal. But there's a way around it if you testify. I need you to explain why Angela and Sofia had to stop seeing each other. It was because you sent someone to deliver the message that the relationship had to end. You didn't tell them to do anything else, to threaten her in any way, am I right Mr. Hushemi?"

"Don't insult me with such a stupid insinuation."

"Of course, you didn't. But now rather than worrying about Troutman wielding your name as a sword, we can use it as a shield. Once the jury learns that Sofia was defying you, and even risked your disapproval by seeing Angela, nobody will think she's a racist."

"Stop fooling yourself Bernstein," Victor stood, pointing his finger. "You know my testimony won't help. The jury won't believe a word I say. And there is nothing in the world that bastard Troutman would desire more than having me on a witness stand. Manipulating my words, maneuvering into something that has nothing to do with the case, and hitting me with at least a perjury charge."

He turned to Sherman. "You're getting old. How can you be part of this? What the two of you are talking about makes no sense. And how dare you make Sofia think otherwise?"

"I'm sorry if you don't like it. But for once it's not your ass on the line. It's your sister-in-law," Sharron bravely responded. "There's simply no better option. Even with Novack and Mikhail dead and gone, we haven't been able to get anyone who'll testify about their racist beliefs and propensity for violence. Your testimony is essential. And if any line of cross-examination by Troutman touches on subjects that concern you, just claim the Fifth. David will be there. He'll make sure you don't incriminate yourself. He's agreed, he will no longer represent Sofia."

Victor's brown and blue eyes cut through Sharron only to have her fearlessly return his look with a dark stare of her own.

"Let me ask you this, Sherman. If you were advising only me, and this wasn't Sofia, would you allow me to take the stand?"

"Stop it, Victor. You know I wouldn't. But it is Sofia and she's on trial for her life."

Victor abruptly turned to Sofia. "If you want me to testify, my dear, regardless of the consequences for me, you know I will."

Sofia did not hesitate. "This is my case, not Victor's, and the only one who needs to testify is me," she said. "I do not want Victor to testify. After all he has done for me, this is not his problem. I'm going to explain everything. I'm not a racist. I'm proud and blessed to know Angela. The jury will hear all this from me and nobody else."

"I don't like this, not one bit," Sharron responded, keeping her eyes squarely on Victor. "The judge is never going to permit Sofia to explain why Angela stopped seeing her after keeping the issue out of the case. We can only bring it in through Victor. It's going to be hard enough for Sofia to stand up to Troutman on cross-examination. If Angela never testified it would be one thing. I was confident I could win the case with Sofia's testimony alone. Now we need more."

The tension in the room took a frightening turn.

"Who the fuck do you think you are?" Victor moved uncomfortably close to Sharron. "You may be the darling of the media Bernstein, but you're nobody as far as I'm concerned. If Sofia wants me to testify I will, but then and only then."

"Sofia, you must make this request of your brother-in-law," Sharron implored, unfazed by Victor. "Your life depends on it."

Sofia shook her head over and over, finally burying her face in her lap. Victor sat back in his armchair, silent and impassive. Sharron wrapped her arm around Sofia and whispered to Victor, "Tough man. Some tough man. You're all the same in the end, aren't you?"

Sherman held his index finger to his lips, now genuinely anxious for Sharron's safety.

Speaking in as calm and soft a voice as possible, refusing any longer to even look at Victor, Sharron comforted Sofia, realizing it was folly to continue to pressure her. "Sofia, I think it would be much better if your brother-in-law testified, but maybe you're right. Your acquittal may very well depend on your winning the jury over."

Fifty-Two

March 25, 2019
United States Eastern District Court
Brooklyn

After saying a tearful goodbye to Ilka, Sofia took her seat in Sharron's BMW to drive to the courthouse. Sharron nodded her approval of the outfit Sofia wore under her overcoat, a navy blue cardigan, a matching skirt that hung past her knees and a white blouse.

Sharron and Sherman had spent countless hours the night before relentlessly subjecting Sofia to cross-examination in preparation for her testimony. Arriving two hours early, only Sherman had a desire for some refreshment. He sipped coffee from a thermos while Sharron and Sofia sat at the defense table in the empty courtroom. Sharron occasionally put her arm around Sofia and engaged in hushed small talk.

After what seemed an eternity, the Judge came out from the back entrance to the courtroom, took his seat on the bench, the packed courtroom quieted, and the jury was summoned. The Judge's inquiry as to whether there were any matters which needed to be addressed before the trial resumed was met by silence and the stage was set for Sofia.

Sharron, wearing a black halo, Saks Fifth Avenue, Jackie O three-quarter dress, captivating the jury even before a word was spoken, rose from her chair. "The defense calls Sofia Hushemi to the stand."

Sharron walked Sofia through her testimony with Sofia growing increasingly agitated the closer she got to the shooting.

"The second I sat in the back seat of Novack's car, I started to have regrets. I told them we should just go back home. They told me to be quiet and let them handle things. I was scared. I didn't know what to do at that point."

"Did there come a time when you saw Mr. Stanley?"

Sofia swallowed hard. "Yes. As we were driving up towards the top of the park. I saw a jogger who I thought might be Mr. Stanley but I wasn't sure because he had worn a hood before. I also was too scared to say anything. I just wanted to leave. Novack and Mikhail started trailing him. I kept telling them we should go, and they refused to listen, instead they pulled in front of him. Mr. Stanley looked up and at that point, I was sure it was him."

Several jurors leaned forward in their seats. Sofia's voice quivered with emotion. "The boys kept shouting at me. I ended up admitting it was him, but I begged the boys just to talk to Mr. Stanley. Nothing more. I swear nothing more."

Reliving the horror, Sofia started trembling. Judge Nicholsby was ready to order a recess, but also knew the re-telling would never get any easier. Seeing the jury riveted in anticipation, Sharron decided no matter how painful, she wanted to keep things going.

Sofia's voice dropped so low, Judge Nicholsby gently asked her to try and speak louder. Sharron slowed down the pace of her questions while showing the video. Creeping up to the shooting, Sofia's anxiety became contagious, consuming everyone in the courtroom as the vile taunts of the two Serbian boys were hurled at Sylvester, and their guns drawn.

"You testified you were watching Novack and Mikhail from behind a tree so as not to be seen by anyone?"

"Yes, Novack and Mikhail were close to Sylvester, only a few feet from him. You can see on the video, the second the guns were drawn and pointed, I immediately ran to Sylvester and tried to stop it."

Sofia's eyes bulged, suddenly she found herself transplanted back in time. "He is not the one! He's not the one! He's not the one!" her screams rang out before she buried her head, weeping.

"You lying bitch!" a female spectator yelled from the back of the courtroom.

Having no option, Judge Nicholsby halted the proceedings a moment before everything spun out of control. He ordered a fifteen-minute recess to allow Sofia to gather herself, and to ensure calm. After the jury filed out, the Judge requested Sofia remain on the witness stand as she was in the middle of her testimony. The courtroom was ominously silent while Sofia bravely regrouped.

With tears still visible in her eyes, Sofia told Judge Nicholsby she felt ready to continue. Sharron ran the video through the rest of the shooting and had Sofia describe in detail going over to Sylvester and kneeling over him.

"Please tell the jury what you were trying to do at this point."

"I don't know, Sofia said, her voice breaking, I was just hoping I could do something to help Sylvester, to stop the bleeding or maybe help his breathing. But then I heard the police and ambulance sirens, and I just became so scared, I ran away. I…I guess I panicked."

Sharron gave Sofia a moment to wipe away some more tears and then asked,

"Did you learn what happened to Novack and Mikhail?"

"Yes," Sofia replied with her voice breaking. "A few weeks after all three of us were charged by Mr. Troutman, they were found dead. If those two boys were alive, they would tell you I tried to stop the shooting."

"Objection!" Troutman rose out of his chair.

Judge Nicholsby was irate. "Ms. Bernstein this is the second time, there better not be a third. The testimony is stricken from the record and the jury is to disregard it completely. Novak and Mikhail are not on trial in this courtroom and their whereabouts have nothing to do with the guilt or innocence of Mrs. Hushemi. And you are not to speculate about what they may or may not have said if they were witnesses at this trial."

Sharron responded with a phony apology. The look on Judge Nicholsby's face showed that he did not accept it. He turned again to the jury to inquire if anyone felt they would have trouble disregarding Sofia's mention of the boys' death. When nobody raised a hand, Sharron resumed her questioning.

"Mrs. Hushemi, are you certain you never said or did anything to encourage or assist Novack in the shooting of Sylvester Stanley?"

"I tried everything possible to stop the shooting. That is the absolute truth. I'll never forgive myself for asking Novack and Mikhail for help. If I had never spoken to them, none of this would have happened. I never meant for any harm to come to Sylvester."

Judge Nicholsbly spoke as Sofia began crying again, "Mrs. Hushemi, I know this is extraordinarily emotional. Would you like another recess?"

Sofia declined.

After answering a few background questions about how and when she met Angela and how close they became, Sharron inquired, "Mrs. Hushemi, there came a time when you and Angela Styles stopped seeing each other, correct?

Sofia's eyes widened.

"Yes," Sofia's response was barely audible.

"Was that because of anything you or she did?"

"No."

"So, why, after being so close, did you and Ms. Styles have such a complete falling out?"

Now it was Troutman who objected.

As counsel huddled at a sidebar, Judge Nicholsby sternly addressed Sharron. "I have no idea why you are bringing this up now, but I am not going to allow it. I will not permit you to bring it out on your terms. If you have a witness other than Mrs. Hushemi who could shed some light on it for the jury, it might be different. But I will not permit Mrs. Hushemi's version of the breakup to come in when Ms. Styles was not permitted to give her point of view."

Disappointed, but not surprised at the ruling, Sharron moved on. "Mrs. Hushemi, you used the Albanian word *zezak* when you spoke to Ms. Styles at the coffee shop. What does that mean?"

"It's a word I heard growing up in Albania used to describe Black people. My husband's family uses the word. I never even thought about it until one day Angela told me it didn't sound right. I then looked into it and learned it is not a nice word. I stopped using it, but I guess that day at Corteleine's, with all the stress, it slipped out before I could take it back. I'm ashamed I used it."

"And how about what Ms. Styles said about your presuming Mr. Stanley robbed you?"

"Ms. Bernstein, I couldn't think or talk straight that day at Corteleine's. I intended to explain everything to Angela, to tell her how terrified I was thinking my wedding ring was stolen, only to discover it was never even lost, that it fell off in the back of my husband's wheelchair. But what I wanted most, what I needed most was for her to understand that I had tried to prevent the shooting. But before I could explain everything to Angela, she became so upset that she stormed away. I don't blame her. Just like I don't blame Angela for testifying here at the trial."

As Sofia laid her head in her lap, a young African American man in the third row jumped up from his seat and screamed, "You racist lying bitch, you won't fool this jury!"

Judge Nicholsby immediately ordered him out of the courtroom. Others murmured in approval.

"Quiet down, everyone!" the Judge commanded. The Judge again turned to the jury and advised them that they must not consider anything other than the evidence or lack of evidence in the case and must not be distracted by outbursts.

At a bench conference, outside the hearing of the jury, Sharron made a motion for a mistrial to protect the record but as expected it was denied. "No matter how many times this case is tried, because of the nature of the charges and its notoriety, there will always be these sorts of problems, emotions intruding from both sides of the table. I am confident that we have a jury that will properly decide the case."

Despite the outcry, Sofia's testimony exceeded Sharron and Sherman's expectations. Her answers went exactly the way they had in their practice session. The pitch of Sophia's voice and the fact that she had to stop at times to pull herself together were a sure bet to capture the jury's sympathy and understanding.

Troutman smugly rose thinking otherwise.

"Mrs. Hushemi, before you came to this country had you ever met a person of color?"

"Objection!"

"No, I will allow it. As I have previously ruled, the issue of Ms. Hushemi's opinions on race is an essential element of the charged offense."

"In Albania, I did not know anyone who was Black."

"Other than Ms. Styles, did you have any other African American friends or acquaintances?"

"Unfortunately, I wish I had but other than meeting a few of Angela's friends, I never had an opportunity to do so."

"Any *male* Black friends?"

"I was fearful of my family's reaction, not my husband, but other members of his family. So even my relationship with Angela was kept private and left little opportunity to socialize with others."

Troutman was so cool, a textbook prosecutor skilled at interrogating a witness with objective questions wrapped in a righteous tone.

"Let's talk about your meeting with Angela the day after the shooting. Mrs. Hushemi, you testified that the word *zezak* came out of your mouth without your realizing it was reprehensible. Are you telling this jury that you had no idea until you researched it, that *zezak* is as bad a word in Albanian as using the awful English label 'nigger' to describe an African American?"

"Honestly, I do not even understand all this fuss about names for people of color. In my neighborhood, I hear the word nigger used all the time by young Blacks to describe their friends."

"So, you are telling the jury that you believe there is nothing wrong with calling a man of color a nigger?"

"Objection, your Honor. That is not what Mrs. Hushemi said. He is twisting her words."

"Overruled."

"I have heard my family members use both *zezak* and nigger often to describe Black men and never thought much about it. But after I saw how much it upset Angela, I researched the word *zezak* and dropped it."

There was no way Sofia could acceptably reply to questions of this nature. Sharron and Sherman rehearsed a hundred different options and concluded there was really nothing to be gained from having Sofia deliver anything other than a candid response. Sofia's answers, however, were noticeably alienating members of the jury, even causing several noticeable discomforts.

Troutman shifted gears, feeling the time was right to show some animosity towards Sofia "Mrs. Hushemi, you've told us all about what Novack and Mikhail did and how you were just dragged along for the ride."

"Ask a question, don't make speeches, Mr. Troutman," Judge Nicholsby admonished.

"When Novack and Mikhail whipped out their weapons, it was no surprise to you, was it?" Troutman asked with escalating sarcasm.

"Surprised? I was so shocked my heart stopped."

"Are you trying to tell this jury that you did not know they were armed?"

"If I knew they had guns I never would have gotten in the car with them."

"You asked for their help to recover the irreplaceable ring you lost?"

"Yes, that is true."

"And you knew they were two men who were hired to maintain order by your brother-in-law, Victor Hushemi?"

"Objection, irrelevant."

"Overruled," Judge Nicholsby said, strangely overlooking his prior insistence that not even a hint of Victor's involvement should come into the case.

"They told me when I saw them earlier at the Albanian Festival that they were hired by my brother-in-law to act as security guards."

"And how did you think they were going to get your ring back from a man you presumed stole it, when it was never taken by anyone. Right?

Sofia bowed her head and tearfully whispered, "Edward found my ring in his wheelchair after the shooting."

"And what did you expect Novak and Mikhail to do, just calmly ask Sylvester if he stole it?"

"I don't know," Sofia answered, anxiously putting her right hand to the side of her head and gently rubbing her temple. "I was hoping they would talk to him and see if he had it."

"Really, Mrs. Hushemi? You knew they were two men who did a lot more than talk. You knew they were armed and would use their weapons if they had to when they confronted Sylvester Stanley."

"Objection! There is no basis for such questions."

"Overruled."

"I was shocked that they were armed. I will say it again, I never would have gotten into Novack's vehicle if I thought they were carrying weapons. Never."

"You do not really expect this jury to believe that do you, Mrs. Hushemi?"

"Mr. Troutman!" the judge reprimanded. "Ask a question and stop the theatrics."

"You hid behind a tree for several minutes and heard the racial epithets Novack and Mikhail directed at Sylvester, correct?"

"Yes, it was awful."

"But at first you did nothing. Is that correct?"

"I didn't know what to do, I was scared. I kept trying to think what to do."

"And what you did was race out from behind the tree towards Novack after he drew his weapon?"

"Yes, I rushed to Sylvester, I looked right at him, trying to make him see that I was coming to his aid. I pointed and screamed to try and stop everything, that he was not the one."

"Mrs. Hushemi, isn't it correct that upon seeing you come out from behind the tree, Novack and Mikhail turned towards you and lowered their weapons?"

"My God, they were armed, and they pointed their guns not only at Mr. Stanley but other people as well. My mind was on stopping them. My mind was on saving Sylvester, not hurting him. Rushing to his aid. Whether or not they put the guns at their side for a second, I have no idea."

"You didn't notice that Novack and Mikhail were paying attention to you, awaiting orders from you?"

"Paying attention to me? That was exactly what I was trying to get them to do."

You can prepare a witness forever but it's never the same once they take the stand in the courtroom. Sofia was beginning to wriggle in her seat.

"Lowering their guns was not listening to you, Mrs. Hushemi?"

"I never saw that."

"Did you never see it, or did that mean they were *not* listening to you?"

"That's not fair, you are twisting things."

"Twisting things? You were sitting here listening to the testimony of Mr. Stanley and Professor Marvel, and you saw the video. Please now Mrs. Hushemi, you know, you saw they lowered their guns."

"Objection," Sharron cried out.

"Sustained. Mr. Troutman, rephrase the question."

"Mrs. Hushemi, I ask you again, didn't you see both Novack and Mikhail put down their weapons at the sight of you?"

"I don't recall."

"You don't recall? How many times have you sat here this past week and seen the video?"

"Objection."

"Overruled."

"Several times."

"How can you not remember?"

"I don't know."

Sharron was thinking about requesting a recess but knew Judge Nicholsby would not allow it.

"Mrs. Hushemi, you ran out from behind the tree. Correct?"

"Yes."

"Novack noticed you running."

"He did."

"And so did Mikhail. You saw both of them turn and look at you?"

"I did. Yes, I did."

"But you never saw them lower their weapons? How could you not see that?"

"Objection! Objection!"

"Overruled."

"Sharron," Sherman called out louder than he should have, desperately imploring his niece to take some action.

"Judge, can we have a short recess?" Sharron pleaded. "Mrs. Hushemi is becoming too upset. She needs a break."

"No, we will continue, it will be better for everyone to conclude the cross-examination."

"I didn't see it," Sofia said, her voice shaking, wringing her hands in her lap.

Troutman smelled blood.

"They lowered their weapons. Put them down the moment they saw you, isn't that what happened?"

"Objection!"

"Overruled.

"I don't know. I keep trying to tell you. I don't know."

"Mrs. Hushemi, they lowered them waiting for you to tell them what to do. Isn't that correct?"

"What? No, no, no..."

"Mrs. Hushemi, they put their weapons at their side and didn't raise them again until you ordered them to shoot, am I correct?"

"Oh my God... no!"

"I ask you again. And I ask you to keep in mind we all saw the video. You ordered, 'Shoot,' more than shoot, your ordered, 'Shoot his eyes,' and they turned back, raised their weapons, Novack aimed right at Sylvester's eyes and fired? Isn't that what really happened? Isn't it?"

"Objection! Your Honor!"

"Overruled."

"No, no," Sofia whimpered.

"You said, 'Eyes! Shoot his eyes!"

"No! No of course not!"

"On *your* command!"

"No, I said, 'He's not the one.' To stop Novack, to save Sylvester."

"Mrs. Hushemi, do you need to look at the video again? You said, 'Eyes. Shoot his eyes. Shoot his head off his body!' Isn't that right?"

"Objection!"

"Overruled."

Sharron and Sherman looked at each other, astonished that Judge Nicholsby was permitting Troutman to virtually assault Sofia.

"No! I said, 'He is not the one.'"

"Isn't it correct that you said, 'Shoot! You shouted, 'Shoot! Shoot!'"

"I did not. I swear under the Kanun I did not."

"You gave that order."

"No."

"You must put a stop to this, your Honor!" Sharron pleaded.

"'Eyes! Eyes shoot his eyes. Shoot poor Sylvester right between the eyes.' Isn't that what you said, Mrs. Hushemi?! Sylvester heard it before he was unmercifully gunned down!"

"Please, Judge," Sharron cried out.

Suddenly, Sofia shot up out of her chair screaming.

"AI NUK ESHTE AI! AI NUK ESHTE AI! AI NUK ESHTE AI!"

The courtroom fell completely silent as Sofia's words bounced off the walls.

"Oh my God," Sofia continued in a voice that instantly lowered to almost a whisper. "This is what must have happened the day of the shooting. That is why Sylvester and the professor think I yelled 'Eyes. Shoot his eyes.' *Ai* sounded like eyes. Nuk *eshte* must have sounded like 'shoot.' Until this moment, I had forgotten.

"Mrs. Hushemi, what did you say?"

"I'm sorry. I just spoke in Albanian. *Ai Nuk Eshte Ai* is Albanian for he's not the one. It must be what I screamed that day. I must have spoken Albanian."

Sharron asked for a sidebar and argued that it was unfair not to grant a recess to permit Sofia to collect herself. Hiding that she would be oblivious to any admonition not to speak to Sofia during her cross-examination, Sharron longed for a recess to devise a strategy consistent with Sofia's defense. Judge Nicholsby ruled against it.

After countless hours of preparation, Sofia found herself being thrown to the wolves.

Troutman narrowed his eyes,

"Mrs. Hushemi, you recall your direct testimony, you insisted you said, in English, 'He is not the one.'"

"Yes, I just remembered now that I said, '*Ai Nuk Eshte Ai.*'"

"Never said that Albanian word that sounds like 'shoot'?"

"No, because I did not remember."

"Mrs. Hushemi, you spoke to the police and the Brooklyn district attorney's office, isn't that correct?"

"Yes."

"Accompanied by your attorney?

"Yes."

"And you swore to tell the truth just like here in the courtroom?"

"Yes."

"And you told them that you tried to stop the shooting by yelling, 'He's not the one.' Correct?"

"Yes."

"In English?"

"I do not know how many times I have to say this, that was what I thought, I didn't realize I spoke in Albanian until just now when you questioned me."

"But, Mrs. Hushemi, that meeting with the local authorities, that took place only a week or so after the shooting not almost a year later."

"That is true, Mr. Troutman, but, again, I never realized my speaking in Albanian until now."

"Mrs. Hushemi, aren't you changing your testimony now to use Albanian words with an innocent meaning, isn't that what this convenient return of memory is all about after hearing the testimony of Sylvester?"

"No, Mr. Troutman, I am speaking the truth."

"Speaking the truth when, Mrs. Hushemi? Now or before?"

"Objection."

"Yes, sustained," Judge Nicholsby ruled. "Move on, Mr. Troutman."

"Let's talk some more about your meeting with Ms. Styles after the shooting. Mrs. Hushemi, you testified that the word *zezak* came out of your mouth before you realized it. Is that because sometimes words come out of your mouth without thinking and other times it's with a lot of thought?"

"Objection."

"Overruled."

"I don't understand your question. I guess it depends on the circumstances."

"And, under oath in a courtroom, is that a time for answers without thinking or responses with careful thought behind them?"

Sofia was trying her best not to fall apart.

"In a courtroom, I want to carefully think about my answers and tell the truth."

"So, your Albanian words which came out a few moments ago during my questioning, and were never said before, were the result of careful pre-meditation, not some spontaneous utterance?"

"Objection, your Honor. Mr. Troutman isn't asking questions; he is testifying with highly prejudicial innuendo."

"No, I will allow it."

"I explained everything, Mr. Troutman. That's not right what you are doing. The stress of your interrogation triggered my native tongue as well as my realizing for the first time that's what I shouted. I can only hope that can be understood."

Could it get any worse? Sharron turned for a moment to see Sherman's distraught face.

"You have spent the past week hearing the testimony of Sylvester Stanley and Professor Conrad Marvel, correct?

"Yes."

"And you heard them testify they heard you yell, 'Shoot.' Not simply shoot, you heard Sylvester testify you said to shoot his eyes. Correct?"

"Yes."

"And knowing if you chose to take the witness stand, you would be testifying that you said something very different."

"Yes."

"And you are aware that 'he is not the one' sounds nothing like 'shoot.' Wouldn't that be fair to say?"

"Objection."

"Overruled."

"I guess you are right."

"And your Albanian phrase, what is it? *Nuk Eshte Ai* in English means he is not the one and conveniently resembles the sound of the precise command to shoot Sylvester in the eyes."

"Well, it does to some extent. You are right about that."

"And isn't that why after hearing the testimony of Mr. Stanley and the professor, you created this version? That you realized it was a far better way to sell your story to the jury?"

"Objection! The question is totally improper."

"Overruled."

Judge Nicholsby was providing Sofia with no room to breathe.

"Mr. Troutman, if I wanted to do something like that, if I wanted to lie, I would have claimed that I said, 'Don't shoot.' That would have been the easy thing to do if I was going to lie."

"Very clever, Mrs. Hushemi."

"Objection!"

"You know better, Mr. Troutman," Judge Nicholsby scolded.

"When you and your attorney spoke to Detective Rodriguez and Assistant District Attorney Bridges and you informed them you shouted, 'He is not the one.' You did not claim you yelled, 'Don't shoot.'"

"Yes, yes."

"So, you are kind of stuck, aren't you? And that's why you had to come up with this Albanian rendition?"

"Objection! Sheer harassment of Mrs. Hushemi."

"Overruled."

"I don't know what you are saying. I am here to testify and tell no lies. That's why I am here. I would never tell lies. It would be a sin under the Kanun, which is the highest authority. I live by the Kanun."

"Really, you would not create an Albanian story to save yourself from life imprisonment?"

"Objection."

"Sustained, now you have gone too far Mr. Troutman, just finish up. NOW!"

"Mrs. Hushemi, you testified on your direct examination that when you went over to Mr. Stanley after he had been shot, you were hoping to provide aid?

"Yes"

"Did you?"

"No." Sofia looked down into her lap. "As I said, before I could think of how to help. I heard the sirens and I panicked and ran."

"Wasn't the real reason you went over to Sylvester to see if your orders had been successfully carried out?"

"No, it was because I was horrified by what those boys did to Mr. Stanley and ran to his aid."

Troutman's open-ended question was a dreadful unnecessary reach by the seasoned prosecutor. The look in Sofia's eyes and the anguish reflected on her face when she responded resonated powerfully with the jury. After all he had accomplished on his cross, Troutman couldn't believe his stupidity. He quickly switched gears.

"Ms. Hushemi, you place a high value on speaking the truth."

"More than high value, Mr. Troutman. It's a solemn oath I must live up to under the Kanun."

"In a courtroom or everywhere?"

"The place does not matter. Swearing to tell the truth is a solemn undertaking."

"Mrs. Hushemi, isn't it correct you would withhold the truth and tell falsehoods to protect a family member from justice. Specifically, your brother-in-law, Victor?"

"Absolutely not."

"Objection!"

"Sit down, Mr. Troutman. Your cross-examination is finished." Turning to the jury, Judge Nicholsby instructed them to strike from their minds his last questions and told the panel, "They never should have been asked."

"Goddamn Troutman," Sharron muttered under her breath. One way or the other Sharron always felt the specter of Victor was going to make its way into the minds of one or more jurors. Which was why it was essential to do it on her terms.

On re-direct, rather than ask for the break, which was what she desperately desired earlier, Sharron simply had Sofia tell the jury that her upbringing instilled a duty to always tell the truth and she would never lie under oath. That her recalling she spoke Albanian was no tactic. Sharron concluded by providing Sofia an opportunity to testify spontaneously and from the heart about her beliefs.

Breathing deeply, Sofia testified. "There is not a hateful bone in my body towards people of color or who are from a different race or religion. There was nothing in my words at Corteleine's or at any other time which should be exaggerated to mean otherwise. Despite what happened at Corteleine's, my relationship with Angela proves it. I love Angela. I have said over and over that I will never forgive myself for what Novack and Mikhail did to Sylvester. I am no racist. I swear by the Kanun that I am not."

A court officer helped Sofia back to the defense table. She placed both hands on it to keep from collapsing, and murmured, "I'm sorry. I'm sorry. God, I'm so sorry."

Fifty-Three

March 26, 2019
United States Eastern District Court
Brooklyn

There was a buzz in the air to rival the seventh game of a Subway World Series. It was like a tin of sardines in the courtroom for the closing arguments. Reporters were permitted to fill the entire second row behind both counsel's tables. Spectators unable to find seats were allowed to stand against the back wall.

In the back corner of the courtroom, with dark sunglasses hiding her face, Sofia caught a glimpse of Angela. To the left of the prosecution's table, Troutman huddled with his team of agents and paralegals. Sylvester and his family were seated directly behind them, surrounded by two rows of Troutman's fellow prosecutors lending their support. Professor Marvel, socially distanced, sat in the adjacent row. Also standing in the back corner, opposite Angela, wearing tinted shades and a gray suit was special Agent Dan Ford.

"Mom," a young voice rang out.

Sofia's eyes locked on Ilka standing directly behind her with Edward in the first row.

"Don't be mad," Ilka said. "We had to come."

Sofia's eyes went wet with tears before she pulled Ilka into a passionate hug.

"I love you, Mom." Ilka sobbed into her shoulder.

Sofia was even more startled by Edward's presence, sitting next to Tomas and Karina. After Sylvester's testimony, they both agreed it would not help either one of them if he forced himself to continue to attend the trial. Edward's deep brown eyes never looked so handsome, as court officers allowed Sofia to embrace him, and he whispered optimistic words of comfort. Even though the case had ended, with the jury yet to commence deliberations, Victor kept his distance.

Court officers tried their best to keep the noise down, but it took Judge Nicholby's arrival to bring a jittery silence. "I would like to thank everyone who has attended this long and difficult proceeding for their conduct and patience. We have had a few disruptions but, for the most part, everyone has kept their emotions in check. We need to keep it that way."

Troutman rose to deliver his summation first. After a few prefatory remarks, he launched into began his argument. "What happened in the park was not some spontaneous encounter. Sofia recruited two young men who were more than happy to do her bidding. And when Novack hesitated, as shocking and horrifying as it is to believe, Sofia looked into Sylvester's eyes and ordered Novack to shoot them out of his head. A vile violent racist command that shocks the conscience."

Sharron overlooked the improper oratory.

"That is what lines up with all the facts and circumstances. Sylvester Stanley was the defenseless victim of Mrs. Huhsemi's hatred and Professor Marvel saw and confirmed it. The video captured it all in real-time."

After dissecting the trial record in his favor, Troutman concluded: "Members of the jury, I respectfully ask you to use your common sense and to look at the evidence in its entirety, which is all you need to arrive at a just verdict. Thank you."

Sharron stood in the stellar turquoise three-piece outfit she reserved for closing arguments, exuding calm confidence.

"Mr. Troutman insists the jury has to choose between truth and intentional falsehood. Whether both Mr. Stanley and Professor Marvel are telling the truth, or Mrs. Hushemi. But the real issue is whether Mr. Stanley and the professor testified as to what they felt in the heat of the moment and emotionally heard rather than what they actually heard. Not that they knowingly perjured themselves to secure a guilty verdict. Mr. Stanley is understandably seeking retribution for what he has suffered and that is why in his heart he believes he heard Sophia yell the frightening words, 'Shoot his eyes.' But his memory of such words did not even exist until months later. And it was a recollection encouraged, reinforced, and, I would go so far as to say, manipulated from his memory by the government."

"Objection," Troutman cried out.

"Ms. Bernstein's words and opinions are not evidence," Judge Nichosby instructed. "The evidence and the facts, are to be determined by you, the jury, and the jury alone."

Without missing a beat, Sharron continued, "The same goes for the government, as Mr. Troutman has thrown some wild accusations/allegations around this courtroom. Simply carefully examine the evidence and see if it does not support my contentions. Professor Marvel first came on the scene when guns were already drawn. He was far away when Mrs. Hushemi ran out from behind a tree. Reluctantly, the professor had to concede during his cross-examination that his certainty came about not only months later, but only after Mr. Stanley recalled that he heard the word shoot. Isn't this newly discovered recollection by Professor Marvel a *marvel* in itself? I doubt it.

"The Professor's memory is the product of fanciful thinking, a memory in support of a beloved friend who has been a victim of an unmerciful crime of hatred. But the haters were not Sofia Hushemi, they were Novack Lukic and Mikhail Markovic. How can you possibly be comfortable concluding that the damning word he put in Mrs. Hushemi's mouth was what he heard rather than what he wanted to hear?

"Sofia tried to prevent the shooting, not cause it. And her Albanian words to an American listener sounded remarkably like the English words, 'Eyes, shoot his eyes.' If Mrs. Hushemi was going to stretch the truth or contrive a self-serving story, would she have waited until being under the duress of cross-examination to create such a version of events? She would have to be a genius and a conniving, unprincipled veteran of the courtroom to do such a thing.

"Mr. Troutman's contention that Mrs. Hushemi blurted out her words in Albanian as a master strategy is preposterous. And why would she even think it would be helpful to testify that she spoke Albanian rather than simply remain consistent and rely on her prior statements to the government that she screamed out in English that Sylvester Stanley was not the one and she was misheard. Mrs. Hushemi's native tongue reappeared in the courtroom before your eyes. You saw her and you are the best judges of whether it was a performance worthy of a professional actress or authentic behavior beyond reproach. Albanian words that were misunderstood and inaccurately heard by Sylvester Stanley and Professor Marvel.

"The question of Novack and Mikhail's overwhelming guilt for a horrible hate crime is not the question before you. Sofia Hushemi is a young woman of virtue. She speaks the truth one hundred percent of the time, whether in a courtroom testifying under oath or simply out on the street."

Sharron concluded, "Sofia Hushemi is no racist ladies and gentlemen. Don't be fooled by any attempts by Mr. Troutman to transform a regretful remark made by Mrs. Hushemi to Angela Styles while suffering from enormous stress and grief as a reason to salvage his weak case. Convicting Sofia Hushemi would result in there being not one, but two victims of the heinous violence perpetrated by these two young men. You, ladies and gentlemen of the jury, *you* are judging Sofia Hushemi's credibility, not anyone else. *You* find Sofia Hushemi not guilty, not anyone else."

Attempting to begin his rebuttal summation to prevent the jury from having any time to ponder Sharron's closing, Troutman immediately sprang from his chair to take full advantage of the government's opportunity in federal cases to deliver the last as well as the first closing argument to the jury.

"Stop right there, Mr. Troutman. We are going to take a ten-minute recess to allow the jury to stretch their legs and digest what they've heard. The parties shall remain in the courtroom, however, because I want to finish closing arguments and proceed to the court's final instructions."

As Sharron returned to her seat, Sherman raised a clenched fist in approval of her summation. Troutman turned and whispered, "You can't blame a guy for trying."

Following the short break, the jury filed back into the courtroom as Troutman stood and gripped the lectern to deliver his speech.

"Ms. Bernstein did a nice job of portraying Mrs. Hushemi as a woman of unquestionable virtue. But is she?

Would she really hesitate to twist the truth in the face of a criminal charge which she fears will take her away from her child and family. Her prior statements under oath prove that is exactly what she did. The changes in her story from her words to the local authorities and here at trial are damning. And nobody can forget Angela Styles' testimony revealing Sofia's racist contemptible labeling of Sylvester as a *zezak*?

"The government has provided you with a trial of Mrs. Hushemi's statements in times of trouble which rips the mask from the saintly picture painted by the defense of poor, innocent, unsophisticated Sofia. Mrs. Hushemi deceived the local authorities when all charges were dropped against her. Don't let her deceive you ladies and gentlemen of the jury. Mrs. Hushemi ordered the shooting of Sylvester Stanley, not simply because she thought he stole her ring, but out of racial animus.

"Finally, even if we indulge for the moment in the idea that she really did yell out in Albanian that Mr. Stanley was not the one, what would Novack's reaction have been? Even if he was so full of hate that he would have pulled the trigger despite knowing Sylvester was not even the person who collided with Sofia, wouldn't he have at least paused before firing? What Mrs. Hushemi is asking you to believe flies in the face of common sense. Novack's reaction to her words was the response to a command, compliance with an order.

"Do not let the fact that Sylvester Stanley committed a crime many years ago when he was young blind you. Nor condemn or misinterpret the admirable passion of Professor Marvel in the face of perceived injustice as reasons to reject his truthful testimony. Mrs. Hushemi ordered Novack to shoot, to 'shoot the eyes' out of Sylvester Stanley. And as distasteful and sickening as the thought may be, the color of Mr. Stanley's skin was the primary reason for doing it. Mrs. Hushemi may well have regrets, but she cannot take back her orders on that fateful day."

Applause and shouts of "Sylvester Matters," reverberated off the walls. Ilka ran to Sofia and they held on to each other for dear life. Sherman and Sharron exchanged smiles of attempted confidence.

"Quiet! Quiet in my courtroom!" Judge Nicholsby shouted to no avail.

But it no longer mattered. Sofia's fate was in the hands of the jury.

Forgiveness

Fifty-Four

November 2019
Brooklyn

The text on Victor's cellphone was from an unknown number. But Victor knew it had to be him. Nobody else had the number.

Tonight. Eleven thirty. Ground level bathroom at Fornino's next to volleyball courts at Brooklyn Bridge Park. Locked at midnight. Don't be late.

But driving to the rendezvous in his black Escalade, Victor wondered if he was the one being set up... if a deal had been made to ambush him. So many sides of the fence were playing with each other, there was nobody to be trusted. Victor smiled, knowing if they tried, he would be the last man standing.

Walking down the pier to the cement block restroom, the rancid smell from the urinals and doorless toilets cut through the late autumn wind. The bathroom was a decent size, making it a perfect place for a hit. There were twelve-foot, wooden posts that surrounded the outside perimeter making an identification of a fleeing assailant almost impossible. Arriving a half hour early, Victor hid in the far stall, reserved for the disabled, which was the only toilet with a door. Hanging his overcoat on the back hook, Victor sat on the toilet, ignoring the chill, preparing for the unexpected.

At eleven, the bathroom custodian turned off the lights. As the entrance door slammed shut and the room turned pitch black, Victor had no idea if he was locked in. With the temperature plummeting Victor's impatience accelerated. If the meeting was called off without even receiving a text, he would blow a hole through the door at midnight and there would be no more meetings. And no more fucking talking. Ever. Just a price to be paid. Like every other motherfucker who dared to play him. Suddenly, Victor heard the lock turn and could see by the illumination from outside streetlights. The flat black entrance door pushed open. Victor stepped out of the stall with his right hand pointing his SR40c revolver at the right temple of the man who entered the lavatory.

"Put your fucking gun down, Victor," Special Agent Dan Ford demanded. "Don't we have enough problems? Why the fuck do you always have to be so melodramatic?"

"I should fucking take you out before another lie escapes your zezak lips. Fucking double-crossing motherfucker FBI ape."

As the unrelenting breeze turned frigid, Victor's gun remained pointed at Ford's temple. Not that it produced the slightest flicker of concern. Ford was more unflappable than Obama. And even harder to read.

Victor continued ranting, "I risk my ass year after year ratting out my friends and what's my reward? You let that piece of shit Troutman put Sofia on trial for her life."

Flashing a contemptuous grin, Ford replied, "Mind your mouth my Albanian friend. I'm afraid you have it ass-backwards. Your reward for what? All these decades after Sherman pulled a rabbit out of a hat with your acquittal, throwing us nothing but scraps of information, most of which we already knew. Your friends? Come on Victor, we both know it was your competitors you were helping us take down. And half of them were old dying capos on their way to Alzheimer's wards."

Victor placed the gun back in his waist. For the time being.

"You and your bosses haven't done shit for me. Troutman? Give me a fucking break. All he'll ever have is wet dreams about nailing me. There's no rats, no wires. No evidence of anything criminal. I don't need your help to do my business. You deserve a slow death for dragging Sofia and her family through the mud. Never lifting a finger to stop Troutman from trumping up charges against her."

Before Victor said another word, Ford surprisingly draped his arm around his shoulder.

"Now, now, Victor," he said in a voice dripping with sarcasm. "I never knew you were such a sensitive soul. I'm hurt you think that my colleagues in your adopted homeland don't care." He laughed.

"Keep it up, Ford," Victor replied, playing with the switchblade hidden in his pocket.

"My friend, let me update you. Without the Bureau covering you, do you really think Troutman never would've discovered you supplied the guns to Novack and Mikhail? And never would have found out you orchestrated the murder of the two boys to keep their mouths shut? Strikes me that's a handsome reward we've bestowed upon you."

Victor abruptly shut his mouth, mystified. How could Ford have known? Who the fuck was his source? *There was no point in asking*—Victor wouldn't give him the pleasure of another smarmy fucking answer. Ford continued his lecture:

"Sofia's prosecution couldn't be prevented. Nobody knows better than you how tight the circle of your cooperation has to be to succeed. Just be thankful she was acquitted. Even if I wanted to, things would have been complicated trying to help her if she was found guilty. Now, let's get back to you."

"What's there to get back to? I told you I'm done."

"I don't think it's quite that easy. You may not have been charged with Sylvester's shooting or Novack or Mikhail's murder, but you haven't been acquitted either. And last I looked, there's no statute of limitations on a murder prosecution. So, your incentive to work with us is far from a mere insurance policy. It's more of a get out of jail free card."

"So why the meeting, Ford? Get to the point."

"Now that's better. Glad you got it all out your system. All that time you've been spending in Albania, you think we don't know your goings on there as well? The connections and money you've been making by adding alien smuggling to your gun and drug trafficking? Time for you to make it work for the protection of your adopted country, Mr. Hushemi. For the stars and stripes."

"I have no idea what the fuck you're talking about?"

"I love when you switch gears and play dumb Victor," Ford smirked, "there's a nice warm bar up the street. We'll get a drink and I'll fill you in on all the details."

Fifty-Five

December 2019
Westchester, NY

The daily news videos of demonstrators turning over cars, store windows being smashed, and shots being fired by enraged protestors had finally receded when Sofia and Ilka returned home from shopping and found Edward unconscious on the living room couch. This time, the frantic efforts of medics could not restart his heart. Doctors warned of the risks of his never-ending cocktail of anti-depressants, but he had no life without them. Sofia also blamed herself for the black hole her husband had descended into after watching Sylvester on the witness stand.

The early winter snow sprinkled the grounds of the barren woods on the drive to the cemetery. Ilka sat next to Sofia in the back of Victor's Cadillac, her wild hair pulled back into a modest, low bun, her forehead resting gently on the glass as she looked out the opposite window. Sofia wondered if her daughter blamed her as much as she blamed herself for her father's death.

Edward would have chosen to be buried next to Chris in Arlington. But Victor would have none of it, he had years earlier picked a beautifully landscaped cemetery in northern Westchester County as the family plot.

No more than thirty people attended the funeral. Apart from a sprinkling of family members, there were nine of Victor's men, all dressed in dark suits and coats, accompanied by wives wearing somber clothing. Victor wore a starched white shirt, a three-piece pinstripe suit of the darkest gray, and a black cashmere winter coat. Despite it being a dark winter day, sunglasses hid his bloodshot eyes.

"My youngest brother faced trauma and tragedy no man should have to endure," Victor began in a quaking voice. "Growing up in Albania, our father was sent to the harshest of labor camps when Edward was only two years old. Edward would never know our father. Later, Edward and Tomas were targeted by my enemies. Loyal friends helped them escape to join me in America. Not even a citizen of this country, Edward enlisted. He ignored my pleas to come work with the family business. For his sacrifice, he was persecuted, disrespected, and devalued. Sent to Iraq, he served with honor. But he returned home damaged beyond repair."

Victor sucked in a deep breath, glanced over towards the trees and noticed two additional observers attending the funeral with a different purpose. They were standing in front of two SUVs less than a foot from the path leading to Edward's burial plot, snapping pictures. Victor fell silent. He walked over to Edward's grave and shoveled a small portion of dirt onto the coffin. When Ilka broke down, Sofia stood strong and wrapped her arms around her as if she were half her age. Seeing a telescopic lens placed on a camera was the last straw. Victor rushed over to the Feds, screaming they were trespassing on a private ceremony.

"Didn't mean to disturb you, Victor," one of them said. "Just doing our job."

As they drove away, Victor muttered, "Motherfuckers, they don't have a clue."

Brooding behind the wheel on the ride back towards the city, there was almost ten minutes of uncomfortable silence in the limousine before Victor finally spoke:

"Everything is going to be fine, Sofia."

"I know, Victor. Thank you."

"Back home in Albania, my most trusted and skillful associate has a great future. I have plans to bring him and his family to America soon. He has a son, Tarik, who would be a perfect match."

Sofia sighed, in no mood even for Victor, she flippantly replied, "Your beloved brother was placed in the ground less than an hour ago. Can't this wait? Are you really that anxious to be rid of me?"

Victor smiled. "My dear Sofia, you'll always be my sister. I meant a perfect match for our Ilka here."

Sofia's stomach did somersaults, grabbing Ilka's hand, she squeezed it so tight, Ilka flinched.

"My daughter, Edward's daughter is not even seventeen."

"Two years older than you on your wedding day."

"She's not her mother. We both know that. But I need time to rest and cannot talk about these things right now. I'm sure you understand," Sofia replied holding herself back from saying more.

"Of course." Victor's smile remained plastered on his face, as he drove in silence envisioning Ilka's future. Ilka's lips quivered, she clasped her hands together and couldn't stop rubbing them. Sofia wrapped her arm around Ilka and mouthed *Never*.

Fifty-Six

January 6, 2020
Brooklyn

Sofia's freedom mocked her. Unable to sleep, she paced the floors of her apartment all night. Victor had offered to move her and Ilka into a far more luxurious apartment, but she refused to leave the marital home. She stopped hounding Ilka about applying to college or even asking how she spent her days. Sofia's hopes of rekindling her relationship with Angela died when she learned a few months after the trial that she and her family moved to Chicago. The only saving grace was Victor's talk of marrying Ilka was on hold. For the past few months, his whereabouts were unknown.

Sofia's silver bullet nightmare had been replaced by reliving the shooting every night. And when not revisiting the shooting, she dreamt of seeing Sylvester on the witness stand being torn apart about smoking a blunt.

One night, staring at Edward's couch, longing for her dead husband, after an hour of pacing, Sofia realized what she had to do. With Edward's passing, she had no path to redemption. Nevertheless, she had to find Sylvester. Beg his forgiveness. Pray for absolution, even if it was the last thing she deserved.

Fifty-Seven

Later that same week
Brooklyn

"Take your time, Syl," Wes Edwards, Sylvester's heavily muscled trainer advised as he guided Sylvester through the handrails.

Sylvester breathed deeply and evenly; his wrists locked beneath his weight as he tried to relax his shoulders. Sweat dripped down his nose as he gazed at his legs, trying to will them back to life. For the past ten months, every morning Loraine or a part-time attendant had taken Sylvester to the gym at the Coney Island Rehab Center.

"Looking good, Syl. But don't overdo it."

"No pain, no gain, Wes," Sylvester gritted his teeth. "I'd rather feel pain than nothing."

"Don't talk. Just breath. Focus."

The same way Sylvester survived prison was the way he battled his condition. He refused to accept the impossible odds against him. Once Sylvester was back in his chair, Edwards lectured him,

"You push yourself too much, Sylvester. I'm not in favor of the intensity of these workouts," he said. "You have no choice but to scale things back. That wrist looks concerning to me."

"Like I said, no pain, no gain," Sylvester replied, hiding his discomfort.

Wes shook his head. "Almost every one of my clients has to be pushed to do more. You're the one exception. I love it, Syl, but you gotta slow down. You'll need to take time off until your wrist fully heals."

The memory of Sofia embracing Ilka, laughing in his face. Walking away Scot-fucking-free, like they all do when a black man is slaughtered, that image provided Syl with eternal motivation.

After PT, Sylvester sat in the waiting area, his backpack hanging on his wheelchair. Flipping through one of the textbooks from his afternoon master's social work program, while waiting for Lorraine, Sylvester looked up.

It couldn't be. Before his very eyes, Sofia.

Sylvester obsessively conjured retribution scenarios, but words were never part of the equation. He felt unprepared for this moment, sick to his stomach, more anxious than a schoolboy finding his first love in the arms of his best friend.

"To what do I owe this pleasure. Have you brought a new posse to finish me off? Nobody else here, Sofia, you can tell everyone I tried to run you down with my wheelchair and steal your purse and you had no choice but to strangle me to save yourself." He paused, then exhaled, "Seriously, Sofia, what the fuck are you doing here?"

Sofia was equally unprepared for reality. Heart racing, unsteady, desperately wanting to flee, she instead tentatively took another step forward.

"I came to talk to you. I was hoping you would hear what I have to say."

"I'm listening, a captive audience thanks to you." Sylvester waved to the small couch in front of him. "Have a seat, just like me."

Sofia sat down, took a deep breath, and looked away, struggling to hold back tears.

"We'll be left alone here," Sylvester said. "Nobody is coming to get me for at least another hour. This is your lucky day, Sofia, my calendar's open."

Staring at the floor, before raising her head, holding her hands tipped towards Sylvester as if in prayer, Sofia rambled, "I don't know... where... how to begin. After being found innocent, you'd think my life would be right as rain. Instead, my husband died two months after the trial, and I can barely function."

Sylvester bit his lip.

"But as much as it hurts and however badly I miss him, it's not Edward's death that haunts me." Sofia paused, terrified of Sylvester's reaction to her next words. "It's what I did to you. And how I assumed you stole my ring and was the one who asked those insane boys for help. And the way you were treated at trial by my lawyer as if you were the criminal. It was all so unfair. So wrong. Sylvester, I never wanted to see you hurt. I told the truth on the witness stand, but without me none of this would have happened. I should be punished. I *am* guilty."

Sofia lowered her head and wept. When she looked up, Sylvester was strangely silent, puzzled by Sofia's spectacle.

After what seemed an eternity, he firmly responded. "Sofia, what do you want from me? Forgiveness? Condemnation? Punishment? Why the fuck are you here?"

Gasping, choking, Sofia regurgitated, a putrid smell filling the room. She struggled to continue:

"Oh God, I have no right to ask, you should kill me rather than help me, but please, I beg, help me, Sylvester. I'm so sorry. I'm such a bad person. I'm in so much pain! Please help me, Sylvester. I'll do whatever you say, whatever you want."

"Enough! Enough! Stop already! Get the fuck out of here!"

Sofia, her arms wrapped around her midsection, staggered towards the hallway. With a look of disturbing despair in her eyes, she turned back, her voice barely audible, begging one last time.

"My husband was wounded in Iraq. He was often in a wheelchair, I learned to care for him. Maybe I can help you from time to time."

Sylvester, looking at Sofia in disbelief, exhaled deeply, and replied slowly, articulating every word, "I've replayed the trial in my head countless times. Lying and sitting all day leaves lots of time for recollection. Know what I mean Sofia… ? Oh, I forgot you don't!" Hesitating, momentarily debating his next words, Sylvester confessed:

"There's no doubt in my mind you told the truth. You tried to stop those animals. I misheard you. How could I know you were screaming in fucking Albanian? But you come here and beg forgiveness and you still don't get it. Don't fucking get it at all."

Sylvester's voice suddenly and starkly, returned to a shout:

"Do you?"

"I'm sorry. I don't know what you mean."

"Of course you don't, that's the problem."

"I don't care what language you spoke! You assumed a nigger stole your ring. A fucking immigrant from Albania, you assumed like everyone else it had to be a nigger who stole your ring. That's why I'll never walk again. Because you assumed a nigger stole your fucking ring!"

Sylvester's lowered his voice. "And now you come here to ask for employment." He wiped tears from his eyes with his right hand, "You're shitting me, aren't you? You came here to ask for employment?"

"I don't want any pay, I just, I just..."

Sylvester interrupted Sofia, putting his hand up, "You're a fucking insane woman, completely fucking insane," Sylvester said shaking his head. "Charity from you. Never," Sylvester shook his head, before continuing, a slight shift in his tone of voice:

"Maybe your insanity is contagious. And what do I have to lose, as much as my friends and family have helped me there are still too many hours where I'm alone and need someone to take care of me. Tell you what, I'll offer you minimum wage to be my aide. You want to make amends, then you can walk the walk instead of just talk the talk. I can't but you can."

No matter how she prayed and hoped, Sofia couldn't believe Sylvester was offering her the opportunity to atone. But he did. Her offer to help was the only way she knew how.

Fifty-Eight

January 13, 2020
Brooklyn

If looks could kill, Sofia would have suffered the slowest and most painful of deaths her first day on the job. Seated in his chair when his attendant showed Sofia into the living room, Lorraine entered from the kitchen.

"Sofia, I would like you to meet my mother, Lorraine. Mom, you remember Sofia, don't you?" Sylvester said with a sarcastic smile.

Lorraine's eyes cut Sofia in two. "I'm not amused, Sylvester," she said. "Whatever you're doing here, I don't want any part of it. Allowing this woman into our home. She should be in a jail cell not dirtying our walls and polluting the air we breathe."

"Mom, you need a break. We need help and Sofia says she wants to help. Isn't that right, Sofia?"

Sylvester's mother stormed out of the room, slamming shut the door to her bedroom. Sylvester turned to Sofia. "Words can't kill you. Not like bullets, ain't that right, Sofia?"

"You didn't tell your mother I was coming?" Sofia inquired in disbelief.

"Wasn't sure you were serious until now," Sylvester shrugged. "So, you here to work? Or you out of here?"

With Lorraine refusing to leave her bedroom, Sofia embarked on her first day at the Stanley residence. Cleaning the kitchen was her sole success. Her first mistake was to assume Sylvester would accept her assistance the way Edward did. The first time she tried to lift Sylvester out of his chair, he snapped.

"Get your fucking hands off me. You think I can't get in and out of my chair myself?"

"I'm sorry," Sofia said, raising her hands above her shoulders. "I should've asked."

"Stupid," Sylvester mumbled, as he lifted his body off the chair and maneuvered himself onto his bed.

"I'm gonna nap for an hour, try at least not to make too much noise." he said, sinking into his pillow with his back turned. Unable to resist another dig, Sylvester added, "Don't get tempted to finish me off."

"What time should I wake you?"

"Jesus, woman, I know how to set a fucking alarm!" he snapped.

Everything Sofia did the rest of the day was wrong: the clothes she picked for Sylvester to wear drew a rebuke, the food she selected for lunch was too rich and cooked incorrectly; the laundry detergent and floor cleaner she used made him "feel sick." Undeterred, Sofia mopped the kitchen floor, cooked two days' worth of food, scrubbed the floors and toilets of both bathrooms until she tore the whites off her knuckles and developed blisters on both hands.

Exhausted, nearing the end of her first workday, Sofia answered the doorbell.

"What the fuck," a black male around the same age as Sylvester, extremely overweight, exclaimed the moment he walked in the door. Quickly moving dangerously close to Sofia, both hands clenched, he shouted,

"What's up with this Syl, the Albanian Assassin. Who the fuck let her in?"

"Chill out Travis, grab yourself a Heineken, and I'll explain. You won't fucking believe it."

Sofia busied herself cleaning Sylvester's bedroom, while she overheard the two men mocking her.

"What do I have to lose," Sylvester explained, "take her in, break her ass, kick her out. House can use some cleaning, the thing immigrants are best at, isn't that what they say?" he laughed. "Risk free too. She told me her Gotti gangsta brother-law is out of the country."

Taking a long gulp of his beer, Travis responded, "Still think you're crazy bro, but your call. If it gets you off making her do shit, cool. Ha, make her clean the shit off your body too while you're at it."

After sucking down several more beers while Sylvester sipped herbal tea, Travis recalled he had to meet his wife in the city, tapped knuckles with Sylvester and rushed off.

After sweeping the last speck of dust from the floor of Sylvester's bedroom, Sofia put the broom and dustpan in the corner of the hallway closet and reached for her coat.

"Interesting day for both of us," Sylvester said as he sat by the front door. "I doubt you could stomach another one."

Sylvester underestimated was that punishment for sin was in Sofia's skin. In truth, she welcomed the abuse.

"We agreed on Monday through Friday, nine to five. I'll see you tomorrow morning."

Never a day missed, never a minute late, Sofia exhausted herself working. Lorraine remained mostly out of sight except to assist Sylvester in the bathroom and to shoot daggers whenever Sofia inadvertently crossed her path. In the face of Sylvester's never-ending disparaging remarks, Sofia spent her days cleaning and cooking, driving Sylvester where he needed to be and running family errands. Lorraine even turned a blind eye to Sofia gathering her clothes and doing her laundry. Sofia obsessively proved herself in other ways. While keeping her new-found employment a closely guarded secret, she contacted a carpenter Tomas recommended to lower the table height and otherwise adjust the furniture in the living room so Sylvester could maneuver more easily. She spent three days reorganizing the kitchen so Sylvester could access everyday items.

One day, in the middle of her cleaning, Sofia found a room which had always been locked, with the door slightly ajar. Sylvester was taking his daily nap, and Lorraine was out visiting friends when she tentatively took a step inside, discovering dozens of paintings. Not on display, just propped on the wall, collecting dust. There was an easel, sketch pads, paintbrushes, and all sorts of art supplies. Carefully picking up one of the canvases, she noticed a signature in the bottom right-hand corner: *Sylvester the artist known as Stallion.*

"What are you doing?" Sylvester's voice was suddenly sitting in his chair behind her.

Sofia jumped back, a shock wave hitting her heart, and almost dropped the painting.

"I'm sorry. I was just..."

"Put that back."

Sofia started to put it back with the other paintings, before bravely offering, "I could hang it somewhere if you'd like?"

"Did you fucking hear me?"

Returning the painting to the pile, she said, "I didn't mean to..."

"What? Ruin my art career?"

Sofia clenched her eyes shut, unable to suppress the tears running down her cheeks.

Sylvester wheeled himself over to several other paintings stacked a few feet away.

"This was my studio. Once upon a time." He let his hand run along the bristles of his paintbrushes.

"My daughter is taking art classes," Sofia said with a shudder.

Sylvester unexpectedly dropped his guard, "Let's see some of her work," he said. "I'll tell you straight up if she's any good."

Stunned, Sofia anxiously pulled out her cell phone and started swiping through photos.

"These are some of her sketches from the art fair at her school her senior year."

While Sylvester took a few minutes to look, Sofia held her breath, anxiously awaiting his opinion,

"Not bad." Sylvester remarked, returning the phone.

Even walking a tightrope, hearing approval of her daughter's work, warmed her mother's heart.

"I know she's starting to try her hand at watercolors now. But she's been struggling a little."

"Bring her here Saturday. I can show her some things."

"Really?" Sofia could not believe her ears.

"Not like I'm doing anything else with my free time," Sylvester said, rolling out of the room. "You'll need to clean this space up though if I'm going to be doing all that."

Left alone, Sofia let out the widest of smiles.

Fifty-Nine

Brooklyn

Riding on the subway with Ilka to Sylvester's brownstone the following week, Sofia was flooded with misgivings. *Was Sylvester going to use Ilka as a pawn to get back at her? Crush her child's confidence as an aspiring artist just to hurt her?* But there was no turning back. Ilka was far too interested in a free lesson.

Walking in, Sofia was startled to find Sylvester already in the studio with a much younger black male, his hair with streaks of orange dye, an earring dangling from his right ear, he had several tattoos on each arm and wore a black and gold Notorious B.I.G. t-shirt and baggy jeans. Sofia, having insisted that Ilka dress modestly for a change, and tie her hair, struggled to suppress a smile. His handsome face bore a striking resemblance to Sylvester. He had paintbrushes in his hand and was covering a canvas with bold colors and abstract shapes.

"You must be Ilka," Sylvester said, wheeling himself around to shake Ilka's hand, with a smile. An uncharacteristic gesture in Sofia's presence.

"I saw your sketches. You've got lots of potential."

Ilka blushed. "I actually brought my portfolio to show you some others, Mr. Stanley."

"Sylvester," he said, a surprising invitation never extended to her mother. "And this is my nephew, Michael. He's also an aspiring artist, enrolled at Berkely, lives out west with my brother Marco. He's in Brooklyn for a few weeks, thinking of transferring.

Michael flashed a sideways smile as magnetic as his uncle's. Ilka took a step closer to Michael's colorful canvas.

"Wow! Is this all acrylics?" she asked.

"I like to do a mix. I primed it with spray paint. It gives it a glossier look."

"I'd love to get my hands on some spray paint!" Ilka said excitedly.

"Have you checked out the street art here in Bushwick?" Michael asked. "It's so dope."

"No, I've never even been to Bushwick before now," Ilka replied embarrassed.

"There's a great mural around the corner you gotta check out." He stood up. "Want to?"

"To...go see the mural?" Ilka stammered. Sofia glanced back and forth between Ilka and Michael. It was like she and Sylvester weren't even in the room.

"Maybe some other time." Sofia interjected. "I'm sure Mr. Stanley has something planned for your first lesson."

Sylvester leaned back in his chair, amused. "Go ahead, guys. I'll flip through your portfolio while I wait."

As soon as Ilka and Michael walked out the door Sylvester laughed so hard, he began to cough. After catching his breath, he was the one looking down. At Sofia.

"Don't worry. She's not his type anyway," he said. "I'm sure you won't have to bring home no—what was the wor— *zezak*? Ain't that what you call us?"

"Mr. Stanley," Sofia sighed, "think what you want about me. But my daughter is a beautiful soul. And unlike her mother, she is free to befriend whomever she pleases."

Sixty

February 28, 2020
Brooklyn

It took Ilka six weeks to work up the courage to show Sylvester one painting which she'd kept hidden in her bedroom. With the door locked, the lights low, and Sofia running errands, Sylvester and Michael remained speechless for several minutes, their attention riveted to Ilka's heart wrenching canvas. It was a haunting painting of two females. Streaks of blood ran down the face and torso of one of the women, the other female was rushing to save her with tears streaming down her body. Other than the deep red blood, and the ghost-colored faces of the women, everything else in the painting was dark black. The sky, the ground, the clothing, lifeless black. The two women looked alike.

"Hmm," Sylvester said, initially focusing on the technique instead of the interpretation, a far easier topic with which to start the conversation. "Your brush strokes tend to be a little heavy here." He motioned to the linework on the canvas. "Obviously, it's quite sad, but I like it."

"Especially the way they're grasping for each other," Michael chimed in.

"It's about my mom," Ilka, said, shockingly unguarded. "She had a sister that she really loved growing up. She never talks about her anymore. But I found some letters that my mom kept in a drawer. She was in an abusive marriage and my mom was trying to help her get to America, but she never made it."

“What happened?” Michael asked.

“Her husband killed her,” she said matter-of-factly. “That’s why I’m never getting married.”

“*Never*?” Michael blurted out, wishing he could take it back.

Ilka shook her head. “I don’t know. My family’s crazy. They think you can sell women off to the highest bidder. I’m surprised I’m not already married to some Albanian guy my uncle picked out for me. I’m praying my mom can protect me unlike her mom who didn’t even seem to give a shit.”

Other than a few trite responses of comfort and understanding, Sylvester and Michael found themselves lost for words. Ilka was the only one attempting to rebound, asking questions about some of Michael’s recent work which he had shown earlier in the day. Sylvester went through the motions and decided to end things early.

Hearing Ilka throw open the book to Sofia’s life of slavery, Sylvester decided if he could never forget, perhaps somehow, he could try to forgive.

Independence

Sixty-One

March 2021
Albania

On his flight to Albania, Victor leaned back in his first-class seat and questioned the plan with which Ford had saddled him. Nothing made Victor's blood boil more than being a puppet on Ford's string. No matter, he would deliver beyond the Feds' wildest expectations, they would immunize him from his crimes, and they would all go fuck themselves. He just had to survive.

Ford had recently been assigned to work with a multi-agency task force on international security. The task force was primarily interested in his contacts with the Albanian mafia. Director Henry Kritz told him that since the defeat of ISIS in Iraq, its fighters were fleeing to other nearby countries and Albania was an increasingly favored destination. The task force felt an urgent need for better and more detailed information about their comings and goings.

Ford knew that Victor's overseas crew maintained secure facilities in remote regions of Albania, where they stored drugs, arms, and stolen goods. Now, after more than a year of planning, he wanted Victor to reach out to ISIS, and offer those hideouts as a refuge. However, Victor could only implement Ford's plan with the consent and assistance of his right-hand man and closest friend.

"Victor, you're out of your fucking mind," Grigor Dervishi responded as they sat across from each other at a back table of their favorite café in Tirana. Grigor weighed at least two hundred twenty pounds and wore a mustache only he adored. He was a warrior just like his father.

"We're going to set up ISIS leaders. Get them to come to Albania and then tell the Americans where they're hiding. Those guys just got here. How are we going to contact anyone of importance, let alone gain their trust?"

"My friend, what's our choice? The fucking Feds know everything. They even knew you and your father provided me refuge in the days leading up to my escape to the States. We don't help with this insane plan of theirs, I'll be shut down and locked up. The Feds will extradite you as well. We have to give them what they want or it's over."

Grigor took a long drag on his Turkish cigarette, reached down to sip his expresso, let out a long sigh and asked, "So how and what exactly do they want us to do?"

"We make a deal with the Jihads to provide them with places to hide out. We secretly report back to the Americans any activity we see happening within the compound. If we're lucky nothing else happens and they never know."

"And what's in it for us?"

"Comrade, ISIS has loads of money. We'll be well paid. But, with what the Feds have on us, leaving me and you alone is fucking more than enough."

Realizing that he and Victor were out of options, Grigor switched gears. "It's not the Feds I'm worried about. Eventually, those sick bastards will find out what we're doing. How do I protect my wife and son with Jihadists hiding around every corner, waiting to blow us up?"

"You think I haven't thought about that? That I would ever not be there for you and your family? Me!

I'm bringing your family to America. And keeping you there."

"My friend, now what the fuck are you talking about?"

Victor smiled, reached into his pocket, took out his cell phone and proudly displayed his favorite photos of Ilka. "I've arranged for the Feds to help get everyone out of the country and for your son to marry my niece. Tariq is the perfect husband she needs. After he's married to an American citizen, he'll be able to get visas first for himself and then for you and your wife. She will love America. Meli will be Sofia's long-lost sister. Trust me brother, it'll all be taken care of. Nothing is more important to me than the safety of you and your family."

Grigor stared at the picture of Ilka and gasped. "My God she is so beautiful." Before he could take his next words back, Grigor said, "She is young Sarah's double."

Victor held up his hand and slammed his fist on the table. "Ilka is nothing like my mother, and Tarik will never find a more faithful and loyal wife than my niece Ilka."

Grigor quickly regrouped. "Comrade, nothing would mean more to me than to see our families joined by the marriage of my Tarik and your Ilka."

Victor waved over a waitress, ordered a bottle of vodka and the two men toasted each other and the impending nuptials of Ilka and Tarik as they sat together, long into the night.

Sixty-Two

June 2021
Brooklyn

Victor took off his summer blazer, hung it up in the hallway closet and made his way to the kitchen while Sofia, as quickly as possible, changed out of her work clothes in the bedroom. Making sure to wear a smile, she walked in wearing a long blue dress and kissed Victor's cheek before sitting opposite him at the small dining table.

"It's been ages since you last stopped by," Sofia remarked. "We've so missed seeing you. Everything is fine, I hope?"

"Business, business, business. More and more it takes me back to our country. When I can breathe, you and Ilka come first." He looked around the room. "Where is my beautiful niece?"

"You just missed her, I'm afraid." Sofia bit her tongue, making sure not to let slip that she was busy with Michael taking a lesson at Sylvester's apartment.

Victor deliberately sipped his glass of water while coffee was brewed, and several homemade Albanian pastries were placed before him.

"I realize my words were too much too soon the day of my brother's funeral," he began, "I spoke out of turn."

Sofia, relieved, started to respond, but Victor continued, "Sofia, you're such a blessing to our family. And so strong. Bringing up Ilka the way you have, all alone, even when Edward was alive, may my brother's soul rest in peace, the burden has all been on your shoulders." He paused as Sofia's heart began to race and an all too familiar anxiety crept up her body.

"The time is more than right, Ilka's turning eighteen. I may have been rushing things before with my poor brother's passing, but we both know her pairing is overdue. My most trusted comrade, Grigor, I'm bringing him to America with his wife and son, Tariq. He's a perfect match for her. Thirty, handsome, a man brought up to follow the rules, with loyalty, the Kanun and Besa the priority. Not only that, I plan on retiring soon and I'm going to name Grigor the head of my organization. Ilka is going to have a dream life. I've made the arrangements."

Sofia became increasingly faint as Victor produced a small decorative box and slid it across the table.

"What's this?"

Sofia rested the tips of her trembling fingers on the box.

"For Ilka to present to Tariq on their wedding day," he said.

Sofia, with her heart in her throat, forced herself to lift the lid. Inside, there was a slender, silver bullet rested ceremoniously on a velvet red cushioned interior.

"In honor of their solemn marriage," he went on. "I've sent your father much-needed funds to endorse their pairing. His farm is in such disrepair and the last time I saw him his back was in terrible shape. This wedding will be a blessing for everyone. I'll even bring your family over for the event."

Sofia fearfully held back her screams. Even if Ilka's dowry were millions and Victor showered a king's ransom on her parents, she would die, they would both die before such a marriage would happen. Victor adored Ilka, in his own sick way, but she would never be a party to his plans.

Ilka was an American girl on her way to explore the world, become an artist and find her own man, if not Michael, any man she chose, black, white or purple. She was going to live the life Sofia was denied. Not even Victor would tell Ilka what to do.

Despite Sofia's fury, she knew and feared her brother-in-law all too well. She gathered her wits before speaking softly and calmly:

"Victor, you know how much I respect you. Always being there for Edward, seeing me through my arrest and trial. Without you, I'd be in prison and would have lost Ilka forever."

Victor held up his hands. "We're family. It's my job to look out for you and my precious niece. That is why I traveled to Albania to convince Grigor to accept the arrangement. Tarik is a worthy and wonderful man. All that remains is finding you the right husband. Edward is never to be forgotten but you're still young and... need to remain productive."

With sweaty palms, her heart racing as fast as when she was on the witness stand, Sofia stood and, regardless of the consequences, made the only reply possible:

"Victor, I'm afraid there's no arrangement. Because neither Ilka nor I are a party to it. Ilka won't accept the old rules and ways. And as for me, maybe I never would have ever grown up without having suffered so. Living through Edward's pain and addiction. Being put on trial for a hate crime. Watching a man get shot and forever paralyzed. I never would have left Edward. But, now that he's gone, if I ever have the desire, my partner will also be my choice and nobody else's. Not yours. And not my father's."

Staying seated and listening, Victor's fists clenching the sides of his chair, his blue and brown eyes widened. It seemed an eternity passed.

"I'm impressed," he began. "Always impressed by your strength and resolve. But Tarik is the man I chose for Ilka. It's an honor for her to be his bride. Tarik will treat Ilka like royalty. He's her fate, her destiny. I've ordained it."

There was no turning back, there never would be. Sofia remained steadfast. "I will not agree or permit it."

Sofia slowly slid the bullet across the table. More stony silence passed. When Victor stood, Sofia recoiled, as if she were back in the bedroom the first morning of her marriage, her face preparing for the delivery of his fist. Instead, Sofia was flabbergasted.

"I'll respect your decision," Victor sighed. "I'll break the news to Grigor and Tarik. And to your father. Of course, he will have to return what I have given him in expectation of the nuptials. Hard to say," he smirked, "which one of the four of us will be more disappointed."

Sofia rushed over, hugged and kissed both of Victor's cheeks. "Thank you, thank you my dearest brother-in-law. Thank you for understanding."

Sofia slowly walked Victor to the door, thinking that perhaps after all, despite his old traditional ways and whatever their ups and downs, and no matter what he may or may not have done to others who stood in his way, Victor truly cared, perhaps even loved his brother's wife and daughter.

She prayed that he did.

Two weeks later, on a steamy early summer morning, with no relief from the clouds or even a slight breeze, Sofia was within a block of Sylvester's apartment when her heart stopped.

Flashing lights were all over the street and a half dozen vehicles blocked ongoing traffic. Sofia feared Sylvester had had a terrible accident or a devastating setback in his condition, or despite their obsessive precautions and multiple vaccinations their worst COVID fears had come true. Racing, praying he was still alive when she got to the corner of the building there were no ambulances on the scene. Instead, it was an all too familiar equally ominous sight: more than a dozen dark blue windbreakers and baseball caps with an FBI insignia.

"Please," Sofia shouted, without digesting her words as she tried to walk past police barricades blocking the building entrance, "I'm his friend. What is happening here?"

"Ma'am, stay back. This is official police business."

"What are you talking about? The man is paralyzed. You're making a terrible mistake. Leave him be!"

Before receiving a response, Sofia saw Sylvester being wheeled out of the building by a male agent, flanked by two others. Another female agent had her right arm on Michael whose hands were in handcuffs behind his back.

Sylvester caught a glimpse of Sofia as he was being placed in an ambulette. Two agents entered the van and sat alongside him as it sped away followed by two police vehicles.

In the blink of an eye Sofia stood alone on the street, knowing a knock on the door to inquire would be met by Lorraine slamming it in her face. Looking up into the sky without even shielding her eyes from the blazing sun, Sofia searched for an answer. She had been making so much progress turning Sylvester around. Their time together was progressing from cordial to friendly. Even personal stories had begun to be shared. He welcomed her arrival and seemed disappointed when her workday came to an end. Lorraine was even starting to come around. Sofia was planning on winning her over with a traditional Albanian feast.

Searching the heavens for an answer, Sofia's screams scorched the streets of Bushwick.

After hearing the news reports, Sofia couldn't make sense of it all. The police found staggering amounts of crack cocaine hidden under the floorboards of Sylvester's room along with numerous weapons. The medical bills were unrelenting and constantly rising. Carrying the house was a never-ending burden even if Sylvester was healthy. Sofia dwelled on the thought of what desperation does to the best of people. Dealing drugs was not an unfamiliar solution.

"You have to get them out, Mom!" Ilka cried as Sofia sat on the edge of Ilka's bed in the late afternoon, explaining what happened.

"If they are innocent, the police will do their jobs," Sofia said unconvincingly trying to soothe her.

"*If* they're innocent? Mom! Of course, they're innocent!" Ilka screamed.

"You're right. You're right." Sofia cursed the small part of her which, no matter how hard she tried, and all she had been through, still harbored the possibility that Sylvester could be guilty.

"What are you waiting for. Get Sharron on the case. Or go to Sherman. Do something. You crippled Sylvester and got off, it can't be so hard."

Before Sofia could react, Ilka broke down sobbing.

Sixty-Three

August 2021
Bergen County Hospital Unit for Federal Inmates
Bergen County Hospital, New Jersey

"You've got to get me out of here," Sylvester breathed through clenched teeth, his arms shaking in anger. "Locked up and a fucking cripple. Not happening."

"Syl, you know I'll do anything to help. Just tell me what to do."

From the day of his arrest, Sofia came to see Sylvester every permissible visiting day. The walls of their past tumbled following Sylvester's re-incarceration. Their bonding was a truth stranger than fiction.

Housed in an overcrowded hospital unit, lying handcuffed to the rail of his bed, for the first time in months, Sylvester snapped at Sofia. "Don't play stupid, Sofia, not now. Don't be acting the clueless poor immigrant girl with her head in the sand."

"Sylvester, what are you saying?"

"There's only one person who would do this to Michael and me. Your gangster brother-in-law. You told me about his plans for Ilka. This is exactly the kind of thing he would do, take out the *zezaks* to solve the problem. Right, Sofia?"

Sofia put her hands over her ears. "I can't listen to this. I'll think of something. I'll get you out. Prove you and Michael have been set up. But it's not Victor. No matter what you think, no matter what anyone thinks, he wouldn't do something like this."

"Visiting hours are over, ma'am. You have to leave," a corrections officer commanded.

"Please, Syl?" she cried as she stood up. "Nobody is as strong as you. In just a little time, that's all, you'll be out. I promise."

Sylvester turned away, disgusted by what a fool he was to not only open the door to a friendship with Sofia, but to trust her, to come to depend on her, to…to…to…..

The visit was over.

Sixty-Four

September 2021
Manhattan and Brooklyn

As much as Sofia wanted to believe Sylvester was grasping at straws accusing Victor, he was still the last and only person Sofia could turn to for financial assistance to secure his defense. She was scheduled to see Sylvester in two days and had done nothing. But what could she do? Sofia couldn't sleep or eat, stayed alone in her bedroom unable to bear the accusatory looks in Ilka's eyes. The few times they nibbled take out at the kitchen table; they barely spoke.

Out of desperation and dread, with the clock ticking on the date for Sylvester's trial, Sofia turned to the one person who might help. After a heartfelt hug, they sat together wearing face masks, on the couch in Sharron's opulent office. Sharron coolly digested hearing about Sofia's stranger than fiction relationship with Sylvester. There was no need to bring Sharron up to speed on the arrest. The case was a news highlight.

"I know this will be a bit hard to swallow. But, let me call Troutman. Despite our skirmishes throughout your trial, we're professionals. We don't hold grudges. He's still my best and most trusted contact. I'll set up a meeting. I'll find out if he's willing to consider doing anything for Sylvester."

Late in the afternoon, Troutman listened quietly as Sofia told him about the close relationship she had developed with Sylvester. She recounted that Sylvester insisted from the outset he and his nephew were being framed and that, in the five months she had been taking care of Sylvester she had never seen any signs of contraband or weapons.

"Nothing you are telling me comes as a surprise," Troutman said.

He leaned back in his chair at the head of the conference table before reaching into a folder and taking out a dozen photographs. Pictures of Sofia in front of Sylvester's home, photos of the two of them on the subway, Sofia accompanying him to classes, and spending time at cafes and restaurants were placed before her.

Troutman went on as Sofia sat in shock, sickened by the invasion of her privacy. Unfazed, Troutman continued.

"I voiced my concerns to the assistant in the office who has brought charges against Sylvester. But it's not for me to question him. Eastwick would only bring a case after a complete and thorough investigation and analysis. And, unfortunately, the search of Sylvester's apartment leaves hardly any room for doubt." He leaned forward and lowered his voice. "But, in all frankness, I more than wonder if Sylvester was set up."

"You do?" Sofia asked, feeling hopeful.

"Come on Sofia, I know you don't want to face it. But there's only one person with a motive, capable of doing something so ruthless."

Troutman dropped one last photo on the table: Ilka and Michael, kissing. Sofia gasped and put her hands to her chest.

"I'm sure your brother-in-law was less than pleased by your daughter's growing friendship with Sylvester's nephew. I've talked to Eastwick on several occasions.

The problem is there's no proof he framed Sylvester and Michael. This past year Victor has not even been around. I'm not sure where he's been and what he's up to, but I've been working on it."

Troutman took out a narrow black box, and inside was what looked like a thin pen. He pushed a button on the top. "Modern technology is really something. It records without a wire. James Bond would be impressed." Troutman laughed. "I bet even you're not familiar with this device."

He handed it to Sharron. She passed it back and Troutman clicked the button twice. A recording of his voice played, his words clear as a bell.

"There's an external wire that plugs into any iPhone, laptop, or computer and the conversation can be downloaded. No tech knowledge required, anybody can use it, even a dinosaur like me." Troutman smiled, impressed with his little display.

"Sofia can engage Victor in a conversation and try to elicit an admission. Right now, it's your only hope to exonerate Sylvester. If I thought it would be discovered, if it wasn't safe, I would never suggest wearing it. She can easily hide the recorder in her purse or blouse, it can't be distinguished from a ballpoint pen. Victor won't suspect a thing. It's not like bulky wire in the old days."

Sharron took no time to respond. "Come on Alan. Talk all you want about your new toy, but I seriously doubt you would ever send one of your agents to talk to Victor Hushemi with it on him. Sofia and I will give it some thought, I'll hold it and let you know. But odds are we'll return it."

Sharron and Sofia stood and thanked Troutman for his time.

On the ride home in Sharron's brand new two-door Mercedes, her certainty and loyalties torn apart, Sofia asked her advice. "We still don't even know Victor had anything to do with Sylvester's arrest and God knows how he'd react if anything went wrong, and he discovered you—even you—wearing a recorder. Even if it's the only hope of exonerating Sylvester, I think it's too dangerous."

"But how can I do nothing?" Sofia wrapped her hands around her head, wrestling with herself, her mind raging in turmoil, and suddenly, with a strange look on her face, she fell silent. A second before Sharron asked what was bothering her, Sofia said, "You know, I think there might just be a way I can do this without Victor finding out. And it's not just Sylvester and Michael, Ilka would never forgive me if I didn't do everything possible to help."

Pulling the car over to the front of Sofia's apartment, the two women went back and forth for another half hour, until Sharron relented, but not until Sofia said she would sleep on the final decision. Before saying good night, Sharron handed over the pen to Sofia and she gingerly placed the recorder in her purse.

Sofia lay awake staring at the pen under the light of the small table next to her bed. An hour before daybreak, she made up her mind. She needed to look into Victor's eyes and talk to him. And even if he had nothing to do with Sylvester's arrest, he could find out who framed him. And she would figure out a way to convince him to help, do or say whatever it took. Even agree to another arranged marriage for herself. She prayed that would be enough.

Sixty-Five

September 2021
Brooklyn

When Victor answered the bell to Tomas' apartment the following morning, Sofia stood before him looking as if she had seen a ghost.

"Sofia, my dear you look frazzled. What's wrong? Tomas and Katrina are out, I'm afraid."

"I'm looking for you actually," she answered, willing her voice to stay steady.

Victor took the spring coat he had gifted to Sofia and hung it in the hallway closet before ushering her into the living room. After gesturing for Sofia to sit on the couch, Victor kicked his feet up on the step stool of his favorite armchair and began polishing his black loafers.

"Work keeps taking me back to our country. I've seen your father more than I've seen you," he said, avoiding eye contact.

Sofia was in no mood for small talk. "What do you know about Sylvester Stanley's arrest?" Sofia inquired, dropping any concern for the emotional sound of her voice. "I know you must have heard about it."

Victor shrugged. "Once a drug dealer, always a drug dealer. Being able to stand and walk is not a job requirement."

"Please!" she cried. "He's innocent! I know you have connections all over the city. Please. Just tell me what you know or heard."

"And why should I care about a man that tried to put *my brother's wife* in prison?"

Sofia threw caution to the wind. "Because he's my friend now. Please. He doesn't deserve this."

Victor looked amused. He licked his lips as Sofia wept and dropped the game they were playing.

"Of course, I know all about you and your friend. I let it go when you started caring for that crippled *zezak* just to ease your feelings of remorse, even though your behavior was sheer madness! But allowing Ilka to spend time with that *zezak* boy? God knows what he's already done… to soil her. How dare you disgrace our family?"

Victor stood quickly, firing his surreal heterochromatic pupils down upon Sofia, causing her to cringe.

"Ilka is promised to Tarik. Your father is pleased with the arrangement and has no desire to return the money he's already spent. As pleased as he was when I sent him a king's ransom for your hand in marriage for granting me refuge in your home. Edward's death has not changed the rules. I decide what's best for you and Ilka. She is to wed Grigor's son and the cripple was corrupting you. Something had to be done."

Ignoring Sofia's distress, Victor shrugged.

"Nothing you can do about it, so I'll tell you. There's a *zezak* I do business with. Despite what you think, I don't hate all *gabels*. Told him I needed someone to set up Sylvester, to inform the feds the cripple and his nephew were dealing crack from his apartment. Large quantities. Even more than in the old days. During one of his doctor's visits, while the apartment was vacant, he planted substantial product, money, and guns under the floor of his bedroom."

"The evidence will speak for itself as well as my *zezak* friend. Sylvester should plead guilty and swallow a decade of time unless he stupidly wants to get another life sentence. And his nephew should do the same. And there's no Obama around to grant them clemency this time."

Victor started to laugh but caught himself, losing the desire to luxuriate in Sofia's pain.

"Who are you? What kind of a man are you.? Have you no conscience?" Sofia screamed. "No feelings? No morals? Sylvester's a paraplegic. He won't survive prison this time! Michael is a wonderful young man. I won't let this happen. No matter what you've gotten away with before, this time you'll pay the price."

Victor's voice softened as the anger left his eyes and the sight of Sofia's hurt finally registered.

"If anyone is to blame, I'm afraid it's you, Sofia. None of this would've happened if you hadn't been so soft and exposed your daughter to Stanley's family and let her fall under some black magic spell."

"I'll tell Troutman if I have to! I won't let you get away with this."

"My dear, darling sister-in-law, get a hold of yourself. Think about it. What are you going to do? What proof is there? I will deny what I just told you. People already think you've lost your mind caring for the *gabel*. Nobody will take you seriously. You want to save the *zezaks* then you know what you must do. I don't have to tell you."

Victor pulled out the silver bullet he had specially made for Ilka's ceremony.

"Once Ilka marries Tarik and proves herself a loyal wife, I give you my solemn word, your *zezak* friends will be free."

Sofia let out a gut-wrenching cry, unlike anything Victor had ever heard.

"I trusted you, I believed in you," she collapsed and cried into the red living room carpet.

Victor let Sofia cry herself out in silence until her sobs turned to whimpers. When she she raised her head he responded,

"No need for anymore talk today. I'm confident you will come to your senses and make Ilka see the light as well. Go home to your daughter."

Sofia turned away and sullenly walked to the hallway closet where she grabbed her coat. Just as she reached the front door, it opened and one of Victor's men walked in.

"Sorry to interrupt, Victor," he said.

"It's fine Andrei, my sister-in-law was just leaving."

Suddenly, a second before Sofia stepped into the hallway, Victor shouted "Sofia, wait!" She stopped in her tracks.

"Andrei, take her coat, and pat her down."

Sofia turned around; this time she was the one staring.

"Have you lost your mind? Haven't you done enough? Said enough?" she gasped.

"You're the one who said you won't let me get away with this."

Andrei checked her coat and threw it over a chair. He touched her chest, felt below her waist, reached inside her pockets, and quickly stroked her backside suppressing a smile on his face.

"She's clean," he said.

"Her phone?"

Andrei picked up the cell.

"44427," Sofia screamed.

"What?"

"The code unlocks it, search it all you like."

Andrei spent twenty minutes examining texts and phone numbers, listening to voicemails, and searching for recordings.

"Nothing," he finally reported.

"Her purse."

"How I wish Edward could see you. What a cold-blooded bastard the brother he loved is. What a heartless gangster he is. Even worse than Troutman knew!"

Andrei grabbed Sofia's purse and spilled its contents on the couch. An unusual looking pen fell out. Noticing a flash of tension on Sofia's face, Victor told Andrei to bring it to him. Screwing it open, Victor pinched the plastic tube and blue ink-stained his fingers. He snapped it in two, took out his handkerchief and wiped his hands in annoyance.

"You may go now, Sofia," he said softly. "Sorry for the intrusion. I know it all seems so bad, but you'll get over it. In time you will see I'm right, I expect you will even love me again."

Sixty-Six

Brooklyn

Sofia walked downstairs to her apartment, quickly locking the door. After glancing into Ilka's bedroom to make sure she wasn't home, she rushed to the bathroom, threw her coat over the shower curtain rod, pulled her dress down and reached into the medicine cabinet for a sanitary napkin. Sitting on the toilet, she reached inside her vagina and slowly pulled out a tampon. Delicately taking it apart, she slipped out the blood-spotted pen wrapped inside. After wiping it off, she replayed Victor's words. After washing herself off, she plugged the pen into her laptop, downloaded the conversation, and e-mailed it to herself and Sharron, writing, *"As my attorney and friend, I trust you to know what to do next."* Still feeling dirty, with tears streaming down her cheeks, Sofia ripped her clothes off and stepped into the shower.

Sofia spent her life refusing to believe the truth about Victor. His being targeted by law enforcement, she dismissed as hatred and stereotyping of Albanians. She even scoffed at Angela's accusations. Victor controlled her life, but there was nothing he would not do for Edward and he seemingly worshipped Ilka. From the moment Sofia arrived in Brooklyn, Victor was a protector and savior. The reality of the man crushed her soul.

Sixty-Seven

October 31, 2021
Catskill Mountains, New York

"I can't do this. I'm not ready," Sofia protested.

"This always happens at the moment of truth," Bill Lawrence laughed. "You guys have been training with me for two months now you're more than ready."

After Sofia and Sylvester streamed the movie *The Upside* in his home, Sylvester became obsessed with paraflying by the disabled. Immediately he began reading every article he could get his hands on and watching countless videos of people who never walked a day in their life being instructed on how to fly. He also loved that training and flying in the open fields provided a rare opportunity to shed the face masks saddling everyone since the onset of the pandemic.

Lawrence was a worldwide, respected instructor and designer of paraglides. He devised cables he secured to parachutes in specially built chairs. With proper training, both the parachute and flight apparatus could be manipulated exclusively by the flyer's hands. Miraculously, some could even fly solo with only Lawrence guiding them from the ground by wireless audio communication. The ability to fly solo, however, required at least a year of instruction and planning. And Sylvester was always an impatient son of a bitch.

After six weeks of intensive training, Lawrence had Sofia and Sylvester ready for takeoff. Sofia may have trained but was far from ready. She swallowed her fear and lied when Sylvester offered to postpone their flight.

"No, I've been training right along with you. It's ok, just a second of panic. I'm ok now," Sofia said as they prepared for the flight.

"Sure as shit you are," Lawrence chuckled. "But we couldn't ask for a more beautiful day. We have the bluest of skies and a window of ten to fifteen mile per hour winds. Perfect flying conditions."

Sylvester calmly lifted himself with the help of an aide from his chair into the glider's flight seat with a secure buckle wrapped around his chest and two Velcro straps fixed to the front of his chair. Sofia was nervously secured into the back of the chair in a standing position with a seat belt that locked into place in five different places. The most difficult challenge was getting the massive nylon canopy inflated and capable of lifting into the sky.

With their backs facing the canopy and their feet planted on the ground. Lawrence stood behind pulling, spinning, and pushing the parachute while Sylvester handled the controls and Sofia held on for dear life.

It took much longer than hoped for the wind to fully fill the chambers of the apparatus. The first attempt at inflation caused their feet to drag along the ground for several minutes until Sofia screamed to stop. Another effort resulted in Sylvester dropping the controls and cursing in frustration. A third attempt had them zigzagging for more than forty feet before giving up.

Sofia told Sylvester it just wasn't their day. The longer it took, the more she worried that after all they both survived, they were fated to perish attempting a frivolous recreational pursuit. Sylvester on the other hand remained confident, the grin on his handsome face undiminished.

"What you think, Professor?" Sylvester asked Lawrence.

"I think your woman should get ready to fly," Lawrence shouted as he tightly wrapped his arms around Sofia, sprinted two dozen steps, and after an enormous push, let go. Sofia looked at her feet in disbelief. They were off the ground.

"Looks like one of us is going to get their revenge after all!" Sylvester screamed in delight as they launched into the sky.

Sofia closed her eyes, expecting to crash any second. Instead, they soared high above their mountain top launch point. Sylvester manipulated the parachute while Sofia did her best to steady the chair. Rising into the clouds as if they had wings, Sylvester and Sofia squeezed each other, erupting in laughter.

Sylvester threw his right arm out into the sky, and Sofia held his left hand, the same as their fateful day in Prospect Park.

"Sofia, I am free. Beat all the odds again! Nobody stops me!" he shouted at the top of his lungs.

"So am I, Syl. Finally! So am I."

Epilogue

November 1969
The Wedding Ring
Albania

In 1950, Albania's communist government confiscated the land owned by Victor Hushemi's family for more than a century. Their large, prosperous farm in Northern Albania was amalgamated into a state-owned cooperative. Production plummeted, yielding only a fraction of the tobacco, fruits and vegetables previously cultivated. The family lived on the paltry wages paid by the state, supplemented by whatever food they could grow on the small plot that was allocated to the family for their private use.

When Victor was nineteen years old, his father Imer was imprisoned on suspicion of anti-government activity. Victor's mother, Sarah, did whatever she could to earn extra money to feed the family. Yet the teenage boy, though starving, went to bed every night feeling his mother was only concerned about his younger brothers, Tomas and Edward. *And fucking Robert.*

It was on Thursdays that Robert, the manager the government assigned to monitor the farm came to check on things. Still only in his twenties, the trim dark confident young man would make his rounds around the farm to view the crops, livestock, and farmhands. Carrying a notebook to record whether the farm was meeting its quota, he sat at the kitchen table matching his daily figures with the accounting Sarah was required to maintain.

A child bride of an arranged marriage, Sarah, at 34, remained a strikingly beautiful woman, despite her life's burdens. The sight of his mother awaiting Robert's weekly arrival enraged Victor. It was the only occasion when she would wear a long dress rather than her work clothes. *Does she think the infidel Premier Enver Hoxha has created a world where a woman can do what she wants, ignore the Kanun, disrespect her husband, forget her place? Before the fucking communists, when customs and tradition ruled, women would be shot for such flaunting.* Such thoughts flooded Victor whenever he saw them together.

Robert looked up from his paperwork, "Just making sure the figures and the inventory are in order. You know the committee will look at my notebook the moment I return. How is everything, Victor?"

"I'm wonderful, comrade. Even with my belly empty, my brothers starving and my father in prison. We're so lucky to have you."

Robert sighed at Victor's tone.

"Victor, you know I did what I could for Imer. I still check on his re-education and when he will be allowed to return. Victor, you must mind your words. You know ears are everywhere. You'll be exiled like your father for talking that way. Control that temper, Victor. If not for your sake, for your mother's."

"Oh comrade," Victor replied with a contemptuous grin. "Your concern is duly noted. Thanks so, so much."

"I try to tell him, Robert," Sarah interjected. "He's hard-headed. Even Imer always had trouble getting through to him. What can I do?"

"I've said my piece. I must be getting back. See you both next week."

Victor watched his mother blush when Robert rolled down the window of his government vehicle and tenderly touched her cheek for the briefest of moments before he drove away.

"You're a dead man," Victor mumbled, shaking his head.

The following Thursday afternoon, while Robert sat with Sarah, Victor went to the barn to retrieve the small truck that was used by the collective to deliver produce to town. Loosening the valve to the back left tire to let the air out, he drove on the woefully maintained main highway until the tire was almost flat. He then pulled off to the side of the road and anxiously waited, while images of his mother and Robert danced in his head.

An hour and a half elapsed before Robert's car finally came within sight. Victor frantically waved his hands. Robert initially passed without stopping, but after a hundred feet he realized it was Victor, backed up, and got out of his car.

"I almost passed by without seeing you. What happened?"

"Just a flat, comrade. I have a spare. But no jack in the trunk. So stupid of me. You have one?"

Robert overlooked Victor's "comrade" taunt. He silently turned and walked to the rear of his car, opened the trunk, and rummaged around for a jack. Just as he found it, Victor swung a large piece of wood he had retrieved from the back of his truck with decapitating intent. Robert crumbled to the ground.

Thirty minutes later, painfully disoriented, Robert regained consciousness, and tried to put his hand to his bloodstained temple only to discover that his entire body was tightly wrapped in rope. A heavy boulder was tied to his right foot, while his harness made even breathing difficult. Victor had tied him to a tree branch by another rope, dangling approximately four feet above a heavily wooded area of Shiroka lake. This rope was wrapped over a thick branch which then ran down to the ground and was tightly tied to another tree.

Robert shook his head clear, maniacally struggling to free himself. Being late November, the area was deserted.

"Comrade, how're you feeling?' Victor's unmistakable voice rang out. "Sometimes I don't know my own strength. I only meant to give you a love tap."

"Victor, what the fuck is the matter with you? Put me down, untie me. Stop before it's too late."

Robert frantically squirmed and shouted for help, both to no avail.

"I ask questions, you give answers. Tell the truth, you come down. Question number one: When did you first fuck my mother? Before or after my father was sent away?"

"What? I never touched your mother."

"Fucking liar!"

Victor loosened the rope from the tree that secured Robert above the water. The weight of Robert's body pulled the rope over the tree branch, and he plunged into the lake.

More than a minute passed with Robert flailing with every muscle to escape his harness.

Victor grabbed the rope, threw it back over the branch, and hoisted Robert out of the water. Spitting up mouthfuls of water, Robert gasped for air.

"Please, Victor. Stop!"

"Again, did you start fucking my mother before or after my father was sent away?"

"Victor, I swear I never touched your mother."

"You're brave, comrade. Brave, but such a damn liar."

Victor dropped the rope, Robert again descended into the lake. Even more time elapsed before Victor pulled him up.

Robert breathlessly spewed, "You want me to lie? I won't. I never touched Sarah. Kill me, bastard. Fucking get it over with."

"Asshole, back you go."

When Victor finally raised him, Robert resigned to his fate, whispered, "I love Sarah, but I swear, I swear on my daughter's life I never touched her."

"Half-truth. Good for you, comrade."

Victor smiled and let the rope go for the final time. Robert's body disappeared into the murky water. Without glancing back, Victor walked back to the highway, looked into the trunk of Robert's car, and grabbed his blood-spotted keys, He drove the vehicle over the unpaved trail that led to the lake until it was no longer possible to navigate the rough terrain.

Victor groaned at the effort it took to push the car up to the top of the hill that perched over the south side of the lake. With a final shove, the vehicle crashed below, but still bobbled on the lake's surface. Victor stared in disbelief, having no idea what to do next. It would be weeks, maybe months, maybe forever, before anyone had any idea what happened to Robert if both the vehicle and his body disappeared. But the sighting of his abandoned vehicle would lead to trouble.

Suddenly the automobile started to sink. A vortex of water formed, and the car was sucked to the bottom of the lake. Victor screamed in delight, so loud his voice ricocheted off the rocks. *Shit someone might hear me*, he thought, then chuckled, feeling total relief and satisfaction, and not an ounce of guilt. With all the evidence gone, there was nothing to worry about. He was merely a young comrade, wandering the woods following a hard day's work, after having a well-deserved drink or two.

Victor took the jack out of the trunk and quickly put the spare tire on. Driving home, he swore to slap his mother, the moment he witnessed any sign of grief upon hearing of her boyfriend's mysterious disappearance.

March 1970

A dinner invitation from the Hushemi family was the last thing Ivan Kramski and his wife Galina ever expected. After Imer was first exiled, Ivan would even sneak over several evenings during the week with some fruit, bread, and potatoes from his family's modest allotment.

Sarah served a meal she could hardly afford. While Victor's younger brothers, Tomas and Edward, kicked a soccer ball outside in the fading light, Sarah slowly worked herself up to address the real reason for the dinner.

"Mr. Kramski," she said in a loud enough voice to arouse her guest, "you've always been there for us, a wonderful neighbor and friend of our family."

"You're too kind, Sarah," Ivan replied. "I've done very little. When Imer was exiled, I felt terrible. I should have done something."

"I know you would have helped if you could. But now we have a different problem, and I'm praying that you might help. I don't know where or to whom else to turn."

"Of course. Anything," Ivan responded, peering into his empty wine glass.

"Manager Robert's brothers have returned from military service and vowed retribution for the murder of their brother. His body was recently discovered at the bottom of Shiroka Lake. The police are so incompetent they cannot find the real killer, so they blame Victor. The party hates our family and are seizing on the opportunity to convince Robert's brothers of Victor's guilt and will turn a blind eye to a revenge killing."

"What can I do?" Ivan asked, knowing the answer.

"I am begging you, Ivan. Grant Victor sanctuary in your home. Provide him with *besa*. It would only be until he leaves the country. He knows he cannot remain in Albania. Guard him until he can safely get away."

If Ivan had not been emboldened by several glasses of cheap wine, he would have asked for time to think things over. But ultimately no Albanian man can refuse a plea for *Besa,* the Kanun's sacred principle, the promise of protection of a guest which prioritizes his safety above all other occupants of the home. Ivan had to agree to provide Victor refuge.

Victor awakened the following morning before dawn and packed his essentials. While Edward remained asleep in the cot they shared, Tomas watched with bloodshot eyes as Victor placed two rifles and a handgun into a narrow sports bag. After emptying his bedroom drawer, the brothers embraced.

"Don't worry, Tomas. Wherever I go, whatever happens, I'll never allow anyone to hurt you or Edward. I'll always protect my brothers. And one day we'll be reunited. We'll all be together, living the life we deserve."

Tomas tightly held on to Victor, refusing to let go. Finally, Victor gently unwrapped his brother's arm. Victor walked into the small family room with the heavy sports bag strapped on his left shoulder and an even weightier suitcase in his right hand. He stopped at the front door and put everything down.

Sarah came over and, in a tremor filled voice said, "If you discover you've left anything important, just let me know."

For several intensely uncomfortable moments, they stood within inches of each other, both with their arms at their sides. Finally, Sarah took a few cautious steps toward Victor and wrapped her arms around him. Tormented by conflicting emotions, Victor tentatively returned his mother's embrace.

"Take care of yourself, Victor. I pray this nightmare ends soon and our family is reunited."

Victor hugged Sarah and wept as he buried his head in her bosom.

"Take care of my brothers. Keep those boys in good health and mind until Imer's return. It's your duty."

Victor opened the door and took a step outside.

"Victor, did you do it?" Sarah whispered, her tears falling to the dirt below her feet.

Victor whipped around, his heterochromatic eyes burning a hole through his mother.

"What did you say?"

"Victor," Sarah mumbled, wanting to stop herself but somehow couldn't. "Did you kill Robert?""

"You accuse me, your first born! The man of our house. All I've sacrificed for our boys… I mean my brothers."

Victor walked back, grabbed his mother's hand so tightly she squealed in anguish, almost pulling her finger off with her wedding ring.

“I didn’t kill your lover, but I wish I did. Now you can look forward to joining your partner. When Imer returns, let him see the ring off your finger. The missing ring will show your infidelity. If he fails to know why it’s missing, his oldest son will make sure he’s informed. And then, if he takes pity on you, a silver bullet will be your fate. If he doesn’t, you’ll be stoned and buried alive. With my help!”

Placing the wedding ring in his pocket, Sarah’s unrelenting sobs mocked Victor. As he walked away, a moment before embarking for the Kramski’s house, Victor stopped and looked back at his mother still standing at the open door. His tears returned, streaming down his face as he watched her for the last time. Victor never saw or spoke to Sarah again. His tears were the last he ever shed.

Author's Note

The two protagonists of my story were inspired by my long-time friend Zylfie Demushi and my former client and close friend Timothy Adams. I have been privileged to have them share their backgrounds, family relationships and legal struggles with me.

Acknowledgements

Ten years ago, after having never written a novel, I set out to write *A Hate Crime in Brooklyn.* The idea was personal and interesting but needed so much support for my vision to evolve. Without the never-ending input, advice and creative suggestions of my brother Keith Secular and my son's fiancé Ashley Gannon it would have remained the work of an amateur. My son Michael has recently joined Ashley in providing graphic artwork for the novel and also deserves recognition.

I have also had the great fortune to have my lifelong friend and colleague and the most dedicated and effective criminal defense attorney in the country, Michael Padden read every draft of the novel and correct its shortcomings. A J Mchugh, a friend and also an amazing attorney, has read and supported every draft and provided great insight. Charles White, another gifted attorney, friend and now a playwright took time away from his insane schedule to read and comment on the novel. My close friend Dave O'Meara also must be thanked for reading and encouraging me through multiple drafts of the novel and, by his life example, keeping me inspired by demonstrating that with dedication and self-belief there are no limits to what we can achieve.

Special thanks go to Justine Brennan, who took time from her overwhelming work as the best and most dedicated immigration attorney I have ever met to help edit and double check the validity of my recitation of immigration laws in the novel.

I have also benefitted from several accomplished authors who provided invaluable advice. I greatly appreciate and thank Charles Holdeffer who taught me in his summer class held at the Iowa workshop and afterwards charitably took the time from his teaching and writing to read several drafts of the novel and provide invaluable advice.

Particular and very great thanks must go to the gifted writer and journalist Jason O'Toole who guided me through final drafts of the novel and saw the limitations of prior versions. British author Tim Lott also tutored me when I took up my first draft and helped me learn and realize the long challenge of creative writing. Thanks also need to be given to Dr. Steven Tuck for reviewing the authenticity of medical scenes in the novel. To so many others I work with and know who encouraged me through the ups and downs of my writing journey that are too numerous to mention, I say thank you.

I also cannot thank enough Linda Langton, my agent and publisher and her assistant Lindsay Watson, who never stopped believing in me and providing support. Vickie Boff, my publicist came on board late, but I would have been lost without her!

Thanks also to my copy editors Marcia Rockwood and Jason O'Toole for their diligence in proofreading and polishing the final draft.

Last and foremost, my family, my wife Sallie, daughters Jennifer and Samantha and son Michael for putting up with me and giving me the space essential to craft the novel.